Never Let You Go

A Small Town, Single Dad Romance

BELLA RIVERS

Copyright © 2024 by Bella Rivers

All rights reserved.

This book is a work of fiction. Names, characters, places and events are the product of the author's imagination. Any resemblance to actual persons, living or dead, events, or places, is purely coincidental.

No portion of this book may be reproduced in any form without written permission from the author, except for the use of brief quotations in a book review.

v5
ebook ISBN: 978-1-962627-00-9
print ISBN (couple cover): 978-1-962627-12-2
print ISBN (discreet cover): 978-1-962627-06-1

· Developmental editing: Angela James

Copyediting/Proofreading: Grace Wynter, The Writer's Station

Cover: Echo Grayce, Wildheart Graphics

Contents

1. Alexandra — 1
2. Christopher — 19
3. Alexandra — 29
4. Christopher — 41
5. Alexandra — 51
6. Christopher — 57
7. Alexandra — 64
8. Christopher — 80
9. Alexandra — 86
10. Alexandra — 95
11. Christopher — 105
12. Alexandra — 113
13. Alexandra — 124
14. Christopher — 133

15.	Alexandra	140
16.	Christopher	152
17.	Christopher	160
18.	Alexandra	169
19.	Christopher	182
20.	Alexandra	189
21.	Alexandra	198
22.	Alexandra	207
23.	Alexandra	213
24.	Christopher	222
25.	Alexandra	226
26.	Christopher	239
27.	Alexandra	246
28.	Alexandra	254
29.	Christopher	266
30.	Alexandra	273
31.	Christopher	284
32.	Alexandra	288
33.	Christopher	298
34.	Alexandra	303
35.	Christopher	308
36.	Alexandra	311
37.	Christopher	322
38.	Alexandra	334

39.	Alexandra	343
40.	Christopher	351
41.	Alexandra	359
42.	Christopher	370
43.	Alexandra	376
44.	Alexandra	387
45.	Christopher	391
46.	Christopher	404
47.	Alexandra	416
48.	Christopher	423
49.	Alexandra	425
50.	Alexandra	433
51.	Christopher	442
52.	Alexandra	449
53.	Alexandra	457
54.	Christopher	461
55.	Alexandra	466
56.	Alexandra	479
57.	Christopher	488
58.	Alexandra	494
59.	Alexandra	498
The Promise Of You		505
Acknowledgements		526
About the author		528

Chapter One

Alexandra

You ever have that feeling that your day started off wrong, and you might as well give up 'til tomorrow?

I'm the opposite.

Take today. January's first Monday morning in Manhattan, sidewalks full of people shoving me to the side so they can get to their nine-to-five, city buses splashing snow and mud and salt on my new boots, my two coffees spilling off the container.

Because of this, I'm looking forward to the rest of the day. It can only get better. Bright, beautiful mornings? They set up the wrong expectations. Trust me—I've been there. At least tonight, I have something to look forward to: microwaved ramen and wine from the box with my roommate and BFF, watching a trashy show. Now, that's a day with an upswing.

My stomach clenching, I slosh through the marble floors of Red Barn Baking headquarters, the chain of industrial bakeries owned by my late grandmother and my current place of employment. As I swipe my card through the turnstiles and make my way to the row of elevators for the first time since her passing, the finality of her death hits me like a slap. What am I even doing here? It's not like she's going to start noticing me *now*.

The pit in my stomach grows while I make my way to my cubicle in the Marketing Department, returning the fake smiles of my coworkers. I quickly switch my boots for the pumps I keep under my desk, smooth my skirt, fluff my hair, and take my two dripping coffees to the office of the CEO's assistant, Barbara.

Her warm smile greets me, but she waves her hands, *No*, across her desk.

"Organic, sustainably harvested, soy milk and honey, just how you like it. Don't you want to make your Monday better?" I've known Barbara my whole life. She was my grandmother's assistant. And from the day Mom died fifteen years ago, she's been there for me. So, although she's now the CEO's assistant and I'm barely above entry level, I take some liberties with protocol. Especially since Rita, my grandmother, died last week, and her constant frown and pursed lips are no longer here to chase me away like she did whenever she patrolled the hallways of her empire.

"Sweetheart, you're the best," Barbara says. A whiff of patchouli hits me like a sweet memory. "I just don't want you to spill it on my desk again, is all."

"Spill already happened this morning, and it wasn't even my fault this time," I say, handing her a messy cup and pulling up a chair.

"Don't sit down, honey. Boss wants to see you ASAP. Conference room."

Oh shit. I'm never called into a meeting with the CEO. It's so above my paygrade. "What about?"

She raises her eyebrows and makes a *my-lips-are-sealed* gesture.

"Does this have anything to do with Rita?"

She tilts her head, *maybe*. "Be smart," she says. Her eyes are kinder than usual. My stomach bottoms out. Am I being let go? This company is the last tether to any form of family I have. *Please don't let it be that.*

I square my shoulders and force a smile. "I'm *very* smart."

"Not that kind of smart. And leave your soggy mess here," she adds, pointing to my coffee.

I put the tray down. "Gotta make a bathroom run."

She shakes her head. "No time for that. Robert already asked twice for you."

Am I really that late?

She waves me out. "They're waiting for you."

Who's they? I clench my bladder and take a deep breath. Doesn't look like the day is getting better just yet. *Ramen and wine, and a trashy show. Focus on the little things that'll get you through the day.*

The big boss, Robert Norwood, is sitting at the top of the conference table with two other people in suits on one side, a man and a woman. Stacks of paperwork are lined in front of them in neat piles. On a side table, a silver tray holds a steaming pot of coffee, croissants, and immaculate porcelain mugs with our new logo on it. I love that logo. It's a stylistic rendition of a red barn, not unlike the one on the giant picture frame hanging on the wall right above. It's been a pain to get everyone to agree on that logo, but after exhausting the patience of two external firms, we ended up doing the job ourselves and—

"Alex! Are you with us?" Robert's voice booms, pulling me out of my thoughts. "Help yourself to some coffee. You look like you could use it." He sounds even more annoyed with me than usual.

"Thank you." I almost take him up on the offer, but my bladder rings the alarm, so I choose the safer route of sitting down and getting this over with quickly. I smile at the people across the table from me. They smile back, lips pinched.

Not good.

"Alex, this is the law firm representing your grandmother's estate," Robert says. He doesn't bother with their names, and for some reason that makes me feel a little closer to them.

I nod their way and smile again.

"They've come here for the reading of the will, as a convenience to us. Save us some time."

My eyes drift from the snow now falling steadily on Manhattan to the picture on the wall. A red barn, horses grazing in a lush meadow in the background, and a guy in a flannel shirt holding a massive round bread, flashing a smile too white to be true. For all its fakeness, every time things felt awry in this company, I've taken solace in the picture that's supposed to symbolize it.

I take a deep breath. This is just a formality. For a minute, I thought I was in real trouble, but then again that meeting would have been with HR. This is all making sense.

"Ms. Pierce," the woman across the table says, "Your grandmother, Ms. Rita Douglas—"

"I'm sorry, I didn't catch your names," I interrupt softly, my gaze darting between the two of them.

The man reaches for two business cards from his suit pocket and hands them to me. Robert shifts in his seat, like he doesn't approve. I'm just being polite. It looks like these people are about to get personal about me and my grandmother. The least we could do is introductions, no?

"We would normally do this type of thing at the deceased's estate, or at our offices, but this seemed more convenient than having you come to Long Island," the woman says.

"This is perfect," I reassure them. "Thank you." My grandmother practically lived here, having founded the company decades ago, and managing it almost to the very end of her life. She had a mansion that was never a home. Not to her, and certainly never to me.

I glance at their business cards while the woman clears her throat and starts reading from her stack of papers, never making eye contact with me. The man next to her is fidgety. I wonder if they're concerned about my reaction when they get to the part where I get nothing. Or rather, when they get to the end of the document and my name never came up. *I bet they rarely see that. The sole heir of a tycoon getting absolutely nothing.* Although, if they want to see me, there must be something they need to tell me. I clench my bladder again. This should be quick.

Rita raised me like that. *You'll never get anything from me that you didn't work for,* she would tell me.

Now, there's something to be said about tackling your twenties with a knack for budgeting and penny pinching. I have Rita to thank for that. Her stinginess made me stronger. It turned out to be her gift to me.

It wasn't Rita who'd recruited me to work for Red barn Baking. I'd followed the standard application process. I never knew whether she was proud, annoyed, or pissed when the head of Marketing hired me. Or how she felt when I quickly became their best asset.

My name comes up in the monotone reading of the will. Rita left me with a sum of money that would have covered maybe three days of her living expenses but amounts to about two of my paychecks.

That's a nice chunk of money. Fuzziness spreads inside me, but I suppress it quickly. It doesn't sound right to feel happy under these circumstances.

I twitch in my seat. Surely this is close to being over. I really need to use the bathroom.

Hearing my name again, I straighten my shoulders. A part of my brain listens while the other part drifts back to Rita. To be honest, I don't *miss* her. I just have to accept that the opportunity to connect with her will never present itself now. I thought that by working for her company it would happen. With time. When I became an adult.

It didn't.

End of story. I need to move on.

"Alex, did you get that?"

I jump. Yes. Yes, I did get that. I internally repeat something totally outlandish. The gist of it is, if I want to be vested in the ownership of Rita's shares of Red Barn Baking, giving me a controlling vote on the board, I have to complete a baking apprenticeship. Said apprenticeship needs to happen in a specific bakery in a village in Vermont.

Um... what? My gaze drifts to the picture of the red barn. Several things don't make sense: Me potentially being at the helm of Red Barn Baking. Me becoming a baker.

And also, why didn't this ever come up before? If she wanted me to take over after her, why didn't she prepare me? At least sit me down, have a conversation?

"Can you run this by me once more?" I ask, and while they do, I wonder what Rita's intentions were. And as usual, when trying to figure out my late grandmother, I come up empty. "What does this apprenticeship consist of?"

Robert snorts.

The man explains, "You would be working part-time at the bakery in Emerald Creek, under the supervision of their baker, a Mr. Christopher Wright. The rest of the time is for you to study the theory and practice your skills in the bakery. You'll have to pass the French baking exam. An examiner is scheduled to visit a culinary school in the state, and he will validate your apprenticeship."

Rita Douglas, founder of an industrial bakery, wants me to undergo a traditional French baking training? "How long is this apprenticeship?"

"It's on the very short side. Five, six months. Lots to pack in, according to the examiner, unless you have solid baking experience and knowledge." He cocks an eyebrow at me, and Robert scoffs.

"Can't I do this here, at a culinary school?" I'm pretty sure I already know the answer, but what's the harm in asking? "If I pass the exam, what's the difference?" I am actually thinking about this.

I know. Crazy, right?

Robert sighs and shakes his head while the woman cuts in. "These are the terms set forth by the late Ms. Douglas. There can be no modifications, I'm afraid. You need to follow the rules of a traditional French apprenticeship, one where you live on site and are under the baker's responsibility for most areas of your life, regardless of your age. The late Ms. Douglas also prescribed the *one* bakery where the apprenticeship is to take place."

Robert is rubbing his face like he's super tired. It's what—ten in the morning on a Monday? "You don't need to worry about all this," he says. "You can't be seriously considering it. You'd be setting yourself up for failure. You realize that, right?" He flicks his pen nervously. "Supposing you pass the exam, do you seriously see yourself presiding over the company?" he snorts.

I would kinda be his boss? That'd be awkward, and I see now why he's more pissed than his usual self. But I can't let that distract me.

"What's the valuation of Red Barn?" I ask him. I should know this, but I don't. I can tell you how my most recent tweak on our latest social media campaign increased click through rate, in what measure this directly impacted each of our five regional territories, and the net dollar amount generated by that adjustment. I can tell you what color scheme in our graphics is sure to generate greater customer engagement. But I've never known the big picture of the company itself, its margins, its real estate holdings, its investments in mills, and all the other components of this empire. Rita never shared this with me, which makes her posthumous offer even more surprising to me.

Robert moves his hands like my question might require an audit.

"At the close of the books last year, what were the assets, what were the liabilities, and what were the revenues?" I ask him slowly, mentally patting myself on the back for remembering Small Business 101. Not too incorrectly, I hope.

His gaze narrows on me. He gives me three numbers, then adds, "give or take a few dozen million."

Holy shit. I swallow hard but hold his gaze. So much for small business. "I'm going to have to think about this."

The woman interjects, "You need to make a decision—"

"This does *look* like a lot of money," Robert interrupts, "but it's more of a headache than anything else. However, in consideration of the circumstances, the board has authorized me to share an offer they want to make." He pulls a paper from inside his jacket and unfolds it.

"What circumstances?"

"Pardon me?"

"You said the board wants to make an offer in consideration of the circumstances." I have to pee so bad, I switch the way my legs are crossed.

"Y-yes. The fact that Rita—Ms. Douglas—didn't provide for you in her will. The board understands that this might be... difficult... and they want to help make it right." He takes his glasses off.

"So the board knew? I thought a reading of a will was like—this surprise revelation."

The woman stacks her papers back into a neat pile. "The late Ms. Douglas, as many prudent entrepreneurs, chose to share her succession plan with her board."

I chuckle. "You call that a plan? It's a frigging monkey wrench." I blush at my near use of the f-word. I don't know what's gotten into me this morning. I'm blindsided, and angry about it, but that's no excuse to be rude.

"I'm sure she had her reasons." She purses her lips. "Though I can't see which."

"That makes two of us." My heart drums hard, pushing words out of me.

Robert extends a pacifying hand. "Rita was... a special person. Very few people could ever understand her. But here we are," he says, gesturing to the sprawling offices, and the stylish logo stenciled on his crystal glass. "So we have an offer. Handsome compensation in exchange for declining Rita's—Ms. Douglas'—offer." He slides a two-pager signed by the board members across the table.

In between a couple of dense paragraphs, I read a number, and I learn the monetary equivalent of the word handsome. I'm speechless.

"It's very generous," Robert says. "They really don't need to do this."

Then why are they doing it?

My bladder is ready to explode now. I stand from the table. "If you'll excuse me a moment."

"We need your decision now," the woman cuts in.

I'm about to ask her why, but I can't hold it any longer. "And I need to pee now."

As I dash past her office, Barbara scowls at me. But when I exit the stall, she's leaning on the bathroom vanity. "How are you doing, honey?"

"Do you know what's going on?" I take time lathering my hands, observing the soap suds form and pop, before rinsing them under scalding water, trying to calm the thrum in my body. Despite my pitiful efforts to be loved by her, Rita barely tolerated me. So, why this?

Barbara turns sideways to face me and crosses her arms. "Robert asked me to prepare a packet, *Just in case*, he said."

I shake the droplets off my hands and turn toward her. "You know why Rita would do that?"

"Red Barn was her family. You were her granddaughter."

The nuance doesn't escape me. It's nothing new, but it still stings. It always will.

"It's the village she was from, you know. Where she was born." Her gaze is on me, soft yet burning. She's hurting for me.

"I figured," I whisper before sliding my hands between the loud air blades of the dryer. I rub them up and down several times, my skin creasing as I do, then lift them slowly out and turn to face Barbara's scrutiny.

She takes my face between her soft hands, and her gaze bores into my eyes. "This means the world to her." She says it as if Rita was still here to watch me make my decision, and in a sense, she is.

I hold back tears. "Why did she do that *now*? Why didn't she ever let me in before?"

Barbara pulls me into a hug, her silk scarf caressing my cheek. "She wasn't good with words. But she did love you, in her own way."

"I only had you after Mom died, and you know that," I say after she lets me go.

It's *her* eyes that well now. "Oh hush. Now go back there and do the right thing," she says. "Never mind the boss."

Of course I'll do the right thing. Rita was my only family, but I never felt like I was *her* family. Red Barn Baking, the business she created on her own as a single mother and grew into an empire, was her family. Barbara is right. This is Rita's love letter to me, and I have no other choice than to act on it.

I've been wanting a family forever, and she's giving me hers—a business.

So because she was my only family, and because this void I always have inside me feels like an abyss right now, I'm going to do what she said.

And also because it's pissing off Robert. Can't discard the little pleasures in life.

"Holy shit, Alex! That's next level," my roommate and best friend, Sarah, says that evening. She hands me a glass of wine and sits on the couch next to me, curling her legs under her. "That's where Rita was born? Didn't you tell me they kicked her out of there when she was pregnant with your mom? Do you think that's why she wanted you to go? And why did she not ask you to go earlier?"

I have all the same questions, none of the answers. I take a long sip of wine, appreciating the fact that we're drinking from actual glasses. A celebration of sorts.

"Did you ever visit there? As a kid?" she continues.

"I went once with my mom." The memory is fuzzy but potent. The air was crisp and smelled of fire in chimneys. There was a dusting of snow on the ground, and it was pretty in an eerie way how it mingled with the leaves that hadn't quite yet finished falling from the trees.

Mom wiped her cheeks a lot on the drive back, but these were happy tears. "I think she was reconnecting with her dad?" My belly clenches. "Isn't it messed up that I can't remember?"

"I'd say it's normal. It must have been pretty heavy duty. Is it a happy memory?"

"Yeah, it was one of those good times. I wish I could remember more."

"Why didn't you ever go back?"

"I guess... it must have been shortly before the accident. Maybe she planned on going back? I'd say that was late fall, and she died right after Christmas. Yeah, it probably was the same year, you're right."

Sarah chuckles but pats my hand softly. "I didn't say anything."

"You're helping me, dude. You're like the memory whisperer." I take a long draw on the wine.

"Alright. Enough with the past," Sarah says, grabbing her phone. "What's the name of this bumfuck place you're going to?"

"Hey. That's my small town you're talking about," I say, swatting her arm playfully. "It's called Emerald Creek."

"Awww. Can't make this stuff up. Alright. Here we go. *Emerald Creek, Vermont.* Kay. *Located at the edge of the Northeast Kingdom.* Whaaaat?"

"*What.*"

"That is a cool name. The Northeast Kingdom."

"I guess. If you're selling tiaras. Or setting a fantasy movie."

"Or moving in with a hot baker."

I glance at her phone. "Is he hot?"

She laughs and sets her phone down. "Nope. Sorry to disappoint. He is so fugly, you are forbidden—"

"Shut up. You don't even know his name. You're full of it."

"True. Just kidding. So—what's his name?'

"I don't remember, and you're not googling him."

She picks her phone back up. "Why not?"

"It's weird."

"It's research," she says, her thumbs active on her phone.

The wine is beginning to mellow me, and the stress of the day, the questions I've asked myself, are wearing me down now that the tension is easing away. "Do you think she was trying to fix something? Rita."

"Maybe? But who cares? This could be a great new start for you, Alex. This is so exciting! The beginning of a new life!" Sarah is always excited about new adventures, big decisions, major projects.

Me, I'd rather keep my life low-key. The truth is, my big-picture items always end up broken. So I focus my happiness on the little things. A cup of coffee with my favorite colleague in the morning, a glass of wine with my roommate in the evening. New boots to hop in the snow, a favorite perfume to wear on performance report day. Every time I've been excited about a big thing, disaster has struck. So I stopped making these things count, and since then my life has been going okay.

"Maybe this will spruce up your dating life!" Sarah continues. "How long since you went on a decent date?"

"Look who's talking."

"Yeah, yeah, whatever. Seriously, Lexie, you should give it a try when you're up there. Maybe you'll meet Mister Right."

"There is no Mister Right, at least not for me. You know that."

"*Ohmygod*. Not The Curse again."

"You're the one calling it The Curse. I'm just saying, it's not in my DNA. My mother was a single mom, my grandmother was a single mom, and I've grown up—"

"I know, I know," Sarah interrupts. "Men only bring misery. Blah blah blah."

"But it's true! For my family it's true. No men for me."

"You're discarding the power of the orgasm."

"And you're confusing relationships and sex."

"Ha! Now we're talking. You need to get laid. It's decided. Speaking of which, who's the baker you're going to be working for?" She waves her phone at me. "What's his name again? Did you look him up?"

I spit my wine back in my glass. "*Speaking of which?* I am *not* sleeping with my boss! Are you out of your mind?"

She growls. "Yeah, yeah. Right." She takes a deep breath. "Emerald Creek bakery. There's like... nothing online. There does seem to be a bakery on the map. Nothing on social. Found a couple of middle-aged men in wife beaters." She giggles and shows me her screen.

I don't even look her way. "You did not. Anyway, my boss is probably twice that age. He's some star baker." In the packet of instructions Barbara handed me after the meeting, there was a short bio of the guy.

"What's his name again?"

"Christopher Wright."

"Ha! Got you. You *do* know his name." She types and her eyes twinkle. "Huh," she smirks.

Tonight I couldn't care less about my future boss, but I should show some interest in my best friend's efforts. "D'you find him?"

"Uh—no, it's not him." She puts her phone down. "Wanna watch something trashy?"

"Always."

A couple of days later, I reach Emerald Creek several hours after leaving New York, and a sense of relief washes over me. Not just because the trip is over, although driving on snow was stressful enough, but because this place is so darn cute it belongs on a postcard. My ten-year old self didn't register that at the time, or at least that's not the vibe that stuck with me.

It's the beginning of January, and the town is still decorated for the holidays. Soft white lights outline the pitch of the roofs and the contours of the houses. Candles flicker behind each window. Wreaths ranging from magnificent to elegantly understated hang on front doors. Fresh garlands and red bows graciously drape white picket fences. I sit still in the rental car, taking it all in before stepping out.

Standing alone on the quiet street, I take a deep breath and stretch my sore muscles. I tilt my head back, savoring the cool tingle of light snowflakes on my face as they flurry softly down to earth.

I grab my duffel bag from the backseat, lock the car, and catch myself as I step on the sidewalk, my new boots betraying me as they slip on the packed snow, and I nearly fall.

The bakery is a Victorian house set back from the sidewalk by a narrow garden, if the round shapes covered in snow are any indication A Christmas tree blinks multicolor lights on one side of the garden, while a snowman stands proudly on the other side of it. A central walkway, free of snow and sanded, leads to the wraparound porch and the front door. The soft glow of the inside of the store spills into the night through wide windows, inviting me to move forward despite the *Sorry, We're Closed* sign.

The door yields when I push it open, and the doorbell chimes. I take another deep breath and step inside.

It smells heavenly of baked bread and sweets, and any lingering stress I had goes down several notches.

A counter lines two sides of the bakery. Behind it, wooden racks are slightly tilted to display the breads. They're empty at this late hour, but some of them have tiny blackboard signs with labels in cursive: Mother Hen, Bob's Favorite, Two Millers, Down the River, Up the Hill, Across the Border. I'm assuming these are the names of the breads they bake here. Interesting choice. Not names we use at Red Barn Baking, for sure.

A large blackboard lists the prices for their baked goods, and my mouth waters as I read. Cinnamon buns, apple muffins, cheddar croissants, bacon maple rolls, apple cider donuts... the list of temptations goes on and on. I fish my phone from my pocket and snap a photo.

Barbara warned me that cell phone coverage was poor in Vermont. She got that right. I have like, one bar. Then none. Spotting the wi-fi password next to the old-fashioned register, right below a cardboard collection box for the local hockey club, I enter it in my phone, then send the picture to Sarah. Caption: *Made it! ttyl*.

A slew of notifications ding once I'm connected. I glance at the screen. Seven text messages and two emails. All the text messages are from Sarah, who must have gotten confused about my itinerary.

The emails are from Robert Norwood, the first one sort of menacing with a bunch of legalese, the second a desperate plea for compromise as he extends the deadline for me to come back to my regular job. My heart rate picks up, and I clench my jaw. I delete the emails. I can always fish them out of the trash folder if I have second thoughts after a few days. I just don't want to see them there.

It's bad digital feng shui.

With that out of the way, I focus back on the here and now. The little things. I slip off my coat, letting the warmth of the room envelop me. The only sound is a voice coming from beyond the wall. It sounds like a one-sided conversation, someone on the phone—a man.

I welcome the wait, savoring this time to myself, this buffer between my old life and what will be my world for the next six months.

I walk to the window. Lazy snowflakes dance in the golden light cast by the lampposts. Across the street is a vast expanse that looks like a park. In the center of it, I notice a lone silhouette gliding effortlessly and gracefully in circles on what must be an ice rink. Peering out, I can make out the string of lights surrounding it and several houses and buildings on the other side of the park, also decked out for the holiday season. Even if the reasons I find myself here are all wrong, I'll do what I always do when life gets weird: I'll ignore what I can't change and focus on the little things that make me happy. It seems there will be no shortage of these here.

From what I've seen so far, Emerald Creek might just be the perfect place to forget the troubles that await me when I return to New York. I'll learn a new skill, meet new people, become stronger. I suspect this is why Rita wanted me to come here. To learn some life lessons.

Footsteps approach from the back of the shop, the door behind the counter swings open, and my heart skips a beat before he even looks at me. Whoever *he* is.

Well over six feet.

Dark, mussed up hair.

Two-day stubble on a strong jaw.

Pecs all but snapping open a plaid flannel shirt, muscular forearms straining the rolled-up sleeves.

Our eyes connect for a split second and a zing of electricity runs from my brain to my core.

He turns his back to me to close the door. Softly. Deliberately. As if closing a door required care and attention.

His hair is a little long down his neck, but not long enough to hide his tan nape. The shirt strains against his shoulders, and my lady parts do a little happy dance before my brain catches up and scolds my body into calming the heck down.

He turns around and takes two steps to my side of the counter. His gaze does a quick swipe of my body, then he crosses his arms and locks his eyes to mine like he's putting all his effort into being professional and not checking me out.

Well, hello to you too.

Chapter Two

Christopher

Skye grabs a handful of my hair to pull my head up so she can see how her pedicure is coming along.

"Wait, sweetie, I'm almost done," I say, applying a coat on her pinky toe with the tip of the brush. She still has a bit of baby fat around the toes, and the nail is tiny.

"Let me see," she says, frowning. "I love it. Do you think you could do my hands?" she asks, extending her fingers like a diva and wiggling her toes. She's spending too much time at my cousin's beauty salon and is clearly picking up on her clients' mannerisms. It's cute now, but I need to keep an eye on this before it gets out of control.

"Don't smudge them, Skye. Be patient." I use my fake big voice. "I'm not doing them over."

"How about my hands, Daddy? Wouldn't the glitter just be the prettiest on my hands?" she insists.

I glance at the time. I'm expecting the new apprentice at any moment. "All right, then. Real quick and promise you won't move." I start on her nails just as the bakery phone rings.

I tuck the receiver under my ear while painting Skye's fingers. The bed-and-breakfast is having a bus tour and wants to add two dozen croissants for the morning and three apple crumbles for tea. I add their order to the four dozen apple cider muffins going to the coffee shop. I hang up, and the phone rings again. I curse under my breath as I pick up. This time, it's the restaurant at the inn, asking for a special order of low-sodium dinner rolls.

Once I'm done transcribing their orders on our log for tomorrow, I resume my six-year-old daughter's manicure. "How is your writing coming along?" I ask her.

"Daddy. You *know* I got an A-plus!"

"Good, because I'm going to need an assistant soon."

She wiggles in her chair. "Caroline says her mom says every good baker needs a wife."

"Caroline's mom talks too much." And she's been wanting in my pants for years. "I'm already the best baker in the country."

"That's what I told Caroline."

"You told Caroline her mom talks too much?" I chuckle.

"Noooo." She giggles. "I told her you're already the best baker in the whole entire world. But she says her mom said it's not true."

"Is that right?"

She pouts. "I hate her."

"You can't hate her. She's your best friend." I do sort of resent Caroline's mom right now for saying that, although I know it comes from a good place. A number of people in Emerald Creek are gently nudging me to compete in the TV show, *New England's Best Baker*. It would attract a lot of outside shoppers and tourists and benefit all the other shops. I know I'm good enough to hold my own on the show and even win the competition. I just haven't given it the time, yet. Skye is my priority.

Being a single dad and growing my business is eating up my days and nights. But, as several friends have pointed out to me, winning the competition or even placing well would help my own business a lot. Other bakers who have won it, even in remote places similar to Emerald Creek, experienced an increase in sales, allowing them to hire more help and increase their prices on high-end products. It would bring the bakery to the next level. It's actually exactly what I need.

It's just not what I want.

"Well, today, I hate her," Skye says as I finish her last fingernail. "Thank you, Daddy." She smiles and purses her lips to give me a kiss. "May I please watch a cartoon, now?"

"Sure, princess," I say, propping her in front of her favorite show. "Don't smudge your nail polish, now. That was hard work for me." I ruffle her unruly hair. "I told you about the apprentice coming to live with us, right? He'll be here any minute. You stay in front of the TV while I get him settled."

She's deep in her show and nods absently. I've had little time to prepare her for the arrival of the apprentice. It's just the two of us, and she's not comfortable around strangers. The downside of growing up in a small town, I suppose. She knows everyone and everyone knows her.

Getting an apprentice all happened over the last couple of days. The foundation that provided the grant for my bakery called to set up an apprenticeship ASAP. They're who made my dream of owning this bakery possible, so although I typically put my apprentices through an interview process, this time I didn't have a say.

Not that it matters that much. Just like I did when I left my family over ten years ago, someone needed a place to land. Maybe someone who needed to get away from some family drama, or who, like me, was just over feeling not wanted and simply felt the urge to do something useful with his hands. Something that expressed love and brought people together.

I only hope the apprentice will be friendly and not as rowdy as I was in my days. All I know about this kid is that he comes from New York City and is arriving today. I offered to pick him up at the bus station but was told it wouldn't be necessary.

I'm on the phone, again, when the door to the bakery chimes. Our shopkeeper, Willow, is gone by now. We're sold out of bread, and the lights are dimmed. It has to be the apprentice, so I wrap up my call and head over to take care of him.

I feel like a tsunami is hitting me as I take in the woman standing in the middle of my bakery. A shy smile, big brown eyes, and a mouth that turns my thoughts dirty against my better judgment. I take my time closing the door so I can collect my thoughts. Calm down.

I like women, but damn.

I take a deep breath and follow the pull that takes me to the middle of the room instead of staying safely on my side of the counter.

There is a duffle bag next to her, but no apprentice in sight. She must be part of the bus tour.

"Can I help you?" I ask. Real original, I know, but my brain stopped its normal functions. And I do want to help her—in more ways than I care to elaborate.

She twists her long, dark-honey hair in a rope and brings it to one side of her body. My gaze follows her delicate hand from her face to her breast to the slope of her waist above her perfectly curved hip. When

I snatch my gaze back up, her eyes are fastened on mine, amusement lighting them ablaze.

In another time, another life, I would have offered to conclude whatever business she has here with a drink at the pub. But those days are long gone.

She takes two, three steps toward me. She looks tired in a beautiful sort of way. Glowing skin, dark circles.

"I'm looking for Christopher Wright?" She sounds both a little worried and happy to see me.

I'm getting more confused and not because there's a buzz in my veins I haven't felt in a long time. I know exactly where *that* comes from. I don't mean to take my time answering, but I keep running scenarios through my head of who she might be. Social services? School? Bank? Lawyer? I've been in trouble with each of those at some point or another. Nothing major, just annoying. It's the duffel bag that throws me off. The most logical answer is that she's accompanying the apprentice.

"Yeah, that's me," I say, scanning the room.

She smiles softly and sighs in relief. My groin starts seriously stirring, begging my brain to come up with a follow-up question that will keep those lips moving.

"You're the baker?" she breathes. "I'm here for the apprenticeship."

I knew it. "Right. Alex, correct?" I say, looking around. "Where is he?"

Her brow furrows, and she tilts her head. "That's me. Alex Pierce. Alexandra?"

Holy fucking shit. I take in the whole package. Her long nails, not good for kneading or prepping or any manual labor. Her tiny wrists—will she be able to lift heavy bags of flour? Her age, on the older side for an apprentice, only a couple years younger than me. That part doesn't bother me, not in the least, but for different reasons, and that isn't good either.

Maybe I should have asked a couple more questions before taking her in. Just to be prepared.

"Of course," I finally manage to say. "Alexandra. Welcome."

She extends her hand, and I take it. It feels awkward. We don't really shake hands with women around here, unless they're your banker or doctor. She's going to be living under my roof, be part of my family for months.

But it's not like I can hug her, so I hold her hand longer than strictly required, relishing the feeling of her soft skin against my palm, noticing the gentle strength of her grasp despite how small her hand is. Her eyes hold my gaze, a shade of pink tints her cheeks, her body inches closer to mine, and her throat bobs as she swallows.

Fuck.

Me.

The doorbell chimes, pulling me from my fantasies. I peel my eyes from Alexandra. The town's official gossip, Sophie, is ogling us.

"We're closed, Sophie; you know that."

"Oh?" she says, quizzically looking at Alexandra and her duffel bag.

I try to scare her away with a frown, but I should know better. That only makes it more interesting to her. "What do you need?" We keep our unsold breads of the day in the back to give to the food shelter. The townspeople know they can always try their luck if they need something.

"You're the best. Two blueberry muffins for the morning, if you have any left over. I have an early start." She turns to Alexandra. "I'm Sophie, the town librarian," she says. "Welcome to Emerald Creek."

Alexandra gives her a sweet smile. "Thank you. I'm happy to be here."

I duck to the back as quickly as I can.

"And I'm happy for *Christopher*," I hear Sophie whisper on my way out. "It's about ti—"

"Sophie, mind your own business!" I boom.

"And a sliced Two Millers, if you please. Or anything sliced!" she replies.

She wants me to use the slicer so she has time to pry, and so the noise covers her chatter.

I hand Sophie her baked goods and the first unsliced bread I could get my hands on and push her toward the exit. "You need a life, Soph'."

She stops at the door. "Did you read my new fairy tale?" she says, a twinkle in her eye. "Did it resonate with you?"

"Be right back," I tell Alexandra as I walk Sophie to the sidewalk. If I don't, she might stay for dinner. "I'll have some cinnamon rolls for your knitting group tomorrow. How's that?"

"It's crochet and thank you. You're the best." Looking above my shoulder at the bakery, she adds, "Who's the beauty?"

I sigh and cross my arms. There's no point telling her it's none of her business. It'd be rude. And it'd be wrong. Everything that happens in Emerald Creek is Sophie's business. "She's a new employee. An apprentice."

"At her age? Is that even legal?"

"*Fine*. An intern. Duly paid. How's that?"

Sophie is also the self-appointed keeper of rules. "Much better. Words carry more weight than people realize."

"You're right."

"Where is she staying?"

Seriously? I chuckle at her nosiness. She's also one of the sweetest people I know, and she always means well. "Here. This internship is modeled after a traditional apprenticeship."

"In the attic?" she cries.

"That's where all the apprentices stay, Sophie. I can't make an exception just because she's..."

Sophie's eyes narrow. Is she actually waiting to see me put my foot in my mouth and say something flattering about Alexandra?

"... *a woman*. That would be discrimination. Right?"

She huffs. "I s'pose so."

"And it's not an *attic*. It's a quaint bedroom under the eaves."

"Well look at you. If this bakery thing doesn't pan out, you could always write descriptions for realtors," she says. "Seriously, Christopher, is that place even clean? You catch more flies with honey than vinegar, you know."

"What are we even talking about?" Pretending to ignore her gist seems to do the trick. She starts walking away.

But then she turns around.

"You'll need to give that child a mother eventually," she says.

Oh no she didn't. My blood boils, and my words bite. "Skye has been doing just fine with her father, wouldn't you say?" I leave it at that. She should know better than to bring that up.

"Not all women are bad mothers. Just saying."

I guess she's into extra layers tonight. "'Night, Sophie."

"That came out wrong," she says apologetically. "I worry about you too. We all do."

I know they do. That's what I love about this small town. They've all been looking out for me since I took refuge here to build my life on my terms. "There's nothing to worry about." And that's the truth. Skye and I are doing just fine.

Back in the bakery, I lock the door and roll down the blinds for extra protection against the busybodies of Emerald Creek. Alexandra lifts her gaze from her phone, pockets it and gives me a shy smile. I hope she didn't hear what Sophie said out there.

I grab her duffel bag before she has a chance to and start up the staircase leading to the bedrooms. "Let's get you settled," I say. I lead the way up to the first floor, where mine and Skye's bedrooms are, then continue onto the second, narrower flight of stairs. The apprentice bedroom is exactly above mine, with only one layer of disjointed hardwood floor between the two rooms.

It's not as bad as Sophie makes it out to be. The bedroom is on the larger side and has an en-suite bathroom. It has everything you need, but nothing you don't. Nothing pretty either.

"Sorry about the room," I say as we reach the eaves.

"This is adorable," Alexandra exclaims. She's a little out of breath, and her shallow panting makes my dick twitch again.

I set her bag down next to the twin size bed. "When I was an apprentice, I shared a room with the master's kids. I thought this would be more than adequate. But we can change things around to make it more comfortable for you. I wasn't expecting a—" *Woman? Sex symbol? Bombshell?* "I was expecting a teenage boy. I must have misunderstood."

"Are you kidding? This is perfect," she says, setting her handbag on the bed. She crosses to the dormer window and kneels on the small built-in bench underneath it, looking outside. "Oh, my god! This is sooo romantic." She pulls her phone out.

"Yeah," I say, scratching my head. "Bathroom is here." I get self-conscious about the dull, thin towels hanging on the rod. "I'll get you nicer towels." I have a visual of her naked body wrapped in a towel while I am literally feet away in my own room. This is going to be near impossible.

She gasps at the clawfoot tub. "Awww, how cute!"

"That's really old—been here since the fifties. The water probably gets cold really fast in there. I wouldn't recommend it."

"Oh, I won't use it," she said. "It's so deep, it'd take up all your hot water."

Good. Last thing I need is to know she's lathering her generous boobs, soap suds floating around her, toes sticking out... *Stop. I have to stop these thoughts.*

"I'm a shower person, anyway."

Yeah, me, too. Do you like them hot and ...

Stop. Stop right now. "We'll have dinner in an hour. You'll meet the woman of my life," I say with a smirk.

Her eyebrows furrow.

"Kitchen and den are all the way downstairs, behind the bakeshop, which is behind the bakery," I continue.

She seems puzzled. Doesn't she know the difference?

"The bakery is where we sell the bread—where you came in. The bakeshop is where we make the bread. Some people call it a lab. There's a door behind the counter that leads to the bakeshop. In the back of the bakeshop is our private kitchen and the den where we hang out."

Her gaze darts intently from my eyes to my mouth as if she can't decide where to focus her attention. She takes another shallow breath, her parted lips revealing the tip of her tongue.

I dash out of her room.

This isn't going to work.

Chapter Three

Alexandra

When he leaves the room, my head is dizzy, and my heart is pounding.

I'll chalk it up to the long drive. Nothing a shower can't fix. I climb inside the antique tub, careful to tuck the shower curtain inside. The bathroom floor is a beautiful solid hardwood I would hate to damage. The tub, sink, and toilet must have been added long after the house was built. The shower handle leaks slightly, showing its age. Everything here is so effortlessly vintage. People in the city would pay thousands for this country feel that is just so authentic here.

As I lather my hair with shampoo, I find myself smiling. This will be good for me. The aftermath? I'm not so sure about. But for now, I will find some self-indulgence in this fantasy land.

The shower gel feels good on my body, and my thoughts drift to Christopher before I rein them in. Yikes! I'm not that person. I can't help but wonder though. What is it like to be with a man like him? I've never dated a guy with such a healthy masculine vibe. Like testosterone wrapped in a flannel blanket. Besides his incredibly good looks, what struck me most about him was his strong confidence that was everything but arrogant.

It felt good to be in his presence.

And the way he treated the sweet gossip, Sophie?

So nice.

Most people I know would have turned her away. She wouldn't have made it through the door. Granted, I come from New York, and this is Vermont. So sure.

But he gave her bread and muffins and whatever she wanted. And then he walked her outside. In the freezing cold. It must have dropped to fifteen degrees out there.

And he was wearing just a shirt.

And he made small talk with her!

Who does that?

I sigh as I exit the shower.

Is it okay to have a platonic crush on your boss? Because your girl can't help it.

As I pat myself dry, my cell phone buzzes with a text message.

Sarah

> How's it going?

>> It's going! Got here not too long ago, getting ready for dinner

> Sooooo. Tell me???

>> Not much to tell yet. The town is so romantic and my bedroom is the cutest ever!

I take a quick video and send it to her.

> OMG is this for real?

> Are those eaves?

> And vintage built-in bookshelves?

< Yes

< everything is so adorable

> Is that a fireplace?

< I don't think it works

> Doesn't matter

> I'm so jealous right now.

< <3

> Soooo

> The baker...???

> ???

< What about him?

> ugh.

> Is he a 10 or what?

> hahaha did you google him

Duh

> He has someone.

Of course he would

On the upside

did you unpack your shit yet

> No

When you do you'll thank me

> What for

I threw something in there

> Awww so sweet what is it

something handy

> thx xoxo

> gtg

<eggplant emoji>

> <3

I throw on my best-fitting pair of jeans and a dark green cashmere sweater and examine myself in the mirror above the sink. I dab some concealer under my eyes and declare myself presentable. The mouthwatering smell of a home-cooked meal wafts all the way to me, and my stomach growls.

It dawns on me that I'm invading these people's privacy, living under their own roof, and didn't even think to bring a little thank you gift. I know I'm not really a guest, and I'm here to work under conditions that were pretty much dictated to me, but I suddenly feel self-conscious of my presence within this home.

I need to do everything in my power to stay out of their way and not intrude in their daily life. Especially given the *very* inappropriate thoughts that went through my mind when I first met Christopher. Granted, I didn't notice a wedding band, but then again, I wasn't specifically looking for one.

I'm vaguely ashamed of myself.

On my way down, I glance at the second floor. The large hallway is lined with several doors, all closed except the one at the end where a child's bed is softly lit.

The bakery is bathed in a warm semi-darkness. I run my hand on the soft wooden counter as I circle to the back of it. I push open the door behind the register and find myself in a large, brightly lit room with metallic prep tables, ovens, fridges, and baking racks glistening. It looks very professional, in stark contrast with the rustic warmth of the bakery.

"Over here," Christopher calls as a door in the back opens, framing his silhouette.

My stomach flutters. I startle and steady myself on a cold prep table, turning my face away from him. "This is very impressive."

"Yeah, it's a nice lab. Can't complain. I got a good grant." He smirks. "Come on in."

I step into a vast kitchen anchored around a large, solid pine table. A child's drawings are taped to most of the cabinets. The smell of sautéed onions and subtle herbs comes from a creamy stew simmering on the stovetop, reminding me again how famished I am. The kitchen extends into a larger space that is mostly dark right now, bathing in the bluish, flickering light of a television set.

"Skye!" Christopher calls out.

I tug on my sweater, curiosity eating at me. A woman who cooks like a goddess (I don't need to taste the stew to know it will be heaven), lives in a storybook village, and is married to a hunk of a man? She's bound to be my inspiration. Forget learning how to bake.

"There's my princess!" he exclaims as a patter of steps sound and a little girl runs into his arms. He picks her up with familiar ease. "Alexandra, meet my daughter, Skye. Skye, meet our new apprentice, Alexandra."

Skye has Christopher's dark complexion, brightened by honey-gold eyes. Unruly locks of jet-black hair cascade on her shoulders. She leans against her father's chest and studies me with widening eyes, her face tilted to the side so that it's flush against her father's shoulder. She seems very intimidated by me.

"You are so pretty, Skye." I smile. "Thank you for sharing your home with me." I cock my head to the side.

She dangles her leg, dropping her slipper, and extends her foot toward me.

"We had a mani-pedi session," Christopher clues me in.

"Ooooh, I love the glitter! Isn't it the best? You look like a fairy!"

Taking a deep breath, she straightens herself off her father's chest and shows me her nails with matching glitter.

"Oh, wow. Love it," I say, gently holding the tip of her hand in mine.

She stretches from her father's arms and reaches for my braid.

A smile warms Christopher's face, and he winks at me. "Time to set the table," he says to Skye as he sets her down.

She puts her slipper back on and starts tiptoeing from a cupboard to the table as Christopher busies himself at the stove.

"I'll help you if you tell me where to find everything," I offer.

She rushes her movements, proud of her responsibility. Christopher stifles a smile as she sets three plates on the table.

"You can grab the glasses," he says to me while whipping oil, vinegar, and spices in a salad bowl. "Top of that cupboard over there. Grab two wine glasses for us. Skye has her own tumbler."

Three plates, three glasses. So it's just him and his daughter.

I can't help the flutter inside my body, but quickly shut it down.

My reaction is all kinds of wrong.

Christopher sets the Dutch oven on the table, his forearms flexing slightly, a vein standing out against his strong wrist.

He plops Skye on a regular chair boosted by a pair of thick cookbooks. "Please," he says, motioning to the chair across from him. Still standing, he leans over my side to pour wine in my glass, and I'm hugged by his warmth and scent—fresh laundry and something woodsy—and instantly feel both relaxed and incredibly wound up.

We feast on the stew that has been making my stomach rumble for far too long. The meat melts in my mouth and is perfectly completed by farfalle al dente and a tossed salad with homemade vinaigrette. It's touchingly clear from Christopher's ease in the kitchen that he cooks everything from scratch, and if that doesn't make a woman melt, I don't know what will.

How is it that he's single?

"So. You met Sophie," Christopher says.

"I looooove Sophie," Skye cuts in. "She writes fairy tales."

"Is that right? That is so cool!"

"She also reads stories at the library. I *love* story time. Do you like story time, Alek-zandra?"

Story time brings up memories from before. From when Mom was still alive. "I used to love story time." It's a bittersweet memory, so I snuff it. "What else do you like doing?" My eyes dart between Skye and Christopher.

"Hockey," they both answer and laugh at the same time, their eyes dancing.

"Jinx! You owe me two stories, Daddy."

Christopher clutches his chest. "Two?"

We all laugh together, and my eyes well up at the easiness going around the table. "I think I saw an ice rink in the park. Is that where you play hockey?"

"That's The Green. It's just for fun," Skye says.

"The Green?" I ask.

"It's really white right now." She nods, like she knows where I'm coming from. "Did you bring your skates?"

"The Green is the park in the middle of town," Christopher explains. "They flood it in the winter to create an ice rink, but it's only recreational. Hockey happens at The Arena, outside of town. Just a couple of miles after the covered bridge."

"Did you bring your skates?" Skye repeats.

"I'm afraid I don't have skates," I say, amused at the bewildered look on her face when I confess that tidbit of information.

"That's okay," she says. "There's a bin of skates on The Green for people who forgot theirs. You can borrow some. Right, Daddy?"

"Can you skate?" Christopher asks.

"It's been a while."

"No pressure. We don't want you to hurt yourself. We also like to fat bike, right? And snowboard."

Skye nods. "Aunt Grace likes to bike with us. Do you know my aunt Grace?"

"Not yet, but I'm sure I'll meet her soon."

"She's my cousin," Christopher explains. "You'll meet her tomorrow. She takes Skye to school each morning before opening her salon."

"Daddy always picks me up from school because I'm his pri-o-rity. Right, Daddy?"

Christopher sets down his fork and leans over to kiss his daughter's forehead. "Yes you are." While Skye turns back to her food, he furrows his brow and ruffles her hair, his expression both worried and tender in a way that stirs me.

"What grade are you in?"

"I'm in Miss Hen-der-son's class." She nods. "She's very nice. I like her very much." She stares at me intently.

"What do you like most in school?" I ask.

"Do you have children?" she asks back.

"Nope," I answer.

"Are you married?"

"Not married."

She scrunches her face. "But you have a boyfriend, right?"

"No, I don't."

"Why?"

"Skye," Christopher interrupts. "You're being nosy."

She barely glances at her father. "Sorry," she huffs. "Do you have brothers? Is that an okay question?"

"No brothers."

She sighs. "Me neither. I wish I had brothers."

Christopher looks at her, surprised, but says nothing.

"Do you have sisters, then?" she asks.

"No sisters either. Just a very good friend." I anticipate her question, so I add, "Her name is Sarah."

"My best friend is Caroline. We just had a fight, but tomorrow we'll make up."

"Oh yeah. You don't want to stay upset at your best friend."

"Do you look like your mommy?" she asks.

Christopher takes a long sip of his wine.

"You know, I'm not sure. I guess so?" There was a time when I spent hours looking in the mirror, seeking a resemblance. I always came to the conclusion that I must look like Mr. Pierce. Whoever the hell he was. "It doesn't really matter," I add on a hunch.

"Where is your mommy?"

Hmmm. Intuitive. "She's in heaven now."

"I don't have a mommy."

"Well, you have a wonderful daddy."

"Was your daddy sad when your mommy went to heaven?"

"No. I didn't have a daddy."

She widens her eyes.

"Skye, you *are* being too nosy," Christopher says and shifts on his seat. "We don't want to make Alexandra sad, do we?"

"It's alright," I answer with a smile for Skye. "It's not making me sad."

A phone rings in the distance, and Christopher stands reluctantly, his gaze darting between me and Skye. He glances at Skye's plate, which is still nearly full, and makes two portions. "Come on, pumpkin, eat at least this much," he says, pointing to the smaller portion before leaving the room.

It's not lost on me that he's trying to change the conversation.

"How old are you, Skye?" I ask her when he's gone.

"Do you like my daddy?" she asks back.

So, that's what this is. "He seems very nice, and I'm sure I'll learn a lot from him."

She dangles her foot under the table, moves her food around her plate. She seems deep in her thoughts.

"Is there something else you wanted to ask me?" I prompt her. "I don't mind nosy," I add on a whisper.

"Are you going to marry my daddy?" she finally whispers back. Her gaze is fierce, her breathing hitched. She clearly gathered all her courage to ask me that.

This is serious business for her. I owe her a serious answer. "Oh, no. Never. I'm only here to learn and work. And I'll be gone in less than six months."

Her eyes widen and her mouth gapes.

"That sounds like a long time when you are six years old, but in grown-up time, it's very short." I snap my fingers. "It goes by just like that."

She finally brings her food to her mouth. Her eyes never leave me while she chews. "And then, you'll leave?"

"And then, I'll leave."

She takes another forkful while I take a sip of wine. I've never been in her shoes, but I lost my mother when I was barely older than her. Stuff like that makes you think about what matters. "That was very brave of you to ask me that, Skye. You remind me of myself when I was your age."

Christopher walks back in from his phone call. "Someone's appetite is back," he comments, mussing up Skye's hair on his way. "How did that happen?"

Skye glances at me.

"Girl talk," I say.

"Really," he says. "What's that supposed to mean?"

"It's polite for *none of your business*," I answer.

Skye giggles and takes a heaping forkful of food.

Christopher looks at me sternly. God help me, he's even sexier when he's upset.

I hold his gaze for a beat.

He doesn't flinch.

"It was nothing, really," I breathe. "A harmless secret."

He looks back at Skye. "You can use that secret anytime you want. Skye finished her plate."

Skye scrapes the last of the gravy with her fork, wipes her mouth with her napkin, and stacks her cutlery on her plate. She slides off her chair and takes her plate to the sink.

"I'll be right up to tuck you in after dishes," Christopher says.

I stand and start clearing the table. "I'll take care of dishes. Two stories, right? That's got to take some time."

He pauses and looks at me intently. "Are you two ganging up on me?" He flashes a quick smile, and my heartbeat picks up. "I bet you Skye'd forgotten already."

"So not true!" Skye giggles. "And you love reading me stories!"

"*That's* true," he says, following Skye. Turning to me, he adds, "You can tell me all about your baking experience when I come back."

That is going to be a brief conversation, mister, unless we're going to compare different brands of mixes. And I don't think that's what he means by baking.

Chapter Four

Christopher

"Teeth, face, hands and nails."

"I knooooow."

"Lemme see?"

Skye grins and opens her mouth, then shows me her hands.

"Both sides."

"Daddy! You *saw* me wash up."

"What are we reading tonight?"

"Sophie's new bedtime story!" she cries excitedly.

I pull a face, and Skye laughs. "I looooove Sophie's stories!"

"I know, pumpkin. Her stories are something else."

"Yes," she nods frantically.

I take a deep breath and reach for the double-spaced, stapled booklet bearing the library's stamp and Sophie's name below the title, *The Baker and The Princess*.

Fuck me. What did she write this time? "*Once upon a time...*"

While I sift through the pages about a baker pulled from his village to bake bread for his king, my mind wanders back to dinner. I'm pacified by how Alexandra managed to bond with Skye already, yet worried at the same time.

I'm concerned Skye will get attached.

"I will only bake bread for Your Majesty if I can marry the princess."

I'm starting to root for the baker in the story, but soon, my thoughts are overtaken by Alexandra. *"Impale the baker! How dare he!?"*

Did Sophie try to write the story of my life? The baker not good enough for the woman hits very close to home. Except I never loved Skye's mother, even if my daughter is the best accident that ever happened to me.

"Oh, wait, he wants to marry the other princess? Good riddance, here you go!"

Nope, not my story. Not getting married and certainly not to a princess.

When I finish reading Sophie's flowery prose, Skye says, "You see, Daddy, all bakers get married."

This again.

"That baker got married only because he wanted to. And you can tell Caroline, he was the best baker in the country *before* he got married—that's why the king wanted his bread."

She has a big smile on her face. "That's true."

"I do not want or need to get married," I say and boop her nose.

Her face gets serious. "Anyway, Alek-zandra said she won't marry you."

"What?"

"I asked her. She said no." She smiles.

"You—Okay." I chuckle. "That's just as well, because like I said, I don't want to marry her either. Or anyone." How many times do I need to repeat this?

Skye feels threatened by women. She has this irrational fear that a stepmother will turn her into Cinderella or, worse, try and have her killed like Snow White. *Fucking tales*. I've talked about it with her therapist, and she says it's to be expected. So, I suppose it's good she's verbalizing. Heck, more than just verbalizing.

I tuck her comforter tight under the mattress, just how she likes it. "You're all I need in my life."

Her eyes grow wide. "But someday my prince will come and what will you do? You'll be all alone. I don't want you to be alone, Daddy."

Some dude taking my only daughter? Over my dead body. Still, I reassure her. "That's in a very long time. And I won't be alone. I'll have Justin, and Aunt Gracie, and the whole village."

"Sophie, Cassandra, Uncle Craig and Aunt Lynn, Miss Emma, Miss Henderson, Kiara, Willow, Autumn—" Skye is counting on her fingers. We're going to be here all night.

"See? Lots of people. I'll never be alone."

"Second story, Daddy!"

"That's right! I almost forgot." She chooses a Christmas story we've read over and over again, and before I'm done, her breathing has steadied and her eyes are shut.

I know it's the comfort of a familiar story that lulls her, so I keep going until I whisper, "The end."

And then she flits her eyes open and wraps me in a tight hug.

"Who do you want tonight?" I ask and go through the list of her stuffed animal family.

"The whole family, Daddy. They all need me."

I stack the stuffed animals above her pillow. "Don't you keep my little princess awake, you rascals!" I growl.

That always sends Skye giggling. She ties her little hands around my neck again and holds me tighter than usual. "I love you, Daddy."

I pull her close to me, inhaling her baby soap scent. She's who gives me strength, day in, day out. How is it that she's already thought about moving out? I don't want her to grow up. "I love you too. Sleep tight."

"And don't let the bed... bugs... bite."

I kiss her forehead, my heart swelling at the improvements in her speech.

I switch on her turtle night-light before turning off the other lights in her room, and glance at her while I pull the door halfway closed behind me. My heart fills my chest almost painfully.

My daughter is everything I live for. To say that I love her doesn't begin to cover it. She's my life, my blood, my heart, so small and fragile. I'm terrified every day and every night that something might happen to her while I'm not around to protect her.

"I'm sleeping, Daddy. You can go now."

When I get back downstairs, Alexandra is wiping the table. The dishes are all done and put away, expect for our two glasses and what's left of the wine.

I've never had a woman alone here, and I know I shouldn't think about Alexandra like that, but I can't help it. It feels too intimate, and I wish I hadn't prompted her to stay up and wait for me. "You must be tired," I try.

"No, I'm great!" she says as she hangs the dishtowel neatly on a bar handle. She plops her fists on her hips. "You wanted to ask me questions?" Her lips seal together in a thin, forced smile. Her breathing is uneven.

Shit.

She's totally freaked out.

I rub the back of my neck. "Look, I'm sorry if Skye drilled you with questions."

Her face softens and she brushes off my concern with a wave. "She's the cutest. You must be so proud of her."

"I try my best. I guess..." I gather my thoughts and pick up the bottle, a question in my eyes.

"Yeah, please," she says and plops in her chair. She looks wound up.

I pour the wine. "I guess I've been trying to get her to open up about anything that bothers her, and it's working a little too well."

Alexandra chuckles, visibly relaxing. "I think it's great. At least she's clear about what's on her mind. Let's hope she stays that way growing up."

"Yeah, she's got time to figure out filters and shit."

"Screw filters," she says, and I nearly spill the wine, laughing.

"Screw filters," I answer as we clink our glasses.

We let a few moments pass in silence, and it's both awkward and so peaceful.

"So. Why do you want to become a baker?" I finally ask, breaking the spell.

She tucks her feet sideways under her thighs on the chair. "I work for Red Barn Baking. You heard of them?"

Fuck. Why am I surprised. They're tied to the foundation that gave me my grant. Doesn't mean I like them. "Tastes like shit, looks like cardboard. Yeah, I heard of them. Soulless big corp. Didn't know they were interested in baking." *Now why would a girl like her work for these assholes?*

Her eyes widen, and a small smile forms on her lips. "Screw filters, right?"

Forget her looks. I like her attitude. Damn. "What did you do there?" I don't mention rumor has it the founder was from Vermont. Speak of a travesty.

"Well, I'm in digital marketing? That's my thing. So, yeah. Here I am!" Her eyebrows wiggle, and she drops her gaze to her wine.

Marketing? What the fuck? "Did you ever work in their labs. In production." Not sure that would be a good thing, frankly. I'd rather start from scratch, not have to deal with bad habits.

She hesitates, then says, "No, they wanted me to come here to have some experience with that."

Again—what the fuck? Although, these guys can't bake, so... "Figures."

"I—I'm confused..." She frowns briefly. The thin crease that forms between her brows stays, a scar of her emotions.

"I asked you why *you* wanted to become a baker," I say.

She bats her eyelashes. Not in a way that wants to be cute. More like she's trying to get rid of something that's bothering her.

"I have to become a baker in order to keep my job at Red Barn," she says. "And they said I have to complete my apprenticeship here. With you. They need me to pass the French baking exam. They told you that, right?"

She seems like a smart girl. So why does she put up with shit like that? "That sounds right," I say. "They treat their employees like shit, just like their customers."

Her eyes widen for a beat and her cheeks color. "Wait—what did they tell *you* about me?"

They didn't tell me anything. The foundation that gave me my grant said I needed to take in an apprentice, and so I did. I didn't ask anything about the apprentice.

"Nothing," I say. I stand and look out the window, my back to Alexandra. Even if I don't have any reason to question her honesty, something's off. City girls who work in marketing aren't the bread and butter of baking apprenticeships. Unless, that is, they've decided to turn their life around and pursue some lifelong calling. Not the case here, from the looks of it.

My brain needs something neutral to focus on. Something that's not the hot new apprentice with questionable motives to be here.

Justin's pub shines across The Green. Although it's been pitch dark outside for a while now, it's still fairly early, and occasionally the door to the pub opens to let a couple or a group in or out, spilling light on the sidewalk. And if you know what you're listening for, you can hear accents of music too. Up on the hill, lights from farmhouses twinkle. A car's headlights gently swerve in the darkness. It's simple, and peaceful.

It's the best place on earth.

"Where do you work? Offices?" I ask.

"Y-yeah."

"Where?"

"Midtown."

"That's—Manhattan? High rise? You have a view on other buildings? What does it smell like?" I can't begin to imagine it.

"Thirty-second floor. No view. No smell."

"That's gotta be the worst. So, let me get this straight," I say, turning back toward her. She sits up and nods like she knows where I'm going with this. Like she's been through the same thought process and empathizes with me.

"You're here to learn enough of baking so you can pass an exam, so that you can then sit in an office and help make an industrial bakery that poisons people, millions more dollars?"

Yeah, she's just as puzzled as I am.

Just not angry about it.

"You could put it that way, I guess?" She squirms in her chair. "Although the poisoning part?" She scrunches up her nose, purses her full, rosy lips. "Debatable?"

And in that moment, I want to debate it with her. Make her understand what baking is about. What food is about.

I also want to kiss away her worry frown.

"So, explain it to me. What is it that you do, daily." I lean against the kitchen counter, towering over her, but from a safe distance.

She starts explaining the stuff she does, and every now and then throws some jargon, but not in an arrogant manner. More in the way of people who're really good at their job. Breathe it. Her hands get animated and tell half of the story. Her eyes squint.

Her lips take all sorts of interesting shapes.

I'm not listening to what she says, but I'm totally digging the passion she has.

What am I going to do with her?

"I guess they wanted me to experience the real thing," she says as a manner of conclusion.

My gaze flicks back to her eyes. There's a quick recognition on her end that she caught me ogling her mouth. "So they sent you here?"

"You're supposed to be the best baker in the country. Right?" She does a quick scan of my body, and I hope that glint is not what I think it is, because if she's attracted to me the way I'm attracted to her... well, hell.

That can't happen.

Her cheeks are rosy, but I'll chalk that up to the wine.

"What made *you* want to become a baker?" she asks, surprising me. I haven't been asked this in a long while. Me being a baker is part of my identity, and on a typical day, no one questions your identity.

I take my seat back at the table. "At first, I was looking for a way out."

"Out? From where?" she presses.

The wine feels good down my throat and in my veins. "Home."

She nods. "Oh."

"Yeah."

"That bad?"

"In hindsight? Nah. But for an angry teenager, pretty fucking bad. At least in my mind."

She stays quiet, giving me space to say more or nothing at all. "Then, I realized how food brings people together. And how bread transcends that experience. How by the simple act of making bread with my hands every day, I was making my life better. And the life of all who I shared my bread with."

My mind goes back to my apprenticeship, which I had all but fled to, and the values I'd discovered there. "After my apprenticeship in France, I stayed with family in Emerald Creek, worked here and there, and had the opportunity to get this space." I skip the part where that was made possible because of a grant I received from a foundation tied to Red Barn Baking. I'm not proud of the fact that the grant money comes from industrial baking. I always thought they'd helped me out because the founder was from Vermont, supposedly even from Emerald Creek, and maybe that was their way of making some things right in this world.

But mainly, I can't ever have my apprentice know that in order for me to keep the grant, she must pass the French baking exam. I can't put that kind of pressure on Alexandra—on anyone. It wouldn't be fair. My finances shouldn't be the apprentice's problem. An apprenticeship is about discovering a trade, an art, and oneself. It's not a financial transaction. And the apprentice should always feel free to walk away if they discover this is not their path. If she knew what's a stake for me, she'd lose her freedom to leave.

I don't believe in tying people down.

We polished the bottle and our glasses are empty. And although I want this evening to drag on, it's not the right thing to do. There's also the matter of me having just a few hours of sleep ahead of me.

I stand and she follows suit. "Let's make a baker out of you, Pierce. And I'll be damned if you spend one day in a fucking office."

"Mm," she says, doubtful.

"Mark my words." I smile. "Not a day in a fucking office." This time I chuckle to myself. There's something about this girl. I don't know what it is yet, but she doesn't belong in a cage in a city. "You'll have the day off tomorrow. Get settled in. Grace will show you around."

Chapter Five

Alexandra

My room under the eaves is so comfy and the town is so quiet (literally, not a noise all night), that I sleep like a log until my alarm rings. I stretch, turn the alarm off, and sit on my bed.

Thank god Christopher gave me the day off to settle in. I don't know how I'm going to be working with him, for him, for months without jumping his bones. I could hear him toss and turn in his bedroom when I went to bed, and my imagination filled in all the blanks with unusual creativity. If I hadn't been so tired, it would have distracted me enough to stay awake.

Dinner was emotionally intense for me. I'm not used to deep conversations, unless I've had one too many drinks with Sarah. Or if life just got too heavy and I give myself a pep talk and head back to my therapist.

Something stirred inside me last night. Sure, there's that man. Tall, dark, and handsome. A puddle for his daughter. Serving me his home cooked meal and pouring me wine. Those sexy vibes after dinner. I'm not going to discard *that*.

But there was more. A feeling of being home. Since Mom died, I haven't had that. Even if Barbara did everything she could to give me the kindness Rita didn't, it was never like that. Simple. Truthful.

Last night, sitting in this homey, unpretentious kitchen, Skye and Christopher both opened their hearts, their insecurities to me, a perfect stranger. As if to say, *Here's who we are. How about you?*

And this morning, I'm not sure who I am anymore. And that's frigging scary, because this girl needs to keep her eye on the ball and become a baker.

So she can sit in an office and...

I know, I know. *Dammit.* I'll need to dig deeper into how Red Barn makes their bread and treats all of their employees, not just those at headquarters. It'll be my responsibility soon, and that's something I know nothing about on the grand scale. My position in marketing didn't prepare me for that. I'll need more info.

Christopher seems to be the kind of person, the kind of *friend* I would need to help me navigate the situation I'm in. I can tell he's had his share of troubles—he told me so himself—and he seems to have found his way. He's someone who would be precious to brainstorm ideas and solutions with.

But I can't tell him who I really am in relation to Red Barn. He made it clear he despises the company. He's definitely not going to help its next owner. The minute he knows I'm really here to guarantee my position at the top of Red Barn Baking, I'll be out the door.

Which means I'll have lost everything.

Not just a job, not just a future.

I'll have lost the only family I can claim.

Yet I'm torn. Forget the physical attraction. He's a great guy. I want him to like me. I've never had that depth of connection with someone I barely know.

And it's not just Christopher; Skye was an open book to me, and even Sophie, the sweet librarian, was so genuinely welcoming in her own way. How do you open up to people while keeping a big part of your life a secret?

It's not something I can solve right now. I'll have to navigate this as it comes.

Right now, I just need to get in the shower.

Then, I'll finish unpacking.

Little things. Focus on the little things, Alex.

I turn the faucet on, and with no warning, it explodes, water spurting horizontally in icy gushes, soaking me head to toe. I shriek, and shriek louder when I reach into the shower to cut the water off.

My tank top is soaked, my bare legs dripping water. Before I can grab a towel, the door flies open, and Christopher barges in.

"You okay?" he asks, out of breath. "What the hell?" he says, looking around the room, then at my half-naked, dripping self. His breathing hitches, and his eyes drop the length of me. He averts his gaze. "You got the order wrong, Pierce. First, take your clothes off. Then, get in the shower."

I grab a towel and bend over to wipe my legs, but from the look he gives me, I stop and wrap myself in it.

"Seriously, what happened? You scared the shit out of me and Skye."

Skye is standing outside my bathroom door, wide-eyed.

"The shower's not working," I say.

Before I can explain, he's reaching in and turning the faucet on.

"No!" I gasp. Water gushes over the two of us.

"Shit," he hisses and turns the faucet off, but too late. "Damn, it's cold," he says, still leaning inside the shower.

Skye is giggling. I start laughing too.

Then, Christopher turns from the shower, and my legs weaken. His T-shirt clings to his torso, molding his impressive pecs. He shakes the water from his hair, then his eyes fall on me. He's hot as sin, towering over me in the small bathroom. I can't keep my eyes off him, all of him.

"Skye!" A feminine voice sounds from downstairs. "Time for school! Where are you?"

Christopher glances at his daughter. "Go get ready with Aunt Grace, honey. I'll be right down."

He grabs one of my towels and buries his face in it, then rubs his hair. The V-shape of his torso leads my gaze down to his midsection. He dabs his shirt then swears, folds the towel on the sink, and pulls his shirt above his head.

For the moments that he's stuck with his arms above his head, fighting to get out of the wet fabric, I feast on the sight of his chiseled abs, wondering how they'd feel under my hands. Under my lips. Over my belly.

His dark hair forms a happy trail, leading my gaze to his jeans hanging low over his hips.

I'm all warmed up now, cold water forgotten, and the wetness between my legs has nothing to do with a broken shower.

"It's freezing," he groans as he emerges from his shirt.

Judging from the bulge in his pants, not everything in him is cold.

He grabs his shirt and steps out of the bathroom. I treat myself to the sight of his large shoulders, his muscular back, his narrow hips.

I've never throbbed for a man until now.

His back still to me, he plants his fists on his hips. "I'll have your shower fixed today, but you can use my bathroom this morning," he says. "Be ready to leave with Grace in about half an hour. She'll give you the lay of the land." He's talking as if we aren't both half naked. As if this is a totally natural situation.

He pauses. Looks at the room. Grunts at the sight of my unmade bed. "Need to get a different bed," he mumbles. Then, his gaze drops to my suitcase, open on the floor. Clothes are spilling out from it, as well as my journal, and the weathered manila envelope I carry around wherever I go.

And Sarah's gift, propped atop its wrapping paper. I opened it just minutes ago and had a good laugh. And grateful appreciation.

Now? My cheeks are burning. I rush to the suitcase to snatch it, but too late.

Christopher stoops over and grabs it. Pointing to the wrapping paper and with his back still turned to me, he says, "Goodbye gift?"

I clear my throat. "Uh, yeah. That a problem?"

He spins around and pins me in place with his intent gaze. "Not at all. From your boyfriend?" His gaze searches me.

We're so close, his heat radiates into my core, and his scent inebriates me. "From my best friend. I don't have a boyfriend," I breathe. Suddenly that detail seems very important to point out, and I chastise myself for it. For all the not-so-hidden meaning behind that tidbit of information. As if to back up my poor judgment, my gaze goes from the vein beating in his neck, to the stubble on his chin, to his lips so temptingly close, and finally lands on his dark eyes.

"Why not," he grumbles.

"S-Sorry?"

His pecs expand with each of his breaths. "Why doesn't a girl like you have a boyfriend."

Why do the words *a girl like you* make me throb? "I don't do boyfriends," I say.

He cocks an eyebrow and smirks. "Okay," he says, tossing the vibrator on the bed as he leaves my bedroom.

CHAPTER SIX

Christopher

She had hungry eyes, and I wanted to give her what she was begging for. Thank god Skye followed me. When I saw Alexandra, with her soaked tank top clinging to her perky nipples, her gaze caressing me, I would have lost it if my daughter hadn't been right there.

And the way Alexandra watched me try to get out of my shirt?

Fuck.

When I finally got unstuck from my soaked T-shirt, I caught her gaze stroking me from top to bottom until it settled right below my belt and her mouth opened a bit.

I can't let that happen.

There's too much at stake for me.

I grab a clean T-shirt from my bedroom on the way down to catch Skye at breakfast before she leaves with Grace. It's tough for me to stay away from the bakery that early in the day, and I'm thankful for my cousin's help. But I always pick Skye up from school in the afternoons.

"I need a favor," I tell Grace as I pour two cups of coffee and hand her one.

"Sure." She sits across from Skye, while I gulp my coffee standing.

"I have a new apprentice—"

"Alexandra?" She smiles. "Skye told me all about her, didn't you, sweetie?"

Skye nods. "She's really nice, and she's staying less than six months, and six months is short in grown-up time. Right, Daddy?" She turns around on her chair and looks up at me, expecting a confirmation.

Six months with Alexandra in the house is going to be very long.

"I guess so." My daughter seems to have it all figured out. I could use some of her candor right now.

"That's what Alek-zandra said." She turns her back to me and dives into her overnight oatmeal.

It's been less than twenty-four hours, and these two women seem to have it all figured out amongst themselves.

I turn to Grace. "Could you show her around town today, help her settle in?" I scratch at my nails. Alexandra has a manicure, and I need her to get rid of it before starting work.

Grace frowns.

"You'll know what to do. She's a girl—a woman. I figured it would be more welcoming if you—"

"Of course, no worries. I could use a new face around here. Is she very young?"

I scratch my head, knowing what's coming. "Twenty-five?"

She says nothing, just nods with this know-it-all look and a huge grin on her face.

I shake my head. *Not a chance.* "I gotta go," I say, kissing Skye on the forehead. "Knock knock."

"Who's there?"

"Figs."

Skye frowns and tilts her head. She's totally into jokes right now, and I'm going to milk it as long as I can. "Figs who?"

"Figs the doorbell, I've been knocking forever."

She erupts in a fit of laughter. "Figs! Fix! Good one, Daddy." She high-fives me. Grace chuckles and shakes her head. "Never gets old, does it?"

"Let's hope not," I say, and duck into the bakehouse to check on my crew. And also so I don't run into Alexandra.

After an hour or so, I go back up to shower. I've been at work since four. Mid-morning, I usually need to reset, and this morning more than usual.

The bathroom is steamy and smells different. As my brain registers that I told Alexandra to use my shower, my dick goes in full-on needy mode. I lock the door and get under the water. I close my eyes, but all I can see are Alexandra's boobs perking toward me, begging to be fondled. What kind of sound would she make if I sucked on them? Would she push my head between her legs? How does she taste? I open my eyes to change my train of thoughts, and my gaze falls on a long, straight hair at the level of my dick.

Alexandra's hair.

I'm done for.

I stroke myself, giving in to my fantasy of lifting her and fucking her standing up in the bathroom, then throwing her on the bed to take care of her pussy and send her pleading, then flipping her and taking her doggy style, making her mine, putting my mark on her.

That's the price I pay for staying away from women for so long. One delicious temptation and it's a fucking revolution in my pants. A full-on coup.

I come in long, powerful streaks that hit her single hair repeatedly. And tell myself my brain is back in power.

My relief comes, but the frustration doesn't ease.

I shouldn't want her now, but I still do.

Jerking off in the shower like a teenager didn't solve the problem. I need to remove the root cause.

I need to send Alexandra back home.

I wrap a towel around my hips and grab my phone.

Sifting through the emails, I quickly find the contact I'm looking for.

After introducing myself to the receptionist at the Red Barn Foundation, I explain why I'm calling. I'm put on a brief hold, then transferred, and I repeat my request to cancel Alexandra Pierce's apprenticeship, this time buttering it up with some bullshit excuse about another apprentice I committed to.

"I see," the woman on the line says. "In that case, we could send her back when you have a spot for her?"

Shit. I take a deep breath. "Look, this isn't going to work. I just need to cancel this apprenticeship. And I'll cover a week's pay for the apprentice, plus her expenses, or whatever you think is fair." I start to wonder what I'm going to tell Alexandra. *You're too fuckable to be living under my roof?*

"That's disappointing. All right, then. I'll send over the rider to the grant."

"Come again?"

"The grant. It's to become a loan if the apprenticeship isn't successful."

Fuck. Right. "But she just got here last night. We didn't get started yet. Can't you send me another apprentice? Anyone else."

"Has Ms. Pierce done something to displease you?"

God, no. "No. Not—Not exactly."

"How do you mean? What happened?"

"Why can't you send me someone else."

"Because these are the instructions of the late Ms. Douglas. Ms. Pierce is to complete her apprenticeship with you, in Emerald Creek. These are the conditions stated in your grant."

When I decided to open my bakery in this small Vermont town, I applied for grants and loans without much hope. Until I received a crazy offer from a New York-based nonprofit: a grant covering the purchase of the whole building and the baking equipment. I didn't really believe it until the money was in the bank.

"I don't remember my grant stating a specific apprentice." What I remember clearly now was the thirty-minute online meeting I had with Rita Douglas, a stern woman who grilled me about my baking. I looked her up online after we hung up. She was the founder of Red Barn Baking, the industrial bakery chain that had hundreds, maybe thousands of storefronts, now synonymous with industrial bread in the US. They embody everything I loathe about baking.

That I got the grant from her foundation is still unbelievable to me.

"Correct. The grant doesn't name the apprentice, but the instructions for the disbursement of the private funds Ms. Douglas donated toward your grant do. We can't go around it. I'm sorry."

What was I thinking? That they'd do the right thing and help a kid learn a new trade, make a living for him or herself? Of course not. They'd use it for their own purposes. Give some training to someone in marketing. Whatever the fuck they're going to use that for.

I made a deal with the devil, and it's pay time.

And the price is a hot, age appropriate, single woman sleeping in my house for six months. She's clueless about baking, but at this point it's a detail. I can work with that. She seems motivated.

What I can't work with, is the lust she's awakened in me.

And maybe worse, the fact that she's *likeable*.

I shut my eyes. I can do the right thing for my business and keep my grant but put my sanity at risk. Because there is no way I am going to let anything happen between us. It would be unprofessional, unethical, and a disaster when Alexandra moves back home. So, the only certain thing is, my dick is sitting this one out.

Or I can send her back and not have to live with the temptation but lose my grant and owe a shitload of money. My business is doing well enough that I could pay it back, but I have bigger dreams for the bakery that require capital. And the real reason I want to grow the business is for Skye. To offer her the best life I can.

So, the dilemma boils down to this. My sanity or my daughter's future.

Also, I'd like to believe I'm better than that. I *can* get her out of my system. I just need to look the other way.

"Do you want to think about it, Mr. Wright?" the voice on the phone says.

"No. No, I'll make it work. Thank you." I hang up and clench my jaw.

There are three reasons why nothing can or will happen between me and Alexandra: Skye, Women, and Time.

Reason number one, Skye. She's my priority in life. She needs stability and protection. She was abandoned by her birth mother. I can't expose her to a substitute but uncertain mother figure. That brings me to—

Reason number two, women. Fickle creatures with often-hidden agendas. I learned that lesson early on. I'm not going to get burned again.

Reason number three, time. Alexandra is not here to stay, but she will be here long enough that any intimate relationship would lead to disaster in one of two ways. Either heartbreak for me and Skye when Alexandra leaves or a total clusterfuck of annoyance at the bakery and at home if things don't work out between us and go south before she leaves.

And, in my experience, things always go south with women. And I don't mean that in a dirty way.

I just hope Alexandra has what it takes to be successful in the apprenticeship, because if she doesn't, I'm losing my grant. But hey, that's a risk I have to take.

Chapter Seven

Alexandra

After showering in Christopher's bathroom, I quickly dry my hair, tie it in a braid, throw on a pair of jeans and a sweater, and grab my puffer jacket, a hat, and gloves.

The bakery smells heavenly, and my stomach growls as I hurry down the stairs. The low hum of conversations grows, then Skye's voice pipes before I can see her, "That's her! That's Alek-zandra!"

And the bakery goes dead silent.

The customers lined up at the register turn their backs to the counter and face me. Most are smiling. Some are plain gaping. Skye is beaming.

A young woman crouched in front of her stands to greet me, pulling me out of my stunned freeze. "I'm Grace," she says, extending her hand. She has Skye and Christopher's jet-black, curly hair, and her dark irises seem to dance with her smile. Her handshake is soft and firm and short. "Let's get you outta here," she says with a side glance to the line of customers, and a giggle.

Skye grabs my hand. I wave faintly to the customers and am rewarded with full-on smiles.

Once outside, I shiver, more from sheer pleasure than from the cold. Sometime overnight it must have snowed again. A pure white layer covers the street, and the sun now glistens over the village. I squint while Grace pulls out a pair of sunglasses.

She shakes her head. "Sorry about the welcome committee," she says as we step onto the sidewalk.

I chuckle. "That was actually cute."

Skye trails her mittened hand alongside a white picket fence, gathering snow in her little fist, then throwing it in the air. Tree branches trimmed with white powder, hang low over the sidewalk. The few cars out this morning tread slowly on the unplowed street.

"Christopher says you drove in last night? How were the roads?"

Dark and slick. I shrug. "I made it."

Grace eyes me sideways with a grin. "What kinda car you have?"

"A rental," is my answer. I don't know anything about cars. "Which I need to return. It's costing me a fortune."

"Ah. I'll ask my brother to return it for you."

Um... "That's not nec—"

"He's a mechanic," she adds as if that was explanation enough. "He loves cars. You'll be doing him a favor. He's always looking for an excuse to drive around."

Well, then. That settles it.

As we reach the school, Skye lets go of Grace's hand. "Caroline!" she calls as she runs to meet a little girl bundled in a light pink coat with matching boots. Caroline is holding the hand of a woman tightly wrapped in a sleek, black puff coat who appears to be her mother.

Despite the frigid temperature, the cold doesn't seem to bother Caroline's mother. She's not wearing a hat, and her beautiful blond curls bounce freely around her shoulders, while her breath escapes her plump, pink lips in cute little puffs as she exhales and smiles our way. "Hey, girl," she says, giving Grace a quick side hug while she glances at me. "I'm Emma," she adds and extends her hand to me.

"Alex. I'm apprenticing at the bakery." I try not to flinch at the strong grip she has on my hand.

"So I've heard. Are you staying with Grace, then?" she says, finally releasing my hand.

"No—I'm... I'm staying at the bakery."

"So it's true." She squints. "Well I guess... Welcome to Emerald Creek?"

"Thanks." I turn my attention to Skye entering the school with her friend. At the last minute, she turns around and waves at me. "Bye, Alek-zandra!" she says at the top of her lungs, a huge, gap-toothed smile lighting her entire face.

I blow her a kiss back. "Wow, she likes you already," Emma says.

"Let's take the long way back," Grace says, looping her arm in mine. "See you later, Ems."

Tilting my head up, I'm taken by the brightness of the blue sky. Plumes of smoke billow from chimneys of the houses up on the hill. The cold air is crisp on my cheeks, the snow soft under my feet, and the faint smell of burning wood holds the promise of coziness and simple pleasures.

A smile forms on my lips. It won't be hard to love my stay here. One slightly abrasive person won't change that.

"I'm sorry about Emma," Grace says once we're out of earshot. "She seems to be having a bad day. She's normally friendlier. She's pretty protective of our little town, I suppose."

"It's alright," I say. "She wasn't rude or anything." *Just destroyed my hand.* "I understand being guarded toward strangers. It's probably even a good thing."

"That's not how we normally treat people here." She chuckles. "Once you get to know her, she's cool though. She became a CPA while raising Caroline on her own."

"Wow." That is pretty impressive. It doesn't escape me that her situation seems to draw a lot of parallels with Christopher's. And my mother's. "I grew up in small town, raised by a single mom too. That 'It takes a village' saying was pretty real for me as a kid. I can see where she's coming from."

I snap a few pictures, admiring the contrast of the harmonies of white with the bright blue of the sky and the dark green of the trees.

"I thought you were from New York City?"

"Nope. As a kid, I grew up upstate. But it got messy after my mom died. I moved in with my grandmother, and she packed me off to boarding school."

"Oh. I'm sorry."

I shrug. "It was for the best. She had her own stuff going on. I don't blame her. I've been living in the city since I graduated college, though."

"I used to fantasize about going to boarding school," she says, chuckling. "I bet it wasn't as fun as it seems."

Well, it wasn't exactly camp, and also Mom would have never done that to me, so... "It was alright." We reach the covered bridge, a long wooden structure with a red roof. "Is that the creek?" I ask, pointing under our feet to the white, unmoving expanse. The bridge seems to be spanning a very flat ribbon of land.

"Yup. That's the creek. It's large around here, more like a river. It gets pretty big in the spring. But right now it's frozen solid." And covered in snow. There is no telling where the river stops and where the banks start. It's all a white expanse shining under the sun as if a trail of diamonds had been scattered.

Once on the other side of the bridge, we walk uphill for a bit, and I slip a couple of times. "I'll have to upgrade my boots," I say chuckling and admiring Grace's fur-lined, thick-soled footwear.

"Sure," she says. "Let's take you to the General Store." We hang a left on a narrow road. The village lays across from us, brick federalist houses and white capes and colorful Victorian houses elbow to elbow, forming a charming and diverse picture. A woman shakes the snow off her trees and stops to wave at a man two houses down shoveling his portion of the sidewalk. I snap a few pictures again, then catch up with Grace. We take a second covered bridge back into town.

As Grace turns around to check on me, I take a photo of her, framed by the covered bridge, the village behind her, her sunglasses reflecting the snowy hill, and her deep red lips curved up in a smile.

"Now, I really know what a storybook village looks like," I say as I close the gap between us and tuck my hands in my pockets. Taking my gloves off just a few moments to take pictures was enough to make my fingers numb with cold.

"Aww," Grace says. "It *is* beautiful. I suppose we take it for granted most of the time." We cross the bridge in silence, our feet loud on the wooden planks. "Did you have time for breakfast?" Grace asks.

"Uh... no, but I'm fine," I lie.

"Tsk tsk tsk. Did Chris pull you out of bed this morning?"

I'm suddenly warmer. *He nearly pulled me out of the shower and looked like he wanted to try my new vibrator on me.* "No, I just... ran out of time."

"Well, I could use a cup of coffee. Let's grab something at Easy Monday's and then we'll hit the store for those boots."

Easy Monday is a coffee shop that smells like a box of chocolates and a mug of coffee had a love baby named Cinnamon. My mouth waters and my nose tingles from the warmth inside. The space is large yet comfy, with shelves overflowing with books, board games stacked on the carpeted floor, and a hodgepodge of armchairs and couches and tattered coffee tables.

"Gracie! It's been a hot minute," a woman about our age says. She's sitting in a deep couch, surrounded by colorful pillows. "And you brought our new resident with you." The woman closes her book and smiles at me. "Welcome to Emerald Creek. I'm Autumn." She stands, her beautiful red hair cascading on her shoulders, and a big smile and the cutest dimples illuminate her face. "I have to go, but I'll catch up with you later."

"My girls!" Another young woman says from behind the counter. "How can I make your day awesome?"

"That's Millie," Grace says to me as she drops her coat on the closest armchair.

Millie gives me a concerned smile. "Tea and honey for you, sweetie? I hear you're sleeping in a drafty attic full of critters."

I laugh. "The room is lovely, and tea and honey sound great. But this morning, I'll just have your house coffee and a muffin," I answer as I take my coat, gloves, and hat off.

"Just house coffee? And what kind of muffin?"

"Whatever's most popular."

"That would be the apple cider donut."

My stomach growls. "Sounds amazing."

A dreamy look plays on her face. "You have simple tastes for a big city girl."

"How'd you know... never mind." I smile.

"Same for me," Grace says.

As we take our seats, she waves at Autumn through the window. "Autumn's family owns the antique shop, and she's trying to make it as a decorator. It doesn't pay the bills yet, but we all have faith in her." As Autumn saunters away, her smile stays with me. People seem genuinely happy here. And why wouldn't they be? Beautiful nature, lovely friends, low stress, as far as I can see. Winning combination.

After we're settled with our coffees for hand warmers, Grace says, "You must be a tough cookie if Chris took you on as an apprentice."

How do I answer her? "I don't know about that."

"He doesn't accept just anyone," she presses on.

Despite what Christopher said last night, I know I won't become a baker. At least not how Christopher means it. I don't want to lie about that.

"It all happened really fast. I was told I had to take the apprenticeship to keep my job." It's only a half-truth. I hate lying, but I need to remind myself that I can't chance Christopher finding out I'm Red Barn's next owner once I succeed in this apprenticeship. He'd cancel the apprenticeship, and that would mean losing Red Barn. Rita's wishes matter to me right now. They're the one thing that tie me to family. "I'm not sure I'm up to his expectations, to be honest."

"Don't let his grumpy ways get to you," Grace says. "He asks a lot of his staff, but he's a softy inside. Just don't let him walk all over you."

Millie sets two huge, dark-colored donuts in front of us. "A softy? I heard there's mice nesting in her bed."

I giggle. I love how she mingles uninvited in the conversation.

"A little late for not being walked all over," she adds.

Unsure how to answer that, I take a bite of the donut, and *oh my god*. I have to close my eyes.

I moan.

"Unh-huh," Millie says as she sways away.

"He makes those, by the way," Grace says.

I open my eyes, blinking at her. Of course he does, he owns the bakery. These donuts are insane. His cooking last night was heaven. His body is a dream. And don't get me started on his eyes.

Grace chuckles. "Yup," she says as if she can read right through me. "I'll be right back," she adds, heading for the bathroom and sparing me the embarrassment of being so obviously smitten with her cousin.

I shake away the thoughts. I can't be crushing on my boss. That would be a really bad idea. The worst. I give myself ten seconds to be back to who I am. Alexandra Pierce, potential heir to Red Barn Baking, here to fulfill her grandmother's dying wish.

A girl on a mission.

Eyes on the prize: passing a baking exam.

And nothing else.

I count back from ten.

I think I'm good now.

While Grace is away, I log into the wi-fi and send Sarah the photos I took. I can't wait to share my excitement with her.

Sarah

> Welcome to my storybook village. [4 attachments]

> So jealous. When can I visit?

I respond with a smiley and shut down my phone as Grace comes back from the bathroom.

"Everything okay?" she asks.

"Just making my friend jealous."

She laughs. "I bet you have a lot of friends in the city."

Nope. Once people know who I am, they either hate my guts or try to take advantage of me. "What makes you think that?"

She shrugs like it's obvious. "You're just so likeable."

"That's very nice of you to say. But actually, people are super busy in the city. Always running somewhere. It's hard to make friends."

"Huh. Well, we have nowhere to run to. Everything we need is right here! Ready for those new boots?"

A huge smile stretches across my face. "Always ready for new boots." We bundle up and head out.

The General Store delivers on the promise of its name. Behind a cute but unassuming entrance on Maple Street, it goes on and on, with a basement level and an upper level, and sells pretty much anything you didn't know you needed.

"Thank you so much for doing this for me," I say as I slip on a pair of Sorels and compare them to the Helly Hansens I just had on.

"No problem. This is fun," Grace says as she tries on fur-lined slippers.

I make my selection, and my eyes fall on the cutest pair of Darn Tough socks—dark green with blue deer. I place them on top of the boots I chose—tall with crisscross laces and light fur lining. "Let's go or I'll keep buying stuff," I say, giggling. "Actually, hold on." I put on the boots I'm buying and place mine in the box. "This will be more comfortable."

As we make our way back to the front of the store, we pass a small room to the side, lined with wine bottles on racks. I hop inside and grab a bottle of white wine to bring back home. I'm not sure what the apprenticeship deal is in terms of food, but common sense tells me it doesn't cover booze.

"At least my hands are full now. I can't buy anything else," I say as we head to the register. "Actually. Hold it." There's a rack of sunglasses, and one of them has my name on it.

"Did you want to look up our mouse traps?" The cashier, an older man in blue coveralls, says when we finally get to him with my boots, my socks, my booze, and my sunglasses. "We have humane ones. Thought a city girl like you might appreciate that. But then again, they might not be enough for the rats you're dealing with. We got pretty much every this and that in terms of traps."

Grace is shaking with restrained laughter.

"I'm... I'm fine. I promise there are no mice, or rats, in my bedroom. Totally fine. Scout's honor. Thanks, though."

When we step out, I have to ask. "What's with all that? Is that some kind of prank they play on newcomers?"

Grace checks her phone and giggles. "It's Echoes. It's a closed social media group, just for Emerald Creek, where people post stuff they're selling, or if they need help with anything. Or whatever complaints they have."

"Lemme guess—it's every gossip's dream."

"You guessed right. The thing is, that's where all the important notices are posted, so we all go there, and we all read it every morning. It's our newspaper. For the people and By the people, sort of. It has all the trivia you need to survive life in this small town. If the library is closing early. If the General Store is having a sale. If there's going to be construction on the one road that goes in and out of Emerald Creek. That's where it's posted."

"If the baker just got a new apprentice," I suggest.

"And that she's sleeping in an attic."

"It's not an attic! It's the cutest room I've ever had." Am I feeling oddly protective of Christopher? The way he felt embarrassed last night comes back to my mind. "You should see some of the places I lived in when I just graduated college." Honestly, I don't know what all the fuss is about regarding that supposed attic. "Plus, his cooking is heavenly."

Grace quirks an eyebrow up and cracks a huge smile at me. I blush as I realize I just defended Christopher when we were just talking about a room. She bumps my shoulder and laughs. "My cousin's the best," she confirms.

I look down and bite my lip, but I know we just had a moment. And it feels great.

"Come on, I have time to show you my salon before my first client," Grace says.

"Sweet." I'm going to milk every minute of my day off.

There's a gentle breeze when we're back on the street. As we walk past the bakery, the wind picks up and light snow blows up and around us, enveloping us and reflecting the sun. It's so magically beautiful, I stop in my tracks, set my bags in the snow, and pull my phone out, taking a selfie video while I twirl around, my eyes closed. "It's... it's like I'm in a snow globe!"

My mouth is open in awe, but not for long. A snowball hits my teeth lightly, shocking me back to reality. Grace is bent at the waist laughing. "Did you just...?"

She wipes the tears from her eyes and pulls my arm. "Let's go."

"Can I just drop my bags?"

"Nope. Chris might drag you to work if you go in there. Plus, I'm just a block away. Over there is Lazy's." She points across The Green, to a pub that seems closed right now. "Justin, the owner, opens around noon, most days. Depends. It's a fun place. Actually, do you have plans for tonight?"

Apart from feeling awkward if I'm having dinner with Christopher and Skye? "Nope. No plans."

"Alright then. Let's meet there around five, five-thirty. You'll love it. And this is me!" She stops in front of a two-story brick house with white columns. Wreaths hang on each of the windows, and a large Christmas swag adorns the stained-glass front door. Lights gently flicker on the window boxes filled with pinecones and greenery.

We take our boots off and Grace flicks the recessed lighting on, then lights scented candles. A subtle cedar and spice fragrance warms the atmosphere. Soon, accents of acoustic guitar flow softly from hidden speakers.

The wooden floors creak under my feet as I make my way through the airy space. Blond leather armchairs strewn with cashmere throws are scattered throughout. Side tables laden with magazines are an invitation to just sit and relax. "I'd come here just for the wait," I tell Grace, running my hand over the soft velvet of a wingback chair. It's set next to a simple pine buffet transformed into a coffee and tea station, complete with a Keurig machine, a kettle, and an assortment of organic loose-leaf teas. On a shelf above, a hodgepodge of artisan-made mugs in earth tones are next to a neat pile of red flannel tea towels.

I pull my phone out and take photos of the many details that make me want to just spend the day there getting pampered. I spot her social media handles on a discreet sign, and my instincts kick in.

"Should we remove those for you before you start work?" Grace asks, pointing at my nails.

I look at the gel manicure I had done two weeks ago. Before Rita passed away. Since then, my life has been turned upside down.

"I haven't thought about that. Should I?" I answer while posting and tagging the brands she uses.

She shrugs. "You're the baker."

"Ugh—not. I guess I should? Yeah. Tells you how unprepared I am."

"So, this apprenticeship wasn't... really planned?" she says as we sit at the nail station, and she soaks my fingers.

Not by me. "Yeah, no." I sigh. The soft music and warm scents are getting to me, making my eyelids heavy. I yawn.

"That mountain air making you tired already?" she teases.

"I've had a rough week."

She tilts her head, ready to listen, but not prying.

"My grandmother died a week ago." Coldness settles at the pit of my stomach. "She was the only family I had."

She pauses her scraping of my nails. "Oh... I had no idea. I'm so sorry."

"We weren't that close, but still. It's just me, now." I don't *miss* Rita. I miss having a family, any family. Someone to call my own, however messed up they might be. "And now, my job is turning from being a marketing geek to becoming a baker."

Her eyebrows shoot up. "That's a lot! Like I said, don't let Chris overwork you. He does that to people. You need to focus on yourself. Get grounded again." She's almost done with my nails. "Tell you what. I'm working on becoming a massage therapist—"

"Oh, that's exciting!"

"—so I'll use you as a guinea pig. How's that?"

"Fantastic. And I can help with your social media, if you need it."

"Yes, please! Now, let me roll up your sleeves," she says, then massages my hands with a lotion that smells heavenly.

"Have you lived in Emerald Creek all your life?" I ask her.

"Mostly. I lived in Texas for a little while, when I was married. Then, after my divorce, I came back here."

"Oh, I'm s—"

"Nothing to be sorry about. We all make mistakes, don't we?" She flexes my fingers back, giving me a relaxing hand stretch. "I like it here," she says, looking out the window. "It's home, you know? My mom lives outside the village, my brother is up the road, Chris and Skye are right here, and the people of Emerald Creek are good people. That's all I really need," she says with a soft smile.

There has to be more to her story, but I'm not going to ask. The truth is, she does seem at peace and fulfilled. Something I will probably never experience. "I have to say, it must be wonderful to be able to build a life here."

"It is. Who knows? Maybe you'll stay," she says lightly.

"Oh, no, I couldn't. I need to get back to New York."

"Of course. Do you like it over there?"

I hate it over there. "It's—It's complicated."

She rolls my sleeves down. "I'm sure."

"You have your family here."

"You'll find yours. Sometimes, the strongest families are those you choose, not those you were born into," she says.

I think about this for a bit. If I weren't the kind of person who constantly attracted disaster, I would probably yearn for a solid relationship. Marriage. Children. Being part of my spouse's family. My heart tightens. "The company I work for in New York, it's like a big family." I've repeated this mantra—one of Rita's mantras—often, believing it wholeheartedly. But, somehow, it feels a bit odd today.

Grace smiles softly, pretending to go along with my answer. People who have a family don't understand people like me, and it's okay. I'm used to that. I just don't have the words or energy to explain that, when you can't have the thing you want most, you just make up a substitute for it.

I pull out my phone and take close-up photos of Grace as she cleans the nail station. "You look so much like Skye, you could be her mother."

"Mm," Grace says, her gaze darkening as she stands.

"Sorry. I didn't mean to—"

"It's all right. Skye doesn't have a mother," she says, confirming what Skye said last night. "It's a touchy subject, mainly for Chris. I think he struggles with how to protect her from the pain." She runs her hand through her hair. "I'm around as much as I can, but it's not the same. There's going to be a day when she asks why. And, deep down, she has to know that her mother didn't want her, you know? It's not like she died tragically or anything."

She doesn't tell me what happened, and although I'm burning to know, I don't ask. I've been here less than twenty-four hours, and she's opening up about family secrets already. Just like Christopher and Skye last night. When was the last time someone opened up to me?

"He takes her to therapy," she continues as we make our way toward the front of the salon. "She'll be okay. She's already okay." Her eyes narrow on me, concern in her expression. "Chris, I'm not so sure. I worry about him, sometimes. He can be so tough on the outside, but inside, he's all mush. You know how men are."

"Not really." I blush as I slip my coat on. She looks at me with curiosity. Although I hate to talk about myself, I can't stay a closed book after everything she just unloaded on me. "No father, no brother, or even cousins. And I've never had a serious relationship. Don't want one. It's not in the cards for me."

She seems amused. "Is that so?"

"Hundred percent."

She looks at me differently, like I'm a mystery to her and she's trying to figure me out, but at least she's not trying to convince me that a man is the best thing that could ever happen to me. I suppose I can credit that to her divorce. It's almost like I can hear Rita's approval.

"You're a good listener," she says. A smile warms her features again. "That's a rare thing."

"I'm sorry if I appeared nosy... regarding Skye." My cheeks heat up again. "It wasn't my intention."

"You're not nosy, Alex. You're caring. I can tell the difference. And I'm happy you'll be staying with Chris and Skye for a while. Skye... she already likes you. And Chris? He needs to get out of his comfort zone." She smiles mischievously at me as the doorbell chimes and her first client enters

The funny things happening in my stomach at her words need to stop.

Right. Now.

Chapter Eight

Christopher

I wrap up a quiet late afternoon in the bakeshop, but I feel more electrified than my usual peaceful, winding-down mood. I double-check all my preparations for the next day and verify our orders for the third time.

I bring out the training material for Pierce: her manual with my annotations and target dates for completion. She'll be done on time if she progresses at twice the average time, which is doable. I dig out baking clothes from our uniform closet, fold them in a neat pile, and stack them next to her manual. I write her name on the cover, and my heartbeat picks up like I'm a fucking teenager. *Get a grip, Wright.*

I check the time. It's only six p.m. Emma called to invite Skye for a sleepover tonight, and I dropped her off an hour ago.

The house always feels empty without my daughter. The huge Victorian is too big for the two of us to begin with, and there's nothing I can do about that. It's where my bakery is, and it's a great location. It's just... huge. And right now, empty.

Ems invited me to stay for dinner, but it didn't feel right to leave Alexandra alone, so I came right back.

And on the way I realized it didn't feel right to be alone with Alexandra either.

So at first, I was relieved to find her note on the kitchen counter about her going out for dinner with Grace.

And then I got pissed.

And now I don't know what to do with myself. Which means, I'm headed to Lazy's, my best friend Justin's pub.

I shower again and put on a clean shirt.

As I push the door to Lazy's, looking forward to some quiet guy time with Justin, there she is.

Her head is tilted back as she laughs wholeheartedly at something Grace is saying. Her delicate neck is the first thing I see, her mouth wide open the next. She straightens in her booth, and her laugh dies as our eyes lock. I nod curtly and make my way to the bar. And nearly trip over Justin's dog, Moose, who's laying in his usual spot smack in the middle of the way. Moose lifts his head and squints at me. I squat and pat him. "Sorry, buddy," I say. He grunts his forgiveness and lays his head back on the floor.

Justin hasn't picked up on this, and it's just as well. He pours me my usual draft IPA. "Shane made a mean pulled pork tonight," he says.

"What's it come with?"

"Some dude's fancy bun."

Huh. I was wondering why they ordered brioche buns from me yesterday. "Guess I gotta try it then."

Shane is Lazy's chef. He used to work for the fancy restaurant next door, and since he left to work for Justin, he's been doing a heck of a job with all the comfort foods that are the staple at Justin's establishment.

"You got it," Justin says. "Grace and Alex are over there," he adds, pointing with his chin. "I'm about to bring them their soups. Should I set you up with them?"

He knows Alexandra by name already? I pull a bar stool. "I'll stay right here."

He cocks an eyebrow. "Whatever you say."

The place is filling up, but all I can hear is Alexandra's laughter and voice. She isn't loud, far from it. It's as though her voice is on a frequency that hits me just below the ribcage and radiates from there.

I've never felt that way about a woman.

My food comes out quickly, but I'm not hungry. I stare at it. Then take a bite. It melts in my mouth. The flavor of the meat is enhanced by the brioche bun, which also has the perfect soaking capacity.

Bread making is an art. A passion. It's not a hobby, at least not in my bakery. Alexandra is going to find out pretty soon.

There's something off with her story. I have the gut feeling she's not telling me half the truth of why she's here. I hate liars, but for some reason, she's giving me a different vibe. Like she doesn't really have another option than to play her cards close to her chest.

I need her to succeed, but not at the cost of her well-being. If she finds out this is too much for her and she walks out on the apprenticeship, then so be it. I'll deal with the financial consequences.

Although the walking out would sting for other reasons.

She's kind and helpful. Smart and funny. Sassy. Sexy as hell.

She has a magic touch with Skye.

She's a gem of a woman.

I'm fucked, right?

Yeah. I'm fucked.

"Something wrong with the pulled pork?" Justin says, interrupting my thoughts.

I zap out of it. "It's delicious." I take another bite and then another before it gets cold.

He frowns and leaves, shaking his head. When he comes back a few minutes later with a tall glass of iced tea, he talks my head off about an outdoor restaurant section he wants to put together for the fair this summer.

At the mention of the summer fair, I have an image of Alexandra in a sundress, the gentle breeze showing her thighs, the sunlight playing in her hair, her laughter cascading down my body. But she'll be gone by summer. I tune him out and agree to whatever he thinks I should be doing on my end.

"So... Alex, huh?" Justin says after a long pull on his drink.

"What about her."

His eyes stay zoned in on me. "She's hot."

My jaw clenches.

"You don't think so?" He says when I don't answer.

I force a shrug. "She's my employee."

"So?"

"So what?"

He looks her way. "Where's she staying?"

I narrow my eyes on him. "How so."

"Where does she live? She from around here? Never seen her before."

"You know where she's staying."

"Won't believe it until I hear it from you."

Justin and I go way back. We have that kind of friendship where I don't need to tell him anything. He knows when something's up with me, and what's up, without me needing to tell him. It's half because we go way back, half because this is a small town, and half because he's the pub owner and bartender on top of having grown up on a local farm.

I know, that's more halves than you need to make a whole, but it doesn't even begin to cover everything that Justin is.

He produces a notebook. "I'm taking bets on how long it'll take you to get in her bed. Wanna see the odds?"

Yeah, he's also half asshole.

I pretend to grab the notebook, expecting him to keep it out of my reach, but he lets me take it. I flip it open to make my point that no one cares but him, but there it is. Three neat columns, with the names of my friends on the left, a date in the middle, and a dollar amount on the right.

Make that total asshole. "You gotta be kidding me," I say as I throw the notebook on the counter like I don't care. "You guys need to get a life."

"*We* need to get a life?"

I nod. "You guys are sad."

He smacks his lips. "You know what's sad? Let me tell you. That girl over there has been looking at nothing but you since you got here, and you're not going to do a goddamn thing about it."

"You're right about that. Not a thing."

"And why is that?"

"Told ya. She works for me."

"Lot to unpack in that answer."

"Yeah?"

"Yeah." He moves to my side of the bar and pulls a stool close to me. Then he leans over. "You coulda said she's not your type. You coulda said it'd be weird for Skye. Hell, you coulda said she's got bad breath." He looks at me, like he's giving me a chance to say something. "But no," he continues. "The only lame-ass excuse you could come up with is that *she works for you*. And that's not a reason at all to not be interested."

He grabs the booklet from the bar, a pen from his pocket, and scribbles his own estimate of how full of shit I am.

It'd be fun if I was the kind of guy who was fine with casual relationships. Someone like Justin, for example.

But I'm not like that. It took me a while to get over what happened with Skye's mother, and I didn't even like her that much.

I can only imagine what it would be like to have a woman like Alexandra, only to see her leave.

Chapter Nine

Alexandra

Too many beers, too little sleep.

I wake up with a dull headache, but still push the door to the bakehouse at six a.m. sharp, right on time for my first day. I'm barely awake, but I need to get through this day, and the next, and the one after that.

However many days to make up the five to six months that separate me from claiming Red Barn Baking as mine and fulfilling my grandmother's wishes.

Small, steady steps, getting me closer to the goal.

No more late nights with too many beers for me.

The good news is, the smell of baking bread clears away my headache instantly.

The bakehouse hums with the sounds of ovens at full speed, the clatter of metal trays against metal tables, and the chatter of a handful of people working. Bright lights shake my system close to awake mode, but my eyes protest and blink repeatedly. A couple of people smile warmly at me, then go about carrying trays in and out of ovens, shaping dough, mixing things.

Strapped in a white chef jacket with a straight collar, Christopher is pacing between two rows of prep tables.

Except for a few stolen glances at Lazy's last night, I haven't seen him since our too-close encounter in my bathroom almost twenty-four hours ago, and I'm not sure how this morning will go.

Minutes into my first day of work, images of my boss's naked torso and wet jeans are superimposed with his smirk as he toyed with my vibrator. My hands are clammy and my knees weak. What's up with that?

I take a steadying breath, trying to act cool and detached as I wait for him to notice my arrival. His back to me, he approaches a petite woman dressed in the same white chef uniform as him. Leaning over, he points to something on the prep table, making her laugh, his eyes dancing in response. Their complicity is obvious, rippling through the room as others smile at their exchange. Even my traitorous body starts to relax.

Until she turns to me, her laughter replaced with an inquisitive look that bounces from me to Christopher.

Christopher's gaze does a full swipe of my body, and I feel myself burn up with embarrassment. "Alexandra's our new apprentice," he says, answering her unspoken question.

She tilts her pretty face up to him. "You okay, boss? You look like you're having a stroke," she teases.

"And this is Kiara, our on-and-off pastry chef."

Kiara plants her fists on her hips. "On-and-off?"

"When she's not chasing some pipe dream in a big city, she graces us with her presence," Christopher says, his gaze not leaving my body.

"Meanwhile, Alexandra's here to stick it to some office-bound assholes."

Kiara seizes me top to bottom, a small smile spreading on her face. "That right?"

"Just ask her," he shoots back, gaze darkening as if I'm still half-naked and wet in the bathroom and really, *what's up with that*?

Her eyes dart between the two of us, curiosity and amusement in her gaze. "I just did. You didn't let her answer."

Arms crossed, which, incidentally, makes his biceps bulge, eyes still pinned on me but trailing down the length of me and that's just downright unnerving, he answers without missing a beat. "She didn't answer 'cause you're too intimidating. I don't want you scaring her away." My spine tingles at his confession.

"Well, I'll be fucked," Kiara mumbles. "I'm scary now?"

Christopher glances at her. It takes him a nanosecond to round her body with his gaze. She's all of five feet, maybe one hundred pounds. Seeing her point, he explains, "Your social skills need polishing."

"Look who's talking." She steps away from Christopher. "Yo, Bambi."

She's looking my way, so that would be me. "Y-yes?"

"Why'd you come all the way to Creepy Creeks to learn how to bake?"

Creepy Creeks? Okay.

Modeling my conversational style after hers, I point my thumb to Christopher. "What he said."

"To stick it to the big guy?"

My lips curl up. "Something along those lines, yeah."

"Huh. I'll need the whole story over a coupla drinks, but until then, I can say I like you already."

Five foot, one hundred pound pastry chef with a pixie cut who's clearly making an effort to not swear like a sailor likes me? I beam. "Thanks. Feeling is mutual."

"Don't get too excited 'til you really know me, honey."

Christopher clears his throat. "If you ladies are done. You. Kitchen," he tells me, pointing his chin to the door. His eyes are drilling through me, and I can almost feel the physicality of his gaze.

I should have used the damn vibrator. Maybe I'd feel more in control this morning.

"First things first. Make some coffee," he grunts when the door closes behind him.

Thank god for that. "How d'you like it?" I ask.

He seems surprised. "It's for you."

Another boss telling me to get some coffee first thing in the morning? I really need to work on looking more awake.

"I take mine hot and naked," he adds.

Holy crap. The heat on my face crawls down to my chest. I stay carefully with my back to him, busying myself with water and ground coffee as he continues, "No cream, no sugar."

"O—okay." My voice comes out a quack. *Get a grip.*

I pull myself together while going through cupboards and drawers in search of mugs and spoons. The smell of coffee completes my calming down process. I find cream and sugar, fix my cup the way I like it, and set Christopher's on a coaster on the farmhouse table without my hand shaking too much.

"Thanks," he grunts, and takes a long sip. Then he points to a pile of papers he's been busy setting on the table. Snatching the top document, he says, "That's the apprenticeship contract. We need to sign it." He drops it back on the table, where it lands and slides with a woosh, and grabs a pen from a drawer.

He scribbles his name on the last page, then hands me the pen.

I flip straight to the last page and start signing my name on the other side of the page, across from his.

"You're not reading it," he comments.

"Should I?"

"Jesus, Pierce. I need to teach you other skills than just baking."

"I can read, if that's what you mean."

"Skills like not getting fucked over."

"*You* didn't read it."

"I *drafted* it. Think I know what's in it."

Oh.

"Nah," I shrug. "I trust you. How bad can it be? I need to work here every day for the next five or six months. Follow your instructions." In the packet Barbara put together, there was a pretty clear description. I was going to have no personal life during this apprenticeship. Having the day off yesterday was a pleasant surprise.

I finish signing and set the pen back on top of the contract.

He huffs. "You're handing me your ass for the next six months."

"I'm fine with that," I reply a little too quickly. "Metaphorically," I add, feeling that darn blush coming back.

The air sizzles.

"Pierce, seriously. You shouldn't be so trusting. No wonder Red Barn is walking all over you." He seems genuinely pissed off. It's cute in a hot kind of way.

I cup my hands around my mug. "It's okay. They gave me the lowdown on how this was going to work. I'll read the contract tonight, as part of my homework. How's that?"

He comes closer to me, handing me the contract. I free one hand to grab it, and our fingers touch briefly, warmth spreading from my fingertips to my core. "If you don't like it, we can discuss it," he says, his body very close to mine.

"I think I'm going to like it just fine."

His eyes dart between mine, hesitating between concern and amusement, making me all sorts of mushy. I could stand there for hours debating which is the most endearing—his frown line or his single raised eyebrow.

Or the heat of his body seeping into mine.

My mood goes up three more notches, but for all the wrong reasons. I need to stay focused in order to complete this apprenticeship. Swooning over my hot boss is not going to help me accomplish that. It'll drive me away from the only reason I'm here.

Focus, Alex. Focus.

He lets go of the contract and returns to the pile on the table. "This here is your bible," he says about the several booklets neatly stacked. "It's the theory part. It normally takes a year, sometimes more, to go through it, but you'll have to cram that in six months." He sifts through the separate booklets, making annotations on their front pages.

"It's totally doable," he adds. "I'm dividing these in sections. There will be a test each week. We'll start with the first section in a week, and so on. In two months, you'll have covered the basics, and you'll start work with me at four in the morning. Until then, I'll see you here at six every day, except Mondays—our day off. I'm going to ease you into it. No point breaking you now."

One year of training crammed into six months, with the basics done in two months?

Sure.

My goal of becoming Red Barn Baking's next in command just reached a new level of highly unlikely.

But sure. I'll do it.

"Next up. Work attire." He rubs his hands and points to a pile of white clothes. "You can wear these on top of your clothes," he says, eyeing my leggings and sweatshirt. "You might get a little hot. Tomorrow, wear only a T-shirt. And your shoes." I'm wearing white Keds. "Get something with more support."

Getting dressed in front of Christopher, even if that means adding layers to already existing clothes, is hot as sin. I can feel his gaze on every part of my body, every move I make.

I trip a couple of times trying to get into the pair of white chef trousers that tie with a string and fit kind of loose. Christopher's gaze follows as I fasten each button of the white chef shirt in thick cotton with a mandarin collar. I finish with a long apron that wraps around my back and ties in the front, and a skull cap.

All the while, Christopher is standing in front of me, legs apart, arms crossed, hips thrust forward, frowning.

I'm melting.

Does he still see me half-naked and wet from a broken shower, or is he just making sure his new apprentice starts right?

"You'll need to tie up your hair under the cap. The cap should cover your forehead. It's meant to absorb your sweat."

Sweet. I roll my loose hair as best I can and try to tuck it under the cap, but it keeps falling back out.

Christopher rummages in the drawer where he found the pen and produces a scrunchy that has to belong to Skye. It has a bunch of green turtles on a pink backdrop. Our fingers touch briefly again as I take it, the warmth of his leaving a burn in mine, this time.

I quickly tie my hair and put the cap on.

He leans in and tucks a stray hair behind my ear. "That's much better," he says in a soft voice.

Ohmygod. Please stay bossy and borderline grumpy. I can't deal with kind Christopher.

"Let's go," he whispers, and my knees buckle.

As we head back to the bakehouse, the kitchen door to the outside slams, and a teenager barges in. Christopher's brows knit. The kid hastily removes his jacket and disappears somewhere.

He reappears minutes later, rushing into the bakehouse in white garb just like the one I'm wearing, except it's embroidered *Isaac Fletcher*. He stands with his feet slightly apart, hands along his sides, and says, "I'm so sorry. It won't happen again."

"Hey, Isaac," Christopher says, and I swear I see the kid visibly relax. "Everything okay?" Christopher asks softly.

Isaac blushes slightly. "Fine. Great. Sorry again."

Christopher grunts. He puts one hand on Isaac's shoulder, and the other on mine. "This is Alexandra. She's new. Why don't you give her an overview of the baking process." He lets go of our shoulders and takes a step back.

"Sir?" Isaac asks.

"Chris," Christopher corrects him. "Your exam is coming soon. Let's hear it. Start with a description of the equipment."

Isaac points out and names the ovens, refrigerators, racks, mixers and their different functions, prep areas and how they are dedicated.

"You have a good memory, Alexandra?" Christopher interrupts.

"Yeah, I think so." I shrug.

"You're not taking notes."

"Oh. Right." I run into the kitchen to grab the first of my training booklets and a pen, and nearly trip on my feet when I rush back.

"What's this for?" he asks me, pointing to a giant mixer that stands directly on the floor. Luckily, I remember that one. Isaac just went over it. I think.

"It's for... kneading dough."

"What is the purpose of kneading?" He isn't looking at anyone in particular, and certainly not at me, which makes it more comfortable, in a way.

I still feel I should answer. "I don't know."

"Isaac?" he says, his arms crossed on his chest.

"Kneading is one of the steps in preparing the dough. It consists of working the dough to release the gluten in the flour," Isaac says.

Christopher tilts his head toward Isaac. "That's it?"

"... release the gluten in the flour... in order to... capture the air during the proofing process."

"The air?"

"The... carbon... dioxide."

"Correct. You need to go over your definitions, Isaac."

"Yes, sir."

"Chris."

"Right. Yes, Chris."

"Alexandra," Christopher says.

"Y-yes?" I'm trying to write everything Isaac just said in the margins of the booklet.

"Relax. It's all there in the manual. No need to scribble all over the damn thing."

"Oh—I thought..." *I thought I was supposed to take freaking notes?*

"I was just messin' with you."

Isaac bites his bottom lip, a silent chuckle shaking him.

Christopher slaps Isaac on the back. "Having fun?" He keeps his hand on the teenager's shoulder and shakes him gently. "Alright, son, show our rookie around. Treat her good, yeah? We don't want to scare her away."

Chapter Ten

Alexandra

The next few days go by in a daze. Mostly, my body needs to adapt. My feet are killing me. My arms are killing me.

The work is hard.

They never said it would be easy. And Red Barn offered me a lot, and I mean *a lot* of money to turn it down.

That's not the problem here.

"Alexandra."

That's the problem.

My hot boss. The way he says my name, rolling off his tongue like a dirty word whispered between sheets we might want to share at some point. A code of sorts.

I tilt my head up.

Yup.

He's looking at me like I'm puzzling and fascinating to him. "You gonna be okay?" He brushes off the snowflakes caught in his hair.

Isaac came in with a bruised jaw this morning, and I talked him into telling me what was going on. What's going on is, his father is an asshole. The major league kind.

I didn't take it too well.

"Me? I'm great. It's Isaac you need to ask."

Christopher leans on the doorjamb. Drops his head. Studies his feet. Looks back up at me. "He knows we're here for him. I had a talk with his asshole of a father just now. I need to be careful. Can't break the link, you know. He's under eighteen. His father says he can't work here anymore, then he can't."

"Can't you report it?"

He clicks his tongue. "Isaac won't. He wants to look after his mom and his younger sister. The way he sees things right now, he's the punching bag, they don't get hurt." He looks up at me, and there's pain in his eyes. It sears through me. "We're working on changing how he sees it. So. Thanks for talking to him too. That means a lot to me." He looks at me, and all of a sudden, we're not talking about Isaac anymore. His eyes are talking about how he sees *me*, and that scares me a whole lot.

"Course," I say, because I don't know what else to say, and the moment is getting too intense for me. Full-on belly clench. It doesn't help that his eyes roam my body, and my nipples don't get the message that it's technically wrong to perk up under these circumstances.

Although.

Damn I like when he looks at me like that.

He finally pushes himself from the door. Before leaving the kitchen, he adds, "I think his father got the message this time."

"Good," I say on an exhale.

I turn my attention back on the late lunch I fixed myself while Christopher was picking Skye up from school.

I was starving, my appetite left during the convo with Christopher, now I know Isaac is going to be okay thanks to my hot boss, my appetite is back.

The good news is, the fridge is stocked with cold cuts, cheeses, and soup, and I'm surrounded by the best bread in the world.

Being hungry around here is a good problem to have.

I'm finally sitting down, a sandwich between my fingers, and *damn*.

That bread is *good*.

So good I tear a piece from the sandwich to savor it alone.

So good I close my eyes and moan.

Pure.

Pleasure.

The scraping of a chair on the floor pulls me from my moment. I keep my eyes closed and swallow, then open one eyelid to see who's interrupting my break.

Christopher.

I sit up.

"Did I wake you." His eyes lift from my throat and glide over my lips.

"God, this bread is sinfully good."

He smirks.

I take a huge bite from my sandwich and feel my cheek bump to the side. I can't be acting cute around my boss. I'm starving, and I'm focusing on the task at hand: getting through this apprenticeship, passing the exam. My earlier bodily reaction to his presence can't repeat itself on a loop.

"What's your favorite bread," he asks.

I point to the baguette and take another bite.

"Apart from that."

I shrug.

"What's that mean."

"I try to stay away from bread."

He quirks an eyebrow. That's his way of asking a question. I think.

"You know. Weight and all that," I say as a manner of explanation.

He grunts. He stands, disappears into the bakehouse, and reappears minutes later, carrying a wooden tray with an assortment of breads.

And he says, "You have the type of body that fills in in all the right places."

Oh.

My.

God.

I nearly choke on my sandwich.

And what are these places, again?

He hands me a piece of buttered dark bread. "Taste this."

Our fingers touch briefly, and I try, and fail, to ignore the fluttering of my belly. He moves to the side of the table and sits, elbows on the table, eyes boring into me.

The bread is warm, soft, and full, its flavor needing nothing, its texture filling.

"So?" he asks. A real question this time. Interesting.

I swallow. Again, his gaze trails the bread down my throat then goes back up to my mouth and slowly locks back with my eyes. The tickle between my legs intensifies, and my eyes can't pull away from his.

He's my boss. This needs to stop.

How do I stop this?

"Describe the taste for me."

I swallow, try to take a steady breath, and look away from him. I can't let him see what I feel. "It's thicker than the baguette. Denser. Much tastier. Almost spicy." I feel myself blush.

"That's a rye *boule*," he says. "It's a mix of 25 percent rye flour. That's the texture and flavor you're describing. An overnight fermentation in the refrigerator brings out the flavor more." He's switched to pro mode, and god, that might be even sexier.

He reaches over and grabs another loaf, ripping it open with his hands. "This one is a house specialty. The flour is whole wheat, with added semolina for extra crunchiness. The fermentation is a two-step process to bring out the bubbles that make it light and airy inside." He points to the larger craters in the bread, then hands it to me to taste it. Our fingers touch again.

I feel the blush spreading on my face.

"Why are you blushing." This he says as a statement, with a hint of irritation in his tone, and amusement in his eyes. He moves closer to me.

"You're watching me eat," I answer, my hand hiding my full mouth.

"Oh, that." He pulls my hand gently away as his gaze trails down to my lips. "Better get used to it," he whispers. His thumb traces the palm of my hand, sending ripples of pleasure through my whole body, then abruptly lets go.

He paces the kitchen and switches back to pro mode. "You have some catching up to do in everything bread related. As your master, it's my responsibility to educate you. We'll work on educating your palate."

His tone suddenly softer, his eyes back on me in that manner that just melted me, he adds, "It's a good thing you're staying in-house. We can use all twenty-four hours of the day."

I have trouble swallowing. Not only is he insanely gorgeous, in that tall, dark and broody way that only exists in books, but he's looking at *me* with those eyes full of want and then, the next moment, full of kindness, and I'm not the kind of girl to swoon over a man but when that man is so objectively desirable and when he just told *me* it's a good thing he's going to have *me* twenty-fours a day in his house?

Color me a deep shade of smitten.

So when he leans in to run his hand like a feather over the side of my face and says, "Does that sound like something you can handle?" —a real question again—all I can do is blink my agreement. Real deer-in-the-headlights moment.

I can't breathe.

I drown in his irises the color of sin.

"You're blushing again," he says in a low voice.

Um? *Yeah.*

He pulls his hand away softly and flicks his fingers. "You had a breadcrumb," he says, and before I can analyze what happened, he's gone, and I don't see him until dinner that night.

The kitchen is empty when I walk into it, but the table is set for four. After a minute, Skye runs in alone. "We're having galettes tonight!" she says, grabbing my hands and pulling me in a little happy dance. "Have you ever been the queen?" she asks, letting go of me.

"I have no idea what you're talking about," I confess.

"It's okay," she says, nodding like it's not the first time she's heard that. "It's from Paris. My daddy lived there, that's why we do it. He bakes the Best. Cake. In. The. World, and hides a bean in it. If you get the bean, then you're the queen. You get a crown," she says, showing me two cardboard crowns set on the table, "and then you get to choose your king." She sighs dramatically. "I hope I'll be the queen."

"Who will be your king?"

She rounds her eyes at me. "Daddy!" Then, seeming to understand, she adds, "You have to choose someone around the table. I s'pose if *you* got the bean, you could choose me as your other queen. That works too."

"Oh, good," I say. "I will do that—*if* I get the bean."

She squints at the table. "It looks like Aunt Grace is coming. Yay!" Right on cue, the doorbell chimes and seconds later, Grace comes in carrying a dish wrapped in foil.

"Hi, Alex," she says. "Can you open the oven for me?"

My phone startles me, buzzing in my back pocket. *Voldemort*. I send it to voice mail and open the oven.

"Where's your dad?" Grace asks Skye as she sets the oven temperature, then takes her coat off.

"I'll go get him," Skye cries out and darts upstairs.

"What's up with him? Why isn't he here?" she asks me.

"I-I don't know. I haven't seen him all afternoon."

Grace adds serving utensils to the table. "Huh. He told me to come over for his galette. Mom made three dishes of lasagna yesterday, dropped one off at my place, so I told him I'd bring it. Grab us some wine, I'll make a salad."

I hesitate. "White? Red?"

"Whatever you'd like. Red sounds good, and then we can have a hard cider from the fermentory with the galette. Speaking of wine, are you free this Thursday night?"

"My social calendar is wide open."

"Good. I'll take you to Game Night. Us girls just get together, drink wine, and come up with our own versions of board games. It's fun."

"Sounds nice. What time and where?"

"I'll pick you up here at five. We'll walk to Cassandra's. She's having it in the back of her store. It's the most adorable space," she says.

"Corrupting my staff already?" Christopher groans, startling us. "Smells good in here." He pecks Grace on the cheek and places a variety of dinner rolls in the oven. "Thanks for the lasagna. My favorite."

"You can thank your aunt."

"I will."

"Skye, hands?" Christopher asks, ruffling his daughter's hair.

"S-craped them s-queaky clean!" She smacks her lips and rubs her hands.

"Good job, Skye!" Grace says. Skye smiles, clearly proud. She seems to look for words difficult for her to pronounce. Seeing her seeking this challenge is both heartwarming and inspiring to me.

I cast a side glance at Christopher. He, too, picked up on his daughter's efforts. Of course he did. He tries to hide his pride, but it's hard to miss. It's in his eyes and in his smile.

He winks at Grace. "She's doing great, isn't she?" he says softly, earning a hug from Skye. I feel like an intruder and try to disappear in the background, but just end up being moved to the core by the love emanating from them.

"Of course she is," Grace says as she sets the heavy dish of lasagna on the table. "Alex, can you grab the salad?" she adds, making me instantly grateful that she also caught my unease and included me. "And, Chris, the bread please. Let's eat!"

While we take our seats, I snap pictures of the breadbasket at the center of the table, contrasting with the colorful dishes. My phone buzzes, again. *Voldemort*. I send it to voice mail, again. Less than a minute later, the voice mail tone chirps. I set the phone on silent.

"Do I need to cast a spell?" Christopher smirks when my phone screen lights up with the same nickname.

I take the phone to the kitchen counter and set it screen down. "No," I admit softly. "It's the office in New York. But there's nothing they can do to me while I'm here, so..."

"So...not answering?" Christopher says.

"That's right."

"What could they possibly want from you?" Grace frowns.

"It's nothing... It's just... work-related."

Christopher sets his fork down with a loud clank. "They can't have you working for them while you're here with me."

The heat coming from him electrifies my veins. I hold on to his gaze as if he's some kind of buoy. "I'm not working. It's—It's complicated. It's about what I'll be doing when I go back."

He frowns.

"When do you go back, again?" Grace asks.

"In less than six months," Skye answers. "That's in a loooong time."

Christopher grunts.

"And they're already bothering you with what you'll be doing when you get back?" Grace asks.

"Yeah. My boss."

"He's not your boss as long as you're with me," Christopher cuts in.

As long as you're with me. My spine tingles. "That's why I'm not picking up his calls," I breathe.

Christopher grunts again—something that sounds like "good."

Grace's eyes dance between the two of us. "How's the apprenticeship going?"

I wipe my mouth. "So far, so good? I guess? The theory is okay, not too hard to memorize." I take a sip of wine and glance nervously at

Christopher. "It's the practice. I'm such a klutz. It's like I have two left hands. I don't know."

"It'll take time," Grace says.

"You care about what you do, and the dough senses it," Christopher cuts in.

The dough what?

"The dough is a breathing, living thing," he continues. "When the baker is in a bad mood, or doesn't care, the dough senses it. Just like a pet. It feels your intention and reacts to it." He drills his gaze into mine. "You are a caring person. You'll never totally screw up your baking."

I reach for my glass for composure, my eyes unable to leave his. The back of my hand hits the stem, the glass tilts away, and Christopher's hand wraps around mine and the glass. "See?" I breathe, my cheeks ablaze.

He gives my hand a squeeze. "You just need to gain confidence. And, sometimes, you'll need the right person next to you at the right time."

He brushes his thumb inside my wrist before removing his hand.

Heat zings to my center.

And confidence sweeps through me as well.

"Nice catch, Daddy!" Skye giggles. Thank god she's oblivious to the subtext between us.

Grace's gaze darts between Christopher and me, a smile dancing in her eyes.

"I don't know about that," I say. "It never works that way."

Chapter Eleven

Christopher

"*It never works that way.*" Why is she so jaded? I've had my share of shit, but I'm a fighter. I don't let go until I have what I want. Although, right now I want her hand back inside mine, but I have to let it go.

For now.

"Ready for galette?" I ask, looking at our empty plates.

Skye shrieks in excitement. We quickly clear the table and set it for dessert. "Alexandra, are you familiar with Galette des Rois?"

"Skye told me about the bean and the crown," she answers. "Sounds exciting!"

I clear my throat. That wasn't the answer I was looking for. She really has no clue about baking. I need to remember that. "It's a pâte feuilletée filled with frangipane."

"Amazing," she says, a small smile on her beautiful face. She still clearly has no idea what I'm talking about.

"Puff pastry filled with almond paste," I add.

Her eyes widen. "Definitely amazing."

Skye sets the galette and a clean dishcloth on the table, then crawls underneath the table. "It's part of the tradition," I say to Alexandra.

Skye giggles. "Daddy! Your feet stink."

"They do not."

"Do to!"

"Oh my god, it smells heavenly!" Alexandra says. "I can't wait."

Grace laughs out loud.

"You hear that, little bug? My feet smell heavenly."

Alexandra turns a bright shade of red. "I mean the galette." She grabs her phone, swipes off a bunch of new notifications, and snaps a few photos of the untouched galette. She's beaming, and my stomach does a funny little thing.

I slice the galette, then cover it with the dishcloth. "Alexandra. Do the honors," I say, handing her the pie server, and for some strange reason, that turns me on. "Just be sure to keep the galette covered, so there's no cheating."

She sets her phone down, slides the server under the cloth and loads a random slice of galette. I call out the ritual question, "Who is this one for?"

"Aunt Grace!" The answer comes from underneath the table.

Alexandra serves Grace, then, sliding the server under the dishcloth, loads the second slice.

"Who is this one for?" I ask.

"Ummm. Daddy!" Skye says, and Alexandra serves me, then loads the third slice.

"Who is this one for?"

"Alek—zandra," Skye calls out.

As Alexandra is ready to put the slice on her plate, she freezes, her eyes zooming in on the fava bean at the edge of the slice, and makes a face. Her eyes dart between me and the tablecloth. I get her idea and lift the cloth while she swiftly switches slices. It's such a treat, for a child, to get the bean.

"And...who is this one for?" I ask while I push the bean well inside the slice, so Skye won't see it right away. Alexandra is ready to set it on Skye's plate.

Our eyes meet.

My chest warms.

"Meeee!" Skye cries as she comes out from underneath the table. Back in her chair, she takes an unsuspecting but hopeful bite. I'm anticipating the moment she finds the bean. But my fatherly joy is soon interrupted.

"Aaaah. This is soooo good," Alexandra moans, eyes closed, a flake on the corner of her lips. Mouth still half-full, she continues, "Buttery. And crispy outside. Mellow inside. Almond... mmm." She swallows and opens watery eyes on all of us staring at her. Then, she starts taking close-up photos of her slice.

Grace keeps looking between the two of us like this is the most fun she's had in a while.

Skye nods and says, "I told you. Best in the world!" Then takes another large bite.

I haven't touched my slice, yet. I'm sure it tastes much better straight from her mouth, and that's where my eyes linger. Until today, I never knew bread tasting could be such a turn on, but after I was done with her in the kitchen, I had two choices. I could take her on the kitchen table, or I could leave.

I left.

"I don't even have the words to describe it," Alexandra says, her eyes not quite on me, as if she's intimidated about giving me a compliment.

My dick stretches painfully against the seam of my jeans. This can't be happening. My own daughter is right here, and so is my cousin, and my dick is having a life of its own, punishing me for too many months—years—of abstinence.

"I've been telling him to enter New England's Best Baker competition," Grace is saying, referring to the bread baking TV show that has viewers glued to their screens twice a year. "He won't listen."

Alexandra looks up at me. "Seriously. This is heaven," she says, and I'm pretty sure what I see is admiration.

Heat spreads through me.

"A competition?" she asks me.

"A TV show."

She narrows her eyes on me. "You don't like the spotlight?"

I hadn't thought about that aspect of it. I don't think I'd mind it. I entered some competitions, back in the day, and although they weren't televised, I kinda liked the public aspect of it. "I don't have time for that." I shrug.

"Interesting," she says, drawing out the word like I'm some fucking experiment.

"Skye, what do you think? You want to see your daddy on TV?" she asks.

Skye rounds her eyes and nods frantically, her mouth too full to talk.

Grace giggles, and I know what she's thinking.

Because I'm thinking the same thing. Alexandra knows what makes me tick. I guess it's not rocket science. Single dad and all, I'm bound to be swayed by my little girl.

"I think your daddy would look *awesome* on TV." She taps her phone, like she's got some footage there to prove it.

I could get addicted to this.

She points to the galette and to the rolls now sitting on the side table. "This needs to be shared with the rest of the world. Seriously." Her eyes land on me, and it's more convincing than any speech.

"I mean, how good are the other bakers?" she asks, looking around the table.

I give her my cocky-smile, silent answer. *Not as good as me.*

But I feel the need to prove that to her, and maybe that's primitive of me.

So what.

I know my worth, and I know I'm one of the best bakers in Vermont, and probably the whole Northeast. But, until now, I didn't feel the need to prove it to anyone.

Grace is silent, smiling. Enjoying the show of her cousin's demise.

Even I'm enjoying feeling myself fall for Alexandra's trap. What's not to enjoy? Look at her face. Wonderment. I did that.

The silence is stretching between the adults, until Skye shrieks and pulls out the bean from her mouth. "I'm the queen! I'm the queen! Where's the crown?"

Thank god for kids. It was getting awkward.

We cheer and applaud. I get the golden paper crown from the console, tie it around her head, and hand her the second crown.

She comes down ceremoniously from her chair and crowns me. "You're my king, Daddy" she says, hugging me tenderly, burrowing her head in my neck. Making my heart beat faster.

I kiss her head and hug her tight. As I lift my eyes, I see Alexandra snapping a photo of us, and I mouth "thank you" to her for giving me this moment with my daughter. My eyes are trained on Alexandra, my arms latched onto Skye, and that damn fluttering radiating from my stomach just gets worse.

It's fucking scary.

After dinner, Skye demands that Alexandra tucks her in. "I'm the queen tonight." She kisses me and Grace good night.

"All right, Your Majesty. Shall we?" Alexandra takes her hand.

I watch them leave the room, my heart hurting at the perfect image. "Teeth, face, ha—"

"Hands and nails," Skye continues.

Grace finishes clearing the table while I start on dishes. "When are you getting a dishwasher?" she asks for the millionth time.

"I don't need one. It's just the two of us."

I expect her to comment on that, but she doesn't. For a few minutes, we work in silence. "Hey, could you babysit Skye for me, a week from tomorrow?" I ask her.

She smirks, a twinkle in her eye. "You're taking Alex out?"

"No."

"Oo-kay? Just asking."

"Just saying. I'm not taking Alexandra out. I'm her boss."

"I see. You're pretending this is a work thing, but you're taking her out. That's cute."

"I'm not taking Alexandra out. Why would I do that?"

"You guys have been eye-fucking all evening."

"We have not."

"Chris, it's fine. You deserve some fun. You're not taking anything from Skye by having an adult life outside of work."

"I need to go over my financials with Emma." Emma is not only Caroline's mom. She's also the only CPA in town.

I see her a lot. Too much, if you ask me.

"Oh, right." She hands me the stack of dried plates. "Why do you need a babysitter? Don't you normally bring Skye so she can play with Caroline?"

I asked myself the same question. That's been the MO between us. Single parents and all. We bring our kids to work meetings. "I guess she wants to meet at the office? I dunno. She asked if I needed her babysitter."

"Huh." Grace shrugs. "Sure. You know I love taking care of Skye. And I'll get to spend more time with your 'apprentice,'" she adds, air-quoting the word with her fingers.

"She *is* my apprentice. That's why I didn't ask her to babysit Skye." Though I'm pretty sure she wouldn't mind. She's been here all of a week, and she and Skye are thick as thieves.

"Huh," she says again.

"What."

"Emma."

"*What*."

"You know what."

"That's history, Grace." There was a time when Emma was coming onto me pretty clearly. She even put it bluntly, once. "*We make sense together,*" she'd said.

"Ya think she's one-nighter material?" I'd asked Justin after too many drinks, the desperation of my horniness getting to me.

"Sure thing," he answered. "One time's all you need. She'll have your balls on her mantlepiece. One and done."

Thank god for sober bartenders. That was the end of that messed-up plan to get me some action.

"She got the message," I say to Grace. "She's not stupid."

"No, she's not. She's just… lonesome."

"Nothing I can do for her there," I answer.

"Oh, I know," she says playfully. "Especially now." She wiggles her eyebrows.

I grab her in a playful headlock and rub my knuckles on her skull.

"Ow! It hurts!"

"I know it does. Trying to drill into that silly skull of yours that there. Is. Nothing. Going. On."

"For now," she mumbles under my arm. "I have a lot of money on you. Don't disappoint me."

I let go of her. "Seriously? Gracie bear. You, of all people. *I* am disappointed in *you*."

I wrap a galette for her parents and hand it to her. "A week from tomorrow."

She pecks me on the cheek. "I'm happy for you, cousin," she says as she leaves.

This betting thing, it's annoying and it's nice at the same time. I know everyone here just wants what's best for me. But Alexandra is a big city girl with a fancy career. She doesn't want a baker.

I got burned once believing I could be enough. I'm not repeating that mistake.

Chapter Twelve

Alexandra

The following Thursday, I bounce into the bakery bright and early in the new running shoes I bought at the General Store. It's not six in the morning, yet here I am, ready to take this day on.

Norwood, a.k.a. Voldemort on my phone, stopped trying to call. He sent emails—same thing. Offering me money to come back to Red Barn.

But I'm right where I need to be. I won't let him ruin my days. Until I'm back in New York, I'll focus on the little things. The rest will take care of itself.

The first couple of hours go like a charm.

"You're on a roll," Christopher says to me, to which Isaac responds, "Working on your dad jokes?"

I giggle, and Christopher frowns. "It's a good one," I tell Christopher. "Skye will appreciate it."

This gets me my own pointed frown, but I don't miss the glint of heat that sparkles in his eyes.

Or his visible relief at seeing that Isaac seems to be doing well.

Around eight, Kiara comes in to start work on her pastries with Willow, and I slide into the kitchen to make coffee, drink a large glass of water, and snatch some sit-down time.

As I'm about to pour Christopher and me our coffees, Emma strolls in, carrying a briefcase and a large bag.

I stop my pour midair. "Hi?" I say. Should I ask her what she wants?

"Oh. Hello," she answers, as if she's surprised to see me here. She plops her briefcase on a chair and opens her canvas bag.

I resume pouring our coffees and put the coffee pot back on its base.

She pulls two mismatched egg cartons from her bag and places them in the refrigerator. Rummages through said fridge, rearranging things like she lives here. Then pulls small glass jars from her bag and places them in the fridge.

Then she makes her way to the coffee machine and starts a fresh pot.

Like she lives here.

"Oh hey, Ems," Christopher says.

Her breath catches as she smiles at him.

"You know Alexandra?" he asks.

"Yeah, we've met," she answers crisply, her smile dying. "I brought you fresh eggs from my chickens and some homemade yogurt," she adds.

Christopher rubs the back of his neck, looking annoyed. "Thanks. You want to set up in the den?"

"Sure."

"Invoices and all that shit's already out there," he says.

I remember now. Grace had said Emma was a CPA. She must be doing Christopher's books. "You got your coffee?" he asks her.

"In a sec." She grabs milk from the fridge, frowns as she closes the fridge, then goes straight to a cupboard that holds random things, pulls a mug that says "Emma's mug" on one side and has a bunch of sheep on the other, then pulls an instrument that looks like a vibrator on a stand but turns out to be a milk frother, and proceeds to make her own little latte like a pro.

The woman *is* a pro. You have to give her that.

She shows up at her client's home to do bookkeeping and brings him fresh eggs and homemade yogurt because she knows he's a single dad and could use the help.

And the attention.

God there's a lot of attention-giving going on right now.

She's wiping the kitchen table she hasn't used. Folding the dishtowels she hasn't used. I'm surprised she didn't bring flowers.

Oops! She reaches inside her Mary Poppins canvas bag.

"There," she says, plopping a pot of blooming bulbs on the table.

"All set?" Christopher asks, still rubbing his neck.

"Yeah. That's better. Much better," she says, and I'm not sure if I should feel mildly offended or hilariously entertained, so I settle for both.

Thankfully, she leaves for the den, a multi-purpose area right off the kitchen, equipped with a couch, a giant TV, and a table, plugs in her laptop, and takes a deep dive into "the shit" Christopher prepared for her.

Christopher grabs the coffee I push his way. "She's my CPA," he whispers to me.

"I got that. I think?" I whisper back.

"I can hear you," Emma says.

"I know," Christopher replies, undeterred.

"I'll need her contract," she says.

"Whose contract," Christopher says.

Her eyes land on me. "For payroll."

"*Alexandra's* contract is in the pile of shit," he answers. Then he pushes himself from the counter and moves to the table where she can't see him anymore, taking this morning's mail with him. "Sorry," he mouths to me while rolling his eyes.

I stifle a laugh and feel all warm. I think back to something Skye told me the other night, after we shared the galette, and my amusement at the situation with Emma turns into a mixture of tenderness and gratefulness for Christopher. As I tucked her in for bed, she couldn't hold it any longer.

"Can you keep a secret?" she asked, then lowered her voice to a whisper. "I helped Daddy choose a princess bed for you."

I hugged her close and promised I wouldn't say anything, and I didn't ask more. But *my* inner princess was doing somersaults. I'm not sure what a princess bed is, but it has to be better than the twin size mattress and frame I'm currently sleeping on. Not that I'm complaining. I'm so tired, anyway, I fall asleep the minute my head hits the flat pillow, and I wake up in the same position I fell asleep in.

Since I know he's planning to upgrade the bed in the room I'm occupying, I figure it's safe to ask a question that's been puzzling me. "So... I've been doing some shopping."

His eyes flit from the mail to me. "M-hm."

"And... I'm a little tight on storage space."

He raises an eyebrow.

"I was trying to open that closet in the corner of my bedroom, but I can't figure it out."

"What closet. There's no closet in your room. We can get you a dresser. I'll get you a dresser."

Gosh, no, I don't want him to get me a dresser. First a bed, now a dresser? No way. I'm enough of a burden already. "No... I don't need a dresser. Just, there's this closet, under the eaves? To the left of the window? It's like flush with the bookcase, in the angle. There are hinges, and a handle, but it won't open."

A faint smile plays on his lips, and his eyes do this thing, just fleetingly, where the dark embers of his irises light up and the corners crinkle just so, while he does a sweep, not just of my body, but, it seems, of the entirety of my being. He nods slowly. "It's not a closet."

"Gotcha. A closed bookcase. Thought I could use it to store some stuff?"

He doesn't answer.

"Never mind."

"You couldn't store anything in there," he says.

"I don't need much space. Just maybe for my shoes and sweaters?"

"It's a hidden staircase."

"A—A wh—?"

"A concealed staircase. Meant for servants back in the day, to get from one story to the other without using the main staircase."

"Oh..." Way cool. A Victorian house with a hidden staircase. All I need now is a ghost.

Wait.

"Where does this staircase go?" I ask, but my stomach jumps. I know the answer. There's no level above me, and under my room is—

"My bedroom. Used to be the grand room. For entertaining."

Right. Heat creeps up from my middle.

"The staircase is locked from the inside. From my side. But, if that makes you uncomfortable, I can nail you—I mean, nail *it* shut." He turns his back to me and rinses out his coffee mug.

My brain strives to gloss over his slip, while my body disagrees, and my cheeks burn. I whisper scream so Emma can't hear. She might be deep in her numbers, but I'm sure she's not losing one word of this conversation. "You mean it's still in working order?" *Yeah right. Pretend like you're just interested in architectural details.*

He stacks the mail and stands. Then leans over me on his way back to the bakeshop. "Perfectly functional."

His scent lingers around me, and I fall into a dreamy daze.

I'm fantasizing on all the possibilities. The scenarios. I wonder if someone before used this staircase for illicit encounters.

Am I crazy?

The existence of this hidden passage is an invitation to use it, right? A permanent what if. What if he came up the hidden stairs? What if he knocked on this door instead of the main one? What if I answered that door? What if I left the door open the next night?

God. I need to snap out of it.

"So *you're* the one," Emma says, effectively pulling me out of my inappropriate fantasies.

"Sorry—what?" I take a few steps to get closer to her.

"*You're* the apprentice Chris got from that foundation. For..."

She trails off, takes a sip of her latte, her pink lips leaving a trace of lipstick on the sheep mug.

"I'm not following."

She pulls her eyes from her laptop and latches them onto me. She has the most beautiful, deep blue eyes, bordered by thick, long lashes to die for—and they're all natural. No mascara. No eyeliner. Full mane of curly blond hair, and she doesn't even need to play with it to make you notice it. She's wearing a sweater that molds her without being obvious. Slim jeans that move with her.

She's the kind of woman who runs for Miss Small Town America and the whole country falls in love with her.

She takes another, thoughtful sip of her coffee, and I realize the sheep on the mug have something to do with counting. I wonder who gave her that mug. If she brought it here herself, with her frother, or if it was a gift from Christopher, to make her feel at home.

That last thought sits uneasy in my stomach.

She smiles at me but doesn't show me her perfect row of pearly white teeth. That smile, she reserves for Christopher. But still, she smiles at me and says, "Never mind. I see he didn't tell you. I overstepped." And she ducks back behind her laptop, taking cute little laps of her homemade latte with her perfect pink, plump lips.

Now, an accountant is like a lawyer. They don't overstep. They know they can't share much, if anything, about their clients.

That right there was not a professional accidentally oversharing and hoping we can pretend this never happened.

I spent my tweens and teens in all-girls private boarding schools. And 99 percent of the girls there were gold. Tight-knit, stick together, to death kind of friends.

And then you had that one girl. It never failed, year after year, grade after grade.

There was always *one* girl who couldn't leave well enough alone. Who had to dig up dirt. Who spent her year trying to sully friendships. I never figured out why they did it, but I learned to recognize their MO.

Innuendos.

Seemingly innocent questions.

Half revelations.

What is Emma's problem?

The door to the bakeshop swings up. "Alexandra." Christopher looks between Emma and me. "I need you back there."

Well. Hot damn.

Emma pushes her chair back. "Chris, you didn't forget our date, right?"

My body freezes.

He frowns. "Date?"

"Next week."

"Oh, right. Tax appointment. Right."

"I'll put it in your calendar," Emma says as she sashays to the fridge, pen in hand, and adds her name on the magnetic calendar full of Skye's playdates.

"Whatever," Christopher says, holding the door to the bakery open for me. He folds behind me, his warmth and scent doing funny little things to my insides.

Still, from this point on, I'm totally off-kilter.

My breads have odd shapes. My muffins are different sizes. And I can't focus on making perfectly calibrated dinner rolls. For the next two hours, Isaac is keeping me on track, looking over my shoulder.

"Alex!" Isaac's voice comes through to me.

"Huh?"

"Hurry!" He's holding an oven door open, waiting for me to load my tray of dinner rolls. The temperature dial is falling.

I try to shake my brain free of thoughts of hidden staircases and Emma, and rush to him. I can't see the floor or anything below the level of the large tray I'm holding, but I already know my way around here, so I don't slow down.

I cut corners.

I hit something.

Something that crashes with a loud bang.

And then, I'm stepping in crunchy, sticky stuff, and I see Kiara's face pale.

Then she storms out.

I can face one mess, but not two. I'm *not* dropping our rolls on the floor. *Focus on your first task, then the next, then the next.* I hop over whatever is on the floor, lose balance, and thrust the tray of dinner rolls onto Isaac's unprepared hands. He teeters and two rolls plop on the floor. I steady myself, grab the tray back from him, shove it in the oven, close the door, and manage to remember to set the timer.

Then, I pick up the two fallen, unbaked rolls, and with my hands full, turn around to face the disaster I just created. An explosion of colorful crumbs and sticky paste awaits me. What was seconds ago the latest batch of fresh macarons is splattered on the floor. Kiara is gone somewhere to cool off—thank god. Willow's eyes are shiny. She's biting her lower lip and seems on the verge of either crying or laughing.

I'm so ashamed of destroying their hard work that a tear falls down my cheek, and I can't even wipe it off because my hands are full. I look at the sticky goo in my hands, get on my knees, and start capturing all the pieces of macarons with it.

"What's wrong with Kiara?" Christopher barks as he enters the bakeshop, then stops in his tracks as he takes in the disaster and my attempt at fixing it. I stand, my hands covered in bread dough, macarons crumbs, and filling like some kindergartener doing finger painting with play dough, tears of shame lining my eyelids.

I blink, and they start rolling down my cheeks uncontrollably.

He runs his hand over his face. "Alexandra, stop," he says in a low growl. "Willow, what happened."

"Alex bumped into the tray that was sticking out—"

"The tray was sticking out?"

"It was."

"Okay then. No more trays sticking out."

"Nope."

"Get a broom and a mop."

"Yup. On it."

He bends over to where I'm crouched on the floor. "Alexandra. Hey. Come here." He pulls on my elbow to lift me up and walks me out. I wipe the tears on my shoulder. Once in the kitchen, he rolls up my sleeves while leading me to the sink, where he opens the faucet.

"What's going on?" he asks.

"Isaac asked—"

He taps my forehead and says, "What's going on in here, and in here," he continues, tapping the approximate area of my heart, which incidentally, is awfully close to my breast. Then both his hands wrap around my shoulders, and he gives them a quick rub.

Then leaves them there.

I sigh deeply. I just want to lay against him.

I fight the urge, close my eyes, and turn the faucet off.

"I'm sorry, I'm—"

"You're exhausted. It's normal." He rubs my shoulders again, and *god* it feels good. "Anything different, I'd think you're superhuman. You take the rest of the day off, yeah?"

"Yeah," I whisper. "First I need to clean up the bakehouse."

"No you don't."

"I made a mess."

"It's on them and they know it. The tray was sticking out. It shouldn't have been. No big deal. Plenty of time to make more cookies." And his hands rub between my shoulders.

"Macarons," I whisper.

He chuckles. "Whatever." He pulls my cap off and tucks some hair behind my ear and ohmygod it's borderline erotic.

With a final squeeze of my shoulders, he sends me off.

"Take it easy," Emma says from behind her laptop.

Shit. I have a meltdown, of course miss perfection would witness it.

Chapter Thirteen

Alexandra

On our way to Game Night, Grace and I spot Skye and Christopher's silhouettes on The Green. Christopher is effortlessly ice-skating backwards in front of Skye. A delicious scent of hot chocolate and sugar comes from a small hut decorated like a ginger house next to the skating rink. Kids are lined up and leave with steaming cups and waffles. "Aunt Grace! Alek-zandra! Look!" Skye's high-pitched voice calls out. We make a detour to join them, and Skye proceeds to race around the rink, upper body leaned forward, hands clutched to the small of her back.

Skye hurls herself to the railing, ducks under it, and talks Grace into taking her to the sugar hut. Christopher's eyes fleet to his daughter and cousin walking away, then he skates to me, eyes on mine. "Going to Game Night?" he says as he comes to an abrupt stop in front me. He's wearing nothing but jeans, a ski sweater, and a beanie pulled down to his ears, hair curling out of it.

I clench my thighs and nod.

"I like that for you, Alexandra."

Um... Okay?

He bends over the railing, like he's about to tell me a secret.

I lean into his space. His *warm* space.

"I hear Cassandra is something of a witch," he says. "Throws spells and shit. Make sure you don't... you know... knock down a tray or something. Retaliation and all that."

Then he skates away, and a slow grin spreads across my face while I stifle a chuckle.

On our way, Grace informs me that Cassandra sells lingerie and that her shop draws clients from three states and parts of Canada. Her shop is located in an adorable white and light-gray cape, with lights in and around the windows and alongside the walkway.

We enter through a back door leading us straight into what's best described as a she-shed. A woman cave. White couches with gold throw pillows. Bright pink, furry armchairs. Wall-to-wall cream carpeting. A crystal chandelier. A white fireplace lit with a gentle fire. Mounted on the mantel, a faux doe head in a patchwork fabric wearing dangle diamond earrings. A mirrored bar in a corner, with a pink neon sign above it that reads, Babes Only.

Okey doke. Game Night is on.

The chatter of the group of women gathered in the room dips when we arrive, only to pick up louder as they greet me. Cassandra, a beautiful woman in her forties with streaks of blue in her hair, hugs me right away. Before moving onto the other ladies, she introduces me to Justin's sister, a young woman named Haley with straight blond hair and pale blue eyes who's at the bar, pouring wine into stem glasses.

"Just what I need," I say to Haley.

She flashes back a smile. "Uh-oh. Rough day?"

"One of many."

She hands me a glass of white wine. "Then you've come to the right place."

Thanking her, I turn around and look for a place to sit. Skye's teacher, Laura, is here, and so is Sophie, the librarian who I met on my first night in Emerald Creek. Willow makes her way to me as I sit on a comfy couch. Lucky for me, Kiara isn't here. Grace joins me on the couch.

Willow crouches next to me and sets her hand on my knee. "You okay?" she asks with a a suppressed giggle.

"Yeah, I'm okay. Better now. I'm so sor—"

"Stop it! That tray should never have been there. And Kiara shouldn't have reacted that way. It was her fault. She's a little—well, a *lot*—hyper. But, when you get to know her, she has a heart of gold."

"Barf Barf. Jesus. Next thing you know, she's gonna stitch that on my apron. Yo, Bambi. Where're your glasses?"

My body goes cold. Shoooot. Just the person I did not need tonight. "I'm so sorry, Kiara, so so sorry, I don't know where to begin."

She's standing in front of me, and even though she's of the tiny kind, she is. Frigging. Scary. She rubs her chin like she's considering my punishment.

"I obviously didn't mean to do that," I continue.

She doesn't say anything. No *forget it*, no *water under the bridge*. Nope.

"And, if there's anything I can do to make it up to you…" I trail off.

Still nothing. She just stands there, watching me squirm.

It was her fault the tray was sticking out. Someone was bound to knock it off the table.

I sit up. Enough already. "You know what, screw it."

"Whooo hooo!" she does a little happy dance. "Fiiiiiinally. Stop taking other people's shit. You gotta work on that. Big boss man told me already, but I couldn't believe it 'til I saw it."

"Christopher?"

Her eyes go soft for a beat, and she repeats, "*Christopher*," all breathy-like.

Is she making fun of me? She's totally making fun of me.

"Jeeze, Kiara, leave her alone already," Grace says.

"Ohmygod," Willow is holding her hand to her mouth, "you're right, she's totally into him. That's so cute."

Sophie is quiet as a mouse, looking at me with mischief in her eye.

"What's cute?" Haley says, coming around for refills.

"Chris and Alex," Willow says.

Please make it stop already. I put a hand out to make them stop. "Guys. Stop spreading rumors. You can't do this. Seriously."

Kiara explodes in a cackle. "Seriously," she repeats, with what's supposed to be a big voice. Then she plops herself on the armrest of the couch, next to me, but higher than me, leans over and says, "Does he snore?"

My mouth opens. "I don't know!" I cry.

"Bambi. You sleep right above his bedroom. You can probably hear him fart too."

"Eww, seriously," Willow says.

"That's gross," Grace concurs.

"He's a man, Grace, but I get it. Dealing with delicate ears here," Kiara says, then puts a hand on my shoulder. "He could use some sweet in his life, after what that bitch put him through," she says to me.

I glance up at Kiara. *What bitch?*

Willow plops cross-legged on the floor in front of me, and Grace sits on my other side. They have me in a tight circle.

"Grace, give her the deets. You're family."

"They mean Skye's biological mother. Chris wanted to marry her, and she pretty much told him he was beneath her."

"That's awful," I whisper. "Were they together long?"

Kiara and Willow exchange a look.

"That's the thing," Grace says. "No. It was just a summer fling—"

"Didn't last a summer," Kiara interrupts. "He just fucked her once or twice."

"Kiara! Really?" Grace says.

"I was there, dude. Almost."

Grace chuckles. "Oh well, then. They had brief intercourse—"

Kiara snickers. "Potato potahto."

"And he still wanted to take care of her, do right by her. When she turned down his marriage proposal—"

"He was stoked," Kiara interjects.

"—he tried talking about laying the grounds for co-parenting."

"She was already looking up adoption agencies," Kiara drops.

"Yup," Grace says.

"Well, shit," I say.

Grace nods. "Now you know. Chris is a good guy. A really good guy. And he was burned really deep."

"He still has a fine ass," Kiara drops. "Built up some upper body muscle too. Bet she'd regret it if she saw him now."

"Kiara! Really?"

"Gracie. Your cousin is eye candy. Right, Willow?"

"Can't say that he's not." Willow has an eyebrow up.

"Right, Bambi?"

The words stay stuck in my throat.

"Right, Bambi?"

I take a long pull on my glass of wine. "Right."

"Kay. You need to know, everything that is said here, stays here. Any information you want to volunteer, spill it. Now, tell me," Kiara says.

"What?"

"What what?" She's exhausting.

"Tell you what?" I ask.

"Everything," Kiara says. "Let's start with why he came down from your bedroom your first morning here bare-chested, hair wet, *I need sex now* written all over his face."

I'm mortified. She saw that too? Who else? *Ohmygod*.

"That's enough!" Grace cries.

"It's okay, Bambi. Your face says it all. Like I said, he could use some sweet in his life. And I like you for him."

"You are making her *so* uncomfortable, it's almost funny," Willow says. "But you gotta stop now."

"I do?"

"You do."

"Kay then." And just like that, Kiara leaves my side.

"She gonna torture someone else now?" I whisper.

Willow takes the seat freed by Kiara and laughs out loud. "God, I love you. You're the best."

I breathe easier, take another long sip of my wine, and look around as Willow stands to greet someone. I know over half the people here, and I relax.

While I'm getting settled, someone takes out a game of Clue, and cards are shuffled and distributed. Willow and Haley are together chatting non-stop, while Cassandra, Sophie, and Kiara twirl the wine in their glasses, focusing on the game.

After that, the evening goes by quickly, and I stifle a yawn.

Cassandra stands and takes my hand. "Come with me before we send you away."

She takes me to her lingerie shop, which is decorated in much the same fashion as the women's cave, expect the most exquisite pieces of lingerie are displayed framed on the wall, or on free standing racks, well-spaced out from one another. "Take your clothes off," she says.

I freeze.

"Most of them."

She gently nudges me toward a dressing room large enough to comfortably fit a delicately carved armchair and matching settee upholstered in a carmine velour.

I don't know if it's the wine or Cassandra's soothing voice and confident manner, but I strip down to my underwear.

She whips the curtain open, unannounced. Before I have time to feel like my privacy is being invaded, she declares, "Mother of god, you are even more beautiful undressed than dressed. That's uncommon. You really have nothing to hide, do you?"

Somehow, she manages to make her comments and invasion of my space sound totally normal.

She eyes my breasts with the gaze of a professional. "Take your bra off. You can keep the panties on."

I guess, at this point, I might as well do as I'm told. I feel like I'm at the doctor's, except I'm a little tipsy and the decor is super sexy. Plush carpeting, soft lighting, and mirrors all around the fitting room.

Cassandra grabs a measuring tape and places it right underneath my breasts and around my back. I raise my arms to lift my breasts farther from her fingers. But then, she swiftly moves the measuring tape up and smack across my nipples, the cold plastic making them harden.

I'm mortified.

She mumbles the measurements and writes them down in a thick, leather-bound notebook. Then, she moves to my waist and hips and does the same.

I'm out of the woods.

Or maybe not.

"Spread your legs for me," she says, and, when I do, in two movements, she measures my height from the base of my neck to my pubic bone, front and back.

The humiliation is real, and my appreciation of her lessening by the second. "Are we done?" I snap.

"That's a good start." She hands me a robe. "Hang tight."

She comes back with a copper-colored bustier that fits me to perfection. The demi bra shows a generous share of my breasts without being tacky. The sheer fabric is delicately embroidered with golden threads. A row of tiny buttons runs from between the breasts all the way to the bottom, but a hidden front zipper makes the garment easy to put on and take off. The bustier stops right below my belly button in a V shape. The back has a decorative set of ribbon ties.

As Cassandra zips up the bustier, she swiftly slides a hand in each bra cup to adjust my boobs up. "Shows those babies," she says.

I'm shell shocked by the feeling of her touch on my sensitive nipples. But she clearly thinks nothing of it.

"Try the panties," she says before leaving the room, handing me a matching thong I slip over my underwear.

When she's gone, I try to breathe the burn off my cheeks. Once I feel comfortable again, I turn around on my toes, arch my back and admire myself in the mirrored fitting room. Who's this sexy, confident bombshell with lush hair cascading down her generous breasts, a thin waist, long legs, and killer ass?

What would Christopher think?

"How much will this set me back?" I ask from behind the curtain, my initial displeasure with Cassandra totally forgotten.

"How's a lifetime of true love and pleasure? If you're ready for it."

I chuckle.

"I'm serious. Don't let just anyone see you in this. You'll be stuck with them. Choose carefully." She *is* serious, her tone tinged with a note of mystery. She writes my name in purple ink on the parchment-like tag affixed to the garments. No brand, just the silhouette of an owl. Then she wraps it all in silk paper.

"This is your talisman, Alexandra. My gift to you. Use it wisely."

Chapter Fourteen

Christopher

An hour before my appointment with Emma, I'm in the kitchen, playing a game of Slap Jack with Skye. Alexandra breezes through, clearly coming out of a much-needed nap, her cheeks rosy, her eyes bright, and a pillow mark on her forehead. No disaster from her in the bakehouse today. That's a win.

She grabs a glass of water and plops herself on the couch in the TV area, then flips through her baking manual. Her feet are wrapped in thick socks, and she draws circles with her ankles as she twists a strand of hair in her fingers. Her head is tucked against the back of the couch. The front part of her is turned away from me, but I can fill it in from memory. From days of stealing glances at her.

She's frowning.

Her lips move occasionally as she repeats definitions and proof times.

She closes her eyes periodically to help her focus.

Then she snaps them back open.

Her phone rings. "Hey, Grace!"

Grace included her in her group of friends, and from what I'm hearing, she fits right in. She's been hanging out with them—a lot. She hasn't had dinner here in several days, at least not with me. There are occasional dents in the leftovers, though.

Is she avoiding me outside of work?

She turns halfway around on the sofa. "He's here. Do you want to—Okay…" She settles into her initial position, her back to me. "No, we're—I mean, *I'm* not going out… Okay… Oh wow…. Is she going to be okay? I see… Oh…okay… No… I don't know… I'll let him know. I'm here all evening. I can look after her… Sure. I'll ask Christopher what he wants to do. You take care of your mom." She twists her head my way. "That was Grace. Apparently, she was supposed to babysit Skye tonight?"

I grunt, "Yes."

Skye pulls a Jack, slaps her hand on the table, and swipes up the deck of cards.

Alexandra continues. "Her mom twisted her ankle, so she wants to stay with her to take care of her and run to the pharmacy. She said you were supposed to go out? She's asking if you could drop Skye off at her mom's place instead of babysitting here? I can totally babysit Skye. I told her you'd let her know."

Shit. I should just take Skye with me to that meeting. It won't be fun for her, being at Emma's office, but it shouldn't be more than an hour.

"She might expect a call or a text message?" Alexandra insists when I don't answer.

Losing interest in our card game, Skye crosses her arms. "I want to stay with Alek-zandra."

"Aunt Shannon makes the best elbow noodles," I argue.

Skye sighs. "If Aunt Shannon twisted her ankle, then who will be cooking?"

"It's not all about food, bug."

"*You* said she made the best—"

"Skye. Enough."

"Whaaaat?" she whines. "Can I just please stay home with Alek-zandra?"

"Alexandra has to study."

Alexandra stops twirling her hair, lifts her arm, and lets her thick mane cascade down the back of the sofa. "That's totally fine with me. I'd love the company." Her arm stays bent over her head, and she keeps teasing her hair with her fingers.

My brain is suggesting creative uses for the sofa. Alexandra's head is perfectly aligned with my hips, so there's that. And there's the fact that the back of the sofa is like a cushioned ledge on which her supple body would fit perfectly, on her belly or on her back, while I—

"*Daddy*! Can I stay home with Alek-zandra?" Skye says, making the point that I'm no fun by stuffing the deck of cards back in its sleeve.

"If Alexandra is sure."

"Oh I'm sure! Come here, bug," she says, using my nickname for Skye.

"I'll keep it to an hour, promise."

"Take all the time you need," she answers.

Skye hurls herself into the sofa. "Can I watch a cartoon?"

"How about... we set up an art studio," Alexandra says.

Skye's eyes widen.

"Come on. Paints. Brushes. The whole shebang."

"The whole shebang!" Skye cries as she gets all her stuff out.

"Um. You sure about this," I ask Alexandra.

"Hundred percent. Go out. Have fun."

Fun? "It's a work meeting. Accountant."

Her eyes fleet to me, something weird passing through them. "Oh. Well. Like I said. Go have fun." Something in the way she says it doesn't sit right with me, but I don't have time to analyze any of this. I should get ready, shower, change, get the meeting over and done with.

An hour later, I'm outside Emma's office. The lights are out, and no one answers the door. I call her cell.

"I'm home," she says.

That's weird. "Be right there. I misunderstood. I thought—Never mind."

Emma lives in a big ass house she kept after her divorce. It's outside of town, up on a hill, and you get there by a long dirt road covered in snow November through April. At least it's been plowed today. But I'm over half an hour late for my appointment.

"Hey," she says as I get there.

"Hey."

There's soft music and candles in the dining room.

"Shit. You're expecting company. Sorry I'm late. I won't be long, promise. Just need to look over those taxes." I throw my coat on the hooks she has in her mudroom, take my shoes off, and head for her kitchen.

She lays her hand on my arm. "Come here, silly. You're the company." And she walks me to her living room.

There's cheese on a board, two glasses of wine, a bottle of red. "Caroline here?" I ask, already knowing what her answer will be. I thought we were done with this shit. Guess not.

She smiles and bends over, grabbing the bottle of wine. "She's at her dad's. It's just the two of us." *Yup.*

She hands me my glass and we clink. "Happy Valentine's," she says.

Shit. Shitshitshit.

"God it's good to be without the kids, right? I mean, I love my daughter and she's my whole life but... well, she's my *whole* life."

Awww Christ.

She kicks off her shoes and scoots up next to me on the couch, her legs under her knees, which hikes her skirt up almost to where it would be indecent.

I reach for cheese and scoot farther away when I sit back.

But I think I know what's coming. It wouldn't be the first time. I run a hand through my hair, as if that's going to help me figure how to get out of this.

My phone dings with the ringtone I've programmed for Alexandra. I pull it from my back pocket. It's a photo of Skye painting, her tongue sticking out, focus written all over her face. I smile.

Emma clears her throat.

"Sorry," I say and put my phone away.

"Was that the sitter? Is everything okay?" She scoots closer to me.

"Alexandra's looking after Skye."

"Ouch. Living the dangerous life."

"What do you mean."

"Nothing. Nobody's perfect. Just saying, seeing how poorly she does at a baking apprenticeship she applied for, you gotta wonder how she fares at looking after your kid. You should—"

"You don't know what you're talking about." I'm pretty sure, now, that Alexandra was forced to take the apprenticeship, and I respect her for that. For not being afraid to up and leave on very short notice. For leaving the big city life for the middle of nowhere. For trying to learn a skill she clearly has no talent for. Maybe even no interest in.

For still working hard at it.

Forget respect her. I admire her for that. "She's great with Skye." That's maybe the most important part of it all, as far as I'm concerned.

"Well, brownie point."

Okay. I gotta rip that Band-aid off.

"Look, Emma. You're an amazing woman, a good friend, and a great accountant."

She sighs and sets her glass on the coffee table with a loud clank. "I get it," she bites out. She stands and smooths her skirt, grabs my file, and sits at the dining room table. "Alright, then. Let's look at this."

We go over my taxes for the next hour or so, maybe less. It feels like fucking forever.

Her eyes are shiny, and I feel bad for her. I really do. I believe everything I told her. She's a great woman, and she deserves someone great in her life. That someone cannot be me. I feel nothing but friendship and respect for Emma.

I don't feel anything else, and I don't want to take advantage of her.

Sure, I'm lonesome, and she must be too. It'd be easy for me to slide into her bed. Right this minute, actually. She's attractive and she has a lot going for her.

We're finally done with our taxes. We both stand awkwardly. She licks her lips and puts her hand on my shoulder. "Chris. You mean a lot to me." Before I know it, her head is on my chest, and she squeezes me.

"Sorry, Emma. I can't be that person for you."

"That's why I love you. You're so *honest*."

I gently push her away. "Emma. You don't love me. We've been through that already. Come on."

I wonder if it's cyclical with Emma. We do have this uncomfortable conversation every couple of years, after all.

I move to put my coat on.

"Can we still be friends?"

"Of course. Just friends, right."

She hugs me again, and I pat her back in what I hope comes across as a friendly gesture, no misunderstanding.

Then I head home to the one woman I don't want to be *just friends* with.

Chapter Fifteen

Alexandra

The front door chimes, followed by Christopher's footsteps up the wooden staircase. He's been gone a couple of hours, maybe three. I didn't keep track. All I know is, the evening is in its second phase.

After Skye was done painting, I heated up some soup for her dinner, cleaned the kitchen, then we went upstairs. I read her a story, we got her ready for bed—which included a heart-to-heart girls' talk that she's very adept at initiating—and now she's all tucked in.

Christopher reaches the landing, and my heart does a little somersault at the sexy mess of his hair. At the way his mouth twitches in a smile when he catches me looking.

At the way his eyes dance on me.

"Hey," he says softly, and my heartbeat picks up at that simple word. At the way he says it to me. He breaks our gaze to flick a floor lamp on, and I take it all in.

The stubble he shaved off this afternoon already growing back. His slightly bloodshot eyes, from being tired, not drunk. His white button-down shirt, stretching against his pecs. He's rolled the sleeves up, and why do I find *that* so sexy on him?

His eyes snap to mine. "How'd it go?" I ask.

"Like a meeting with an accountant," he huffs.

My gaze slides down his body, then my blood turns to ice. "Really."

"What."

"There's lipstick on your shirt." Jealousy sears through me like a tornado, a violent reaction I never saw coming. It devastates me.

It devastates me that he was out with another woman.

It devastates me more that I care this much. That I'm possessive of him although there's nothing between us.

This I never felt for anyone.

I try to show nothing on the outside. But my heart hammers so hard inside my ribcage, I'm pretty sure he can hear it.

He ducks his head down to the spot, pulling on the collar so he can see. "It's not what you think," he says. We're both talking in muted voices, so Skye won't hear us.

I try to make as if I didn't care. "I'm just saying, you might want to spray something on it before it sets in. Whatever it is."

He continues rubbing it.

"You're only making it worse," I tell him.

He grabs the back of his collar, pulls his shirt off with the T-shirt that's under it, balls up both, and throws everything toward his bedroom door.

He faces me, his bare chest heaving, and ohmygod.

I can hardly breathe. I've seen his chest before. I can confirm: I like it. So do my lady parts.

He's a mass of muscle and pure sex. Does he know that? Does he know what he's doing right now? Or does he think this is just laundry?

And does he really need to put his hands on his hips? It makes his sculpted pecs bulge. Or is that natural?

And do his biceps always flex that much? I never noticed *that* before.

He takes two steps toward me, until he's too close for my sanity and I frown to force myself back to normal. A smile forms in his eyes but doesn't quite reach his mouth. He's holding it in. "Anything else you don't like about my appearance, please. Tell me."

I need to change topics. Fast. "Skye was a doll."

His gaze softens at the mention of his daughter, and it does nothing to lessen my attraction to him. Quite the opposite. "Thanks for the picture," he says. "That was... cute." His turn to have trouble holding my gaze. His eyes fall on the rest of my body.

I need to get out of here, fast, before I do something I'll regret. "I'm headed out. It's karaoke night at Justin's."

He furrows his brow. His Adam's apple bobs up and down. "Bakers go to bed early."

My eyes dance from the file on the table to his shirt on the floor to his chest too close to mine. Does he not know how that dusting of dark hair is an indecent invitation? It starts where his dark brown nipples mark the apex of his torso and traces a trail all the way down to where his pants hang low on his hips. If I stay here any longer, I'll be running my hands all over him. "I'll be on time in the morning."

He takes a step closer to me. "You're under my supervision."

"For the professional part." *God, why does he need to look so good?*

"For every part of your life. It's in the contract you didn't read."

The double meaning of his words stirs up a storm in my ovaries. "I read it. You're responsible for my well-being. My well-being requires

I let off steam by having unsupervised, adult fun at least once a week. Surely, *you* can understand that." I glance at his shirt on the floor, the lipstick stain my witness.

"I need you at one hundred percent in the bakeshop."

The words *I need you* heat up my insides. "Right."

"I'm making a baker out of you, Pierce," he whisper-growls as he brushes closer to me while he goes to his daughter's bedroom.

"So," I say, now that there's a safer distance between us, "Skye has it in her mind that there might be something going on between Emma and you."

He stops in his tracks but doesn't turn around. "Skye doesn't like any woman who gets near me."

"Of course. Just thought you should know. I said you were an adult and free to have other adult friends, and that doesn't mean you love her less."

"Emma is my accountant."

"Right. But still, I asked her if she'd love you more if she didn't have any friends. And she said no, it wasn't possible. I showed her how it was the same for you, and she understands that now."

He nods. "That was unnecessary, but thank you."

"Why was it unnecessary?" I push.

His gaze avoids me, and he runs a tired hand through his hair. "You know and I know and even Skye knows, there is no space for a woman in my life."

I wouldn't know about that, so I'm not about to give him the wisdom speech that would come at this precise moment in a sappy movie. Something about making space for what's important in life? Still, I'm ashamed to admit the relief that floods through me. Having a first-row seat to a romance unfolding between Christopher and Emma would have sucked.

I need to snap out of this, fast. As Christopher slides into Skye's bedroom, I rush upstairs and pull out my skimpiest dress, a strapless, sequined little thing that molds my ass just so. Cassandra's lingerie, because it makes me feel like a goddess.

And a pair of fuck-me pumps that will replace my sensible boots once I'm inside the pub.

The night is mine.

Justin eyes me with a question in his eyebrows that I answer by ordering a drink and wandering around the packed room. The crowd is fun, swaying to the music while patrons take turns following lyrics with varying degrees of harmony and success.

Drink in hand, I spot the usual suspects at a high table. Grace, Kiara, Willow, and Haley wave me to their table from across the room. They've folded me into their group like an old friend, and it feels good.

"Is Sophie coming?"

"She's probably in bed already," Kiara says.

"Or writing another story," Willow offers.

Grace sums it up. "She never goes out."

A string of pop songs lifts the tempo, and I find myself jumping up and down halfway through my drink. Does Christopher like to dance? Did he dance with Emma, which would explain the lipstick on his shirt? A slow dance will do that. I down my drink just as Kiara comes back to the table with a tray of shots.

Thank god for Kiara. She downs hers and heads for the mic.

The shots help me forget that for the first time, I find it hard to just enjoy the little things and be okay with everything else.

"Wanna go next?" Grace asks, looking at the stage where Kiara is destroying Taylor Swift and doing so with no shame at all.

Nope. Not me. I shake my head.

"Come on, you could use some fun, yeah?" Willow says.

Kiara wraps it up, and her eyes fall on me. "Yo, Bambi," she says into the mic. "You're next."

Nope. I shake my head. "Give it up for Bambi, you guys!" she says with laughter in her voice. "Alek-zaaaaandra!"

The bar erupts in applause, and it seems everyone is looking at me.

I guess I'm the new person in town. Probably everyone knows my name.

I still shake my head, no.

"You don't wanna chicken on Kiara," Haley says. "She's like a dog with a bone. Won't let it go. Here." She hands me yet another shot, and with that liquid courage, I make it to the small stage.

The girl in charge of the karaoke smiles as I grab the mic. "Life Ain't Fair" by Maddie & Tae pops on the screen. She questions me with a look, and I nod. How did she know I liked that song? Even if I'm bound to sing off key. The music starts and right away the bar crowd sings with me, covering my voice, as if they knew I needed this.

I'm feeling a hundred times better already.

I don't need any one person to be happy. Just a good drink, and a good song.

And a village looking out for me.

"Woo-hoo! I'm on the Titanic." The room swerves around me, and I partially miss my mouth with the shot. The feeling of the cinnamon-flavored liquor gliding outside my throat is hilarious. "It's on the wron' side of my throat," I tell Grace, pointing to my skin. "Should be inside, yeah? It's outside." I hold onto her as I roar in laughter.

Grace shoves a glass of water in my hand. "Honey, drink this," she says.

There's two Graces in front of me, and they look soooo funny. So kind too. They are my two best friends. "You think?"

She grabs my waist to keep me from falling. I don't know why the dance floor feels like a boat... Oh. *Am I drunk?* I try to focus.

Maybe?

That's so funny. Sarah would be so proud of me. I get into a fit of laughter and pull my phone out, but my fingers are all rubbery. I need to tell her I love her.

Grace holds the glass of water up to my lips. "Come on, bottoms up."

"I love you," I tell her. "You're my best friend. My second best friend. No. My best friendsss. You're all my best friends," I say, looking at the blurry faces of Kiara—my new cheerleader—Willow, Haley, and Grace.

They all laugh. I *am* funny, right? I take little sips of the water, and by the time the glass is empty, my eyes get back into focus.

And they focus right smack on a broad chest, dark curls, and brooding eyes boring into me, melting my core.

"Oooooooh. You came!!!" I swoon. There's nothing else to do but swoon when Christopher Wright is towering over me, frowning, biting his bottom lip like he's keeping himself from saying anything. "See? You're fun! Let's have fun," I say and grab his hand, pulling him to the dance floor.

I might be a little tipsy, but I don't miss the fact that his palm nests flush against mine and his fingers wrap snuggly around my hand. *Mmm. So good.*

But he stays right where he is, and a simple flick of his wrist pulls me back, right into his chest. I bounce against it. He's wearing a dark Henley shirt, tight around those pecs.

Those pecs.

He smells like pine and fresh laundry but mostly I notice his whole body is cold. He just walked in from outside.

"Where's Skye?" I ask softly, and he tilts his head down toward me. It's loud, so I get on my tiptoes and repeat in his ear, my lips all but touching his lobe, "Where's Skye?"

He leans into me and answers, "Asleep in bed. Come on, let's go."

"I can handle myself," I say, vaguely upset he helped me put my boots and coat on and is now pulling me by his side with one hand, my fuck-me pumps in his other hand. I'm not too drunk to notice he settled my tab—I tried to protest, but one glower was all it took. He won that argument.

He walks long strides across The Green, and when I trip trying to keep up with him, he slows his pace. That's when I notice. "You're not wearing a coat. Or a hat. It's gotta be twenty below." My teeth chatter and I trip again, forcing him to stop.

"Yeah. It's a little nippy." He lowers himself and before I know what's happening, he's hoisted me over his shoulder and starts hustling toward the bakery. "You okay up there?"

Am I okay? Am I okay? "Mmmm. Yes?" I giggle, my voice bouncing with his steps. "Are *you* okay?"

"Never been better." We cross the Green, then the street. He hops up the steps to the bakery, still carrying me, swings the door open, and sets me down in front of him. He kicks the door closed and cups my elbows in his wide hands to keep me from falling back.

I feel a little nauseated, but there's something I need to tell him.

Something that here, in the warmth of the bakery, behind the privacy of the drawn blinds, bathed in the soft light seeping from the lampposts, is the perfect moment.

"She was wrong about men. You're a perfect gentleman," I whisper, my hands crawling up on his chest, resting right below his neck.

He chuckles.

"I wouldn't mind it if you kissed me," I add.

He tilts his head, his hands still on my elbows holding me away from him. "Let's put you to bed."

My insides sink a little, but I soldier on. *Tonight or never.* "I like you very much. And I think you might like me a little bit too?" I bite my bottom lip and lift an eyebrow in what I hope looks like a question.

He tucks a stray hair behind my ear, and I lean into his hand. "You've had too much alcohol to know what you really like right now, Alexandra."

See? Perfect gentleman. So infuriating.

"I'm not in-ebriated. I'm un-inhibited. See? I can say long words. I'm perfec'ly functional." The bakery tilts around me, but my knight in shining armor is there to stabilize me, his hands on my shoulders.

Oh my god. I really am drunk. What an embarrassment. Tears pool in my eyes. "I'm sorry." I try to turn around to take the stairs and have to steady myself on the wall. My stomach feels queasy.

Christopher scoops me up in his arms. "Hold on. I got you."

I hold onto him, like he asked me to. One hand around his shoulders, the other fisting his Henley shirt. Isn't that the funniest? I start laughing hysterically.

"Shhhh. You're gonna wake Skye up," he says, chuckling as we reach the second floor.

I turn my head against his chest to muffle my laughter and damn it's nice there. It smells... comforting and exciting at the same time.

It feels *safe*.

My hands take on a life of their own and wrap themselves around his neck. His muscles roll under my palms, and my thumbs explore his jaw. The stubble does a nice little thing to my core. "Mmm... it's nice," I whisper.

His answer? A growl.

"My grandmother was wrong. Men don't always bring misery," I say and snuggle deeper in his arms.

But then he sets me down, and the second he does and I find myself on my feet in my bedroom, the whole universe around me swirls and my stomach decides to take a part in the dance. "What did she say?" he asks.

"Never mind." I stumble to the bathroom, somehow have the presence of mind to close the door, and drop to my knees in front of the toilet.

That's my price to pay for overindulging.

And I'm fine with that.

What is not fine, and I mean not fine at all, is the door opening.

And Christopher walking in—I can see his jeans.

I wave him off. "I'm fine." *Oh god just please, please go away.*

But Christopher's hand threads through my hair to hold it back. "Come on, baby, let it all go."

Can I please die now?

My stomach revolts against the injustice of it all.

He places one hand on my forehead while I retch repeatedly.

My nose stings as vomit makes its way through it, while the warmth of Christopher kneeling right behind me sends a confusing signal to my body. "Please leave," I whimper between two liquid spurts. "Please."

Is it too hard to understand I really, really don't want him to see me like this?

His hand just gets stronger on my forehead, the other knotting my hair tighter around his fist. "I'm not going anywhere until you're better. You might as well let it all out. Come on. Keep going."

He holds me for what will be forever etched as the longest, most shameful minutes of my life.

But at the same time, *god* his hand feels good.

I wake up to an agonizingly shrilly noise that howls through the pulp that is my brain. Groaning doesn't help. There's no one to put an end to this. I force my sanded eyes open and manage to turn a light on. An old-fashioned, cartoon-like alarm clock is responsible for the increase of my headache, and I manage to figure out how to turn it off.

My head feels like it's split in half, until my eyes fall on my nightstand. There's a glass of water, three aspirins, and a travel mug of coffee.

Aspirin and water down, I take a sip of the coffee.

Then a second. It's made to perfection, just like I like it.

Except better.

Yesterday night's events slowly come back in focus in uneven spurts, the memories jogged by the fact that I'm still dressed in the skimpy dress—stockings and all—and my pumps are neatly set at the foot of my bed.

Ohmygod.

I came back drunk.

Correction. Christopher picked me up drunk from Lazy's. Where the whole town witnessed my shameful behavior.

And I remember asking Christopher to kiss me.

And then I threw up, pretty much, in his arms.

All this after throwing a fit because I saw lipstick on his shirt.

Well of course he'd rather hang out with Emma than with me. That woman has her shit together. A business! A kid she raises on her own! And chicken that make fresh eggs that she brings to him!

You wouldn't catch her drunk at friggin' karaoke.

I'm such a disaster.

This morning, the proverbial walk of shame is going to have a whole new meaning.

Chapter Sixteen

Christopher

I hear her steps early.

She slept like a log. I didn't. That's how I know how well she slept. No tossing and turning. No getting up. Nothing.

Me? All night, I went over what she said when she was in my arms, in no state to say anything sound.

And I also go over what I said to her before she left for Justin's, when I came back from Emma's. That there was no space in my life for another woman.

I think back at what she told me she said to Skye, to appease her.

I think back at how she looked at my shirt. At that spot of lipstick, that she clocked the minute I got back. How jealousy ignited fire in her eyes.

I think back at how she looked at my bare chest.

Thirsty.

I want her right there. God, I want her right there, right where she was after being at Lazy's. Coming onto me. Begging me to make her mine.

But I need her to do that sober. And I need her to take the first step. And the second.

Hell, I need her to take all the steps. To define what she wants, so I can hold myself to that.

Because I want her all the way. And I don't know *what* she wants.

That's where I'm at when she comes in, early, into the kitchen.

Her eyes downcast. *Such* a turn-on. She doesn't even do it on purpose, I can tell. She's genuinely struggling to look me in the eye after what happened last night.

I wish again she hadn't been so far gone when she came onto me. I was this close to giving in, but in all consciousness, I couldn't.

But hell, I'm holding onto the memory of her supple body nestled in my arms, her delicate hands lacing behind my neck, her throaty voice whispering in my ear.

Sweet.

Sexy.

So damn tempting.

Her eyelashes flutter, and she raises her gaze to meet mine. I chase away my lust-filled thoughts and focus instead on the fact that it's ten minutes before six, and that I'm impressed.

Very impressed.

I didn't expect to see her that early.

She's holding the mug of coffee I made for her in one hand, and the alarm clock in the other. I didn't want to try and mess with her phone, so I figured that would do.

"I have several things to say, and I want to say them without being interrupted," she says.

"Okay."

"First off, I am very, very sorry for getting drunk last night at Justin's. I'm sure I broke all sorts of clauses in the apprenticeship contract. If you need to fire me, I understand." She takes a breath, maybe expecting me to say something, and when I don't, she continues. "Second, I'm so sorry you had to carry me upstairs. Third, don't ever, ever stay with me when I am puking again. Ever. Fourth, thank you anyway for staying with me when I was puking. Fifth, thank you so much for the coffee. It was the best coffee ever, and I need to know your secret. Finally," she takes a deep breath and her eyes lock with mine, "I believe I might have said certain things last night that weren't exactly savory, and for that, too, I am sorry."

"Not exactly savory?"

"Unsavory."

Is she still drunk? "Define unsavory."

She clears her throat and tucks her hair behind her ears. "Things you didn't like."

"There was nothing you said last night that I didn't like," I say without hesitation, and I see the shock registering in her.

"Really? 'Cause I'm pretty sure..." she frowns and licks her lips. "I think I remember... I said things to you."

Yeah, you said things to me I'd wish you'd say again when you're sober. "You said things to me that you were too drunk for me to take seriously." My heart hammers really hard in my chest. I don't like games. I don't like lies. Just because I can't be with her doesn't mean I should lie to her. So I take the jump. "It doesn't mean I didn't like these things you said. It just wasn't a good idea."

She seems disappointed. "Right. Not a good idea."

Maybe stupidly, I decide to keep that door from closing entirely. "At the time."

"At the time?"

"You'd had too much to drink for any kind of decision." I see her thinking through this. I can't really make myself clearer. Surely she heard me. She understood me. Right?

"Right." She sets the alarm clock on the table. "This device from the previous century is the work of the devil. I never want to see it again. Thank you but no thank you." Then she sets the coffee mug next to it. "And this, I'll say it again, is the best coffee I've ever had. I'd love another, or at least I'd love to know your secret."

I take her change of topic for what it is. A diversion from a heavier conversation. I'll let her draw her conclusions on what I said, and I'll let her take the lead. It's not like I'm in a position to make a move on her. I'm her boss.

But moreover, it's not something I should want to invite in my life.

But I'd love to make her coffee every morning, just to see that look on her face. Content. Peaceful. Safe. "Maple syrup," I say.

"Huh?"

"Maple syrup, not sugar. In the coffee."

She makes a little O with her lips. Fuck, she has to stop doing those things with her mouth.

Needing to turn my back to her, I settle for making coffee. "So, men only bring misery, huh?"

"Sorry—what?"

"That thing your grandmother told you. Men only bring misery. That true?"

She slumps on a chair and folds one leg under her. "Oh god. What else did I say?"

Things we're not discussing now. "Nothing wrong with that. I was just wondering."

"My grandmother was a single mom. And so was my mom. So yeah. I was raised to not get my hopes up. And I mean. Not. At. All."

"That must have been tough."

She chuckles. "Not getting my hopes up?"

I have to give her that. Hungover, she still has a sense of humor. "Being a single mom."

She frowns, her honey eyes soft on me. "You're a single dad. You would know."

I set two cups of coffee on the table, one black for me, one the way she likes it. Cream and maple syrup. "Was it tough being raised by a single parent?"

A smile brightens her features. "Best years of my life were with my mom. My grandmother, different story. But my mom? She was perfect. She gave me the best childhood I could dream of. We didn't have money. My grandmother could have helped, but she never offered to, not that mom would have accepted anyway. So I was always crashing at a neighbor's place depending on what her shifts were at whatever flavor-of-the-month job she had, but it was her and me against the world." Her gaze is lost somewhere in the past. "Best years of my life."

She focuses back on me. "You got nothing to worry about with Skye. My mom wasn't the best role model in terms of career, if you get my drift." She blinks away the tears rimming her eyes. "You, on the other hand, are the total package single dad." And on that, she takes a long sip of coffee. "Mmmm," she moans.

Christ, she has to stop doing that. The compliments. Now the moaning.

She continues. "I get where you're coming from—not having space for a woman in your life. You don't *need* one."

My initial chuckle dies down quickly. No, I don't *need* a woman. But seeing Alexandra here in my house. In my life. In my arms, even if for the wrong reasons.

I can see the appeal.

She blushes. "*God* what a stupid thing to say. I need to stop putting my foot in my mouth, don't I?"

"It's rather entertaining." I'm full-on smiling right now.

"Anything else I said last night we need to clear the air about?"

My eyes drop to her lips. "Not right now," I decide.

"M'kay." She focuses back on her coffee, but not for long. After a short silence, she says, "What's your family like?"

"What do you mean."

She shrugs. "Mom, dad, siblings?"

"Mom, stepfather, two half-brothers."

"Dad?"

"Nope."

She nods. "You don't like to talk about it."

"Nope."

"Fair enough. I have another question for you." She shifts in her chair, and her eyes gleam with excitement.

"Yeah?" I breathe easier.

"That baking competition."

"What about it." Funny, when someone else brings it up, I'm annoyed. When it's her, I want to talk about it.

"Why don't you want to go for it?"

"Long time ago, I did a few of those. Back in France. It wasn't a circus on TV like it is here, but it was maybe even more serious and challenging."

"And? You hated it?"

I shake my head. "I fucking loved it."

"So?" she straightens on her chair, her eyes gleaming with excitement.

"I dunno. Life. Skye. I'd need to be gone for a couple days."

"Are you kidding? Skye would love you to go. She's got a bunch of people here who can look after her."

"Skye wants me to go?" I'm really surprised. She's never really asked me, although all that talk about Caroline saying I wasn't the best baker in the country...

"And see her dad on TV? Duh. But this has to be about you, Chris. Don't do it for anyone else other than you. And let me say, anything you do for you, you do for Skye. What did you like about it back then?"

I'm brought back in time, my emotion tapping into my younger self. "The constraints and how that boosted my creativity," I say. "The limited time. The challenge. Winning." Yeah, those were fun times.

Her voice goes soft. "D'you feel like sometimes, you're caught in the same routine? Baking what sells best, watching the bottom line—"

"Watching the weather and the holiday calendar to figure out my quantities so I'm not left with too much inventory but still made enough to meet demand? Fuck yeah. It's the business, but..."

"It's draining," she finishes.

"Yeah, exactly."

"You haven't lost your spark, but..."

"It'd be nice to fan the flames." A slow smile spreads across my lips. This woman gets me.

My eyes fall to her lips. Again.

She must sense the vibe because she stands quickly from her chair, rinses her cup, and slips into the laundry room to change into her baking clothes.

"There's a community dinner at Justin's tonight," I tell her when she comes back out. "You'll come, right? Everybody goes."

"Yeah, sure," she says, her smile a welcome pang in my chest.

Chapter Seventeen

Christopher

Justin's monthly community dinner is packed, like it usually is. It's the cold that's been going on for months now, and the early nights. People get literal cabin fever. They feel the need to get out. Get together.

Tonight, it looks like the whole town showed up. The business owners, the troublemakers, the gossips.

And those in need of a free meal, wearing their best clothes. It's one of Justin's proudest accomplishments. That he can help people in need.

At the bakery, we do our share to help out, and Alexandra and I are carrying the last of the stuff we made. Isaac brought the bulk of it earlier and stayed to enjoy himself. A welcome reprieve for the kid, one he can chalk up to "working" as far as his father's concerned.

When we walk in—Skye skipping ahead, Alexandra in front of me, and me closing the back—there's a card game going on in a corner, with a couple of the firemen, the pastor, the owner of the General

Store, and my cousin Colton—Grace's brother, who's usually more of the hermit kind.

A group of women greet Alexandra loudly from afar, and my chest warms as I watch her plop the pies she's carrying on the bar counter, hang her coat up, and join them.

This town has a way of pulling you in, and I love that for her. She's not open about her life in New York, but I'm not getting a homesick vibe. If I'm counting right, she has one good friend in New York. And no family. She's had an active social life here. And I like it.

So damn much.

This town saved me.

Alexandra might not know it, but she needs saving too. She's too fucking lonely.

I strain to keep my eyes off her and focus instead on the laughter coming from behind the doors to the kitchen. Hoisting Skye on my hip, I kick the swing doors open and walk in on Justin stirring a sauce while sipping wine, and Shane, his chef, pouring carrot ginger soup in a chafer. They erupt in laughter as Wendy and Todd, the owners of the inn, deliver the punch line of one of their guests' shenanigans. I plop Skye on the prep table next to Shane, who starts quizzing her on school and life in general.

It's only minutes before Grace pops her head in. "You guys still think you're the cool crowd? We're too old for that. C'mon!" She grabs a bowl of potato salad and goes back into the pub. "Dinner's served!" she announces, her voice not carrying at all, but knowing we'll feel compelled to follow, as we should.

Soon, there's a line at the makeshift buffet laid out on the bar, then we all take our seats at different tables. Isaac joins me, and I sit back, taking a slow drink of my beer. Skye is sitting at the kids' table, laughing and eating. Alexandra is on the opposite side of the room, deep in conversation with Grace, Kiara, Autumn, and Cassandra. Her fingers dance on her phone, which she shows around the table. The women nod, then the conversation resumes. She sips her wine in tiny laps, her eyes dance, shiny. Happy. She says something, and everyone listens to her.

"Alex said she hopes you'll enter the baking competition," Isaac drops before shoving a heaping forkful of food in his mouth.

"She did?"

"Mm-hm," he answers, and swallows. "She really hopes so. Heard her talk with Kiara about it."

"That right."

"Kiara was saying how you don't give a shit. And Alex said you should start giving a shit or you're gonna turn into an old fart."

My head whips to him. "She said that."

"Yup." He finishes his soda in one long pull and stands to refill his plate.

My eyes flit from him to Alexandra, and I catch her looking at me. Pink tints her cheeks, but she holds my gaze.

Smiles at me.

Isaac takes his seat next to me. "She meant it in a good way, you know. I think." He shrugs. "Never really know with women."

"You know much about women, dude? You're what, sixteen?"

"Seventeen. And I *do* know how she looks at you when you're not looking, so I know she meant it in a good way."

Alright. I'm done with this high school bullshit. I don't need a seventeen-year-old filling me in on who in class has a crush on me.

But I am going to throw my hat in the competition.

"I'm *not* an old fart," I tell Isaac.

Justin slides a chair next to me. "Isn't that what all old farts say?"

Isaac chuckles.

"What's this about?" Justin asks.

I glower at Isaac, but he ignores me, and says, "Alex*andra* thinks the boss should enter the baking competition, so now the boss has his panties in a tizzy because he doesn't want to bother with that, but if Alex*andra* wants it..."

Justin's shoulders shake as he tries to hold in his chuckle. "Dude," he tells Isaac. "Don't ruin a good thing, okay? We've all been trying to get him to do it. Don't be jealous because some hot chick from the city rolls in and has him wrapped around her finger and he doesn't even know it yet. You're his teenage male employee. You're in a different world. Just be thankful he's going to do something good for himself. And for us. For the whole town."

"I'm not jealous," Isaac says. "Just saying, Alex*andra* comes in—"

"Why d'you say her name like that?" I cut in.

"He's totally jealous," Justin says to me. "Teacher has a new pet."

"Jesus H. Christ."

"So. You're doing it?" Justin asks me, ignoring Isaac.

"Doing what," I ask Justin.

"The competition."

I pull a long draw on my beer. Since Alexandra talked to me about it this morning, it's been nagging me. She's right. I'm at risk of losing the passion, of being only focused on my day-to-day. I need a challenge. A risk. Even if there's no real consequence and it's all for show.

I also want to prove to her I'm the best.

"I'll do it," I say, and the minute I do, I realize I have to win. I *will* win.

For her.

"Yessss!" Isaac punches the air and high-fives Justin. "Mission accomplished." Then he stacks his cutlery and napkin on his empty plate and stands. "I gotta go."

"Take some pie home," I tell him, smirking.

"You gonna tell her?" is his answer.

My eyes flick her way. "Enough with the high school shit, Isaac. Time to get your ass home now." We both stand, I give him a quick bro hug and a big slap on the back. "You need anything, you lemme know, yeah?"

"Yeah," he sighs. We both hope his father won't give him too much shit for being out tonight. "You gotta tell 'em. All of 'em," he says, his hand motioning to the room.

Justin stands. "I'll do it," he says.

Once the applause, the cheers, the backslapping, and the hooting die down, I search for Alexandra's face in the crowd.

She and her friends seem to have barely registered what happened in the rest of the room. They're hunched together. There's something in their world that's way more interesting than me entering a fucking baking competition, and that's fine by me.

Last thing I need is Alexandra clued into the fact that she made me do that.

Still, I make my way toward Alexandra's table. My excuse is, Skye is sitting on her lap. I gotta check on her.

It didn't escape me, all evening, how comfortable she is with Alexandra. My daughter feels at home around the woman I want, and all alarm bells go off. Is this a good thing or a bad thing?

Fuck if I know.

Then I remember what Skye told me on Alexandra's first evening with us—that Alexandra didn't want to marry me. That can only mean one thing. That Skye doesn't see Alexandra as a threat.

I need to keep it that way.

I also need some adult fun, like Grace says.

I also know that drunk Alexandra wants me to kiss her. Sober Alexandra can't be that far out.

Sober me also knows once I kiss her, I'll want more. And I'm ready to bet she'll want more too.

But for now, I need to know what's so interesting on Alexandra's phone. And Skye has given me the perfect excuse to creep up to her, smell her, maybe even feel her hair.

Fuck man, get a grip. Your daughter has a sixth sense about you and women.

"So, that's how you measure your click-through rate, but keep in mind that only matters if you have a qualified audience," Alexandra's saying.

The women are all drinking her words in as if she's some kind of oracle. Even Emma moved from her table to stand within earshot, looking at Alexandra, arms crossed.

"That's why your branding is so important. Know your target." She shows them something. "Before and after," she says, and they all oooh and aaaah.

"Daddy!" Skye exclaims as she spots me.

Alexandra blushes, and she's so obvious I immediately regret coming over to her table.

"You guys stealing my apprentice away already?"

"Shhhhh... She's showing us something important," Grace answers.

They all hover back over Alexandra's phone. It's full of beautiful pictures of the local businesses, their products, their people. It looks like professional photography to me. I know she spends a lot of time taking photos with her phone, but I didn't realize she was so talented.

It makes me wonder again about her motivation for this apprenticeship. I'm concerned about her.

"How come I don't see the bakery?"

Skye grabs my hand, and I'm so close to Alexandra her scent intoxicates me.

She glances my way but continues swiping through her phone. She switches screens on her phone and pulls up a social media app. It's her account, and she has a lot of photos of Emerald Creek. "I do have some photos of the bakery." She types something on her screen and a slew of photos of the bakery appears.

They're filled with warmth and really make it look great. I never realized my bakery was so... wholesome. There are photos from the outside looking in, the darkness of the street framing the lit windows like a promise of what's inside.

Willow smiling as she hand wraps confections. The line of customers chatting together. Isaac carrying trays of cinnamon rolls out of the oven. Close-ups of full shelves of breads.

Then, I see photos of me working in the lab, carrying bread, talking to customers. I generally hate seeing myself, but I have to admit her photos make me look embarrassingly good.

I clear my throat. I need to get out of here. I lean over to kiss Skye on the head and am about to tell her to be good before I get myself back to the safety of my table.

I'm impressed and proud at how good Alexandra is. I should freak out over the stakes I have running on her, but I'm not. The fact that, if she fails, I'll need to repay my grant barely registers in my mind. What

I'm concerned about is, why the hell is she wasting her time trying to get a grasp of baking, which she doesn't have a talent for, when she could make a killing following her true passion?

The words fall out of my mouth. "You sure you want to continue the apprenticeship? Seems to me you have a customer base for your own business. Right, ladies?"

The ladies approve loudly.

"What was all that ruckus about?" Grace asks me.

"What ruckus."

"The clapping and stuff," she says, gesturing to where Justin is.

"Oh, nothing. The guys got a little excited that I'm throwing my hat in the baking competition."

"You are not," Emma snaps.

"That's great!" Grace says at the same time.

"That's ridiculous," Emma counters. "He's got a business to run!"

"Oh," Grace backs away. "You gonna be okay with that?"

Alexandra is looking at Emma, me, and Grace. Skye's face is ecstatic. The way Alexandra and Skye look at me, both excited, is all I need. "'Course I'll be okay," I say as a slow smile spreads across my face. "It's gonna be fun."

I wink at Alexandra, who turns a sweet shade of pink, and ignore Emma's disapproving grunts. "Ladies, sorry for the interruption."

Back at my table, I'm met with Justin's smirk and a pint of beer. "Spill it," he says, leaning forward so only I can hear him. "How far did you take it with her?"

"The hell you'talking about."

"You forget I saw you carry her out of here last night. Cross The Green with her on your shoulder. Hell, half the town saw you guys. And she liked it. As in. *Liked*. It."

I fight the urge to punch the smirk off him. "Fuck off."

"She's only staying a few months, you know."

"And."

"And, either she works out and you only have a few months to make her see that. Or she doesn't and you only have a few months of fun ahead'a ya."

"Fuck off."

"Gotcha."

Chapter Eighteen

Alexandra

It's been a week since Christopher announced that he's running for New England's Best Baker, and since then, he's been getting up even earlier than usual.

Early isn't the right word. He literally gets up in the middle of the night. His floorboards creak, water runs in his bathroom, his door opens, and he goes downstairs.

And I can't fall back asleep.

My bedroom is cozy. Ish. I bought a throw blanket on sale at the General Store, thick and plush and soft, white with soft pink deer and grey bears. It looks awesome rolled on the little bench under the window. And I borrowed a few mystery books at the library and a couple of romances from Easy Monday's stash. Just the sight of them on the shelves, lit with the full moon, makes this feel like home.

Autumn mentioned they had some cool second-hand furniture at her family's antique store. I've promised to visit, although I know I won't buy anything, because that would make it look like I'm settling here.

Darn it, I'm fully awake. I should curl up on the reading nook with a book.

But I feel responsible for talking Christopher into doing that competition. And, full disclosure, being with him right now is more enticing that snuggling under the throw blankets.

I pull on some jeans and a sweatshirt, tie my hair in a messy bun, grab my phone, and tiptoe down the stairs.

I find him in the semi-darkness of the bakery, wearing nothing but faded jeans and a tight white T-shirt, his apron still folded on a table behind him. He's leaning on one of the prep tables, reading from a thick book plopped to the side with notes sticking out, a mound of flour on the other side, pots and pans and shit lined up in front of him and behind the book. He looks like the wizard baker he is, making his magic. A hot wizard.

"Hey," I say softly.

His head jerks up, and his face softens when he sees me.

God he's beautiful. "Hey," he replies. Half a smile spreads across his lips, then he says, "It's early."

"I feel guilty, so I came for moral support. Plus coffee, whatever. Also, I figured I could shoot some candid videos. You know, for when you're finally worldwide famous. A making of." I wave my phone at him.

"What do you feel guilty about."

Funny, that's the only thing he picks up on. I choose not to answer. "Coffee?" I ask.

"That'd be nice."

Minutes later, I hand him his hot and naked coffee, and cradle mine—creamed and mapled.

"What do you feel guilty about," he repeats.

"Talking you into doing that competition and—"

"It's true," he interrupts me. "It was you who convinced me."

Air whooshes out of my lungs. "Um... well, I'm not sure it was such a good idea. Seeing how you now barely get any sleep."

"It was a fucking awesome idea."

"Emma said—"

"Emma doesn't know shit about me. Except my numbers. And last time I checked, I'm not a profit and loss statement. 'Cept maybe for Emma," he says.

"Right," I say on an exhale.

He takes a long sip of his coffee, his eyes on me. "Thanks for the coffee."

"Anytime."

"Careful. Might take you up on that."

"Huh?"

"Making me coffee anytime. I kinda like it." A smile dances in his eyes.

Oh my. "Might be the price I need to pay for talking you into a show you now think you need to prepare for when, really, you could walk in there tomorrow and win."

His smile now spreads to his whole face. "But where would the fun be in that, when I could have you in the middle of the night right here with me," he says.

His heated words hit my nether regions in very pleasant ways.

"Making me coffee," he adds.

He's not fooling me.

He looks at me pointedly. I do clearly remember what he told me the morning after The Big Shameful Evening When Alex Got Drunk, that nothing I'd said to him he didn't like.

That he just needed me to say these words sober.

Right.

There's a reason they call it liquid courage. He knows and I know I meant every word. At the time. Drunk. Now, sober me is struggling to get out of her shell and express the same things to him.

"Gotta take risks," he says.

What?

"Gotta take risks in life or it gets boring." He tips his coffee mug to me. "I got you to thank for that. I'm having fun, taking a calculated risk, at the same time finding the passion again. So thank you."

"Okay," I whisper.

"Come here," he says, sending a flash of fire down my middle.

I round the prep table. When I'm close to him, he grabs the folded apron and slides it above my head, the warmth of his body sending chills down my spine as his arms graze mine. His scent pervades me—I'd recognize it anywhere. He crosses the belt behind my back, the heat of his fingers singeing through to my belly. My knees get wobbly, as they tend to when I'm close to him.

While he knots the strands of the belt in front of me, he talks, his voice caressing my insides. "Recent techniques make it so that bakers don't have to get up at two in the morning to ensure people have their bread ready by six or seven. Now, we have mechanical kneading and slow, overnight proofing. Although this allows bakers to have a good work-life balance, it's keeping us from having intimacy with the dough, from the real, ancestral experience of making a product come to life with our own hands from beginning to end. That's why it's a good idea to come back to these fundamentals, time and time again." He tightens my belt and lets both his hands rest on my hips while his eyes dive deep into mine. "You can do your video stuff in a little bit.

Right now, since you're here, you'll be kneading bread by hand. It can get physical."

Oh boy. "You got up in the middle of the night to practice—"

"I got up in the middle of the night to reconnect with the essence of baking. Teaching it is even more effective. Consider yourself my muse." His hands, still on my body, give my hips a squeeze before leaving.

He steps a safe distance away and quizzes me on the theory. I fire back the answers, my memory not failing me yet. "Not bad," he says. "What is the water proportion for a classic baguette."

"Sixty-five percent?"

He nods. "Get started."

I take a deep breath.

I wash my hands thoroughly up to my elbows. Then, I weigh the flour, salt, yeast, and water, add them to a large trough and start mixing all the ingredients directly with one hand. The mixture offers resistance, and I power through. When it's halfway homogeneous, I stretch my right hand and massage my forearm. There are still clumps of flour and pools of water that won't blend. The mixture is really heavy, requiring me to muscle through it.

Christopher cocks his head to the side, an amused grin brightening his eyes. He doesn't smile often, but when he does, it melts my heart. I'm trying hard not to think about what happened, or didn't happen, between us. But the feeling of his hands on my body, the caress of his breath on my face, are impossible to forget.

My right arm cramps. "I don't know if I can do this."

"Of course you can." A lock of hair falls over his forehead as he lowers his head and shoots me a glance hot enough to melt my core. "I'll help you," he says in a deep and reassuring voice. He washes his hands and forearms, dons a baker's cap, stands by me, and shows me how it's done: big movements that span the length of the trough, then rapidly crisscross back, fingers open to break the clumps of flour.

I get the hang of it and emulate him. His body is close to mine, and his cedar scent mingles with the sweet, earthy notes of the bread dough being formed. Our fingers touch on occasion, whether or not we want it. The dough is sticky, and the trough starts shifting. Christopher removes his hand from the dough, wipes it, and holds the trough for me. The veins in his hand stand out, the muscles in his forearm tensing each time I move the dough.

"You're good," he says when I've reached the end of the first step, but his words get me all hot and bothered again.

I cover the trough with a clean dishcloth and set the timer to ten minutes. This first pause is to ensure all ingredients hydrate homogeneously. "I'm okay with the theory. It's the practice I'm concerned about," I tell Christopher while I wipe my hand in a clean kitchen towel, my back to him. Ten minutes can be a very long time when there are unsaid things hanging between two people alone together. I need to reduce the awkwardness between us. "This is physically hard. I'm not sure I'll be ready for the exam this spring."

"You won't be asked to knead dough by hand," he says.

"Kay," I say. Then I turn to face him. "About the other night. I'm sorry."

He frowns. "The other night? You gotta stop apologizing for shit. What night are you talking about now."

"When I got drunk."

"You already apologized. Not that you needed to. I didn't fire you. You're here. We're good."

"What I said."

His eyes light up with interest. "You're gonna have to be a little more specific."

I take a deep breath. "What I said about wanting you to kiss me," I breathe out.

"And."

"I'm sorry."

"I'm not. Thought I made myself clear."

I blink several times.

"The thing is, you want something, you have to go after it," he says, his tone low and gentle. "Seems to me you're the kind of woman who knows what she wants, seeing as you decided to leave a comfortable office to come here and work in the middle of the night doing something you don't think you have a taste for, just so you can go back to that office job that means so much to you right now, but I can see myself fighting you on at a later time. Going by that, I'd say you know how to get what you want. Sometimes, it's just as simple as asking for it. In this case, I made myself clear. I think."

Wow. That was a long speech, for Christopher.

Yup. I'm clear. Very clear. But how do I even begin asking for what I want? *I want your hands all over me, your mouth claiming mine. And anything else you'd want to give me.*

The timer rings and I jump out of the hold his dark eyes have on me. "Dough needs tending, sweetheart," he says.

Sweetheart.

The dough. Right. My hands unsteady, I flour the prep table and plop the heavy dough on it. It spreads lightly like a deflated ball.

He uses his boss voice now as he guides me through the process. Strong tone, clipped orders.

Still so hot.

"Sprinkle flour on it, then fold it in half.... Now, lift it to extend it slightly, set it on the table, fold it in half, turn it one quarter counterclockwise and fold it again.... No... not quite. No hesitation,

Alexandra.... Try, again. Lift, fold, and turn. Lift, fold, and turn." He shows me, his movements strong and quick, the veins on his forearms bulging again as he flexes his muscles, the dough perfectly obedient in his knowing hands.

My thoughts drift again to dangerous territory. How would it feel to be handled by him?

More importantly, do I want to be handled by him?

Enjoy the little things.

"The baker's gestures need to have the energy to make the necessary changes happen. The repetition, the succession between these three movements, make four fundamental but separate elements—flour, water, yeast, and salt—become one to create dough, a living thing."

There's nothing left from the initial mess that was in the trough. Instead, there's a bouncy, even ball that's pliable and reacts to his movements.

My takeaway? He definitely has good hands.

"Your turn," he says.

A tinge of disappointment at myself helps me through this next leg of the work, giving me the false energy to lift, extend, set, fold the dough, and repeat.

"Give it a little more love," he says.

"Wh-what?"

"The dough. Give it more love. You're projecting a weird energy into it."

My hands falter, and the dough slips, collapsing on itself. "I'm not good at this," I mumble, then grab the dough again and get back to it. *I have to master this. I will master this.*

"Hey," Christopher says after a few beats. He comes next to me, his arms crossed. "You're doing great. Give it one more turn then set it to rest another ten minutes." His voice is deep and kind.

"Kay" I whisper.

Christopher leans against the prep table. His arms are uncrossed, his hands now holding the edge of the table, his head hanging down. He seems very focused on his shoes. I focus on everything else about him. The way locks of his hair fall on his forehead, and how it would feel to run my fingers through his dark curls. The curve of his full lips and the wonder of how they would taste against mine. His powerful arms and how they'd held me and carried me and made me feel precious and wanted.

The scent of his skin.

The ticking of machines, the purring of the overhead light are the only sounds apart from our shallow breaths. They fill the whole room. Christopher clears his throat. His knuckles are white, his hands flexing on the table. "What is your motivation for this apprenticeship. Deep down."

God. He seems worried about my chances of success. I owe him an answer I can live with. One that's not too far from the truth. "It really is to keep my job. And also, I like to think it would have made my grandmother proud."

"She the one who thought all men were shit?"

"What?"

"You said that, the other night. Something about misery and stuff. She's the grandmother who made you believe that?"

"Yeah, she's the one. She also didn't think I amounted to much, so me being here, being successful at this apprenticeship, it would probably make her proud."

"She sounds like a piece of work."

"That's putting it nicely."

The timer rings.

I push myself up, wash my hands, and grab the dough. It's larger and seems heavier. I'm having difficulty managing it. The last leg involves more technical movements. Christopher moves behind me and guides my hands.

"You need forceful movements, Alexandra. Like this."

His front to my back, he cups his hands over mine, and I abandon myself to his guidance. He accelerates my movements, lifts my forearms higher so the dough can extend more, and slaps it down with energy. I'm molded to his body, encapsulated in him. His pecs flex against my shoulders. His thighs are spread on each side of my hips. His voice resonates through my bones as he comments on what we're doing. Then, his comments die down, and it's just the sound of our labored breaths as we work the dough, arms tangled, my body pinned under his, surrounded by his.

"One more round," he says, the low growl of his voice vibrating through my entire being, his breath tingling my neck. The front of his body still flush against my back, I rock against him as we move in unison for the next round.

A tremor takes hold of me, an unfamiliar weakness in the knees that seems to be the signature mark of Christopher's presence around me. I let go of the dough and hold onto his forearms as he completes the last fold. When he's done, he stays right behind me. With shaking hands, I cover the dough with the clean cloth.

"You did it," he murmurs, his hands caressing my bare arms. "Such delicate hands," he adds, his fingers trailing from my wrists and up.

Shivers run through me. I close my eyes, lean against him, and rest my head against his chest. He smells like clean linen and cedar, a unique scent that drives me crazy. His chin strokes the top of my head. His hands cross my body and he pulls me tight against him, my back still to his front, and I feel his heart booming.

I whimper.

"Babe?" he growls, a question.

"Mm—hmph?"

"I'm gonna need you to be clear about what you want, like I said. We're adults and all, but I'm your boss, technically, although at this point, I'm going to be the one doing what you tell me to. So yeah, spell it out for me."

All while saying this, he brings one hand to my jaw while his other slowly cups my breast, then he drops his face and trails his tongue along my neck, his last words said against my skin the best kind of torture.

I tilt my head to give him easier access and moan as his fingers tease my nipple to hard pebbles.

He turns me around gently and caresses a strand of hair away from my mouth. His gaze stays there for a while, exploring. Although he says nothing, I've never felt so wanted in my life. My lips open on their own. Something passes through his eyes that looks like pain, then goes away.

"Let's hear it," he says.

I don't have words for what I want from him.

His hand against my back strokes up and down, then he trails both hands up my sides until he's cupping my face. My body rocks against his. He pushes me against the table. He's hard against my belly. I lift my hands to the back of his neck and press my breasts against his torso. He lowers his mouth closer to mine until our breaths mingle. His lips graze my lower lip, then trail to the corner of my mouth. His breath hitches.

"Alexandra," he whispers. "I'm dying to taste you."

I close the gap between our mouths. His lips encase mine, strong and soft.

Our mouths mirror our bodies, molding to each other.

I part my lips, inviting him in. His tongue explores my insides, slowly at first, almost tentative. His taste makes me pulse, and I moan.

Our mouths fit perfectly, there's no figuring each other out. Nothing awkward, no adjustment needed.

His tongue explores deeper, and I take him all in. He's strong and soft at the same time, claiming and giving, so hot and so tender.

I trail my fingers in his hair, pulling him harder against me, and soon the sensory overload makes the room spin. I flinch. He wraps his arms around me, lifts me, and sets me on the table.

Wanting to have him against me again, I wrap one leg, then the other, around his hips. His kiss deepens, our tongues deliciously mingling. I nibble at his, and he groans. He cups my ass and rocks his hips against my pelvis. I lift myself off the table and latch my legs around him. He pulls his mouth away from mine, only to trail it down my neck, licking and sucking me softly in the most delicious way. His hands under my ass trail up in between my thighs. Through the light fabric of my leggings, he teases me. I moan loudly and bury my face in his neck.

He sets me back on the table, unfastens my apron, and lifts it off me, pulling my T-shirt up at the same time. I arch my back. He lowers his mouth to tease my nipple through the lace of my bra. A shot of pleasure sears between my legs and I moan. He pushes me gently down on the table, pulls the cup of my bra down, and sucks on me.

"Oh, my god, yes," I whimper. I run my fingers through his thick hair, nudging him to keep going. I can't believe he is doing this to me. Here. Now. He looks at me with hooded eyelids.

I've never been so wanted, so desired.

"Oh, fuck, Alexandra. We better stop."

I take one last inhale of his skin, his hair. He pulls me up with him, and as he straightens himself, I let my mouth trail down his neck, to the spot that pulses when he talks. I lick and suck on it gently, claiming it as mine.

For now.

He pulls my T-shirt back down and molds my breasts with his hands. "You make me crazy, Alexandra." I'm hot and wet between my legs, and if he keeps talking to me like that, there is a strong possibility I will orgasm to the sound of his voice. "But you still haven't said what you want from me, beautiful."

"Whatever you give me, I just don't want you to stop."

Chapter Nineteen

Christopher

She's pliable under my hands, answering my strokes like a field of barley in the wind. *Fuck, and she's turning me into a poet.* I suck on her earlobe, and she exhales a moan that almost makes me come.

"Whatever you give me, I just don't want you to stop," she says in my neck. "I want you to let go with me."

Daaaamn.

She shouldn't talk like that.

Because me letting go means her clothes are ripped off, I'm getting drunk on her sweet juices, and I'm making her come before I even unzip my jeans.

Then I'm pounding her.

"I'm not the gentleman you think I am," I growl and pinch her nipple, to which she responds with a full body tremor and back arching. "But I'll act like one. Don't want you running back to these office types too soon."

The thought of Alexandra back in New York in a few months, moving on with other guys, doesn't sit well with me. If anything, it makes me harder. Angry hard.

"I can't wait to suck on your adorable toes."

"How do you know my toes are adorable?" she asks, her middle grinding against my cock, as if he's the one giving the answer.

"'Cause they'll match those delicate fingers of yours."

She nudges one hand between us, her nails scraping through the thick fabric of my pants.

"Those fingers?"

I push her hand gently away from my dangerously throbbing cock. "Beautiful, you're going to make me come before we even get started."

"So?"

I chuckle. "So. Ladies first."

I circle my tongue around her hard nipple and trail my hand between her legs.

She's so hot down there. And *wet*. "Fuck, you're drenched."

"Oh god, Christopher," she meowls, her hips bucking under my fingers.

I fucking love the way she draws out my name.

Love the way she moves under me.

"Beautiful," I say, taking her lips again. Her mouth is so sweet, and she gives so much. She wraps her hands around my neck like she's about to drown, and she gives me access to her mouth, and also she sweeps inside mine as if my pleasure is more important than hers, and god I want to give her everything but she's giving me so much already. I pull back just enough to look at her beautiful face, and her eyes open just enough to drink me in, gaze unfocused, irises so deep.

She rakes her nails softly against my back, trails them down to my ass. "God I want you so bad," she whispers.

I tug her leggings and panties down in one pull and sweep my hands across the silky flesh of her inner thighs.

She whimpers.

"Yeah," I growl.

My fingers find her folds, so sweet, so soaked for me. I slide two fingers inside her, my thumb on her clit, and just like that, she falls apart under me.

She's loud. A beautiful wail, my name on her lips.

God.

She's perfect.

"Fuck." My dick is furious for all this teasing. I pull back from her, pull her pants back on, slowly release her breasts, her hips, her whole body.

I keep her head cupped in my hand.

She frowns. "You look upset."

"You're perfect," I explain.

A slow smile spreads on her face. "That sounds like a good thing."

Not really, but my mind is too fuzzy to get into that right now, and I don't think I can find the words to explain how her being perfect is really not a good thing for me. "We need to keep this to ourselves," I summarize.

"Okay." Her voice is small.

I move one hand up to her adorable face and play with a strand of her hair. "I need to keep it professional between us. In appearance. At work. In town. It would create too many problems."

"Of course," she whispers. Her eyes get bigger with understanding. "Skye can't know."

She *gets it*. I knew she was perfect.

"Yeah."

"I don't want her to hate me, and I don't want her to get hurt."

"She'd never hate you. She'd just get it in her head that you'll stay with us. And, when you leave, she'd feel abandoned." I almost say abandoned *again*. I don't know if there was ever a particular moment in her life when Skye realized that her mother had left her. It's more of an ongoing feeling of not having ever been wanted by her. I can't have her feel this, again, even differently.

"She'd hurt," Alexandra repeats.

I cup the back of her neck. This woman is so different. So wholesome.

"I guess I'll just go out with the girls," she says. "I like going out," she adds as a manner of apology.

I picture her in that little fuck-me dress and those fuck-me pumps, shaking her ass on the dance floor, me on the sidelines because I don't want the gossip mill to hurt Skye.

"I know you do. I'll take you out. Couple counties over."

"You don't have to—"

"I want to."

Her eyes widen. "You want to?"

What does she think? That I just want to fuck her? Christ.

"We also need to protect ourselves," I say.

She frowns. "I'm on the pill. You have condoms?"

That's not what I mean, but speaking of which, I'm not sure I do. It's been too damn long. I make a mental note to order condoms online, next day delivery. It's either that or drive two counties over to save appearances. "I mean, no expectations, right. We're just two adults letting off steam, having some fun until you leave."

"Yeah, yeah, of course." She smiles softly, but her gaze drifts to the side. "I always knew that."

"Knew what?"

"Whenever life throws me a curveball, I focus on the little things, and that makes me feel good again."

"And the curveball is..."

"This apprenticeship."

I wince.

"I mean, no offense, Christopher," she says, her eyes on me, now, "but this is really not my thing. I'm just not cut out for this." She's lucid. That's good.

Except, I have a lot riding on her apprenticeship, so I hope I can get her to pass the damn exam. "Right. And the little thing..."

"Well, you."

Ouch. "I will have you know, there's nothing little about me."

She giggles adorably and kisses the bottom of my neck. "That's not what I mean."

"Regardless. I can't wait to disappoint you." I lightly stroke her back. Fuck, she's back in my arms already. "There will be nothing little to focus on."

A shiver runs through her, and she arches her back under my hand, rubbing her belly against my erection. "Yeah, I got that impression," she whispers.

She is going to be lots of fun. I need to keep that in mind. Just fun. All good.

We only have half an hour left before my crew starts coming into work, so there's barely time for us to straighten ourselves and the kitchen.

I lean into her to kiss her one last time, and the fucking bakehouse phone rings. It's only five-thirty in the morning. I untangle myself from Alexandra and look up the caller ID.

"It's Red Barn Baking," I tell her.

The rosy glow she'd built up under my hands vanishes. She's more than pale. She's gray.

"Oh, no. He's been calling my cell. I blocked him."

A male voice announces himself as Robert Norwood. "Bring Alex Pierce to the phone."

"Not happening."

"What? Who the hell is this?" he barks.

I can tell Alexandra is straining to listen. I lock my eyes with her while I talk to the asshole. "This is her master."

"Wright? Is that you, son?"

"Norwood, listen carefully. You are not to call Alexandra on this phone or on hers. You are not to contact her in any form during her stay here with me."

"Fuck off."

"For the duration of this apprenticeship, she's entirely mine. You know it. *I* own her. *You* fuck off."

I hang up. Alexandra's colors are back. My hard-on is painful.

"What did he want?" she asks.

I close the space between us. "Don't know. Don't care. You heard me." *You're mine.*

She lowers her eyes and clings to the back of my neck.

"Will you tell me what's going on over there?"

Her body tenses. "Y-yeah. Just not right now, please?"

There's something that bothers me, and I'll get to the bottom of it. She up and left a job she clearly loves, for a boss she clearly hates. Why does she put up with his shit? She could do the same job for a different company. A company that wouldn't require her to go do a full-on baking apprenticeship.

It doesn't make sense.

I want her to trust me enough to open up to me about that.

I've never had a real relationship with a woman. Lots of hookups, some repeats. Never had time or patience for a relationship.

And I know she's leaving in a few months, but for the few months that I have her, I want to make her life better.

I want her to entrust her troubles to me.

So I can lighten her load.

And if that looks like a relationship, so what. Sounds pretty fucking awesome to me.

As long as I don't get Skye hurt.

Chapter Twenty

Alexandra

Between Christopher's scent wrapping me in a daze of need, the sight of his hands working the dough when they could be working me, his clipped orders that are so far removed from his tone earlier, and his commanding eyes that see right through my clothes, I'm dying, and I think it shows.

I fumble the simple task of cutting the croissant dough into triangles. Christopher extends his hand to help me, then steps back. "Best for both of us if I leave you to it," he growls.

I nod, words escaping me when I'm close to him.

My eyes follow his body as he retreats from me, and I fall into the best daydream.

"You okay, Alex?" Isaac asks, startling me.

"Huh? Yeah, I'm fine. You?"

"You've been staring for five minutes," he continues. "I kept track." He comes closer to me. "Are you high?" he asks in a low tone.

Yeah, I'm high on our boss. "Wh-what? Are you crazy?" I scoff. I jump out of my daydreaming, and my gaze hones back on Christopher.

He's talking on his cell phone, eyes shut, free hand running through his hair. "You need me to come jump-start your car...? Colton. Okay... How long's he gonna be?" He glances at the clock on the wall, at the activity in the bakehouse. "Don't worry about it, Grace. I got her," he says. Then he hangs up and takes a deep breath and brushes his hand over his face.

"Want me to load these in the oven for you?" Isaac asks me. I eventually managed to cut, roll, and brush the croissants with egg wash without too much damage or waste.

"That'd be great, thanks," I tell him while I make my way to Christopher. "D'you need my help with Skye?" I ask him.

He looks at me like he didn't remember I was here at all. "Grace is going to be late. I—"

"I can take care of her," I say. I avert my eyes from him, or I might jump him in front of everyone. His jaw clenches, and it takes all I have not to suck his bottom lip right now.

"You sure?" He looks around at the bakehouse, buzzing like a beehive at this time of day. Even though everyone knows what they need to do, Christopher's presence is essential for everything to go smoothly.

Then, he locks eyes with me, and as his magnetism pulls me in, I teeter. "Of course," I say, taking my apron off quickly. I need to put some distance between the two of us, at least for now.

"Can you make me a French braid like yours?" Skye asks when we're in her bathroom.

"Sure." I smile and get to work immediately, so she's not late.

"Today is casting for the spring show," she explains.

"Oh! Right." With everything going on with Christopher, I forgot about that, and I feel guilty. That's another reason why Christopher and I could hurt Skye. By getting wrapped into our own stuff. At least me. To the point of forgetting today is one important day for this little girl. "Are you nervous?"

"No. I'm wearing my good luck sweater." It's her bright orange sweater with small green turtles. It has a happy vibe and looks great with her complexion. It's pilling along the sides, and I'm guessing Skye feels she needs good luck more often than not.

The sleeves are also getting short. Next year it won't fit her. "It's very pretty," I say. Yeah, I'm not great with kids. In case anybody is still wondering, another reason not to have a serious relationship with a single dad. Seriously, what do I have to bring to the table?

Minutes later, we're in the kitchen, and I'm going through the motions of making her a hot chocolate to even out the bowl of cold cereal she's eating. It's a short walk to school, but temperatures are in the single digits. She'll need all the warmth she can get. I know, it's a lot of milk, but I'm short on ideas. So, cereal *and* hot chocolate.

While she's eating, I brew myself a strong coffee. Between the four a.m. start time and the hot makeout session with her father, my eyelids are fluttering already, and the sun is barely up.

I don't know when or how it happens, but halfway into a quiet breakfast, I hear a squeal and a wail. Skye's hot chocolate is splattered all over her sweater and onto her pants.

"Oh, nooooo!" she cries.

I wipe the mess off the table with paper towels, but that's not what we're concerned with here.

Skye pulls on her soiled sweater. "Whu-whu-whuddama gonna do?" she sobs.

That, I think I can help with. Been there myself more than once.

I bring her upstairs, and while she changes her pants, I run the sweater under water, pat it dry between two towels, then get to work on it with the hairdryer while Skye keeps sniffling. That does the trick.

"All right, Skye, look! No more crying." I hand her the clean and dry sweater. She puts it on and hugs my legs.

Crisis averted without adding to Christopher's load of stress. I'll call it a win.

But it was a close call, so I crouch to her level and lift her chin. "Having good luck clothes or objects helps, but remember that you are the one who gets to decide what your good luck charm is. You can change it. It's what you believe that gives the sweater its power. Understand?"

She frowns but nods, humoring me.

"You're the wizard of your own life. Don't you ever forget that. You have the power."

Look at me, doling out lessons to a six-year-old I can't even follow myself.

She wipes her tears and takes a deep breath. "Okay," she says.

Minutes later, I take her tiny hand in mine as we walk outside. Our gloves make it hard to feel the connection, but it's there. She doesn't try to remove herself, and something deep and strong churns in me. She trusts me. Counts on me. Looks up to me.

It's another bluebird day, with the sun shining low on the horizon, the snow glittering all around us, and the sky a pale blue this early, with promises of deepening during the day.

So gorgeous it hurts.

I take a deep breath, inhaling the gift that this moment is. A moment that won't last. I take it all in and store it in my little bank of happy memories for later. For when I'll need memories of happy times.

We get to school with a few minutes to spare. I crouch and Skye wraps her little arms around me to say goodbye. "Good luck with the casting, sweetie pie," I whisper in her ear.

She surprises me by kissing my cheek before running into her classroom.

As I walk out of the school building, I wave at Emma helping Caroline out of her car. It's a small town. I need to play nice with everyone, even if Emma is not my first choice for making friends.

I feel happy and light today.

Walking back toward The Green, I make a detour to buy some flowers. I want to bring my happy into the bakery, and a bright bouquet of flowers will do just that.

I know it makes Christopher happy.

On my way out of the shop, I bump into Emma again.

"Do you have time for coffee?" she asks me. She has perfectly coiffed hair despite the weather requiring hats. Her makeup is right on point, including lipstick the exact shade I remember too acutely being on Christopher's shirt. She even has the kind of teeth described as pearly in kissing books.

She's so perfect it's intimidating.

Me? I got up at four and barely glanced at myself in the mirror. Granted, that hot make out session with Christopher did make me feel like a million bucks, and my morale is off the charts right now, but come on. I need to stretch that capital of self-confidence as far as I can.

So, coffee with Emma? Maybe not just yet. Plus, I'm getting a weird vibe from her.

Okay, I'm not totally over the Lipstick Incident. Yet.

"Maybe next time?" I smile as genuinely as I can. "Gotta rush."

"Oh, don't be silly," she says, looping her arm in mine and dragging me to Easy Monday.

On our way in, we run into Autumn. Rather desperately, I latch onto her. "Have your coffee with us!"

I need a friendly presence.

Her eyes dart between Emma and me, and she looks a little panicked. "I-I'm on a job," she says.

"A decorating job?" I'm so excited for her.

"Yeah."

Why does she look anxious? "Ohmygod, Autumn! That's fantastic. Take some before and after pictures, okay? For your social media. I'll handle it." People don't realize it, but putting other people's work in the spotlight actually brings me joy. Autumn probably thinks it's a chore, but this is fun for me.

"Will do," she says as she scampers away.

Even stressed out, Autumn's sunny disposition, and the news that she's finally starting her new business, just made my day better. "Sorry about that," I say to Emma with a small smile, then place my order with Millie, who informs me that today I'm to graduate from the pot of drip coffee to a Sweet Surrender. "Trust me," she whispers.

"Kay," I whisper back.

"So, did you get a new position?" Emma asks once we're seated.

"A new...? What?"

She takes a dainty lap from her green tea, giving my discomfort time to grow. "I heard about the baking disasters," she says with a patronizing smile. "It figures Chris would move you to doing other things. I have to say though, trusting you with Skye is impressive. I never thought he'd make the leap."

I stop with my own cup midair. "What—oh. Oh no, Grace had car issues. I just jumped in and took Skye to school, that's all." I'm going to let that little jab at my baking skills slide. Maybe she didn't mean anything by it. But I do need to set the record straight. "I'm still very much apprenticing with Chris."

"I see. How long are you here for?"

Funny, I thought she knew. Thought she'd read my contract and all. Maybe she didn't pay attention. "Until mid-June. Another few months until I go back to New York."

"I bet you miss the city. Do you live in Manhattan?"

"Brooklyn," I say and take a long sip of my coffee.

She rolls her eyes and manages to look really cute doing it. "You must find our little town so boring."

"Not at all. It's charming and peaceful. The people are lovely. I've been keeping super busy outside of the apprenticeship and making more friends here than I have in Brooklyn, actually. Matter of fact, I *have* started helping some businesses with their social media, on the side." She witnessed my interaction with Autumn just now, and I saw her linger around my table during the community dinner. I already have ideas of what a CPA could do to get more clients through social media.

If she asks me, I'll help her.

"And how are things with Christopher?" she asks instead, surprising me.

"Things? What things?" *Does she know already?* How could she?

Emma lets out a small laugh. "Work, darling. What other things could I possibly be talking about?"

I tame the flash of heat going through me. Right, work. "Work is good. It's hard, though. Hard work."

"Mmm. How about the boss?"

"Christopher?"

She raises her eyebrows. "Do you have another boss?"

What's up with the interrogation? "He's... he's great."

"Got you tongue-tied, doesn't he? I bet he does." She smiles at me like we're both in on some secret. "He's quite the package, isn't he?"

I widen my eyes, not sure what I'm supposed to say to that.

"Oh, come on. You can tell me. Don't tell me you don't ogle that tight little ass."

I feel myself blushing. Give me an hour, and I'll have a ton of comebacks.

I don't have an hour.

"Well, this has been nice," I tell Emma, putting my coat on and grabbing the flowers. "I should get back while I still have a job."

Emma laughs. "Oh well, if all else fails, he could definitely use a nanny."

"Right," I say.

The cold air snaps me back in shape. I was all out of sorts there for a bit.

When I get back to the bakery, all I need is one look at Chris and my mood is back on the upswing. His hands that were on me just two hours ago are shaping breads, molding rolls, flouring cookies. The tight ass that has Emma all turned on is flexing as he leans into ovens and carries loads of confections. I peel my gaze from him, put the flowers in a vase, and focus on my tasks for the next four hours.

When lunch time comes around, I'm beat. It's just the two of us in the kitchen. The rest of the crew is either gone or helping in the store. He's standing, as usual, eating a sandwich. I'm too tired to be hungry. "I'm going to take a quick break in my room," I tell him.

"No," he says. "Stay here. Get your feet up on the couch if you need to."

I don't move.

His sandwich finished, he licks his fingers and turns around to wash his hands at the sink. "I'm having some guys refinishing the steps to your room. You can't go up there right now. They're going to need a couple more hours at least."

I'm exhausted. The couch sounds good, so I plop on it and close my eyes.

"Hey, sleeping beauty," he says, startling me.

I open my eyes. Did I fall asleep? I must have. I'm totally drowsy.

"Time to work on educating your palate. Everyone's gone," he says, taking my hand and pulling me up. When I'm standing flush against him, he dips his lips to mine, and his tongue trails lazily inside. I close my eyes. He's *such* a good kisser. His full lips pull on mine just enough to increase my arousal. His tongue is now more aggressive, fucking my mouth.

God, I want him inside me.

Now.

I drop my hand to his erection, and he rocks against it. My fingers find his zipper, but he stops me, pulling my hand away.

"We still have some work to do, beautiful."

"We do?" I breathe, my mouth tasting the saltiness on his neck.

"Mm-hm. Blind tastings. Should be fun."

Chapter Twenty-One

Alexandra

Christopher locks the bakery and kitchen doors. "I don't want any interruptions," he says as he brings a tray covered in a clean dishcloth. "I need you to focus on developing your sense of taste."

I'd rather taste the baker, but okay.

Sometime during my nap, he dropped the master baker attire. He's wearing a dark gray flannel shirt that looks soft and warm. It's tucked into faded jeans held tight around his hips by a worn leather belt. I lick my lips.

He pulls a chair and motions for me to sit down. He's standing to my side, and his hand stays on the back of the chair. "Define *viennoiseries* for me." How is it that his bossy voice makes me all mush?

But seriously. French words again? Who has time for that? But he lived in France, didn't he? I bet he can say dirty things in French.

"Alexandra," he growls when I don't answer.

Thankfully, I have a good memory. I like him a little upset, but I'm keeping my eye on the ball. I need to pass this freaking apprenticeship.

"*Viennoiseries* are sweet confections that place them in the tasting scale of pastries but are made according to baking processes of fermented dough, either with yeast or with levain, and long proofing periods of time." His approving glance warms my middle. Pleasing him on different levels is a turn on to me.

He moves away from the chair and stands in front of me, arms crossed, legs slightly apart. "Examples."

"Pains au chocolat, croissants, brioches." I wonder if he's going to correct my pronunciation. It'd be like him to focus on these details that no one cares about but him.

He does that thing with his body when he's talking about baking, where he rocks back and forth on his heels. Does he know how it turns me on? "Give me an example that's not in the book," he says.

Kay. "Cinnamon rolls?"

His nods his assent, his gaze heating up. How can he focus on work right now? "Good example. Do you know why they're called *viennoiseries*?"

I stifle a sigh. Can we just move on to the tasting and maybe continue what we were doing when we were so rudely interrupted this morning? I did memorize the interesting tidbit of history he's asking about though, so I parrot out the answer. "*Viennoiseries* were introduced under Queen Marie-Antoinette, when the bakers of Vienna followed her to France and popularized their creations in the country."

He grunts, then circles around me to the back of my chair and lets his fingers run through my hair. My spine tingles, and I lean into his touch. He grabs a clean dishcloth and rolls it tightly. "Close your eyes," he whispers and ties the cloth on my eyes as a blindfold. "Good girl," he growls. My breath stutters in my chest. The itch between my legs I've had since this morning becomes hard to ignore. I cross my legs tightly. With no sight, I'm more aware of his scent, of the sounds he makes as he moves away from me, presumably to the tray of breads.

He clears his throat. "First sample," he says, and places it on the hand I extend.

The crust is irregular. I bring it to my lips and sniff it before taking a bite. The tanginess makes me salivate. "Mmm," I moan, then swallow.

Christopher lets out a low growl.

"It's a sourdough," I say.

"Good. Easy though. Anything else? What flour?"

I press the remaining piece of bread between my fingers and smell it again. "Whole wheat and... potato?"

A faint metallic sound comes from where Christopher stands. I pull the blindfold down a notch. My breath hitches. He's pulling his belt off his jeans. They hang low on his narrow hips, just high enough to cover his pulsing bulge. I bite my lower lip and wipe my sweaty palms on my pants. Pulling my eyes from his crotch, I rake my gaze slowly back up to his pecs molded in his shirt, his biceps flexing as he tugs on the leather belt, the triangle pulsing at the base of his neck, his jawline accented by just the right scruff.

"What are you doing?" I breathe.

He leans over me, his molten eyes drilling into mine, stoking my inner fire. "Keeping you from cheating. Hands behind the back of your chair."

"Touching is cheating?" I whisper as I bring my hands together behind me.

He kneels on the floor and wraps my hair around his fist, pulling my face slightly back, forcing me to arch my back. "Peeking is cheating. Touching is also cheating, today."

He brings my hair to the front of my body, the gesture so soft it feels like a caress. How can this strong, bossy man be so tender and careful with me? His hands graze my shoulders then trail down my arms, gently pulling them together until my wrists are flush against each other.

He rolls his belt around my wrists and ties it loosely. "Is this okay?" His face is right next to mine, and his voice sends a hot tremor down my core.

I tilt my head slightly toward him. "Yes," I whisper.

A low growl escapes him as he adjusts the scarf on my eyes. Blindfolded and tied up, I'm at his mercy.

And I'm loving it.

The heat between my legs becomes more uncomfortable. I squeeze my thighs together. With my hands tied behind me, my back arches naturally, exacerbating the pulse in my nipples.

"Keep this going, and I will lose it, Alexandra."

Yes. Please lose it already. "This is all your making," I say. I've never had anything close to this level of heat with a man, and the power play between the two of us brings my arousal to levels previously unknown to me.

His fingers tilt my chin. "Open wide." He deposits food on my tongue. My mouth is dry, and I chew with difficulty. The scraping of a chair being pulled over startles me. I swallow. A ruffling sound indicates Christopher seating himself very close to me. His knee brushes against mine. His raspy voice comes from directly ahead of me. "So. What is it."

"It's—It's hard to tell." My mouth is so dry, it seems full of sand. "Could I have some water?"

The chair scrapes the floor. Christopher's footsteps fade out and then back in. He cups my nape. "Careful," he says as I take a sip then dip deeper in the glass. He lifts it, and water trickles down the corner of my mouth, along my throat, to my collarbone. When I'm done, he wipes my lip with his finger. I nibble on it, and his breathing hitches. Freeing himself from me, he lets his hand follow the wet trail until it rests on my collarbone, above my breasts. I tilt back, willing his hand lower, and my hips move toward him.

"What do you want?" he murmurs in my ear, his breath and voice setting my core on fire.

His hand trails down and palms my breast. He growls. I arch my back more, pushing myself against him. Through the fabric, he finds my nipple and rolls it between his fingers. A moan escapes me. "I want you," I finally answer.

He takes a deep breath and releases my nipple. His fingers behind my nape knead my neck.

He presses his finger against my lips, and I take him in my mouth. I close my lips around him, hold him tightly between my sheathed teeth, and wrap my tongue around him. He takes a sharp inhale but does nothing to remove his finger. I suck on it and run my tongue slowly around his finger.

He pushes a knee between my legs, demanding. I spread my thighs and tilt my hips. He runs his free hand slowly from my side down to my waist and in between my legs, teasing my middle through the fabric of my pants.

"Stop teasing me," I pant.

He fumbles with the zipper of my pants.

Yes.

I push myself off the seat so he can push my pants down to my ankles, then drop back down, thighs shamelessly spread open.

His finger trails the side of my thong. I rock myself against him and release his finger from my mouth. Both his hands trail up my ass then down my thighs all the way to my knees, and back up, bringing my arousal to dangerous levels. Then his hands move to the insides of my thighs and slowly make their way up. The higher they get, the harder I breathe. I writhe under the teasing of his large, warm hands so close to my pulsing middle.

"Fuck, Alexandra, you're so soft." He teases the fabric of my thong then grabs my thighs and pulls them wider apart. With painful slowness, he makes his way to my center. He rubs my clit through the fabric of my G-string. "You're soaked. You fucking soaked your panties," he growls. "My turn to do a tasting," he says as he slides under the fabric and dips his finger in my folds, causing me to stop breathing under his knowing hands. He circles my clit teasingly, the only sound my hitched breathing and his heavy panting.

The feeling is so intense and so good, I want it to last forever. "Oh, my god, Christopher, don't stop. Don't stop. Keep going."

He stops, and his fingers leave me.

I whine and push my hips toward him. "Please."

A sucking sound comes from him. "Oh, fuck. You taste delicious. So sweet. I shoulda known."

He pinches my nipple through my top, and I moan again. He pulls my top and my bra down and takes my breast in his mouth while the palm of his hand gently presses my nub. The drumming of his fingers on my clit intensifies my pleasure, and when he pushes the fabric of my thong to the side and teases my folds, making slow circles around my clit without ever touching it, I nearly lose it.

He nibbles on my breast with sheathed teeth, bringing excruciatingly delicious almost-pain that travels to my insides. I move my hips to the side to try and meet his finger with my clit.

He presses the flat of his hand on my pelvis to make me stop, then drums his fingers on my clit before finally, finally stroking it steadily, full on.

I moan, pleasure mounting in me like a tidal wave under his constant caress. His scent intoxicates me as I lean into his head. "Ohmygod, ohmygod Christopher, don't stop, don't stop, don't stop."

He takes his mouth off my breast.

"Please," I beg him.

He takes my other breast in, and I squeal as he sucks the nipple then nibbles on it, the intense pleasure rapturing my body.

My orgasm builds in my toes, and as Christopher sucks harder on my nipple, a low wail escapes my mouth. Pleasure strikes through me like lightning, and as I come undone, he plunges two fingers inside me, his thumb still working my clit.

The tremor that seizes my body is such that the belt that ties my wrists comes loose. I hold onto it for dear life. My blindfold slips off, and the sight of Christopher working me right here, in the middle of his bakehouse, only occupied with my pleasure, might be my undoing. His curls tickle my skin as he sucks my breast, and his dark hand plunges between my pink thighs, the veins on his flexed forearm bulging. As I let out a cry, he gently presses his free hand to my mouth, stifling my sounds of ecstasy.

I come undone, shaking and out of breath, my heartbeat at its max. He slows his motions, cups my pelvis, and leans down to kiss my belly, gathering the last tremors of my orgasm.

I slowly come down from my high, drop the belt to the floor, and bring my hands to his head.

Ohmygod what is happening. Since I've gotten out of my own way and told him I wanted everything from him, he's given me the best kiss ever, and not one, but two orgasms in one day, and he hasn't even dropped once piece of his own clothing.

Yet.

He moves my panties back in place, pulls my bra, my tank top, and my pants up, then brings my wrists to his mouth and kisses them.

I wrap my arms around his neck while he helps me to stand on my wobbly legs.

His erection pulses against my stomach as he holds me tight against him. "God, I want you so badly," he says, smoothing my hair, his eyelids hooded.

I start to lower myself to him, but he won't let me.

"Not here," he says, his mouth grazing my temple. "Not now." His voice is raw with want. "Not like this."

Men might bring misery, but I'm discovering they can also bring pleasure beyond my wildest imagination.

These were the best orgasms of my life, and he only used his fingers. And his mouth.

My god, his mouth.

He lets go of me.

"Is the *tasting* over?" I ask.

He chuckles. "For now. I have to go pick up Skye." He presses his lips to my head and sends me off with a quick slap on my butt.

"Stairs okay now?" I ask him.

"Huh?"

"You said you had guys refinishing the staircase."

"Right." He checks his phone. "Yup, all good."

I feel like lingering in his arms, kissing his full lips one last time. Who knows when the next opportunity will be? But it's just sex, right, so I guess I shouldn't. I can't let my needy feelings get in the way with him. It would ruin everything.

But darn it, sex has never felt this good. In the past, at best, I was happy if it was not too messy. Sometimes, I'd feel some arousal from the friction, that I'd take care of in private, later, without the guy.

But this afternoon, as I walk up the stairs to my room, I feel relaxed and energized.

More than that.

I feel alive.

Alexandra two-point-oh.

And when I reach the top of the stairs and push the door to my bedroom open, as I'm reflecting that I didn't notice anything different on the staircase, I'm stunned.

Oh.

My.

God.

My bedroom.

Chapter Twenty-Two

Alexandra

My twin-size bed is gone. In its place stands a queen-size, four-poster pine bed with a fluffy, cream-colored comforter, a variety of throw pillows at the head and a light pink and slate plaid blanket at the foot of the bed, inviting me to snuggle. It's so cozy, I just want to jump on the bed, but first, I try to process the other changes.

The room is entirely transformed, and I'm glued to the entrance as I breathe in the smell of beeswax and firewood.

The bed is framed by two matching side tables on which simple brass lamps softly gleam. The large bench under the dormer window has been turned into a reading nook, all cushioned up and lit by a floor lamp. A large dresser occupies the space on the right of the window, topped with a mirror framed in matching waxed wood.

To the left of the door, there's a rocking chair with an off-white throw blanket and a lumbar pillow with a moose cutout. Next to it, the copper details of the mantel are polished to a shine. The fireplace is stocked with wood, and a wrought iron log holder is stacked to the brim.

Skye understated it. It's not just a princess bed. It's a princess room in a storybook village.

Standing at the entrance of the room, I'm still awestruck, and questions start to stumble in my mind as I kick my shoes off.

Why?

How?

How much?

Why (again)?

What does this mean? I wonder as I flick the light on, and a brass chandelier bathes the room in a warm glow. I tread barefoot in my new cozy retreat, my feet relishing the feel of the wool carpets that cover the wooden floor in the center of the room and on each side of the bed.

I run a finger along the crisp comforter and the soft flannel pillows. There's a white pillow in the center, with ruffles and lace. Lifting it to the light, I notice an elaborate capital *A* letter embroidered in its center. *A for Alexandra*. My heartbeat picks up.

I'm drawn to the window. My throw with the pink deer and gray bears is rolled up on one side of the newly upholstered bench, making it a truly cozy reading nook. Mohair pillows are on the other side. As I run my hand on them, caressing their softness, feeling their warmth and light weight, I take notice of all the new details.

The cushions and pillows here are in harmonies of soft pinks and beige, brightening and softening the room's wood paneling. The bookcases lining each side of the nook are no longer empty. They hold paperbacks—romances and mysteries, my favorite—alongside old editions of classics, giving the room a lived-in air and making me want to just curl up and never leave.

I open the carved cedar chest at the bottom of the bed and find my shoes neatly arranged in boxes.

The chest of drawers is soft and warm to the touch and smells faintly like roses. I pull open the drawers and find them lined with delicately perfumed paper. Unable to resist any longer, I run to the closet, retrieve my stuffed clothes, and start arranging my underwear, T-shirts and sweaters in the drawers.

I can't believe Christopher did all this for me. I'm overwhelmed with gratitude, and also embarrassed. Again, *how much did this cost him?*

"Hey." His voice startles me and pins me in place. I'm holding the lingerie I'm about to put away. His gaze drops briefly to it, then back to me. He has a mischievous smile. "You like?" he says.

"Oh, my god. I—I don't know what to say. Why?"

He shrugs. "Why not?"

I drop the lingerie in an open drawer and twine my arms around his waist, pressing my body against his, feeling his heartbeat pick up. "Thank you," I whisper. "But this is too much."

"Bunch of old stuff." He shrugs. "Autumn has been looking to get started as a decorator, so..."

So this is why Autumn didn't tell me. But more importantly—*A decorator? For me?*

"Couldn't let you stay much longer in this room the way it was." He pushes the door closed and takes my hand, leading me to the bed.

"So, I was thinking," he says in a low growl as he sits me on the edge of the bed, stands between my legs, and wraps my thighs around him, "maybe it's time to use this old house the way it should be." He rocks his hips toward me. "Look inside my pocket."

My middle throbs. The bulge in his pants is obvious enough. Why his pocket? I make for the belt buckle.

"Tut-tut-tut. Pocket, beautiful. Your mind is in the gutter." He smirks as he trails my chin with his finger. I slide my hand down his pants and tease his erection, my nails barely scraping. He growls. "Witch." Hissing, he adds, "Search my pocket. I think you'll like what you find."

With my legs spread around him, my middle yearns for his touch. I let myself drop on the bed, hands over my head, offered to him, and rock my hips up. His eyes are molten, and his nostrils flare, but he doesn't budge. "Babe. Skye is right downstairs."

I jolt upright. "Sorry."

He grabs my wrist, pulls me up, and shoves my hand down his pocket, where it meets a metal object. "Take it," he grunts.

I pull out a small, ancient key. "A chastity belt?" I smile.

"Now, there's an idea," he says, chuckling. "Take another guess."

I sigh. I have other games in mind.

"Come on." He moves to the side and, with two fingers, moves my chin slightly to the side, so my gaze is on—

"The hidden staircase?" I gasp.

He grunts and pulls me fully off the bed, his hand on the small of my back, leading me to the narrow door. "You decide," he says, "when you want to keep it locked or open it for me. Yeah?"

I'm too overwhelmed to answer. The door opens softly when I turn the key, revealing a wooden spiral staircase. I stroke its handrail, softened by use, and set a foot on the first carpeted step, then the next. Recessed lighting turns on as I progress down, the old steps creaking softly under my weight.

"My bedroom door is locked," Christopher says. "Skye sometimes comes in when she has a nightmare or whatever. I can't have you down there." I see the door to his room, now, and retreat back upstairs, unable to meet his eyes.

"I have to head back downstairs," he says. He trails his lips across mine, my arousal increasing as his stubble grates on me. "See you at dinner."

I kiss him back, his full lips leaving me wanting more.

After he's gone, I fight my sense of overwhelm by grabbing my phone and snapping photos. I love making other people's work look great, and for now I can put all my questions about Christopher and what he just did for me on the back burner.

I focus on making Autumn's magic look its best by editing the photos I take. Then I find the accounts she uses for her decorating endeavor, make note of the hashtags that bring her most engagement, and start posting, adding #emeraldcreekvt.

I get lost in the moment as the little hearts start popping up on my screen. I notice the posts I made of Christopher preparing for the baking competition are getting great engagement as well. I need to talk to him about setting up his own online presence.

Before I get down the rabbit hole of posting more about Christopher, I turn my attention back to my room. I fuss in it for a little while, putting my clothes away. Questions start popping up in my mind. When did he start planning this? Why? I could have added a few more comfort touches myself if I wanted to—I had actually planned on doing just that. I noticed pillows at the general store and a pretty vase at the antique shop that was reasonably priced. He didn't need to do that. Clearly he'd never done it for the other apprentices before me.

Why for me?

I'm afraid of the answer.

I'm afraid I'm misreading him.

He said it was nothing, a bunch of old stuff.

He said we were just having fun until I leave.

But it doesn't feel like that to me. It's more like he wants me to feel at home here.

Is that what it means to him, or is he just feeling pressure from the gossip about this supposedly being an attic?

I should call Sarah to hash it out with her, but I know I'll get overly positive, sunshine-and-butterflies, diamonds-in-the-sky answers.

I'm not this person Sarah thinks I am. I don't deserve what Christopher is giving me.

I need to talk to someone who understands that.

I fetch my phone and hit Barbie Doll on the screen. Barbara is a little woo-woo and flower power and stuff, but she's always given me solid advice.

So I call her.

Chapter Twenty-Three

Alexandra

"He did what?" Barbara asks. She is in her seventies, but she has a young voice. I picture her sitting in the lotus position in the zen room of her Village flat. Outside of Red Barn, she's a total hippie. Nothing normally surprises her.

"You heard me. He totally decorated my room. *Furnished* it. Hold on." I switch the call to video to show her around.

"Honey. Don't do the millennial thing with me. It's rude."

"What millennial thing?"

"The video."

"What's wrong with that?"

"I'm naked."

"Eww."

"Excuse me! I look great."

Please remove the visual from my brain.

She lowers her voice. "I'm not alone."

Kill me now. "I'llllll call back." I hang up.

The phone lights up. *Barbie Doll calling*. I pick up the phone with two fingers. Hesitate. Hit the green button and close my eyes.

"Don't you hang up on me," she says. "Now. I get it. He fixed up the room, yada yada yada. I heard the room was more like an attic, so it looks to me he did the right thing. Now, tell me something I don't know."

How did she know about the attic rumor? I let that slide for now.

"Barb. It has a *reading* nook. And *mohair* pillows. And a *cedar* chest. And and and... he hired a *decorator*!"

"It's not about the room."

"Exactly! Why would he do that?"

"You're not calling about the room. What else happened with Chris Wright?"

I plop on the super comfy, super soft bed and let out a deep sigh. "What didn't happen."

"Honey, you've been there a few weeks already. Thank *god* you're having sex." Her voice is all matter-of-fact. "I mean the guy is—" she lowers her voice, "he's *built* for sex."

Barbara having these thoughts about Christopher is confusing to me, and I don't need more of that now. "Barb! I did not have sex with him."

"Oh." She seems disappointed.

"We just kissed." *And fooled around. He gave me an orgasm. Or two.*

A perky, "oh," this time.

Gaaah. "Why am I even calling you?" I say, at the same time she says, "Why are you calling me?" After that, we stay silent for a while, her presence comforting me, even when we're both silent on the phone.

"Why are you freaking out, honey?" she finally asks.

"I'm scared," I admit.

"Of what?"

"Of losing myself. He's just so... so..."

"So what?"

"So *man* and so *gentle* and *strong* and *perfect* in every way. He's a great dad, been raising his daughter alone since she was born. And he works with his hands, and he's smart and so generous. Everybody loves him," I finish on a whisper.

"And my Lexie loves him above all," she says in a low voice.

My throat constricts, and I don't answer.

"And what's wrong with that?" she presses.

"Everything. I can't. I can't do it. I won't."

"And why is that?"

"You know why."

"Honey, I loved your grandmother, but she had some seriously twisted ideas about men and family and life in general. Happiness and success to her meant a very different thing than it would to you, or to a lot of people, for that matter. Tell me all that BS she fed you didn't stick, did it?"

"But it's true, Barb. It's *true*. We're not cut out for love. We're not meant for normal *families*."

She clears her throat, and I hear her whisper thank you off the phone, then there's the telltale sound of her taking a sip. I picture her in a kimono (she would have thrown something on before calling me back, I won't have it any other way), looking lovingly at a man leaving the room after handing her a cup of freshly brewed, organic, sustainably-grown-from-a-small-farmer-somewhere-in-India, evening tea. Having pondered my freaking-out outburst with a spirit now elevated to Gandhi-level wisdom, she says, "Let's talk about it once you've had sex with him."

Seriously. "You're incredible," I say, sighing and acting upset. Meanwhile, I'm overtaken by visions of Christopher lowering himself over my body, and the feel of his hands still burns my flesh.

"I know, you're welcome."

"I didn't mean that as a compliment. Not this time at least."

"I know that too. But you will, eventually."

There's nothing to say to that, so I don't respond *to that*, specifically. Instead, I say, "How's it going at Red Barn?" Which is not, in my mind, a total change of topic because everything that's happening here is so entirely tied to Red Barn, and everything moving forward will be as well, in ways that are incompatible.

"Alright. I'll come up and check him out in person," is her non-answer to my question.

"Wh-what?"

"You need reassurance, I get that. Plus, I'm curious to see the man who woke up my Lexie. I've heard good things."

"What—who?"

"Honey, I have my sources."

My cheeks are burning. What the hell is going on? "Barbara," I say, putting all my focus on steadying my voice and making it sound mature and responsible. "You will do no such thing. There's better use of your time than pursuing..." What's the word I'm looking for? Aaagh. "Trivial... hunches." There.

My phone seems to vibrate, she laughs so hard. "You're good! You're good." She laughs, again. "Practicing your board voice? Rita used to do that in her bathroom before going to see bankers, at the beginning."

"You knew Rita at the beginning? I thought she hired you as an assistant later on."

"We were roommates when she just got to Brooklyn. Your mom wasn't even two years old, yet." She takes a breath. "I practically raised her for a while."

The line goes silent for a moment.

It's too much for me to handle right now, so I go back to my previous question. "How's it going at Red Barn?"

"The jerks are getting ready to fire my ass, so I'm prepping for that. Once that's done, I'll have time to come up."

I gasp. "What? Can they do that? Are you lawyering up?"

"I don't need to lawyer up. You'll rehire me in a few months. No, I'm downloading all the data I need, a little at a time. To help us strategize what you need to do when you return."

"What data?"

The sound of fabric ruffling comes through the phone. "Let's talk about it later, okay?" she says, a smile in her voice.

Then there's the muted sound of *giggles*, clearly not directed at me. "Love you," she finally says to me before hanging up.

I'm trying to process the idea of Barbara getting fired from Red Barn. Barbara having sex with a man. And Barbara being so aloof about the state of my evolving relationship with Christopher.

Barbara thinks I love Christopher. But in Barbara's world, everyone loves everyone. If you don't love someone, it's because you haven't had a chance to know them yet.

In Barbara's world, you love people who are cool and haven't hurt you. In my mind, I'd always add "*yet*" at the end of that sentence when it applied to men, since they were bound to hurt me eventually, and I had family history to prove my point.

Christopher is cool and hasn't hurt me (yet), so in Barbara's world I love him.

I didn't have the heart to set her straight.

But when my phone rings again and this time it's Sarah, the conversation is going to go very differently.

"Lexie! I misssss you. Can you talk, right now? Is this a good time? Is it not too late? At what time to bakers go to bed, again?"

I laugh at her non-stop questioning. I miss her too.

Sing-songing the words, she ends with, "How's Emerald Creek? And the apprenticeship?"

"The apprenticeship part—I'm not gonna lie; it's harder than I thought. It's just not for me, you know?"

"I hear you." She sighs. "You have regrets?"

"No. I have to do this."

"Not really, you don't," she grunts. Then changes the topic. "How about the non-apprenticeship part? You doing anything fun?"

I look around the room, wondering when and how to tell her about the bedroom makeover. I close the door to the hidden staircase and store the key away.

"Yeah, I started working on some of the businesses' social media." I mention Grace and her spa and other businesses I'm beginning to help.

Sarah laughs. "I'm talking about real fun."

"Oh, yeah. Wellll. Something crazy happened today. Actually, lots of crazy things." And *that's* when I tell her most of what's happened between Christopher and me since the middle of the night. My cheeks are burning just giving her the gist of it, so I leave out most of the graphic details.

When I'm done, she says, "Jesus Fucking Christ, that is hot. Like really, *really* hot. Man. When are you gonna *do it*?"

"I don't know! It's not like this was planned or anything."

"Hmm. But wasn't it? Deep down?"

I ignore her mind games. "He has a kid. We can't just jump on each other once the bakery is closed. We'll have to wait for Skye to be at a sleepover." *Well, looks like I've already given this some thought.*

"Where d'you think you'll do it? Your bedroom? His bedroom?"

"Who cares?" It's always been that way. Sarah needs a plan while I need to go with the flow so I don't counteract what's bound to happen and create more mess in the process.

"I do! It's important. His bedroom would carry meaning, you know? Like he wants you in *his* bed. Now, your bedroom is cute, and then you'd have his smell on your pillow. That's a plus. But wait. Isn't your bed twin-size? I wonder if that's a pro or a con."

"It's not anymore." I try to hide the excitement in my voice.

"What do you mean? Did you get a new bed? When did this happen? God I hate that you're so far." The last part of her words are mumbled, and then my phone beeps. Sarah is asking to switch to video. "Spill it," she says, her face filling the whole screen.

I turn the video on my phone. "Here's what I walked into earlier today." I have to lower the sound on my phone when she shrieks, "Ohmygod" non-stop for the first fifteen seconds of the tour I give her.

Once I zoom in on the details—the books on the shelves, the pottery vase on the dresser, the candles on the mantel, the watercolor of a barn in the snow over my bed—she gets sort of quiet, like she might be hyperventilating. She's squinting and mumbling.

"Oh, my god, Lexie. That's. So. Hot."

"What do you mean? What's hot?" It's nice, it's over the top caring. But hot? Okay, maybe a little.

Maybe more than a little.

"He's got feelings for you. I can tell. And you have feelings for him."

I huff. "Sarah, we don't have feelings for each other. We're just fooling around."

"Why can't you have feelings? Don't be so cynical."

"It's just—You know how it is. I'll get attached, and then, I'll have to leave."

"You don't *have* to leave Vermont. You'll be a gazillionaire. You can run Red Barn from anywhere. And, if you fail that exam you seem to think is freaking hard, you'll marry him, he'll put a bun in your oven, and you'll live happily ever after selling his delicious croissants instead of Red Barn's industrial shit."

I chuckle at her preposterous ideas. "You're such an idealist."

"Realist! I'm a realist, Lexie. And you're a closet romantic. This is what your life should be! Aww, I'm gonna miss you," she says, pretending to whine. "Will you have a guest room for me? Oh, wait! That bedroom will be the guest room."

"That's not the plan for me."

"Whose plan? Your grandmother's?"

"Yes. And I know what you're going to say. That she's gone, and I'm free to live my life, now. But it's not that easy, you know? It's my family legacy, and maybe she wanted me to go back to the roots of baking and bring it back to the family business. That was her way of getting me on board, of continuing the mission."

"First off, it was *her* mission. Not yours—"

"You know how family's important to me. And Red Barn is the only thing that connects me to my family now."

"Lexie. This is your life to live, not anyone else's. Just go with the flow, seize the opportunities."

I wish I could, but there are layers of my life that even Sarah can't understand. "I am. The opportunity is to have fun while I'm here, possibly amazing sex, and that's it. I'm seizing it."

"All I'm saying is, don't deny your feelings."

I shut my eyes. "I can't allow myself to have feelings. Christopher doesn't want a relationship. He's got his daughter, and he doesn't want her to know about us. He wants to protect her." Easier to blame it on him than to argue again with Sarah about why I won't allow myself a normal life.

I carry a burden of guilt that no therapist has been able to shake off, and I deal with it by no longer wanting things I can't have.

Like a real family.

"Hmm," she says. "Okay, I get it. He just wants to fuck you in a decent place. Good for him for having taste."

"Oh, wow. Classy, Sarah."

"You don't want to hear about feelings, girl. Deal with it." She has a point, even if I don't like it that much. "Oh and, let me know how your first full-on sex goes. And since there are no feelings, I'll want all the juicy details. I'm in a sexual desert, right now, so I'm going to live my sex life by proxy."

Chapter Twenty-Four

Christopher

I can't do this.

I know I said it'd be great to have some kind of relationship for the time Alexandra is here, but I'm freaking out.

Last time I opened up, laid it all out, set to buy a ring at the same time as a crib, the woman walked out on me.

It shattered me, and I didn't even care about her as a person. I only cared because she was carrying my child. I was doing the right thing. The *fucking right thing* to do.

The day after I kissed Alexandra, I could not look her in the eye, knowing how she'd felt in my arms. How I wanted to help her out with whatever shit was going down with her boss. Just like I'd wanted to help Skye's mother.

She's been the only thing on my mind. I burned the inn's special order of muffins and forgot Justin's dinner rolls because... well, because.

Alexandra.

She's been the only thing on my mind, and the only thing not on my body, and why the hell do you think that is?

Because she's too much. She affects me like no other woman ever has. Like I didn't even know was possible.

My thinking is, if one kiss and a make out session made me this way, what will a night with her do to me?

I won't be able to let her go.

Now, I may have the instincts of a caveman. I may want to tie her to her bedposts, brand her with my cock, fuck her so good and so hard and so often she'll forget there are other males in the human species.

But I'm civilized. I have a twenty-first-century veneer that will prevent me from doing anything—*anything*—when she leaves. She's a free, independent woman, and her choices are hers.

This, her presence here, in my bakery, in my life, has a shelf life. There's no child to link us together. She has a job to go back to.

She's definitely leaving.

Me? There's just so much I can take. And I know I can't take this any further.

So for three nights, although I know she leaves her door open, I don't go up to her room.

But she comes to the kitchen. Every. Single. Morning.

I should say night, because it's still dark out.

She shows up around four every morning, makes me coffee, brings me a glass of water.

She doesn't say a thing. She pulls out her phone and takes pictures and videos and shit.

I try to ignore her because I'm supposed to be focusing on preparing for the competition.

And then I notice, something funny happens.

I'm more creative when she's around.

My senses are heightened. I'm attuned to her sight, her smell, the memory of her taste, and that inspires me. It gives me a kick in the balls, an incentive to perform even better. And she's watching every move I make.

"Tell me if I'm bothering you," she says the first morning after our kiss, after she's been there an hour and we haven't talked.

I don't answer, and she makes to leave.

"Stay right here."

She freezes.

"Please."

"You sure?"

"I said please."

"Alright then," she sighs and sits on a prep table.

I pop my head up. I'm being such a dick. Why is she even here? Why does she put up with my shit? "I'm sorry," I say. "It like it better when you're here," I finally admit to her. "It helps me focus."

Her cheeks get a deep pink, and my god, just for that, I'm going to learn to apologize more often to her. "Okay then," she whispers, a small smile on her face.

And it's true. I'm in the zone, and she's right there in it with me. She just doesn't know it.

I still don't go to her room that night. Because like I said, there's just so much I can take.

Three straight nights of not going up there, imagining what I could be doing to her, and having the strength not to, just to protect myself. Hearing her come and go, and not joining her.

Not taking advantage of that door that I know she leaves open for me.

That takes a lot of courage.

Enough that I don't have any left to face her in the morning, answer her silent questions, make it right.

There's just so much I can do.

I'm starting on my fourth night of this ordeal, and I don't hear her ordinary noises. The water rushing down the pipes. Her footsteps. The bed creaking.

I turn my lights off, and there's no streak of light coming from her room through the disjointed floor.

I hop into the secret staircase and find her door locked.

Using the main staircase, I go upstairs. Her room is dark. And empty.

It's past ten at night on a Friday. Tomorrow is a workday for her.

I grab my phone.

Chapter Twenty-Five

Alexandra

Three nights in a row, I prepped myself for him. I showered. I shaved my legs. I slathered lotion on my skin. I did my hair in lush waves. I applied nude makeup. I slipped on my sexiest lingerie.

I studied poses on the reading nook. On top of the bed. On the freaking rocking chair.

Three nights in a row, he didn't come. After the kiss we exchanged and the orgasms he gave me. After the room he gave me and the key to his stupid secret staircase.

Angry at myself for being a docile puppet, I repeat the mantra—*Men only bring misery*—and will myself to not let it be true.

So, on Friday, I take Grace up on her offer to go out. I wear my sexiest lingerie again—the bodice that Cassandra gave me, with the garters and silk stockings that Sarah made me buy when I was trying to spice things up in the bedroom with my last boyfriend. It didn't work at the time, but Sarah knows her shit.

The boyfriend was the problem.

Not me.

Right?

Or *is it* me?

Because why has Christopher been ignoring me for the last three days and nights?

Maybe *it is* me.

I fasten Cassandra's bodice and think back to what she said when she gave it to me. Something about being careful who I wore it with? Well, if it brings me luck, I'll owe her.

Then I shimmy into the short red dress that hugs my shapes just right.

Now if *that* doesn't get me lucky, I don't know what will.

Don't judge me. Christopher ignited a fire in me that needs to be taken care of, and if he won't be my fireman, someone else might. What else is a girl to do? Just because relationships aren't for me doesn't mean I don't have needs.

I've recently discovered sex is totally for me.

And I want more than the taste Christopher gave me.

The Growler, an actual barn in the hills turned club slash event space slash game room, is the locals' favorite nighttime hangout. Tonight, it's packed with bikers showing off their tats on their bare arms, outdoorsy types and farm hands in flannel shirts, and office types with their button-down sleeves rolled-up. The troublemakers and the trouble seekers, both looking for relief after a week of whatever it is they do. There's a small dance floor off the main bar that's manned by a deejay, and a live band somewhere in the back.

The place is huge.

The women travel in packs, showing lots of glowing skin. I fit right in with the piece of red fabric barely covering my ass.

Everywhere, there's the urge to either douse or arouse the sexual tension with too much alcohol.

It's the kind of night I need. A night to make a mistake I won't regret.

Drink in hand, I sway with Grace and her girlfriends on the small dance floor, looking for a suitable mate but seeing nothing. Surely, someone will make his way to me and replace the face that's haunting me—dark eyes, curly hair, shadow of a smile—with something equally appealing.

No one does, yet.

Wandering hands make their way under my skirt, and I whisk them away when they don't have the right feel. The one feel I'm looking for.

A strong arm grabs my waist from behind, but I don't like the way his veins don't bulge. I snake away.

After a couple of hours of this hide and seek, the girls and I travel to the bathroom.

I check my phone for no particular reason and see a text message from Christopher from an hour ago.

We go to the back of the barn, where a local group is performing live. I lift my arms and jump in the air with the crowd. A wet kiss smacks my neck; a hand grabs my boob. I shake off the intruder and catch Grace's eye. She's our driver. She points her chin to the door. I'm beat and follow her out, welcoming the sobering air. She greets me and the other girls with bottles of water as we pile into her Jeep.

I take out my phone and look at the last messages from Christopher.

What the heck. I've got nothing to lose.

1:17 am

Me: What will I get in return?

I watch as the bubbles wave up and down on the screen on his side, stop and start again. Does he never sleep?

The bubbles stop, and minutes later, Grace drops me off.

Shoes in hand, I tiptoe up to my bedroom. It's chilly in there, so I keep my dress on to clean up.

There's a full-length mirror in the bathroom now, and after brushing my teeth, I take time brushing my hair and looking at myself.

I lift my dress, revealing the bodice and matching thong.

I would fuck myself in that thing.

What a waste. I let the dress slide back around me.

I skip removing my makeup, dab some cream on my lips, and step into my bedroom.

And freeze.

Against a bedpost, wearing nothing but sweatpants, his arms crossed over his muscular, naked chest, one bare foot hitched over the other, Christopher stands, the image of fury and desire.

"This what you wear to go to that place?" he growls, his hungry eyes raking my body.

I indulge for a beat in being under his scrutiny. Why doesn't he kiss me, touch me, hold me? I can tell that's what he wants. But he only looks at me, and from that alone, my breasts swell, my nipples tingle.

"What's wrong with that?" I finally say, a little out of breath. "This dress is *sexy*."

He closes his eyes and growls again. "Fuck, Alexandra. Do you know what kind of guys go to that place?"

Really? That's the reaction I get? "I was *just* there. I saw," I clip.

His nostrils actually flare but his gaze finally meets mine. "And?"

"And no serial killers. No rapists. I'm back in one piece, thank you very much. And there's nothing wrong with me, and nothing wrong with my dress either. Everything in perfect working order." Tears of frustration start gathering behind my eyes, and I take a deep breath that comes out shaky, but helps me recenter. "Now if you don't mind, I'd like to go to bed, please?"

He pushes himself from the bedpost and takes three long strides that bring him an arms' length from me. "What the fuck is that supposed to mean."

"Bed. Sleep."

"*Everything in perfect working order*. What the fuck is that supposed to mean." He takes another step toward me that places him entirely in my space, his warmth and scent wrapping around me.

God he's beautiful. And the way he looks at me? He drinks me in, caresses me with just his gaze. It's unfair what he does to me.

But he's *so* frustrating. "After the way you kissed me. After everything you gave me. The room. The key to the friggin' hidden staircase. After all that and what I thought it meant, you ignored me. You already gave up on me!"

I blink back tears of frustration. Why am I even upset?

It's always like that.

"You're upset," he says.

"Am not. Just needed to figure out if there was anything wrong with me."

His gaze deepens travels around my face, down my neck, leaving a burning trail. "You got frustrated with me because you felt I was ignoring you, so you went to that place dressed like that, and what did you find out."

"There's nothing wrong with me."

He closes his eyes. "Of course not. Everything is right about you. Everything," he growls. He lifts a hand to tuck my hair behind my ear.

I resist the urge to lean into his caress.

And I further pretend to ignore his sweetness and plant my fists on my hips. "Now, if you please, I'd like to get undressed."

A slow grin spreads across his face. "Sure, don't mind me." He steps back to the reading bench, plops on it, his arms splayed on the windowsill, his thighs spread-eagle, and my traitorous eyes rake his bulging pecs and tight abs and stop right where his happy trail disappears under his sweatpants.

"You're unbelievable," I whisper, and I mean it in both ways, but I hope my tone says I mean it in the not-good way.

He stands back up, closes the distance between us, and takes my wrist. The pad of his thumb strokes the inside of my forearm. "Of course there's nothing wrong with you. You're perfect. You think it's fun, lying on my bed, resisting you?"

Because of the way he's holding my arm, my hand falls naturally to his hip. I inch it up to where his skin is naked. My voice is small when I ask, "Why are you resisting me?"

He moves his hand up my arm, to my shoulder, to my neck. Ends up cupping the side of my neck and gently stroking my throat with the pad of his thumb. Desire shoots from where his hand rests down to my center.

"Because... the way your body feels so right under my hands... the way your lips taste so good," he says and dips his forehead to mine. "Fuck, Alexandra... the way you kiss without holding back." His hand is up to the back of my head, holding it against his.

My hand rakes up his back. "I don't kiss without holding back," I whisper.

His face goes back up. "You do," he says against my temple.

I close my eyes and deeply inhale his manly scent, cedar and clean laundry and something else. "Maybe I kissed *you* without holding back. Maybe I shouldn't have."

His body tenses. "See, that's what I mean. Was hoping to get you out of my system. Not happening. Dangerous."

That hurts a little, although it shouldn't. My heart stutters.

It's a good thing, him wanting to get me out of his system. It's what I want as well. So I tip my head up and volunteer, "You have a few months to get me out of your system."

He bends, his face to mine again. His stubble grazes my nose, then my chin. "What if I don't. What if you get so totally under my skin, I never want to let you go," he says, his lips brushing against mine.

That is *so* not going to happen. I'm not the kind of girl guys don't want to let go. I'm the opposite. He doesn't know it, but it's in my genes. And if I want to, cynically, get that side fun I've been entertaining, I need to enlighten him. Reassure him. We can do this without any consequences for him.

"Not a chance," I whisper. "Anytime I got under a guy's skin, it wasn't the good kind of getting-under-his-skin. You're safe with me. You're not gonna get attach—"

His mouth drinks my last word as he leans into me fully and kisses me hard.

So hard.

So good.

See? You tell a guy there's no chance of getting attached, they give their best.

His hand at my nape is fisting my hair, his other arm is at my waist, forearm the length of my back, plastering me to his length while his tongue captures me. Then his teeth tease my lower lip, and the arm that was at my waist trails down, grabs my dress, bunches it up, and his fingers reach the naked strip of skin above my garter.

I moan.

"I see," he whispers in my ear. His teeth lightly worry my earlobe, then his tongue does some exploring behind my ear, and the shivers it sends down my spine curl and heat up between my legs.

I press my hips to the tops of his thighs, my stomach to his erection beating through his sweatpants.

And I moan again.

"So you're saying..." he stops talking to lick his way down my neck to the other ear. "You're saying," he whisper-repeats once on the other side, "odds are, you're going to get under my skin, but the kind where I'll be relieved to see you leave?" He dips down to worry my nipple through the dress's fabric. I lose the connection with his cock but gain the pleasure of his mouth on my breast. *God.*

"Un-hunh," I answer, then, "Oh *god,*" as his mouth works my nipple harder.

His strong neck is bent over me, and I trail my fingers through his thick hair, my other hand raking his naked, muscular back.

"Guess we'll find out," he says as his hand deftly unzips my dress and he comes back up to face me.

The way he handles me, strong and gentle at the same time, exploring what I like, making me come alive under his hands, placing me before him, I know one thing.

He's under my skin, and he's here to stay.

I'll deal with the consequences later. Right now, I can let go.

The dress drops to my feet. He grabs my ass and hoists me to his hips, twirling me around. "Fuck, baby, you're beautiful." He kisses me deep again, walking us to the reading nook. He places me on the bench under the window, my back to him.

"Get on your knees," he says, "and hold on tight."

"C-can't people see us?"

"Kneel."

I do as he says. My hands grab the windowsill and my knees spread apart on the pillows. My back arches, my ass begging for Christopher. I turn my head, and for a beat, our eyes lock. In the half-light of the streetlamps, I see him reach inside his pocket and throw a condom on the windowsill.

Then, he kicks his sweatpants off, freeing his thick, bobbing cock. My mouth waters and gapes at the beautiful sight, and my center clenches. I drink him in.

This.

This is a man.

His jaw tenses, and his breathing is heavy, but his hands are warm and comforting as he traces my back and cups my hips. I tilt my face back to the window and look at his reflection as he positions himself behind me. He caresses my ass with one hand, a breast with the other, then makes his way along my bodice, kneading his thumbs at the sides of my waist then fluttering his fingers along the length of my torso.

Slowly, he plucks one single ribbon open from the dozens that line the back of the bodice. He could have chosen the buttons in the front, where I could see him. There's also a faster way.

"There's a zipper," I whisper, pushing my ass against him, desperate to get him skin to skin.

"Lovemaking is like breadmaking, Alexandra. If you rush the preparation, if you skip some steps, you won't have the right result." He tightens a ribbon sharply. "Understood?"

"Understood." I squirm.

"I'm going to knead every inch of your body until you've lost the capacity to talk."

His heat warms my back as he slowly unties my bodice. He sets one foot on the bench so his cock grazes my shoulder while his hands are occupied behind me. I tilt my head, licking my lips at the sight of the precum on his tip.

For the first time in my life, I'm getting soaked at the idea of giving head.

"If your pretty little mouth gets any closer, I am going to lose it." He groans. "Look outside," he orders.

I swing my head back, and my hair gets caught on his erection. I linger there.

"Witch," he says, removing his foot from the bench.

I don't look outside. I look at our reflection in the window. His hungry stare, his careful movements. The wild desire emanating from his body, constrained. I'm giving myself this. The way he wants me is intoxicating.

The bodice is halfway undone. He rolls it partly down my waist and wraps himself behind me, rolling my nipple in one hand. With the other hand, he slowly makes his way between my legs, grazing my clit through my panties, stroking my thighs. Holding me tightly in his embrace, he presses his chin on top of my head. "Fucking beautiful." He pushes himself against me, his cock firmly against my lower back, his rhythm matching mine as I rock myself against him. With soft strokes, he massages my nape, my shoulders, runs down my stomach.

Eyes locked on my reflection in the window, he whispers, "Gonna take my time savoring you, beautiful."

I whimper in response.

He drops to his knees and kisses my ankles, licks his way slowly up my calves, his hands fluttering up my thighs. After several minutes of this infuriating teasing, I feel my wetness drip down my leg.

"Gonna give *you* the time you deserve."

I circle my hips to try and ease the need.

"Soaked for me?" he growls.

"Only for you," I whisper.

He tears open a condom wrapper. "That sounds right, beautiful."

"Only for you," I repeat.

This gets me another growl. And makes me even wetter.

He sheathes himself, and I ready myself for him, dropping my head between my arms, tilting my ass up to him. God I want him so bad.

He's flush behind me, his legs inside mine, his cock banging against me.

"Take me," I plead.

"I'll take you when it's time," he answers, his voice commanding.

He grabs my breast with a full, strong hand, then rolls my perky nipple between his fingers, sending spikes of want through my pussy. "I-I think I'm gonna come," I breathe.

He slaps my ass lightly, making me shriek in surprise. "Only when I tell you to, Alexandra." He grabs a fistful of my hair and gently pulls my face to his, raking his stubble against my cheek.

It's not painful. It's just right.

So right.

"B-But you're making me so wet and so... so—"

"So what? Say what I'm making you."

I can hardly think straight. "I— I don't... have... the words," I stutter. "So needy."

He growls in response but continues to worry my nipple with his fingers. He kisses and sucks my neck, adding to the arousal. My legs are weakening, a tremble taking hold of them while a hot wave builds inside me.

"I think you're ready for me, now," he whispers in my ear.

"I—I... been ready... forever."

He moves his powerful hands to my hips and finally thrusts himself inside me. His cock fills me so much I jerk up and lose my breath. He pulls almost all the way out then shoves back in, finding my tender spot and rubbing it continuously. I reel back in sheer pleasure, shrieking faintly, my hands holding the windowsill for balance, his pounding finally building up to the release I've been wanting for days.

"Try to keep it down, beautiful," he says into my neck. "Shoulda known you'd be loud," he mutters, then drops a kiss on my shoulder.

His manly scent mixed with the smell of sex and fresh sweat envelops me, and I breathe it in. My pleasure is so deep it's hard to keep my eyes open, but I catch glimpses of us in the window as he takes possession of me—his head hanging down, his pecs and biceps rolling as he pulls me onto him, my breasts bouncing back and forth with each of his pumps.

The sight of us is so hot.

"Christopher," I pant.

"Alexandra. Come for me. Now."

I keen, my knees tremble, and my arms grow weak as I let out a wail that doesn't begin to match the undoing that tears my insides deliciously apart.

He places a hand over my mouth. "Fuck, baby, love the way you scream for me." He's still pumping in and out of me, harder and stronger and faster, one hand wrapped around my waist as the first tremors of my orgasm render me unable to hold myself up, while his other hand muffles my wailing. I arch against his front as my orgasm rolls out, seizing me body and soul. His thrusts increase until he stiffens, his arms clamp around my body, and he growls against my ear as our eyes lock again through the reflection in the window.

We stay like that several moments without breath, heartbeats wild, hair matted, my limbs weak, his strength alone carrying us both.

Then he lifts me into his arms and sets me on the bed. He takes care of the condom and lies on his back, pulling me onto his chest.

His heart is still beating fast, and I love the way his hand plays in my hair.

I love it and it scares me.

Chapter Twenty-Six

Christopher

For three days, I resisted having sex with her.

When I couldn't take it anymore, I told myself this would be a fuck session of the basest kind. I was going to blow my load and get out.

With all the other women, I'd begin to lose interest after the first time, anyway. The novelty wore out.

It'd be the same with her. Especially if I kept it raw. Sexual.

That's the promise I made myself when I broke my personal commitment and went to her room.

That I wouldn't do anything tender or sensual.

I wouldn't give.

I'd only take.

So when I saw her in that dress, I was ready to take. But what I saw in her eyes the minute she started talking?

So vulnerable.

So tender.

So fragile.

I forgot her body for a hot second.

I wanted to take her, all of her, and not in a sexual way.

Then she said something about leaving. About me having a few months to get her out of my system. And I got it. She's too good for me. She's not gonna stay. So what? I can still have her, sexually, I thought, as long as I protect myself.

So I came up with a plan, fast, while we were still standing, but she was already panting, her hand exploring me, her body already against mine.

The plan I devised while we toyed around and bickered and figured our shit out, was: Avoid looking her directly in the eye while I fucked her. Avoid having her wrap herself around me in any way that could be tender. Therefore, use doggy style. Blow my load like a caveman. Leave.

Fucking her in front of the window—the whole town was asleep, there's no chance in hell I would let anyone see her magnificent tits—was in line with the plan.

What was *not* in line with the plan, was the way she reacted to every one of my moves. The way she liked everything I did to her. Genuinely *liked* it.

The way she said my name.

The way she trusted me.

The way she felt fucking *made for me*.

The way our eyes locked in the window.

Even with her back to me, I felt it. The connection between us.

It was unlike anything I'd ever experienced.

She deserved more than just a quick fuck. I gave her that, and she gave back. Made me feel so powerful and lost at the same time.

And now, I want more.

I pull her into me, and she fits right into the crook of my arm, on my chest, soft and supple, one hand on my neck, the other on my opposite arm, trailing little circles.

She hitches one leg up on my middle and lets out a contented sigh when she feels my cock hardening.

Then her hand trails down, and she strokes me and makes some little purring sounds and writhes her body against mine.

I was going to take care of that sexy underwear she's wearing, but instead, I flip her off of me and onto her back and grab another condom.

I lay on top of her, on my forearms so she can breathe, dig my face in her neck so I don't drown in those big brown eyes, and in one thrust, I'm right where I belong.

Inside her.

I'm not gentle. I move the way I like it. I take. Rough. Hard. Unforgiving.

Hoping she'll ask me to stop, so I get back to my senses.

"Ahhh, that's so good," she whispers in my ear. "Yes. Harder."

Fuuuuck.

She wraps her legs around my hips and pulls me deeper into her, that lace thing she's wearing scratching my skin, her breasts unbelievably soft above it.

She buckles under me and digs her nails in my back. "Oh my god. Ah. Aaaaah. Aaaaaah."

Her pussy clenches around my cock, sucking me in, her walls contracting, pumping me. She milks me into a toe-curling orgasm that lasts forever, my heartbeat at its max, my arms shaking.

I just want to stay inside her. Burrow my face deeper in her neck and forget myself in her.

Instead, I pull out, take care of the condom, and fall next to her on the bed to catch my breath.

Before I can let my guard down again and pull her into me like I'm dying to, she slips out of the bed and shimmies to the bathroom.

She looks like a fucking porn star with her naked ass, garter and silk stockings, her bodice half off. I pull the sheets up to my waist and grab another condom.

When she comes back, after what feels like forever, her hair is fluffed just so, and her lips are pouty.

"Come here, beautiful."

She gets on all fours and crawls to me on the bed, her hair falling to one side.

"Turn around."

She sits, her back to me, and I slowly untie the ribbon holding that thing together.

I'm dying to rip it off her.

But I don't.

I want to give her time to want me again.

Once the top is off her, I unbuckle her garters, move her around so she's facing me, and roll her stockings to the sound of her shallow breathing.

I give her breasts some attention.

Her nipples are hard, her eyes semi-closed.

She's way sexier completely naked.

And that scares the shit out of me.

She sets herself up on her knees, closer to me. She doesn't talk, just strokes my chest, her breasts swaying slightly with her movement.

My hand drifts to her ass. As if on cue, she lifts her thighs off her knees, giving me access to her middle.

She's soaking, my exploration making her pant with want.

Her eyes fall to the tent my dick makes in the sheets, and widen. She bites her bottom lip and pulls the sheets off, then makes an O with her mouth.

She lowers her full lips to my dick and kisses the tip. My hand goes to her head and I gasp as she licks my shaft. She locks eyes with me and takes my cock in her mouth, twirling her tongue against me, sucking on me, her hands on the base of my shaft. "You're very big," she apologizes as she comes up for air. "I'm not used to it."

I nearly come at those words spilling out of her sweet mouth. Hissing, I pull her off me.

"What's wrong?" she asks. "Am I not doing it right?"

"Beautiful, you're doing it way too right. I just want to see your breasts," I explain, cupping her. "Ride me so I can enjoy them."

I also want to see her face up close this time when she comes for me.

I slip the condom on before she straddles me, then my hands naturally land on her thighs.

She's so soft.

Way softer than those silk stockings.

She's so soaked I slip right into her tight pussy when she lowers herself onto me, making her cry out in pleasure. She bites her lip, trying to be quiet.

Moving her luscious hair to the side, I cup her magnificent breasts as she descends on me. I pinch her nipples, and her pussy clenches right back.

"Oh my god, Christopher. More."

Reaching down, I take one nipple in my mouth and nibble on it while my fingers tease the other one. She pumps up and down on my cock, the slick noise of our colliding sexes mingling with our labored breaths.

I suckle her nipple and feel the telltale sign of her trembling, and the dirty talk she gives me in a pleading voice that I've come to recognize as her pre-orgasm announcement. "Christopher. Fuck me harder. Deeper."

I don't point out to her that she's in control of the fucking. I know what she wants. So I let go of her breasts and clasp my hands on her hips.

I take control, pumping her body on mine. I do as she says—I fuck her harder, deeper, and the more I do, the more she sucks me in, our bodies becoming one.

I lock my eyes to hers.

As she comes undone, I register the spectacle of Alexandra flailing around me, the sheer beauty of her features as she's filled by me, her eyes lost in mine, our souls becoming one.

When she finally collapses on my chest, I pull out softly from her and tuck her against me.

It's not long before she's fast asleep, her breathing slow and peaceful, tiny little snores making my dick twitch again.

What was it she said, earlier? *"Anytime I got under a guy's skin, it wasn't the good kind of getting-under-his-skin. You're safe with me. You're not gonna get attached."*

I hate that she feels this way about herself, and in that moment, I wish I could give her everything she needs and deserves.

I stare at the ceiling, gently stroking her hair, like the fool I am. I don't want to think about the guys she dated before me.

I tuck her closer to me.

I don't really want to think, either, about how different this was from anything I've ever experienced. How could I ever want anyone else?

I'll never get enough of her.

She feels fucking *made for me*, even though I'm trying to stay on the surface. Unconnected.

As I lean over to brush my lips to her temple before heading back to my bedroom, I wish I could just lock her up here. Wall the main staircase in. Keep her like this chick from Skye's storybook, locked in my tower.

I'm already attached.

Chapter Twenty-Seven

Alexandra

Once we get started on work later that day, Christopher is quiet. He focuses on Skye, as if he feels guilty and is trying to compensate. She got a small part in the spring show, and he's helping her memorize her lines.

I love seeing his interaction with her. He's funny but strict, forgiving yet demanding. I didn't grow up with a father, and seeing them interact could be bittersweet to me, but it's not.

It's uplifting, and I can't get enough of it.

But I understand how important it is that this unique relationship be protected, and I would hate to cast a shadow on it. Skye is a perceptive child, so I keep my distance from Christopher when she's home.

They have their family dynamic, and I need to stay out of it, even if they're constantly including me like I'm family. I can't let myself fantasize about a life like that.

Later that week, I decide to send Barbara a selfie of me in my baker garb. She'll get a chuckle out of it. I send it from my phone to her work email, so it's easier for her to print. She'll like having it pinned to the corkboard she keeps next to her desk with all her memos and reminders.

I upload the photo, add a quick note, and hit send.

Then I put the kettle on for tea. Christopher went to pick up Skye at school, so the place is quiet for now. I pour my tea and enjoy the moment. The warmth of the kitchen. The clock ticking the seconds away. Snow lazily falling outside. My manual open in front of me. I'm memorizing processes, but then my thoughts drift to Barbara and I check my phone.

The email came back. Invalid email address.

I used the email I always use for her. Maybe they have a firewall now that prevents external emails? That wouldn't be very helpful. Just in case, I log into my work email.

Access denied.

Ugh.

It must be some technical issue, so I text Carlos who works in IT at Red Barn's Headquarters.

I take a sip of my piping hot tea while I wait for his answer.

Carlos IT

> Sorry, Alex. Me and a bunch of others were laid off this week. How's Vermont?

> Whaaat? Why laid off?

> They don't need a reason. At will employment. Shit got real after you left. Gotta go, interview for new job now :) wish me luck

I send him a hug emoji and a four-leafed clover emoji right as Skye barges in from school, pecks my cheek and washes her hands, momentarily distracting me from the stunning news.

Then a low funds alert from my bank pops on my screen. I log in, and sure enough, I haven't received my paycheck. Which makes sense, in a way.

I email HR anyway, from my private address, and this email doesn't bounce back.

Hands clean and dried, Skye goes straight to the cupboard. She pulls out an almost empty jar of maple butter, the one with her name on the lid, and unscrews it. She goes to duck her finger in the pot, but glances at me and grabs a spoon. Settled on her favorite chair, she loads the spoon and licks it like a lollipop, then loses patience and closes her lips around the spoon, wiping it clean. Ducks the spoon, again. Repeats the process.

I'm queasy just looking at her eat so much sugar. Should I say something?

Nope, that wouldn't be right. Would it?

There's already an email from the HR Department at Red Barn, but no answer from Barbara yet. "How was school?" I ask Skye as I start reading.

"Alright," she says, shrugging.

"That good, huh?" My eyes are stuck on the email. "Where's your daddy?"

"Doin' stuff upstairs. What are you reading?" she mumbles, her mouth full.

"Not sure yet," I mutter as I'm jerked from the warmth of Christopher's bakery in Emerald Creek to the coldness of corporate life at Red Barn. Just as cold as I remember my grandmother, the email reads:

When you accepted the terms of the offer made by your grandmother, Ms. Rita Douglas, in her will, and subsequently took on the apprenticeship she organized as a condition of your ownership of her shares and appointment to the board, you implicitly lost your status as a Red Barn Baking employee.

We look forward to welcoming you back at RBB as a fully vested leader of our great company, should you succeed in your current endeavor.

Yup. Makes sense.

I log back into my bank account app.

Christopher pays me a decent wage for the apprenticeship, but it's nothing close to what I used to make. Of course, I won't get paid for a job I'm no longer doing.

I have some savings to see me through the next couple of months, plus the small lump sum Rita left me in her will. It won't be enough to cover my Brooklyn rent until I come back, though, so I'll have to pick up some side work while I'm here, and I'll talk to Sarah about subletting my room for a little time, if I can find someone.

Both The General Store and Millie at Easy Monday have already approached me about managing their social media and marketing, and others might be interested. Even if I'll charge them a very reasonable fee, that might be enough to make up for the gap in income until I return to Brooklyn.

I move some money from my savings account to my checking account from the app on my phone and settle my attention on Skye.

Her jar of maple butter is now almost empty. She goes to the cupboard again and grabs a second jar, this one with *Daddy* written across the lid. She swiftly swaps both lids and puts back a nearly empty jar of maple butter with the name *Daddy* back in the cupboard, then digs into the mostly full jar.

I try not to chuckle. "I saw that, you know."

Her spoon freezes midair. "Are you going to tell on me?"

Good question. "No."

Her legs are dangling faster and faster under her chair. "What are you going to do?"

Another good question. *God, I love this kid.* "I think I'm going to watch how this turns out for you."

"Like what?"

"Like... is your tummy going to hurt? Are you going to throw up? Are you going to feel guilty when your daddy has no maple butter left? That sort of thing."

"Why?"

"What else do you want me to do?

"Adults are s'pposed to tell kids what's right and wrong." She licks her spoon, the sticky paste clinging to her tongue.

This time, I laugh out loud. "Oooooooh-kay. So, you would want me to tell you what you did is wrong? Or maybe I should take the jar away from you?"

She shrugs. "I don't know. I'm just a kid."

She's funny as hell, and at the same time, there is something so mature about her that breaks my heart. I reach across the table to wipe a dollop of gooey maple butter off the tip of her nose. "You already know it's wrong. But, in case you forgot, your belly is going to remind you of it. Come here, sweetie. Here's what we can do." I take her hand and lead her to the countertop where the grocery list sits. "Just write down *Maple butter* right there. Put a little heart next to it, for extra points."

She stands on the tip of her toes and sticks her tongue out as she forms her letters. I ruffle her hair when she's done, then pour her a glass of apple cider. She puts her hand in mine, and we go back to the kitchen table. She snuggles on my lap. Her unruly hair tickles my nose, and I comb it with my fingers.

She grabs my phone. "What were you looking at, earlier? Bad news?"

"Something I didn't quite think through."

She brings the phone level to my face so it unlocks, then goes through my pictures. "Are you going to need a lawyer?"

I'm taken aback. "Aren't you a little young to know about lawyers?"

"Daddy always says we're not in real trouble until we need a lawyer."

"That's very true."

She nods pensively. "So, you're going to watch how this turns out for you?" she says, repeating the expression I used earlier.

This kid. "I'll figure it out," I say and kiss the top of her head. Although my financial situation just got a little trickier, a weight has lifted. I'm done doing things to try and please someone who doesn't deserve it. From now on, the things I do, I'll do for me, for what *I* believe in.

It's liberating.

Skye snaps a selfie of both of us, but it comes out blurry. I show her how to focus, and she tries, again. "Let's save that one."

"Can I have it?" she asks.

"Sure. I'll email it to your daddy. You'll just need to ask him to print it."

"Silly face, now," she says, and we push out our tongues. I cross my eyes, and she laughs hysterically, imitating me and taking a slew of photos. I show her how to edit them, then email a couple more to Christopher's address.

"Hey there."

We both look up as Christopher materializes in front of us. He's leaning against the door frame, his head tilted to the side, his thick hair all mussed up. The top buttons of his flannel shirt are opened, revealing his dark chest, the sleeves rolled up on his muscular forearms. His faded jeans hang low on his hips, his leather belt loosely fastened.

"Hey," I answer.

Half a smile floats on his lips, his eyes are fixed on mine as Skye snaps a photo of him.

"Daddy, make a face!" With his hand splayed across his face, he makes a piggy face, duly captured by Skye on my phone.

"Can we please delete this, now?" he asks, coming into the kitchen while Skye continues to snap photos of him.

"Absolutely not," I object, to Skye's delight.

He frowns, but his lips curl up as he reaches over to peck Skye on the forehead. He smells of soap and something earthy. Skye wraps her arms around his neck and latches onto him, and as he picks her up in his arms, the back of his hand brushes against my breast. I feel myself blushing and straighten in my chair.

"Guess what?" Christopher asks, his eyes between Skye and me.

"Whaaat?" Skye shrieks, beaming at good news she hasn't even heard yet.

"Lynn and Craig are back from their cruise."

Skye shrieks louder and applauds. "Can we go tonight?"

"Not tonight, but soon," he says, his eyes darting between the two of us. "Lynn and Craig are the owners of King's Knoll Farm."

"Oh right," I say, happy I'm starting to know who is who in Emerald Creek. "Justin and Haley's parents?"

"That's right. You know Haley?" A small smile forms on his lips.

"From game nights," I inform him.

"Right. Well, you'll soon meet the whole family. Craig and Lynn have a bunch of people over for dinner once a month. We have an open invitation. Skye loves it, and you will too. Right, Skye?"

"Are you sure I'm invited?" I say. "I think I'd rather stay h—"

"You're coming."

Is it normal that my panties heat up? And not because of the word he used. Because he's ordering me around, and I *like* it.

I glance at him, my cheeks flushed.

"Alek-zandra has lawyer problems, Daddy," Skye cuts in.

Christopher faces me, and Skye wiggles in his arms to look at me too.

I tuck my hair behind my ear and clear my throat. "It-it's nothing. Skye, it's nothing to worry about. No lawyers," I add, suddenly concerned I'm causing her some stress. Clearly, she's used to being in tune with grown-up problems, and I feel the need to shield her from that.

"What's going on?" Christopher asks.

I shake my head. "Really, nothing."

His gaze goes right through me. Is it care I see in his frown? It warms me to the core. "We can handle '*nothing,*' right, Skye?" he says, and she nods. "And, if it becomes something, I'm here for you."

I'm here for you. When was the last time someone said those words to me, except Sarah on one of my rare drunken nights?

Chapter Twenty-Eight

Alexandra

The day Skye has been so excited about finally arrives. Sunday dinner at King's Knoll Farm. After we sell out of bread, Christopher hangs the *"Sorry, we're closed"* sign, and I run upstairs to get ready. I keep my shower short but still wash my hair. Not gonna lie, I'm nervous about meeting so many people at once. Nervous but happy.

I wrap my hair in a towel and slip on the plush robe that magically appeared in my bathroom the day Christopher had my whole bedroom redecorated. I'm applying foundation when Christopher knocks lightly on the half-open door.

"Hey, come in." I close the bottle of foundation and grab my makeup pouch.

"You almost ready?"

"Just need to finish my makeup and blow dry my hair. I'll be quick, I promise."

He closes the door behind him. "There's no rush," he says, wrapping his arms around my middle and kissing my neck. Our eyes connect in the mirror, and we both grin. I pause my blush application midair.

He leans into me to grab the small beige bottle off the countertop. "What is this."

"It's foundation," I answer. "It unifies the skin tone." I dab some powder on my face but am more interested in what Christopher is doing now than in my makeup.

With both arms still around me, he drops a dollop of foundation on his finger and plops it on the tip of his nose, then spreads it around. "Like that?" he says.

"That's totally too light for you," I giggle. "You look like you've been in the sun with a clown nose on."

He groans and wraps his hands back around me, nuzzling my neck. "You smell so good."

"I just showered."

"Unh-unh. You always smell good." Taking a deep breath, he straightens himself, pulls the towel off my head, and runs his fingers through my hair, then massages my scalp.

I groan. His fingers knead the right places, instantly relaxing me, and I close my eyes for a second.

"Tired?" he asks.

"No. Just… a little nervous."

He stops his skull massage and turns me gently in his arms so I'm facing him. "About what?" His eyes are searching me.

"Meeting all these new people," I admit with a shrug. I know they'll be lovely.

"They're like family, Alexandra," he says, tucking my hair behind my ear.

"I know," I whisper. That's probably why I'm nervous. "That's... intense."

"They'll love you." He runs a hand inside the opening of my robe, quickly finding my breast and stroking it, making me moan.

I bite my lip and boop his nose. "Then let's not make them wait," I say reluctantly, then turn around and grab the blow dryer.

"Let me," Christopher says, and takes the dryer from my hand. He slowly runs my brush through my hair, first to untangle it, a delicious feeling, the tingle zinging from my scalp to my center and back up to my nipples.

"Shouldn't you check on Skye?"

"She's ready and watching Princess Dragon." He turns the blower on, and I lean into the sensation of his hands on me, his attention on me, his eyes on me. A slow grin spreads across my face as simple happiness takes hold of me. He's gentle in his gestures and slightly awkward in the most adorable way. I close my eyes, letting him take over, swaying under his touch.

When he's done, he turns the blow dryer off and pulls me in his arms. "Beautiful." His arms wrap around me, and he hoists me easily onto his hips. "Man, this bathroom brings back memories. Not gonna lie, been wanting to make you mine the minute I saw you in my bakery."

My middle clenches at his words.

"But the first time I almost did was right here, you dripping in that T-shirt, eye-fucking me."

I pretend to look offended. "I was *not* eye-fucking you!" *I totally was.*

He chuckles. "Yeah, you tell yourself that." He dips his head to my neck, licking and nibbling.

"And you made fun of me!"

He pulls his head back to look me in the eye. "Made fun of you? I was *so* hard for you. You kept looking at my dick. Didn't help."

I giggle. He's right. "The dildo," I say, getting us back on the track of him making fun of me.

He trails his face down my throat. "Oh yeah. What happened to that little guy?" he asks.

I rock against his hard muscles, my middle connecting with his belt buckle. "I haven't had much use for it."

"Not much, huh?"

"None at all."

His hand trails under my robe and kneads my bare ass. "I wonder why?"

"Been busy."

"Who's keeping you busy?" He slides two fingers inside me.

"*God*, Christopher."

"Second time I almost fucked you, was at karaoke," he says, moving his thumb over my clit. "Couldn't stand seeing all those guys looking at you in that sorry excuse of a dress, shaking your sweet ass in front of everyone."

I'm about to come. "Chriiiis. Please."

"Come for me, beautiful."

I do, digging my fingers in his shoulders, riding every last tremor in his arms.

He sets me carefully on the floor, turns my hair in a rope to my side, kisses me softly on the lips, and says, "Best makeup I know is giving you an orgasm."

"Yeah?"

He trails my cheekbones. "You get all pink here. Your eyes are brighter." He kisses my hair. "You glow even more than you usually do." He wraps me tenderly in his arms, his beating erection between us. "We should get going," he says with a deep sigh. "I need to get out of here," he adds, chuckling. "How much time do you need?"

"I'll be downstairs in five, but hold on."

"What?"

"Let's get rid of that," I say, swiping a cotton pad with makeup remover on his nose. "There, better."

He leans into me for one last tender kiss.

Minutes later, we bundle up. The air is sharp with cold, the sun again so bright on the snow, I wear my sunglasses. We pack several pies Willow made this morning with Skye's help and climb into Christopher's SUV.

His hand on the gear shift brushes my knee when we pull out of the driveway, and a small smile floats on his lips. He glances at me, mischief in his eye. Skye is looking out the window, singing the tune of the spring show.

My mind rewinds to what just happened in my bathroom, and I blush.

"Alexandra," he growls.

"Hmm?"

"Stop." He lifts himself off the seat and adjusts his jeans.

"Oh, sorry." *Not sorry.* "You gonna be okay?" I ask, teasing.

He chuckles. "Probably not."

Trees cast long shadows on the snow when we get to the farm, a large, white Victorian house with a wraparound porch. Several cars are parked in front, and I recognize Grace's Jeep.

A massive red barn towers over the farm, built alongside a hill. Several outbuildings dot the majestic landscape of snowed-in, fenced pastures framed with thick woods.

"Wow," is all I can say.

"Right?" Christopher says. "The land we've been through since we left the main road is all theirs."

"It's so quiet," I say as we circle around to the trunk, the crunch of our boots on the snow the only sound.

He meets me behind the car, and grabs my hand.

"I wish... I could—" he stutters.

"I know." I smile at him. "We're keeping it professional. No worries."

He nods in silent thanks and gives my hand a last tug before unlocking Skye's door, then unlatching the trunk where we grab the pies and breads. "Come on, little bug," he says. "Let's go."

"Aunt Lynn and Uncle Craig!" Skye cries, running toward the house, slipping on the driveway's packed snow as she does.

A handsome couple in their fifties, both blond, fit, and tanned, are coming out of the house and pause on the top of the steps.

The woman glances my way, a kind expression on her face, then turns to Skye with wide open arms and lifts her into them.

The man kisses the top of Skye's head and comes quickly down the steps. "Give me this, sweetheart," he says to me, relieving me of the bag of breads I'm carrying. "You must be Alexandra. I'm Craig."

"I am," I say, glancing at Christopher. "Nice to meet you, Craig."

"You trying to keep her a secret, son?" Craig says. "I knew about your new apprentice the minute she got here. Lynn was about to go snorkeling, and I was at the pool. I'd just ordered a daiquiri. I'll never forget that moment."

Christopher grunts, but his eyes are happy. "Knock it off."

"That's exactly when Sophie texted," Craig continues. He turns to me, a twinkle in his eye. "Welcome to Emerald Creek, where your business is everybody's business. Lynn is beside herself finally getting to meet you."

Lynn greets me with a hug. After we leave our coats and boots in the mud room, she hooks her arm through mine and takes me to the great room, where everyone seems to be gathered, the men right behind us.

A fire is roaring in the hearth, and groups of people are scattered, talking and laughing. Grace is next to a window, a glass of red wine in hand, chatting with Cassandra and Sophie. Willow is plopped on the floor in front of the fireplace, playing a game of cards with people I don't know.

Craig claps Christopher on the shoulder. "So, I hear someone finally got through to you and convinced you to do that TV show?"

I glance at Christopher and warm at his small smile. "You could say that," he answers.

My belly flutters as I watch him and Craig walk away, talking about the competition as they join a group of men.

"Beer? Wine? Tea? Hot spiked cider?" Lynn asks me.

"Hot spiked cider sounds awesome," I say and follow her to the open kitchen.

Haley is ladling mac'n cheese in baking dishes. "Can I help?" I ask.

"Nope, got it," she answers. "You do enough food prep all week. Sit down," she says, indicating the bar stools lining the island.

"Here," Lynn says, handing me a steaming cup decorated with a cinnamon stick. "Our own apple cider doctored with local bourbon. Should warm you up."

I smile. "Thanks."

She sits next to me, nursing her own steaming mug. "So, tell me. How is our Christopher treating you?"

I nearly choke on my drink. "Everything's great. He's a good boss."

"Good. It helps that Skye is a sweetie. Christopher can be such a grump sometimes, but she softens him. How are you liking Emerald Creek so far?"

I tell her I love it here, and the back and forth continues effortlessly between us. She's motherly in a way that brings tears to my eyes, asking who I've met in town, inquiring about my likes and dislikes in terms of food, and then asking me if I miss Brooklyn. All without ever putting me on the spot. Never making me feel like I should say something fake just to be nice. "But it must be so hard to be away from home," she insists when I tell her how much I love living here.

"I'm not sure where home is," I say. Although I'm already on my second mug of hot, generously spiked cider, it's not the alcohol talking. It's this woman. She's so kind and deep, I feel like I could just crawl onto her lap and cry my sorrows, and she'd make it all go away.

"Awww," she says, giving me a side hug, "we got ourselves another misfit." Wow. Even Lynn, who I've just met, and is the nicest person, can tell I'm not cut for having a family. I guess it really is something in our DNA. People sense it.

Lynn sighs lightly, as if she hadn't just said the most true and painful thing for me to hear. I can't hold it against her. Actually, I'm grateful to her for the gentle reminder. This—the big family—is not for me, and if I had any fantasies popping into my head just by being here, I should nix them right away. I lean into her side hug, thankful for her levelheadedness, while she looks up at Haley and two tall, handsome guys who look just like Justin.

"Mom," one of the guys says, shaking his head, "you're crushing her."

"I am not. This is my son Hunter," she says to me, "and his brother Logan."

"I'm not your son? Just his brother?" Logan says, looking dejected.

"It's the same, Logan," Lynn says, rolling her eyes as she stands from the barstool.

"Not the same to me, if you don't mind," Logan says, wrapping his mother in his arms.

"Awwww, baby's gotta a heartache," Hunter says, his hand on his heart. "Boo-hoo."

"Shut up, Hunter."

"Get over it, I'm her favorite."

"Guys, really." Haley rolls her eyes. "D'you have brothers, Alex?"

I shake my head, laughing at Logan and Hunter.

"You're not missing out on much." *It feels to me that I'm missing out on a lot.*

"Hey!" They both turn on their sister.

"Who picked you up drunk from that party your first spring break from college?" Hunter asks.

"Who covered the tracks in the snow under your window *junior year of high school*?" Logan asks.

Yeah, definitely missed out on a lot.

"Kids, enough," Lynn says, but her eyes are narrowed on Haley.

"Mom! You know they're lying!" Haley says, her fists on her hips, her eyes throwing daggers at her brothers.

Hunter and Logan leave the room, laughing.

"Hey! Come back here!" Lynn says. "Bring the food to the table."

Dinner is ready, so I grab two baskets of bread and set them on the massive table, then quickly move away to find the bathroom.

When I come out, my eye is attracted to a gallery of family pictures on the wall. It's a mix of birthdays and Christmases throughout the years, candid photos at the lake and on the slopes, graduations and other more formal photos. One of them catches my eye.

It's an old, black-and-white photograph of a man. I feel like I've seen it before. The way a lock of hair falls along the side of his face. The tentative, lopsided grin. I rack my brain and come up empty.

I must be mistaken. I've lived vicariously through so many of my friend's large family stories and paraphernalia, pretending that I was a part of these large, messy, happy bunches, that I'm imagining things.

I need to stop this and just enjoy what the present is giving me.

As I head back to the dining room, Emma is walking in from the cold. Caroline dashes in front of her, cuts me off, and throws herself in the arms of a man I do not know. "Daddy," she cries as he hugs her. Emma smiles at me and joins the crowd.

I have to give it to her. She even has the co-parenting mastered. She has it together. I'm impressed.

Before I get too deep on how Emma is this perfect small-town woman and I'm a hot mess, Lynn calls out, "Sit wherever you'd like." She pulls two chairs out and adds, "Alexandra sweetheart, come here." She's patting the seat next to her.

"Welcome to King's Knoll Farm!" Hunter bellows from across the room. "Where you're invited to act as you please, then told what to do."

"Hunter! I just want to get to know Alexandra. Unless you wanted to? You can have her for dessert."

"Mom!" Haley cries out. The room falls silent, then erupts in laughter.

Lynn giggles. "Oh silly, that didn't come out right, did it? You know what I meant."

I'm laughing and blushing at the same time and can't help but glance toward Christopher. Emma is pulling up a chair to sit next to him. And he's glowering at Hunter.

Craig seats himself on my other side. "I feel suddenly very important, seated between you two," I say. "It's intimidating." I don't know why, I feel comfortable opening up to Craig and Lynn.

"We're really shielding you from this crazy bunch," Craig says. "We want to make sure you don't go running back to New York before you have a chance to know us." He leans closer to me, pretending he doesn't want Lynn to hear. "Although I'm not sure my wife is the best at this social thing. She tends to put her foot in her mouth, in case you hadn't noticed."

"I do not," Lynn says, passing a dish of venison.

I'm seated across from one of their farmhands and his wife. He tells me they're getting ready for sugaring season, and that I should come and check it out when they get started. A wail erupts from the kids' table, and his wife jumps out of her chair, but Haley is faster than she is. "Stay right there, I got it," she says.

"Thanks, Haley," the man says when she comes back. Then, to me, "We had our first three years ago, and then twins a year later."

"Didn't waste time," Craig chuckles.

"She's exhausted," the man says, circling his hand around his wife's shoulders. "I'm not much help at home."

"You work your ass off all day," his wife says, leaning into his arm. "Pardon my French," she adds. She turns her face to him and kisses his cheekbone, right above his beard.

In another life, I would have wanted just that. The understanding. The messiness. The paycheck to paycheck.

The family.

The love.

I shake these thoughts away, and they're replaced by others about Rita. I don't remember her ever having barbecues or pool parties or any type of get together at her home where she'd invite staff.

This, here, feels like a family company to me. A place where you go to work, but where you also gather to relax, share a meal, be together.

I've never seen that at Red Barn.

After dinner, we all help clearing dishes and agree that we need a break before moving onto dessert. The kids go outside to make maple candies in the snow. I stretch and am shooed away from doing dishes, so I pull out my phone and take pictures of their beautifully restored farmhouse.

The massive fireplace, the cozy breakfast nook, the whimsical light fixtures in reclaimed barn wood, and so many other details, belong in a catalog.

"Would you like to see our cows?" Lynn asks me. "I bet you they'd look great in pictures. Someone said you're really good at social media. Maybe we can hire you away from Christopher, huh? Hunter! Why don't you take Alexandra to the barn?"

"Mom! Stop it already!" Haley huffs.

"I'll take her," Christopher says, coming out of nowhere.

Lynn's eyes flit between us. "Oh. Oh, sure."

Craig chuckles and shakes his head.

Chapter Twenty-Nine

Christopher

On our way to the barn, as soon as we leave the pool of light that surrounds the farm and we reach the shadows, I wrap my arm around Alexandra and pull her close to me. She lifts her face, then buries it in the crease of my shoulder. My heart does a little skip, and I hurry our steps.

The warm, animal smell of the barn brings back memories of make out sessions when I was a teenager. Justin and I would hang out here with whatever girls we had managed to bring to the farm, playing strip poker in the hay loft.

I don't remember any of the girls.

I do remember, though, a dressing down by Craig when he caught us, for fooling around in a workplace.

Then, he lectured us on the importance of being protected. That was soon followed by frequent distribution of condoms.

I chase the thought away.

It feels so good to be alone with Alexandra. Just simply alone.

"I'm not gonna turn the lights on," I say. We can see enough with the halo from the exit signs.

We open our coats, and I slip my arm around her waist while we walk around the stalls.

"They're so skinny!" Alexandra says.

"They're jersey cows. That's how they look. Don't worry about them, they're well fed," I say as a cow presses her nuzzle toward us.

Alexandra pets her. "Look at those eyelashes," she says. "Lucky you."

Hunter would have been way more qualified than me to give this tour, but no way was I going to let him be alone with Alexandra in the barn. I know it's primitive.

But that's who I am.

We walk away from the cow with the long lashes and Alexandra tenses under my hand.

"Are you bored? Are you cold?" I suddenly worry and pull her closer to me.

Her breath is shaky. *What the fuck?* Normally, I'd tell myself that's the reason I don't do relationships. It's just too exhausting to read women.

With her, it's different. I can tell now, she's miserable.

But if I don't understand why, I can't fix it.

And, if I can't fix it, what am I?

Worthless.

I turn her to face me and hug her, my hands stroking her back, soothing her nerves. "Hey," I say. "Talk to me." I trail kisses along her hair, inhaling the flowery scent of her shampoo. "Please?"

"I—I feel... overwhelmed."

That gets a chuckle out of me. I tilt her chin up so her eyes are on mine. "You're talking to a pro at being overwhelmed. Too many balls in the air. Just choose the ones that are the most important. You'll pick the other ones up from the floor when you're ready. They're not going anywhere."

She takes a deep breath.

"What's got you overwhelmed?" I prod.

"Right now?" she asks, worrying her bottom lip with her teeth.

"Let's start with right now."

She waves a hand toward the farm. "This—this is so... great. And us," now she waves her hand between us, "doomed. It's hard." She shuts her eyes and shakes her head.

"Yeah," I say slowly, kneading the back of her head, feeling her relax under my touch. "What Lynn and Craig built, that's pretty great, right?"

She nods.

"When I moved to Emerald Creek, I used to hang out here all the time. It was packed at my aunt and uncle's, with Grace and Colton still at home, and everything they had going on. They took me under their wing, and they helped me out just as much as my own family. Lynn called me her misfit. Just like she did you, earlier."

"You heard that?"

Of course I did. "I hear everything, when it comes to you."

Her eyes travel over my face, so tender. "You never talk about your family. What is your mom like?"

I shrug. "She's... I dunno. A nice person. Too nice. Gets walked all over."

"By your stepfather?"

She remembers I have a stepfather? "For example."

"She must miss you."

"We're in touch," I say, feeling a little defensive.

"You felt rejected. *Were* rejected," she corrects herself and clasps her hands behind my neck. Then she lays her head on my chest, her fingers twining in my hair.

She feels good right there.

"Felt rejected," I admit.

"Too sensitive for your own good," she says softly. "But you're learning to deal with it."

I growl. "Yeah, not sure about that." If I were learning to deal with it, I'd protect myself better. I wouldn't be holding her in my arms, swapping family history and aspirations.

"Tell me about your brothers."

I chuckle just thinking about them. "Ryan and Trevor. Twins. They must be eighteen now."

"That's nice," she says softly. "Do your brothers work at the bakery during the summers?"

"Naah. I haven't seen them in a while. We keep in touch via video though." I kiss her hair.

"Hmm. That's too bad. It seems like it would be fun for Skye to have her young uncles around to be goofy with. And I bet you they'd love working with their big brother." Her fingers are trailing circles on my back, soothing me.

"You know what? Maybe they would." I pull her head back softly to look her in the eye. "I'll mention it to them."

"Why did you leave home?" she asks.

I won't ruin this moment with my shit. "Beautiful, I don't want to talk about it right now."

"Mmm. Sorry." She leans her head back on my chest, and I stroke her hair.

"Don't be. I don't want to bring back bad memories, that's all. Bottom line is, I fought for what I wanted, and I got it."

She squeezes me. "You deserve to have all that you want, Christopher Wright."

I squeeze her back. "I have most of it. The rest, I'll keep fighting for. You can count on me." I spoke too fast, and I hope she doesn't ask me what that is.

"Good," she sighs. "I'll tell the events committee they can start working on the party."

"What party?"

"For when you win the competition."

I laugh. "That may be a bit cocky. I said I'll fight for it. Doesn't mean I'll win it."

"You always fight for what you want?"

"Yeah."

"Why do I have the feeling that when you fight for something, you get it?"

That makes me pause. The major milestones of my life sift through my mind. "If I really want it, you're right. I get it. When I don't get something, I realize I never really wanted it to begin with." That would be true for Skye—I wanted her. And for her mother—I didn't care for her. And for my bakery. "How about you. You a fighter?" She must be, if she came all the way here to get a promotion at work. Truth is, we don't talk about Red Barn Baking, because I hate those bastards and she knows it. There's no point ruining a good thing between us by bringing them up.

"I try not to be," she tells me. "Whenever I fought for something that meant a lot to me, I ended up losing more than I had. So now, I don't fight. I'm just grateful for what I have and don't wish for more."

What a bunch of bullshit. "What makes you believe this."

She takes a shaky breath. I try to pull her face from my chest to look at her, but she resists and nuzzles deeper. I wrap my arms tighter around her to comfort her.

"When I was a little girl, the only thing I wanted was a big family. Brothers and sisters, cousins, a grandma and grandpa... I only had my mother, and I didn't realize that was all I needed. One year, I insisted so much we at least spend Christmas with my grandmother, she gave in... It was not the Christmas I was hoping for. They fought a lot, and eventually, my mother left for a few days, promising to pick me up right after New Year's. She never did."

My heart thumps at her words. I think I can fill in the blanks from things she shared before, but I don't say anything. I give her space to let it out, on her time.

"She died in a car crash on New Year's Eve," she confirms, her body tightening. "Some guy she'd just met was driving. I remember my grandmother calling me into her office to tell me." Alexandra's voice is so small, even in the quiet of the barn, I have to strain to hear her. "She said, that's what you get when you wish for what you're not meant to have... and when you forget that men only bring misery."

I growl my disapproval.

"It's true for us, you know," she says in a firmer voice. "My grandmother and my mom. Sure didn't have any luck trying to build a family. And when *I* tried fighting for more than I already had?" She lifts her face to mine this time. "My mom died because of me. She *died* because of me. So... done fighting for stuff I shouldn't have." Tears line her eyes, and it nearly kills me.

"Beautiful. She didn't die because of you. That's just shit that was fed to you, no disrespect to your grandmother. You need to let go of that."

"I'm trying," she says, her eyes widening. "It's not that easy."

"Of course it's not easy. But there's nothing you shouldn't have." I kiss the tears off her cheeks. "And if there's ever something I can help you get, I'm here for you. You know that, right?"

She takes a deep breath and wraps her arms tightly around me.

I dip my lips to hers, our mouths seal to each other, and our tongues engage in their familiar dance. "You'll be fine, beautiful," I say as we come up for air. "Whatever's overwhelming you, it'll work itself out."

Chapter Thirty

Alexandra

I can't sleep that night, so I scroll through the pictures I took at the farm today. Laughing faces around the long table, farmhands and owners side by side. Parents and children hugging. Pride in their hard work obvious in every detail.

A sense of peace radiates from every photo, and a new resolve takes hold of me. *This* is what I want for Red Barn.

I keep scrolling mindlessly back, thinking about how to bring the small family business vibe to an industrial company, until I land on the photo of myself in baker attire. The one I emailed Barbara but she never received. She would love it, so I text it to her.

A voice message comes back. Impressed with Barbara's mastery of our constantly evolving technology, I open the message.

"Hello Lexie exclamation mark thank you so much for the picture heart emoji you look fantastic exclamation mark how is everything eggplant those bastards sacked me explosion emoji skull emoji Rita must be turning in her grave black broken heart emoji anyway we'll get them strong arm emoji I'm going to come up to Emerald Creek to strategize period love you heart emoji heart emoji heart emoji period."

Okay. Major emotion overload right there. I'm kind of laughing about her confusion between dictation and voice text, but really:

She was *sacked*? So they did it. She was right.

I need more info.

I sit up in my bed and call her.

"It'll be alright," she says as a greeting.

"Why would they do that!?" I didn't really believe it when she said they were getting ready to fire her.

"I opened my big mouth once again. Didn't like how and who they were replacing, and made it known. They're even sacking the store managers who are up for a raise, just to save money. Couldn't sit there and say nothing."

My heart is beating fast, too fast. When she'd mentioned the possibility of being fired and said she'd be okay because I'd rehire her when I came back, I thought she'd been joking.

"Barb," I say. "Are you gonna be okay?" The words barely get out my throat. Carlos had mentioned "a bunch of others" were let go too. What is going on at Red Barn Baking?

"Cash-wise, yes. It's just the good old ego." She laughs and makes a drawing sound like she's smoking, then exhaling.

Barbara doesn't smoke. "Thanks, hun," she whispers, not to me.

"Are you with someone? Is this a bad time?" I'm torn between slightly jealous, irritated, amused, and happy for her.

"It's Jerry. You know Jerry, right?"

I definitely don't know Jerry.

"You'll love him," she says, confirming it's the first time I've heard about him.

"I can't wait to meet him," I say. And truthfully, I can't. My heart beats little tunes of happiness and hope. The all-too-familiar sensation of what could be, takes shape in my mind. Barbara, a substitute grandmother, warm and understanding. Jerry, a grandfather image, loving and caring. Before I can chastise myself, I've given into the fantasy.

Damn it.

"Last time, you said we should strategize," I say to get back on track. "For when I go back."

"Sure, darling. Are you still down for that?"

"Well, you saw the picture."

She laughs. "Dress the part. You got that covered," she says and takes another draw. *Is she smoking weed?* "But is that what you want? Bunch of snakes there, you know."

That's the whole point. My thoughts are beginning to take shape. "Can we change that?"

There's some ruffling on the line, like she's getting comfortable, settling in for a long conversation. "What are you thinking?"

"You know why I accepted Red Barn Baking—why I accepted Rita's offer. I saw it as the only family I'd ever have. I thought if this was her family, then it would be mine. I thought this was Rita's love letter to me."

"Mm-hm. I know."

She knows where I'm going with this—it's in her voice. But I need to get it off my chest anyway. I need to spell it out for her and, mostly, for me. "Well, Red Barn is not run like a family business, and it's certainly not a family. It has no moral values, and no values that relate to the business of making bread." I pause. "Rita was full of shit."

"It's more complic—"

"I don't care about Rita anymore. I never should have cared about her. But in the end, I don't regret my decision. I did what I thought was right at the time." I lower my voice. "And now I'm here. And the thing is, I can do something really good. I feel it in my bones. I can make Red Barn Baking a really good company." I have a responsibility to the people who make the company—the employees—and are treated unfairly. People like Carlos, and the hundreds of others I don't know about. "For the first time in my life, I can make a difference, Barb."

"Okay, Lexie," she says softly.

"I have ideas for some drastic changes, but I need to think it through before I share them." There's one thing we can start discussing, though. "We'll probably need a consultant to help us out, since it will only be you and me."

"Okay... What about Christopher Wright? He's knowledgeable."

"No! God no, he can't know anything." The idea makes my palms clammy. He would end me in a heartbeat.

"Why not?"

My mouth is dry. How will he react when he eventually learns the truth? "Believe it or not, he hates Red Barn with a passion. I don't know how I kept my apprenticeship here once he knew where I worked." I'm whisper-talking now.

"Oh. So he doesn't know about you? Being Rita's granddaughter and the whole inheritance deal?"

I tug my knees up against my chest and bring the comforter up to my chin. "No, and he can't. It would jeopardize everything. I guarantee you, he would cancel the apprenticeship, and you know what that means." As the words leave my mouth, I realize what I fear losing is Christopher, not Red Barn.

Barbara grunts. "I'm sorry to hear that, Lexie. That can't be easy for you."

"I'll be fine." All I need to do is focus on the good things. "I like the idea of you and me working together to change Red Barn."

"Me too, sweetie," she says in her warm, honey voice, the one she has when she's truly happy. There's some background noise, and then the telltale sign of giggling.

Ooooh-kay. Time to go. We hang up.

That was a good talk. Good decisions. Moving forward.

But meanwhile, I need to make immediate financial decisions to avoid being in the red.

I call Sarah, tell her I need to sublet my room for now. It's getting late on Sunday night, and she has work tomorrow. Our call is short, and to the point, and ends with a plan for her to visit after the snow melts.

And no questions about my sex life.

Yay!

The next few weeks, winter storms pummel us, and the accumulated snow is impressive. Tree branches are heavy, and repeat plowing created small snow walls along the sidewalks. Last week we went back to King's Knoll Farm and helped with sugaring.

I've been thinking more and more about Mom lately, no doubt because of the talk I had with Christopher in the barn. And also because at the farm, I observed the young women of Emerald Creek, and how they seemed to have solid role models around them, and I didn't. It made me think how the structures we grow up with set us up for the future. How mine is set to be so different from theirs. It also opened up a dam of memories, and they come in gusts now, flooding me.

I don't try to resist it anymore. I just let the memories resurface, like they do right now, out of the blue, while Skye pours a glass of milk, places it in front of me next to the cookies she assembled in a neat little pile, then climbs on my lap.

I used to do that too.

Skye twines her arms around my neck and whispers in my ear, "It's Daddy's birthday today."

My heart does a little flip, and I make a big *O* with my mouth. My mind is back in the present, in the best kind of way. I have Skye to thank for that, as often happens.

She's a gift, one I have only for now.

"Don't tell him I told you," she continues whispering. "I know because Grandma Trish called on the video this morning. He doesn't want a big fuss."

Of course he wouldn't. "Why not?" I whisper back.

She lifts and drops her shoulders dramatically. "I dunno."

"Okay."

"Maybe we can make a little fuss?" She takes a bite out of the first cookie, a maple shortbread, the crunch of her mouth matching the wheels turning in her head.

"You know what? I think that's a great idea," I say. "What did you have in mind?"

She sighs. "I dunno." She glances toward the bakeshop, making sure Christopher doesn't walk in on us, then dunks the cookie in her milk.

"Let's see. What's something he doesn't have or doesn't get to do?"

She shrugs again. "He doesn't have breakfast with me."

It hurts me that she misses him for those special moments.

"He doesn't have breakfast at all," she adds.

"That's an idea. Why don't we make him breakfast for dinner tonight?"

She perks up. "I love breakfast for dinner!" She whisper-shouts. "We do it all the time at Aunt Gracie's."

"It's settled, then. Let me handle it."

"I want to help."

"Oh, you'll help all right. You'll set the table, and make him a card, and flip the pancakes."

"Okay." She slides off my lap, puts her glass in the sink, and gets on her tiptoes to open cabinets.

"What are you doing?"

"Looking for pancake mix," she stage-whispers.

"I have a recipe," I say, my throat tightening. I haven't used that recipe since before.

Before mom was gone.

But it's time.

As I pull the notebook from the envelope in my room, a photo falls on the dresser. It's a Polaroid of Mom and me—a selfie before cellphones. Our heads are tilted together, and we're smiling big, crazy smiles. There's a huge Christmas tree in the background.

My heart clenches at the memory.

Our last picture together.

I rub my eyes and try to steady my breath. I barely register a shuffling next to me and jump when I feel a brush against my hair.

"Are you okay?" Skye's voice seeps through the ringing in my ears.

"Oh—Yes." I hastily wipe away my tears. "I'm okay, now." I hug her, needing comfort, despite my assurances. She pulls the picture I've been holding between my fingers.

"Who's that?"

"The little girl is me. And this is—*was* my mother."

"She's very pretty. Just like you."

A chuckle makes it through my throat. "Yes, she was very pretty."

"I don't have a mother," she says matter-of-factly. "Come, let's go make pancakes."

She pulls on my hand to get me to stand. I slide the picture back in the envelope, grab my childhood recipe book, and follow her down the stairs.

I manage to read the recipe in Mom's handwriting without bawling again—Skye's constant chatter a welcome distraction. And, here it is, at the bottom: *Enjoy with VT maple syrup*. And a little heart.

Tonight, it feels like she's here with me.

And it feels good. It feels like I'm going to be okay.

"How did you know that was exactly what I needed?" Christopher asks much later that night, after Skye is asleep and he's spread eagle naked on my bed, sheet up to his hips, my head on his chest and his hand threading through my hair.

I love the way he plays with my hair when he's thinking through stuff after sex.

I'm still trying to catch my breath.

"You mean when I licked your balls?" That's not what he means.

He chuckles softly. "Beautiful, you're incredible in bed."

My belly does somersaults.

"But I meant breakfast for dinner on my birthday."

Warmth spreads all over my body. "That was Skye's idea."

His chest does a jerky motion to move my face sideways and meet his gaze. "Really?" A big smile brightens his features, and he sets my head back comfortably on his chest. "Thank you for making it happen." He kisses my head, and I feel panic taking over.

"Hey," he says. "You okay?"

God. Why can he read me so well?

"Yup," I squeal.

His hand strokes my arm, soothing.

"I'm glad Grace and Justin came too," he says. "I liked sharing this," he says.

I nod in understanding. "I love dinners at the farm."

His body shifts, and something passes between us. "It's—that's what... Oh well, whatever." He stops stroking my hair. I know what he means.

Lynn and Craig sharing their home. Their love for each other. These big family reunions. These are the things people like us yearn for.

I clasp his hand in mine and look up at him, bliss and pain fighting for control over my emotions. "We'll take what we can, right? Misfits can't be too demanding."

He shifts us so we're now lying on our sides, looking at each other. "I tend to want a lot of things I shouldn't have." He tucks my hair behind my ear. "And I always find a way to get them."

Is he talking about us? His intense gaze tells me he is, but maybe that's just me fantasizing. Letting myself go down the slippery slope again.

"You can too," he continues. "Soon as you let go of the past, you can start building your future."

Right on about me and Red Barn. But he's talking about us, right? A lump forms in my throat.

"My mother called today," he says, the change of topic welcome. "She spoke with Skye too. We're talking about her going to Maine for a bit this summer."

"That's great," I say. "How does Skye feel about it?"

"Excited." His gaze circles my face, caresses my eyes, wanders to my ears, to my mouth. "You're good for me," he says against my lips, then starts exploring my mouth, his hand grazing down my side.

When our lips start to part, I ask, "How so?" wanting the compliments to keep coming, the moment to draw out.

Again, his eyes drag from my eyes, to my hair, to my neck, then to my cheek, then back to locking with my eyes. "You make me want to do good things. Things I didn't care about before. Like making sure Skye grows up knowing her family. And running for New England's Best Baker—"

"That wasn't me," I say. Everyone was telling him to run way before I'd even heard of the competition.

"It was. It is. You're the only reason I want to do it, now. I couldn't have cared less before. Too much hassle." He's talking in a low voice, his lips trailing my earlobe, shooting desire straight to my middle.

Still, I try to keep a straight head. "Well, then, don't. I don't want to be the reason you do something—and why? Why am I a reason at all?"

"Shhhh. It was all you. And it's a good thing. I got back in touch with old friends, bakers I haven't seen in a while. They're gonna come over, take turns to help me train."

I'm both happy he has friends who have his back and are going to help him, and worried about all the time and effort this is taking him. But I don't want to be nagging, bringing him down, when he has this fire in his eyes about his passion.

He rubs his nose against mine. "You're my good luck charm, Pancake."

"Pancake?" I giggle.

"Yeah," his voice trails. "You're the queen of pancakes. Did you see how many Justin ate? And he couldn't stop talking about them. It'd drive this baker crazy if he didn't... like you so much." He dips his head to my neck and inhales. "God, you smell so good."

I snake my hand down his stomach until I feel him come alive again.

I need him.

I want him.

Now.

Chapter Thirty-One

Christopher

"Hmm," she says. Her hips take on a little rocking motion. Her hand that was on my chest has been raking slowly down, and that's enough to get me going again.

After weeks of sleeping with Alexandra, I'm the opposite of bored. I want more of her. And I want her more than in my bed. I need to talk to her about that. Maybe I'll broach the topic more clearly tonight, once she's done with whatever she has in mind. My hints earlier clearly didn't hit the mark.

By the time her hand slowly reaches my cock, I'm hard. She gives me a couple of strokes. I reach for a condom, but she takes it from me. I cross my hands behind my neck, watching her take over.

Her eyes locked on mine, she gives my dick a couple of strokes, then takes me in her mouth, her full lips wrapped tight around me. Her tongue does creative things, then she lets go and rolls the condom on me. Her small hands on my thick length are way more erotic than I ever thought possible. I let out a groan.

Before I know it, she's riding me. She slides so easily she must be soaking wet. I reach two fingers to her clit. She's dripping. I lick my fingers and trail my hands to her sides, just so I can feel her better. Soon, my hands are cupping her breasts, pinching her nipples just the way she likes it.

She pumps me faster and faster, up and down like I showed her. She's such a good student in bed. She's made for sex. Sex with me.

"Oh my god, Chris," she pants, fucking me harder and harder. Her eyes flutter and her neck stretches. She lets out a low groan as her pussy clenches around me. I let my own release take over. Before her orgasm pumps every last drop of cum out of me, I flip us over.

I want her pinned under me right now.

Minutes later, we're catching our breaths. I'm flat on my back again, and she's tucked against my side. I'm absently stroking her back, looking at the ceiling.

"Why are you really here, Alexandra?" I ask out of the blue, surprising myself.

She tightens in my arms and stretches her legs before giving me a non-answer. "What do you mean?"

I started this, so I might as well finish. I need to get to the bottom of it, and now seems like as good a time as ever. "I can't make sense of a marketing person sent to do a baking apprenticeship. Why didn't they send a baker?"

She pulls away from me and sits on the bed, her back to me. "I told you. They want authenticity in our marketing. Back-to-basics kind of stuff."

Bullshit and she knows it. That's why she can't face me. Something else is going on. Suddenly I bolt upright, a crazy thought hitting me. "All those pictures you're constantly taking, that's not for them, right? I mean, the photos are yours, but the content, that's mine. I never agreed to my products and my bakery being used in Red Barn marketing material."

She turns around and narrows her eyes on me, but in the dim light I still catch the quivering of her lower lip when she whispers, "Holy shit, Chris, that's messed up." She picks her shirt up from the floor, slides it on, and wraps her arms around herself.

I jump to where she's standing, me naked, my cock soft but still long, her trembling fingers grabbing at her elbows. I grab her shoulders softly, giving her the option to shake me off if she wants to.

She doesn't.

"You have to admit, it's weird. No?"

She shrugs. "I guess?"

"I mean. A full apprenticeship? I can understand an internship. Like an observation or whatever." And *why me?* is what I really want to know, but then I'd have to be honest and come forward with the grant condition.

I can't put that kind of pressure on her.

She's still silent, and she looks totally shocked.

"I'm sorry I said that, Alexandra." Her skin is so soft under my hands, I can't help but caressing it as I speak. "You're ...." I'm afraid of what I'm about to say, so I stop. Also, I need to get back on track. Fix what I just broke. "I was just trying to figure out why your former boss was harassing you. What's so important about your presence here that a big shot like him needs to check in on you."

Her voice is steadier, but she's still upset when she says, "How do you know he's a big shot?" Another non-answer, but I'll let it slide.

"We have Google here too."

"For what it's worth, my pictures are mine. I only use them on my personal social media. But I can see your point. I'll stop taking photos of the bakery."

I have my answer, but does that fix things? "No. Don't. Please. That's not what this is." I tease her hair. "I'm just—I feel something off with this whole situation. But looks like it's just me being too protective. I need to step back."

She raises a steely gaze at me. "Maybe you should, yeah."

I'm hurting like fuck, but I brought this on myself. I couldn't leave well enough alone, could I? So now I'm paying the price. Fair enough. "So... we're good?"

She takes a deep breath. "Yeah, yeah, we're good," she says, climbing back into bed. She has those hiccupy movements that just fucking hurt me. She turns her back to me and buries her head in the pillows. "'Night," she mumbles.

"Right," I say, picking up my clothes strewn across the room. When I'm halfway dressed, I pull her into me, and I breathe better when she doesn't resist me. I kiss her hair and whisper, "I'm sorry, Alexandra. I didn't mean it the way it came out. Please forgive me? I can't—we can't be having a fight. Please."

She turns around, and I don't wait for her to talk. I close my mouth on hers, my tongue asks for permission to come in, and she yields. Her body wraps around mine, her hands clasp with desperation on my nape, and her tongue responds to everyone one of my moves like we are full-on having sex again.

We're definitely good.

When we break the kiss, she nuzzles her face in my chest for a while, and I'm pretty sure she's breathing my scent in. I do the same, my face in her hair, because I know this might end too fucking soon.

Then I leave her room, because until I'm sure she's mine to keep, I'm not getting used to sleeping a whole night with her.

I say I'm a fighter, and I say I win my fights, but who am I kidding? She looks exactly like a fight I'm going to lose.

Chapter Thirty-Two

Alexandra

Despite our small argument last night—or is it because of it?—I still come downstairs shortly after four the next morning. Christopher isn't in the bakery, and I feel a cold draft coming in from the kitchen. The side door is open, and the garden lights are on.

"Daisy! Shoo!" Christopher shouts under his breath.

What is he d—?

Ohmygod. There's a cow in the back garden. A big, black, cow. Staring Christopher down.

I slip on the boots I always leave by the door and wrap my arms around my chest against the cold. I take a tentative step out, careful to stay behind Christopher.

The cow shakes its head at me and exhales loudly, steam coming out of its nostrils. I stifle a yelp.

Christopher chuckles. "Babe, it's Daisy."

"Babe," I snap back sarcastically, "we haven't been properly introduced."

Christopher looks back at me, an are-you-for-real look on his face. He reaches for my hand and pulls me into his side, a large grin on his face. "Alexandra, this is Daisy, the Kings' one and only Angus. Daisy, this is Alexandra. My girl."

His girl? All the air in my lungs wooshes out while my lady parts fire up. Up until now, I thought of myself as a progressive woman. The kind who doesn't take kindly to being called a man's *girl*.

I'm reconsidering.

"What's an Angus?" I ask.

"It's a breed of cow. They're raised for their meat. Best steak you'll ever have. Hunter's take on Daisy's escapes is that she resents the farm's jerseys, who are raised for milk, while her kind are raised for meat. Headed for the slaughterhouse."

"Awww! Poor baby," I say and the huge, black animal tilts its head my way. "That's so sad!"

"Babe. They gave her a name. She ain't going to the slaughterhouse," he says, kissing my hair.

"So what's she doing in our garden?"

He gives me a squeeze at my involuntary use of the word our. "Having breakfast."

"Wh—?"

He points to the potted snowdrops and crocuses I'd placed in the garden. Only the pots are left. The blooms are all gone.

"Daisy!" I huff.

"Okay," he says, patting my ass as he turns us around. "You've met Daisy. Time to get to work."

"Are you going to let Hunter know where she is? So he can pick her up?"

"Nah. There's no picking up Daisy. She'll find her way back. Surprised you haven't met her already."

"I'd heard of her. Never believed it till I saw her."

"Believe everything you hear about Emerald Creek, beautiful. This place is fucking nuts in the best possible ways."

We share a cup of coffee, and then Christopher gets his groove on and starts baking while I stay on the sidelines, refilling glasses of water and cups of coffee, taking photos and videos. Silently cheering him on.

At six, my formal workday starts. As I do nearly every day, I meet Isaac at the task board. He blows a low whistle. "Wow, that is really the fast track. You're making puff pastry." He gives me an encouraging slap on the back. "Good luck," he says as Christopher walks in and starts to demonstrate how to make pâte feuilletée, the famous flaky dough.

"Alexandra, everything clear?" Christopher's voice startles me. I've been daydreaming about how he called me his girl. About our lovemaking last night. About our argument, also last night. I've been letting my mind wander to a lot of things except pâte feuilletée.

My eyes jump to meet his. "I—I might need—Maybe Isaac can walk me through this, again?"

He shut his eyes briefly. "Scrap the puff pastry for today. Make three kilograms of brioche dough instead. I'll swing by later to check on the yield and your shaping technique."

I open my mouth to tell him I've never made brioche dough before, but he's already gone, and my eyes fall on Kiara looking at me with undisguised amusement. "Why does the boss have his panties in a tizzy? What did you do to him?"

My mouth drops open as I look around to see if anyone heard us.

She laughs. "Bambi! What's with the deer in headlights look?" She chuckles at her own joke.

"Christopher asked me to—" *Shit.* I do say his name a special way. She's going to make fun of me again.

"What'd he ask you to do?" She rolls her eyes. "In the bakery."

I huff. "Brioche dough. Three kilograms. Or was it five? Darn."

"Three sounds right. You already did this on your own?"

I shake my head.

"Here are the proportions," she says, handing me a laminated sheet she fishes from somewhere. "Make sure the milk is lukewarm, not hot. Anything else, you'll have to ask *Christopher*," she ends on a chuckle. "It's pretty straightforward, but good luck anyway."

I glance at the thing and get to work. It doesn't sound too complicated. Once all my ingredients are in the giant mixing bowl that stands directly on the floor, I attach the correct hook (I think), set the machine at low speed, and the timer on thirty minutes. I look over it for a few beats, but nothing happens. I speed it up. Now we're talking.

While the dough kneads, I clean my workstation then decide it's time to go for a coffee break. On my way out, I check on the dough. It's nice and bubbly, almost to the surface of the bowl.

Wow. *Really* proud of myself, now.

I'm not yet halfway through my coffee when I hear shrieking coming from the bakehouse. "Oh my god! What's going on?" Uninterested in other people's drama, I close my eyes and enjoy a few moments of bliss.

"Alex! Alex!"

I guess they need my help. It's good to feel useful, I realize. There's a problem in the bakehouse, and they're counting on me as well to help. My spirits up, I down the rest of my coffee and head back to the bakehouse.

Kiara and Willow are standing a few feet back from the mixing bowl, mouths wide open, hands on their hips. Isaac is scratching his head, looking at me with what looks like pity.

A bubbly, grayish liquid pours from the mixing bowl to the ground and seems to crawl everywhere. It's thick yet nimble, like a creature from outer space.

"What the f—" Christopher booms as he enters from the bakery. "Somebody stop the fucking thing!"

Willow backs up two steps as the alien-like mixture reaches for her feet. Kiara follows suit. They both look at me. I scurry and lean over to hit the stop button, but I can't reach it, so I step bravely into the muck. As I'm about to reach the control panel, I lose my footing and slip. I try to hold on to the edge of the overflowing bowl, but my hand slips, and I land hard on the floor.

Sharp pain sears through me, then embarrassment, as I try and fail to get up, my limbs uncooperative, my feet slipping through the yucky, thick liquid. My left arm is instantly numb, and I feel like a cartoon character as I see stars dance around me.

"Are you okay?" Willow says, her eyes wide on me, teetering between concern and amusement.

Am I okay? I'm broke, I lost my job, I lost my apartment, I lost the joke of a family I had, I'm sitting in a pool of sticky muck that smells like warm beer, and I can't move my left arm.

And the man who's making me reconsider everything I thought I knew about men acted like a jerk after making crazy love to me yesterday. Granted, he apologized, and we made up.

And then this morning, he introduced me as his girl. Okay, to a cow. But still.

All this is A. Lot.

My body starts to tremble, my chin wobbles, and tears stream down my cheeks as I look at the mess I am. I try pushing on my feet, but they just slip miserably on the floor.

Willow bravely steps in the muck, reaches under my arms, and tries to pull me out. But she ends up falling over me, and insanity takes over as I laugh uncontrollably.

She's clutching at me, trying to pull me to dry ground, but as my hysteria takes over me, she pauses and says, "Are you laughing or are you crying?"

"I don't knooooow," I wail softly.

"Holy fucking shit, Bambi, you're a mess."

"Everyone back to work," Christopher's voice booms. Willow crawls back to dry ground, Isaac moves away, but Kiara stays put, hands on her hips.

I'm pulled by two muscular arms and slide onto a hard chest against my back. Christopher's voice vibrates against my ear. "Are you okay?" My knees buckle, and as he strengthens his grasp against me, I wince at the sharp pain awakening my arm. "Where does it hurt?"

"I'm so sorry," I say. "I don't know what happened."

"You got the proportions wrong," he says. "I should have stayed with you, that's what happened. Now, tell me where it hurts." He doesn't wait for my answer, just narrows his gaze on my hand hugging my elbow.

"It's fine," I say and flinch as he gently removes my hand.

He slips my apron above my head then unbuttons the long-sleeved chef's shirt I wear on top of my T-shirt and slides it off. I draw a sharp breath as he cups my elbow.

"Can you bend it?" he asks softly, and for a moment, I'm lost in his gentleness, and I forget I'm hurting. "Can you?" he insists, worry creasing his eyebrows.

I bend it slowly and nod. The pain is so acute, it radiates to my leg, and I teeter.

"Sit down," he says. "Someone get me some Arnica gel," he barks, louder. "Should be in the kitchen. Second drawer below the microwave." He holds my hand in his. "And a glass of water."

Willow scurries to the kitchen, and when she comes back with the required items, Kiara wiggles her eyebrows playfully while Christopher applies the gel himself.

I roll my eyes and look away from her, focusing instead on how Christopher is taking gentle care of me.

After we've determined nothing's broken, I'm dismissed for the day and instructed to rest my elbow.

But, before that, I get to summarize my mistake to the whole team, because "*We all learn from our mistakes, and we can also try and learn from the mistakes of others.*" (Barf).

Turns out, I misread the instructions and swapped the quantity of flour and the quantity of yeast. *Oops*. And the decision to speed up the process just made it worse. And, here, we get a lesson from the master on how important time is. Not as in, *Let's not waste it*, but as in, *Let's use as much of it as we can*.

Certainly not something I would have heard in New York, and that's exactly the point he's trying to make.

My elbow bandaged, I plop myself on the couch in the den and start sorting through all the photos I took in the bakery. Just because I'm off baking duty, doesn't mean I won't earn my keep. So, I get to work on what I do best.

On what I love.

Showcasing other people.

It's easy when you're dealing with a passionate individual like Christopher, who knows to surround himself with genuine people who clearly love what they're doing.

I open my laptop and organize the photos I took in categories—People, Process, Products, and Place. I don't need much time to decide on the color palette I want for the brand. I'll follow the down-to-earth, authentic feels of the browns and golden hues of the breads. Simple painted pottery and plaid stadium blankets will complete the look.

I'll keep it real by incorporating photos I took at Justin's of Christopher's slices of country breads and rye rolls in wicker baskets or directly on wooden boards, nudged between a cut of Ballyhoo cheese and a chunk of Bayley Hazen blue.

A picnic basket for a prop would be awesome. There's still snow on the ground, although we're moving fast into mud season. I'll take photos in the green lush fields once the snow is entirely melted.

I get to work, sorting, cropping, retouching, applying filters to get the effect I want.

At noon, my eyes are tired, and I welcome the lunch break.

"So, you don't have social media accounts," I say to Christopher when there's a lull in the conversation, which has been mainly between Willow and Isaac, since Kiara left before lunch.

He grunts, a raised eyebrow the only effort he's going to put into the conversation. *So what,* I translate.

I'm not going to ask why not, because that would corner me exactly where I don't want to be: arguing why he would need an online presence. "Would you mind having some?"

"Couldn't care less."

I clear my throat. "Does that mean you'd be okay having a social media presence?"

"Depends."

"If you didn't need to do anything? And it would bring you business?"

"Depends."

It's annoying how I can interpret exactly what he means. He's concerned about the content and the image he'll be projecting. He might act as if he doesn't care what people think about him, but I'm ready to bet he can't afford that luxury, yet. And he might act like he doesn't know squat about social media, but that's just alpha posturing. He has a kid who will be a tween in a few short years. He knows.

"If it was on brand?"

He doesn't grace my buzzword with an answer. Points for him.

I let it go and spend the afternoon continuing to work on my pet project. The only work that actually makes me happy and doesn't feel like work at all.

"Skye, come here," I say. "I want to know what you think."

We just finished dinner, and I want to kiss the feet of the man who can cook a clam chowder and shepherd's pie *and* bring me a glass of wine all at once. But I can't kiss him—not right now—so I decide to woo him with a creation of my own. And, given the cold reception I got earlier, I'm coming up with a little scheming.

I didn't know I was the scheming kind. Note to self: Men might bring misery; they also make women scheme.

This apprenticeship is turning out highly instructional.

Skye stands from the floor where she's been coloring and tucks herself against me, my laptop on both our knees. Christopher is flipping through TV channels, ignoring me.

Step One.

"So beautiful!" Skye exclaims as I scroll slowly through a mock-up feed I created. The photos that Skye finds so beautiful are breads and confections in different arrangements. In a wicker basket, on a china plate, on a wooden chopping board, on a silver tray. No matter the backdrop, the star is the bread. The bread always generates the emotion.

"I love it," Skye says, her little hands clasping at her heart.

Step Two.

"The... Wright... Ba... Ke... Ry," Skye spells out. "The Wright Bakery!" She shoots a huge grin at me and wiggles her feet in happiness after she's deciphered the elements of a logo. I feel, rather than see, Christopher glancing at us. I lock my eyes on the screen and keep scrolling.

Step Three.

"It's Daddy! And Willow! And Kiara! And Isaac! And Daddy again!" Christopher wiggles in his chair but stays put. "Daddy, come seeeeeee!" Skye calls out to her father. "Is that me?" she asks, pointing to a child's fingers tearing apart a cinnamon bun.

"Yes, that *is* you," I answer.

"Daddy come seeeeeee!" she cries louder.

He stands.

Step Four.

"What the actual fuck."

Chapter Thirty-Three

Christopher

This is what happiness looks like. The woman of my dreams sharing a moment with my daughter at the end of a day of hard work.

Skye's excitement gets me out of my head. I do everything for my daughter, so if she wants me to check something out, I do. Leaving my chair to go stand behind the couch where Skye and Alexandra are sitting, I pull on Skye's pigtails because that's what they're for and look over Alexandra's shoulder to her laptop.

What I see stuns me. "What the actual fuck."

There's like a mosaic of pictures of the bakery, each one carrying more emotion than the previous. There's Willow handing wrapped breads to a beaming customer. Isaac proudly taking croissants out of the oven, his uniform impeccable. Kiara focusing on the finishing touches of a myriad of colorful cupcakes.

Although people occupy most of the screen, my eye is always drawn to the products—the breads and pastries. I notice those are sharper and realize Alexandra placed the focus on them, in a subtle way. It's very professional, as far as I can tell.

She scrolls through the photographs, and then, there are several of Skye's hands tearing open breads, smearing jam on her fingers. We never see her face, and I appreciate how Alexandra's thought of protecting her privacy, while being clear to the viewer that this is a kid having an awesome experience eating bread.

An authentic, sense-driven experience.

The photographs that follow show our kitchen table set for four, and again, the bread is at the center, bringing the family together. And I know that's exactly what she's doing here. She's imparting my vision of what bread is.

Not hers.

Mine.

And she captured it exactly. So well, I'm having trouble swallowing.

When she moves to the next batch of photos, I freeze. These are all photos of me, and this time, she's not protecting any privacy.

I'm embarrassed to see myself, even if these photos are professional and there's nothing inappropriate about them. I avert my gaze for a while and notice her hand trembling slightly as she moves through that batch: my forearms clenched around a fifty-pound bag of flour; my eyebrows furrowed as I examine a tray of petits choux straight out of the oven; my back flexing under my uniform when I'm hand-molding breads; me beaming behind the counter, a line of customers in front of me, a bright bouquet of flowers to the side.

I remember when she took that picture. It was her first day here, and I'd sent her away with Grace to get her bearings. She'd been taking pictures all day, and she had finally returned. She'd brought the flowers to brighten the bakery, and she's been doing that a lot since. My smile wasn't meant for the camera.

It was entirely meant for her.

Alexandra finally breaks the awkward silence. "It's just an idea. Here's what it could look like," she says as she switches screens and shows me what look like mock-ups of social media accounts. Each photo is accompanied by a comment and hashtags. The postings are diverse, showing different facets of the bakery all at once. I see a logo appearing at intervals, bold and warm at the same time.

I don't know what to say. I'm overwhelmed with emotion. It's not just the work she put into it. It's how she sees us—how she sees me. The best of who I am. And I know not anyone could pull this off. It takes talent and skill.

It also takes emotion.

Connection.

That scares the shit out of me.

That she sees that in me.

And now what?

"Here's the account I created for Grace." She pulls up an actual live account on her cellphone of Grace's spa and hands it to me. While I scroll through the feed, she stands next to me to walk me through some of the functionalities she's enabled and explains how it's been helping the spa's visibility online.

Next, she reaches over, so she can switch views and show me the back end, and the side of her breast presses against my bicep. I'm trying to focus on what she's telling me about the data she collects, but her scent gets to me, her body gets to me, her soul gets to me.

I shove the phone back in her hand.

I run a hand through my hair. "That's... That's fucking awesome. The work you did."

Her cheeks flush, and she exhales sharply. "Oh, good. I was afraid you'd be upset. Nothing's live, you know? It's all just ideas? You can decide whatever you want to do. I just thought—"

"You're perfect—I mean, *it's* perfect." *Get a fucking grip, man. Your daughter is right here.* "Yeah, just go ahead with it."

"What—like, everything?" She looks like a kid in a candy store. Shiny eyes and huge smile. I'll let her post anything if that's my reward. I've never seen her so happy. So alive. And, although I can't relate to online stuff making people happy, I know passion when I see it.

She's passionate about that.

"You sure about that baking apprenticeship?" I ask, half joking, weighing her counter-performance this morning at the bakery (Who the hell mixes kilos of yeast and grams of flour and expects anything but a disaster?) with the work of art she put together with just a phone. "Seriously, Alexandra, you're wasting your time here. Why don't you tell Red Barn to go screw themselves and go work for another company? Or for yourself?"

Sure, if she were to quit now, that would mean I would lose my grant. But I'd rather lose my grant than see her wither away in a shitty company. She doesn't belong there.

"No, I have to stay there for now. I've got no choice," she says, her shoulders slumping.

"You do, though. You can tell them to fuck off." I could kick myself for having wiped the smile off her face. "Well, you can keep doing that on the side as far as I'm concerned," I say when she remains silent.

I turn back to the photos on her laptop. "How come there are no close-ups of the breads," I ask. "Like you did for Gems," I add, referring to the jewelry shop.

"Oh, you saw that?" she says, blushing slightly. "The camera on this phone isn't good enough. I'd need to clip a special lens on. I could try and buy one online. Gems had professional photography from a while back that I was able to use."

"No, don't buy anything," I order her. No way is she spending money on me.

I've been wanting to spoil her, and she's just given me an excuse.

Chapter Thirty-Four

Alexandra

A few days later, I find several packages on my bed, all wrapped and tied with ribbons.

There's a note attached to it:

Be you

C.

I unwrap the packages, and my heart fills with something new. Gratitude. Gratitude for being seen. Heard.

Understood.

Inside the small box is a clip-on lens for a camera, to take close-ups. The larger boxes hold two ring lights, a tripod, and a mike.

This means the world to me.

It means he cares about what I do, he sees me for who I am, and he's not trying to force me into a mold I'm not cut for.

He's encouraging me to do what I like.

Allowing me to be me.

No one has ever done that for me.

I'm not sure how to thank him, so I write a thank-you note and sneak into his bedroom to tuck it under his pillow.

I've never been inside Christopher's bedroom. It's large, simply furnished. Masculine. There's a king-size bed with a mahogany headboard and a navy-blue comforter. The furniture matches the headboard. The room is bare, with no decorations or objects, except for a photo of Skye when she must have been about two years old, all round cheeks, large dark eyes, and curly hair flying in the wind.

Apart from the picture, the only sign that this is Christopher's room is a low armchair with his dark gray cable-knit sweater swung over it.

I trail my hand on the edge of the bed as I silently make my way to the head. I was planning on dashing in and out of the room, tucking my note on or under the pillow for him to find tonight, but I'm hypnotized and can't pull myself away.

This is where Christopher sleeps, where his body lays at night, right below my own bedroom. Where his dreams take place, and his hopes carry him and unravel. I imagine his body splayed across the bed, tangled in the sheets. I run a finger on the pillow and tuck my note under it, leaning in to inhale the scent of his sheets.

"Find something you like?"

His voice startles me. "I—I just came to say thank you," I say, straightening myself. He's still adamant about me never being in his room, and I feel like I'm trespassing. "I left you something," I say, blushing as I make my way to the door.

He kicks the door closed and pulls me against him. Trailing his hands lightly up and down my back, he breathes in my hair. His erection, now familiar to my body, finds its habitual place against my belly, its pulsing unraveling an urgent desire I didn't feel moments ago.

My heart stutters at the knowledge that we're in his bedroom.

And I've gone from emotionally overwhelmed to sexually crazed in less than sixty seconds.

"Thank you for what?" he says, his voice raw.

The bakery is quiet, and there's still at least a half hour before he needs to go pick up Skye from school.

I reach behind him to lock the deadbolt, pull him by his belt hooks, push him into the armchair, and kneel between his legs.

He groans and fists my hair while I get to work on his zipper and boxer shorts. "Fuck, Alexandra, it was only a small lens." He smirks and then shuts up with a hiss when I pull out his heavy cock. I twirl my tongue on the tip, my gaze on his. His hooded eyelids are heavy with desire, and I tether myself to them. Never breaking eye contact, I take him in my mouth, inch by inch, teasing and licking and sucking. His hand is light in my hair. "Fuck, Alexandra," he whispers, petting me.

I cup his balls in one hand, dig my nails in his hip with the other hand, and take him deeper. He pushes himself into my mouth, groaning. I didn't think it would be possible, but he gets harder and longer. I adjust my angle so I can fit him and alternate the sucking and licking, teasing him and fulfilling him.

I love the feel of him in my mouth. His smell. The salty taste of his precum, the way his hands softly cup my head.

What I love the most is the power I have over him. The power to give him that release.

"I'm not going to last much longer," he hisses after a little while. He tilts his hips back and tries pulling my head off, but I swat his hand away and bob my head up and down, sucking him rhythmically, both my hands cupping the base of his shaft, now that his balls are high and he's entirely in me. His cock hits the back of my throat, and every time it does, I suck on it, longer each time, priming my throat for what I know is coming.

I will not let a stupid gag reflex ruin this moment.

Until Christopher, I didn't enjoy going down on a man, but holy hell, am I drunk right now, on the pulsing of his cock in my mouth, on his heavy breathing, on his growling curse words at me. Shivers run through my spine at every sign he's giving me of the effect I have on him.

I'm throbbing with pleasure at the sexual power I hold over him, right now. This is an experience like never before. I'm totally and only pleasuring him, totally at his mercy.

But I want more.

I bring his hands to my head.

I want him to direct my movements.

I want him to be in charge.

I want him to fuck my mouth.

He takes control, and for a few more moments—seconds or hours—I'm this pleasure thing for him, and I almost come. My spine arches, my breasts are painful with pleasure, and my middle is pulsating, mistaking the seams of my jeans for the magnificent cock in my mouth.

Christopher tenses and hisses my name like it's a swear word. I lock eyes with him as he comes in long, powerful streaks down my throat. I take it all in, the saltiness hitting the back of my throat as I swallow, again and again, for as long as it lasts, tears lining my eyes as I strain to be what he needs.

After the last tremors die down in his body, he pulls me up so I'm straddling him. I unzip my jeans and slide a hand inside my panties, and before he can take over, I come against his chest.

"Is there something wrong with me that I just want to be your sex plaything?" I ask in a small voice, wondering what just happened to me but, suddenly, trusting him with all the answers.

His cock answers for him, but after a beat, he says, "That's a question with too many degrees. I'm too spent to think about it, right now."

He lifts us off the armchair and pulls up his jeans. He runs a hand through his hair and gets ready to leave and pick up Skye from school. He has sex written all over him, and I can't wait until the next time we can spend the night.

"I didn't want memories of you in my bedroom," he says before leaving, and suddenly, I feel off-centered.

CHAPTER THIRTY-FIVE

Christopher

I smile to myself as I get into my truck to go pick up Skye.

It was only a stupid phone lens and a couple of things I threw in there because I thought it'd make her happy. But, fuck, I didn't expect that reaction from her.

What I should have expected was my reaction at seeing her in my bedroom. The force of it surprised me. It felt too good. Too right. Totally within my reach, yet so far.

Granted, when she got on her knees, my focus was on the first-class treatment my dick was getting, so it was easy to let go and just enjoy the ride.

I get hard again thinking how she licked me and sucked me, then... ah fuck... all but begging me to fuck her mouth. Guiding my hands on her head and pleading with her watery eyes.

She's a fucking fantasy.

Body of a goddess, and so eager to please me.

Fuuuuck.

But when she got up and nuzzled against my chest and fucking *orgasmed* on me, I was close to being overwhelmed by my feelings.

And, yes, it was sexual, and yes, it was hot as hell, but it was more than that.

Having her in my bedroom was more than just sex to me.

Drunk on her, I crank the music up so it fits my mood. As I get out of the car, moments later in the school's parking lot, Emma ambushes me.

"You look good." She smiles, patting my chest. Fuck, I wonder if she can tell I just got the best blow job ever. I self-consciously comb my hair with my fingers while she continues. "So... when can you come for dinner?"

"Come again."

She sighs. "Whenever I invite you over, you always have something going on. And I get that. I do. So, why don't you pick the date? I'm totally free for you."

I ignore her innuendo. Truth is, she's been nothing but friendly since I set her straight about my absence of feelings for her several weeks ago. She clearly got the message. There's no point keeping her at a distance.

I've been putting her off for too long, now, and I know I'm being rude. Her inviting me over to her place shouldn't mean anything more than that. We're the parents of two best friends, and at this point, I can't keep refusing dinner with her.

"End of the month work for you?"

She pulls a face. "Wow. Are you that busy?"

"I'm training for the competition. Have some mock sessions scheduled with some buddy bakers. Can't really get out of them."

Her face pinches. "I *told* you it was a mistake."

Here we go again.

"You're focusing on the wrong thing," she hammers.

I rub the back of my neck, fighting the itch to tell her to fuck off.

"You're just trying to make yourself look better for that uppity apprentice of yours..." she trails looking in the distance.

My blood boils.

"... But she'll be gone before you know it."

I clench my teeth. "Whatever you say, Ems." I can't deny that she's probably right about that last bit, and I'm working hard enough to forget that. I don't need her to throw this in my face. Why the fuck am I agreeing to dinner with her again? *Skye. It's for Skye.* "Hope you don't talk shit like that when Skye is around, yeah?"

Her mouth opens but no sound comes out.

"You understand me, Emma?"

"Yeah, Chris, I understand you," she says quietly.

"Then I'll see ya end of the month," I say and go pick up Skye.

Chapter Thirty-Six

Alexandra

Barbara gets to Emerald Creek early afternoon. She's fully embraced her boho side, not trying to hide it under a pencil skirt and a blazer, like she does in New York. Her long, thick hair flows in the wind, her eyes are done smoky but not too much, and on top of her long wool dress there's a large, gold and silver pendant in the shape of a moon. Multicolor feathers dangle from her ears, and dozens of colorful bracelets clink happily around her wrists. All this is wrapped in a long, brown leather coat with an intricate carving on the back and a bunch of leather laces crisscrossing the front.

Much like Grace had done with me my first day here, I take Barbara on a walk around town as soon as she gets here.

We reach the main covered bridge just as the ice cracks on the river, big blocks of ice breaking free, the water gushing under it. "So beautiful," she says, leaning on the bridge's railing as we stand mesmerized at the elements underneath us. "The force of nature. Seasons. The universe talking to us. Telling us to let it go. There's no resisting it." Barbara is smitten with Emerald Creek, and I like that.

I show her around like this is my town.

We walk on the other side of the river, back through the second bridge, after catching a glimpse of the lake still white in the distance, the roofs of the resort glistening at the edge.

"I don't understand why Rita never wanted to come back," she tells me when we're settled at Easy Monday.

I glance around nervously. The place is empty, except for Millie "making our day awesome" by fixing our drinks, and Noah, the owner of the general store, who's here with a man in a suit. They're far enough away, in deep leather-like couches, seeming to mind their own business, but you never know. That's three people who can hear us. "Shh. People can hear you."

"Okay," she whispers loudly, rolling her eyes. Then, "I wonder where that red barn is."

"What—oh. From the logo? Do you think it's from around here?" I whisper back.

She shrugs. "That's the story. Maybe not."

Yeah, maybe not. Everything about Red Barn Baking, the company, is so fake. I didn't use to see it that way. It took coming here to open my eyes. Maybe that was why Rita needed me to come here. To fix things.

I need to talk with Barbara about this, but Easy Monday is probably not the ideal place.

Thankfully, Noah and the other man stand up to leave. Noah trails behind. "Alex, nice to see you," he says, nodding at Barbara with a smile. He's handsome and soft spoken, almost to the point of being shy. All I know about him is that his family owns the general store, and he's the Chairperson of the Chamber of Commerce. "I heard you were looking for some side work. Social media and things? That true?"

My hands flutter with excitement. "Yes! Are you interested? For the store? I love your store. We could do sooo much just with the local products. The leather work gloves, the carved wood, the alpaca sweaters, the maple syrups from several farms. Oh my god and the new pottery line made by Willow's friend? And then there's your family, the historic building... I could create content for three years without ever repeating myself!"

He blushes and I realize he's very young. He always looks so put together. "Yeah, we're also talking with a glass blower, some young guy starting out. But uh, we wanted to talk to you at the Chamber. We're looking at ways for businesses to pool their efforts."

"I love it! Yes, that makes perfect sense. Something cohesive, to bring more visitors to the town."

"She's awesome," Millie says strolling up from behind the counter. "Autumn told me she got three new clients in two weeks just from the posts Alex made on her social accounts! Big jobs too. One of them is a *whole* house. A second home, owners are from Boston." Her eyes shine with excitement for Autumn.

Noah nods silently and glances at Barbara, then looks back at me. "I'm sorry to impose. Maybe we can meet later? Everyone's been talking you up. And we'd rather give the job to someone local."

Happiness lodges in my heart. Working with small businesses, living in Emerald Creek, sound like a dream life, the stuff fantasies are made of.

After he leaves, Barbara comments. "Hmm. Someone local, huh? So, you're staying?"

"That's too much for me to think about at this point." Like Christopher said, I can't focus on all the balls I have in the air right now. "First, I need to figure out what to do with Red Barn. That's all I can think of right now."

"Holler if you need anything," Millie calls out from behind the counter. "I'll be next door." Next door is 420, the weed shop Millie just opened.

"Let me settle, then," Barbara offers, rummaging through the pockets of her coat.

"On the house!" Millie says with a hand wave as she leaves.

Now we're totally alone.

"Okay. Let's get this out of the way," Barbara says. "Red Barn. What are your thoughts?"

I take a deep breath to calm down. I *have* given it some thought, but I've been needing someone to brainstorm with. This is my chance to find out if my ideas hold any weight. Any possibility. Here we go. "Down the line, and in a nutshell, each bakery would be owned and operated by a baker. These bakers will automatically become part of a co-op that owns the rest of Red Barn's assets—the mills, trucks, etc. Red Barn Baking provides training, technical support, and zero-interest loans to buy the bakeries. There would need to be some sort of mechanism to ensure that these bakers follow some quality guidelines, like buying supplies locally as much as possible."

I take a breath. Barbara hasn't interrupted me yet. That's a good sign, right? "We offload the overhead by closing the New York headquarters. Management works from home, with stipends to get set up with a home office. We organize regional training, brainstorming sessions for products that are in tune with local traditions and culture. Our strength is to be locally owned, globally supported." That's a hodgepodge of my thoughts, unorganized.

Barbara's eyes are narrowed on me. "That's a lot."

"I know. It's a total redesign of how we consider bread and food in our society."

"And where do you fit? What do you see yourself doing at Red Barn once the transformation is complete?"

I've already given this a lot of thought, and what Noah said earlier confirmed my decision. "I want out of Red Barn as soon as possible. We'll need to make that part of the plan of turning the company into a co-op. I see myself in a small town like this one, helping small businesses. That's what brings me joy."

Her eyes sparkle. "I like it."

She likes it? Like, I'm not crazy, pie in the sky?

"But that's going to take years," she adds.

Oh no. I'm not spending years working on that. "If we take years, it won't happen. This needs to be decided immediately. And implemented by the end of the year."

"The beauty of youth," she murmurs with a smile on her lips. "How are you going to do that? It sounds like a mix of franchising and co-op."

The heck if I know. "The only real problem is to find a law firm that will be okay fronting the work without seeing a dime until I take over. We'll need contracts ready to sign. I'm thinking most of the current store managers will be on board to become owners. It's just a matter of having the paperwork ready."

Barbara's bracelets jingle as she fluffs her hair. "Okay, honey. Time for a reality check. The whole part about turning Red Barn Baking into a co-op, I can still follow. It's a dream, but it can become a project. Now, asking a lawyer to start working before being paid, that's a delusion. Not gonna happen. Revise your expectations."

Wow. That's a better reaction than I expected. "Okay then. We hire them the day I take over. Can you take care of finding a firm ready to move when it's done?"

She raises an eyebrow. "Let's say, I can start sending out feelers."

"We'll need a consultant. I don't want one of those posh firms. I need someone who has personal experience, and vision. And the charisma to carry this out."

"Someone like Christopher."

Someone *exactly* like him. "Yes, except not him. We've been over that already." Christopher would be perfect for the task. If only he weren't so stubborn about his hatred for Red Barn. Unfortunately, that means I can't tell him anything before I pass the exam. And once I do?

Just the thought of it twists my stomach.

Barbara takes my hand across the table. "Honey. Don't do this."

"Do what?"

"Exactly what Rita did. Sacrificing yourself for Red Barn. It's not worth it."

"I'm not sacrificing myself for Red Barn. I'm doing it—and it's not a sacrifice—for the people who have been wronged by Red Barn Baking. I'm giving them their livelihood back."

"It's a sacrifice. They're grown-ups. They can look after themselves. You're all Knight in Shining Armor on a Mission. Why are you doing this to yourself?"

"Because ... because... I have no choice!" Can't she see that? "I can continue running Red Barn Baking the way it's always been, or I can do some good in the world."

"Doesn't matter. You shouldn't be lying to Christopher about this," she says. "He means something to you."

He does, unfortunately. I'm getting very, very attached. And I'll deal with it. But that doesn't mean I need to cut this short now. And because he'll kick me out of his life the minute he knows who I really am, yeah, I can totally keep that part of my life to myself. "That's exactly why I can't tell him, Barb. So I can protect what we have now.

Once I do, it'll be lost. And I'm not really lying to him. I'm just not telling him everything."

"If he cares about you, that won't matter to him."

"You may be right. But it's too risky." What if I'm wrong about him? What if he judges me and lets me go? Everything would be ruined.

She doesn't like it. She ums and groans and shifts in her chair.

"He's better off not knowing for now. I mean, we have this arrangement, it suits him. Why ruin it?"

"But does it suit *you*?" she presses.

"Of course!" I don't have a choice, do I? I throw her a bone. "The sex is great."

Her eyebrows shoot up. "I can tell. You look fabulous."

And on that note, we go to the resort, where she's decided to stay. "It's off the beaten path," she declares when I ask her why she didn't stay in town. "I need to reconnect with nature."

Good thing that's her plan, because the resort is in dire need of TLC. But it's a sprawling property on the lake, with a view of the village in the background. If she's planning on spending time outdoors, this is the place to be.

"I wish you'd taken the board's offer. I bet you still could," she says out of the blue, while we're walking outside once she's all checked in.

I stop in my tracks. Has she not been listening? I've finally been offered a chance to make a contribution to society. To make a difference for my family business. Why would I let that go? I've come this far, I'm not crawling back to Robert Norwood with my hand stretched out. No way. "Barbara," I say softly, "this is my destiny. We rarely get to choose what we're given. But we can choose what we do with it. I've been given the opportunity to so some good in the world, and I'm taking it."

Later that evening, we meet at Lazy's for dinner. She'd suggested something fancier, but I said, "First dinner in Emerald Creek needs to be at Lazy's. That's a rule."

And so we're seated at a booth in the back when I ask, "Tell me about this guy Jerry." I'm tired of talking about me. I need some gossip on Barbara.

"I met Jerry a few months ago, when your grandmother was diagnosed. She asked me to find him."

"Find him? Is he an oncologist?"

"He's... your mom's father."

Jerry is my mom's father? Rita asked Barbara to find him when she was on her deathbed? So my mom's father—my grandfather—is no longer some shadow figure from the past? As in, I could meet him? I'm elated.

Wait. Jerry, Barbara's *lover,* is *my mom's father*? I'm horrified. "Are you saying you're shagging my grandfather?"

"Do people still use that word?" Barbara frowns.

"It's gross!"

"Not a fan of that word either. It makes it sound like less than what it is." Her eyes turn dreamy.

And then it hits me, and I'm deliriously happy. For myself. For Barbara too, but for myself first, selfishly. I squeal, then giggle nervously. "When can I meet him? Where is he? Why didn't you bring him here?"

"He's uh... He's taking his time."

I can barely contain my shriek. "Taking his time? He's like, fifty years taking his time." That doesn't make sense at all. "How long have you been together? Like, did they split up because of you?" Oh my god that's totally it. He loved both women and couldn't make a choice. "Are you his *other woman*?" Horror again.

"Boy! You've got quite an imagination. I met Jerry when your grandmother was diagnosed. I told you. She asked me to find him for her."

Right. She did say that. I forgot already. Ohmygod my world is swirling. Does she not see how wonderful this is? I'm bound to lose track of the details. Still, I can't pass on the opportunity of a jab at Rita. "Sounds like her. Asking you to do her dirty work."

Barbara waves the concern away in a jingle of bracelets. "Honey, she was terminally ill. It put things in perspective for her. Also, it kind of drained her energy."

"So did they meet? How was it?"

"They met, oh, a couple of months before she died. He came to New York. It was awkward and sad. They were two very different people."

"And he didn't think to meet me? When he was in New York?"

"He did. He carries a lot of guilt too. I'm helping him through it."

He was not my dad, he was my grandfather, and I never missed or imagined him materializing at our front door like I used to with my father. Jerry had never been a concern for me, except when Mom met him, and she was real happy. I thought I would get that happy, too, someday, meeting my own dad.

"He met Mom once—that I know of," I say, remembering those weeks before she died.

Barbara nods slowly. "He's dealing with this too. Letting Rita get away with taking their child. Not doing the right thing."

If Barbara is with him, he has to be a good guy. I need to give him the benefit of the doubt. "What ever happened between them?"

"They were very young. The pregnancy was unplanned, of course. And his parents didn't approve. The town turned against her. She was a nobody, and they blamed her for getting pregnant. His family came from money, hers didn't. They put pressure on him to let her go, gave her some money in exchange for leaving. She took the money and never looked back.

"I met her shortly after, when she was in Brooklyn, baking from her kitchen, selling to local stores. He didn't try to reach out, not at first. And when he did, she pushed him away. Got a restraining order on him, although according to him, he hasn't done anything wrong. But by that time, the roles were reversed. Now Rita was a respected member of the Greater New York business community, while in New York, Jerry was a hick from Vermont. She struck back, and it stung. She never forgave him."

"Until she was on her deathbed."

"You know, I don't think her reaching out to him was about forgiveness. It was more about taking care of loose ends."

Not surprised. Rita was not into forgiving. She'd need to have a minimum of empathy for that. I can bear testament to the fact that she had none. "What loose ends?"

Barbara sighs. "That's not a good choice of words, but... yeah. They discussed you. Rita wanted you to have him in your life."

"That makes no sense at all. She hated men. She hated *him*."

"Maybe that actually was her way of forgiving, in the end? Of fixing things? She knew she'd screwed up with you, not being able to build a connection with you. She knew you wanted a family. She was trying to give you that."

"Why didn't she tell me?" The words are so hard to come out, it's barely a whisper. The injustice of being deprived of my family is making me want to scream, yet the only sound that comes out is thin as air. I can't breathe.

"Why do we even ask 'why' when it comes to Rita?" Barbara says, and it's true.

I shake the frustration away. "You're totally screwing my grandfather. That's the most horrific and wonderful news I've had in a long, long time. And you kept it from me!" I give her forearm a gentle slap.

And that's when I smell his manly scent before I hear him, and my body does its normal thing in his presence. Limbs mush, middle ablaze. My mind, though, freezes. Did he hear what I just said?

"I'm Christopher Wright," he says as he extends his hand to Barbara. "Does that mean I can call you Grandma?" He totally heard what I said. His grin does nothing to soothe the panic I feel rising. I do not want to talk about my grandfather, because I do not want to talk about my grandmother with Christopher. Not yet. I spot Skye in the back, petting Moose. At least she didn't hear that.

"Does that mean you're marrying my Lexie?" Barbara answers without missing a beat.

Ohmygod what is going on right now?

"What are you doing?" I ask both of them, hissing. "Is this a prank? Do you *know* each other?"

Christopher winks at me. "Relax, pancakes, we're just pulling your leg."

"Yeah," Barbara cackles. "No way he's calling me Grandma."

"You don't look like a grandma." This is coming from Justin, who brings a cheese and charcuterie board large enough to cover half the table, and plops himself next to Barbara. "This guy doesn't know how to talk to ladies," he adds, pointing to Christopher. "And that's why—"

"Alright, that's enough," Christopher cuts in.

"Testy," Justin says, wiggling his eyebrows at Barbara.

"You think?" she says, giggling.

And just like that, she's part of the group.

Chapter Thirty-Seven

Christopher

I had a little time alone with Barbara, before she had to go back to New York. I gave her some breads to take home. Mostly, I wanted to thank her for visiting. There was no way Alexandra wasn't missing Barbara, even if she's acting all tough around me.

"What you need to understand about Lexie...." Barbara said. "She's bottled so much in. When her mom died, her grandmother was pissed about having to take her in. Can you imagine what that does to a kid? I stuck around just for Lexie, to tell you the truth. At that point I was done with Rita. There's so much a friend is going to do, you know? And do you know what she told my Lexie once, when she saw her crying? "No wonder your father left when you were a baby. Bet he couldn't stand the crying."

My blood boiled in my veins, and I didn't know what to say.

I could tell it was the same for Barbara. "She was ten years old! Can you imagine? She wasn't even allowed to mourn her mom, and on top of it, she's blamed for her father leaving. All in one little sentence. Rita... what a bitch."

My heart broke thinking about what Alexandra went through when she was barely older than Skye. I clenched my jaw. "But you stuck around..."

"I stuck around, as much as I could. For Lexie. That girl is a treasure. Believe me. All humans have a fear of abandonment," Barbara continued. "But Lexie lived it several times in her life, to the point where she's internalized it as something that is bound to happen to her." She paused and looked me straight in the eye, and although she didn't give me the *Don't you hurt her* speech, she might as well have. "Her father left when she was a baby. Her mother died. And her grandmother, her only family, never loved her. Lexie is always preparing for the next letdown." Barbara shook her head. "I'm overstepping. I shouldn't have said that. What do I know? You seem to make her happy," she added with a small smile. "Just thought I'd give you a little context on why she can appear closed off sometimes."

"Appreciate that." I hope Alexandra will open up to me. Tell me more of these things about herself. Make it less heavy for her to carry.

The days after Barbara leaves, Alexandra seems preoccupied, but it's nothing she feels the need to talk about. I think back to what Barbara said, but I don't push her. Instead, I try to read her. I'm sure finding out she's going to meet her grandfather soon has to be a little nerve-racking. Not to mention that he's with Barbara. That's a plus, but I bet it's awkward.

Speaking of awkward, the dinner at Emma's is tonight, and man I'd like to find a valid excuse to get out of it. But I can't. She's my CPA. If not a friend, a solid acquaintance. Our daughters are BFFs. And this is a small town.

There are certain things you can't get out of.

Let's get this over and done with. I'm showered and changed, Skye is already over there on a play date after school. I just need to drag my ass there and come back asap.

"You look good," Alexandra says as she looks up from her book. A sad smile plays on her face while her gaze sweeps me top to bottom and back up.

"Hey," I say as I approach her. She's stretched on the couch, her long legs propped up. I'm late already, but I don't want to leave. Why did I commit to that stupid dinner, when I could be having a night in with Alexandra? I scooch her legs over and plop on the couch, my torso turned to her front, my hands naturally falling to the sides of her face, down to her neck. "Are you sure you're okay with this?"

She bites her bottom lip and does the tiny little hiccupy breath that nearly kills me. "Of course," she says.

She's definitely not okay. "You can come with," I say. "I'm sure Emma would love to have you."

We both know it's a lie. Even if Emma has remained strictly friendly with me, and been friendlier to Alexandra the couple times she's been here to do the books, we both know Emma would have invited Alexandra if she'd wanted her there.

"I'm sure she would," Alexandra plays along, "but that would make us a couple, right? I mean, assuming that an invite to you extends to me."

"Right."

"Which we agreed, we're not. Right? We're not a couple."

My hand finds its way under her sweatshirt, up to her breast.

She hisses, "Chriiiiiiis." Her nipple hardens under my fingers, and her hips buck up.

I tug the lace of her bra to the side. She's so soft, her pearly nub hard just for me. I pull her sweatshirt up and lower my mouth.

"Right?" she repeats, killing my half boner.

Not a couple. Right.

Not right.

"About that," I say, placing the bra back over her breast and pulling her sweatshirt back down. "What is Red Barn's policy about working from home?"

She frowns, like she doesn't understand my question.

"Mmm?" I insist.

Her eyes bore through me like she's somewhere else. "I don't know," she says.

"Why don't you find out." I dip my head back down, to her face this time, grazing my lips against hers. "Sick and tired of this shit, beautiful. You're totally under my skin, and in a good way, and I want to take this further. You and me."

"Chris... what if it doesn't work out? You and me. What about Skye?"

Well, first things first, I need to know if she wants this. If she wants more with me.

Or if I'm just the distraction.

"Let's talk about it another time," I say.

She nods almost imperceptibly. "You need to go."

I trail my hands down her sides and cup her hips, giving them a squeeze. *I can't wait to have you again.* "I shouldn't be back too late."

She shrugs. "Don't worry about me. Grace texted me to hang out. I might take her up on that." She dives back into her book.

I want to worry about her. "Good." I stand up, relieved that Alexandra won't be alone tonight. Feeling less guilty. "Alright, lemme get this out of the way," I groan, talking about my evening with Emma.

"Have fun," she says without looking up.

I lean over to kiss her temple, and almost say *love you* as I do, the words coming to my mouth naturally, she's so ingrained into my life.

When I get to Emma's, there are candles on the side tables in the living room. She takes my coat and sways her hips when she goes to hang it up. She's wearing a short, tight skirt and a blouse that shows her bra pattern, especially when she leans over to pour me a drink and pass the nuts.

I'm annoyed already.

Skye and Caroline provide me with a much-needed relief from small talk when they come down to show us their costumes and perform a little play they improvise. Then, we move to the dining room.

The table is set for four with flowers, a fancy tablecloth and napkins, and stem glasses for the adults. She went all out. Or is she always like this?

Emma's conversation is lively and probably fun if you're into whatever shit Emma does. She's a great mother. I can tell by the way she looks at her daughter and engages in conversation about her friends, the school, and her ballet. After a while, I have to admit she's more interesting than I ever gave her credit for.

After a couple of glasses of wine, I relax and start to actually enjoy the evening. Except she's placed me so that I have a view through the kitchen door of her ass every time she leans over to check the roast in the oven, and her cheeks flush slightly when I talk to her, and she bites her bottom lip when she smiles.

And this evening is turning into the trap I thought for sure it wasn't going to be.

My mind wanders to Alexandra all the fucking time.

"When is Alexandra leaving again?" Emma asks when Skye mentions her for the millionth time.

There's no way she doesn't know that. She's put her contract under a microscope, trying to get me out of it without losing the grant.

She failed.

Before I have a chance to answer her first question, she fires a second one. "Did she finally find a place to live? I heard the bed and breakfast was offering long-term rentals on their rooms with kitchenettes."

Skye smacks her lips. "She lives with us. I *love* her. She lets me braid her hair." She whispers something in Caroline's ear, and the two girls giggle.

Emma cocks an eyebrow. "She's still living with you?" Her voice is strained. "Why, you should have brought her along." She stiffly taps the corner of her mouth with her embroidered napkin.

"She's pretty independent," I say. "Does her own thing."

"Normally, she has dinner with us every night," Skye chimes in, not realizing she's contradicting me, "but tonight, she's going out with friends because Daddy has plans."

She's going out with friends? Why do I not know this? She said she was hanging out with Grace.

"That's nice," Emma says.

Skye nods. "She says she loves it here, and her heart will break when she has to leave."

"When is she leaving again?" Emma repeats.

"Who is she going out with?" I ask Skye at the same time.

"She is leaving at the beginning of summer," Skye says with a sigh. "But she said I could visit her in New York."

I mentally count down the time I have left with Alexandra, and my heart tightens a bit. That's why I wanted her in the beginning, I tell myself. Because she wasn't going to stay. Wasn't going to have demands or disrupt the balance of my life with Skye.

Everything is different now, and I need to have that conversation with her.

When Emma stands to clear our plates, I don't make a move to help her. Instead, I pull my phone out while she has her back to me.

> Me
> **Where are you**

Alexandra might find that too demanding. I shouldn't impulse-text like a fucking teenager.

> Me
> **Skye says you're out with friends**

Better, but not quite there yet.

> Me
> **Let me know if you need a ride back**

That seems like a legit excuse to text and ask questions. That's three text messages in a row, though, so I put my phone away.

I have it on vibrate, but no message comes through. The thought of her *out with friends* is driving me crazy. Another impulse, and I send Grace a message.

> Me
> **You girls out somewhere?**

I know I have no right to ask questions or have expectations, seeing as I'm having dinner at Emma's, and she's putting on a show.

Even if I don't, and if I've been clear with my intentions regarding Emma, there's clear indications she's treating this as a date.

Maybe even a pre-nup visit. Taunting me with the goods—the gorgeous house, the impeccable food, the nice hostess manners.

I didn't think I'd ever want this, but I do.

I want this. I want this with Alexandra.

A big house full of our babies. A large backyard opening to the woods, a big tree with a swing for Skye and a hammock for Alexandra. Lots of open space. A back patio with a barbecue. A hot tub.

I would turn the upstairs of the bakery into a couple more apprentice rooms. Turn it into a school.

Or maybe Alexandra would rather stay in the village. God knows there's enough empty rooms in the upper level of the bakery. I could easily turn them into bedrooms and playrooms. We'd watch our kids through the window as they'd walk themselves to school and skate on The Green.

I can see my life like that, clearly, and I want it to happen.

Now.

Emma sends the girls upstairs to play in Caroline's room "while the *parents* clear the table and do dishes." I'm getting more uncomfortable, especially when Emma pretends to accidentally brush her body against mine or when I hand her the dishes to load the dishwasher. There's a domestic quality to this that suggests months or years of living together, and I feel like I'm cheating on Alexandra.

As if to confirm my suspicion, Emma says, "This was nice. I could get used to it. We should do it more often. Make it a habit." She's leaning against the sink suggestively, her hands clasped on the edge so that her back arches and her breasts are pushed toward me. I feel a little sorry for her.

"I wouldn't want to get the rumor mill started," I say. I wipe my hands on a rogue kitchen towel—I don't want to get closer to her by reaching for the ones she neatly hangs next to the sink. I call Skye from the bottom of the stairs. Time to go.

Emma snorts. "Says the guy who has a gorgeous, single woman sleeping under his roof for months. Actually sharing his life."

I shrug. "It's work. I didn't pick her. And she's leaving soon."

"Speaking of which," she says, crossing her arms in front of her chest. "Do you know she's helping other businesses with their social media?"

"Yeah, she's great at that. I have no problem with it." Emma is seriously getting on my nerves right now. "I actually encouraged her."

"Seriously, Chris?"

"What."

"Aren't you worried?" She turns her back to me while she hand-washes a pot.

"About what."

"About her failing her apprenticeship."

"I want what's best for my apprentices. Always. If they find out during their stay with me that baking is not their path, that's fine."

"Chris," she says, turning around, her eyes pleading. "For whatever reason, she's got you wrapped around her finger, and—"

"Emma—"

"Let me finish. As your longtime friend, and as your accountant, I can't just sit there and watch you jeopardize your business because of her. Because of anyone, or anything, for that matter."

"The fuck you talking about."

"Your grant! That's what I'm talking about. You do know that it's owed back within the year if she fails her exam, right?"

I close the kitchen door. Not that Skye would understand, but she'd get that we are arguing about Alexandra. Hell, she's so sharp she might even understand the gist of it.

"From the looks of it, she's spending more time outside on her phone than in the bakery, Chris. Does *she* know what's at stake for you?" Emma continues.

Blood thrums in my veins. She thinks she's looking out for my best interest, but she's messing with Alexandra, and I can't tolerate that.

"You stay out of this, Emma. This gets out, I know it was you. You're the only one who knows. I know why you're doing it, and I appreciate it. But you're crossing a line."

I want Alexandra to thrive doing something she loves. And I can handle the financial repercussions of losing the grant. I don't need someone to tell me how to run my business. Not even my accountant.

Emma frowns. "She should know, Chris. It's not fair to you. She's like a frigging teenager, spending more time outside on her phone than in the bakery, for chrissakes. She needs to know what's at stake for you. Hopefully she has enough decency not to let you down once she knows."

I was annoyed at first, but now I'm angry. "You only know this because I gave you access to privileged information. Confidential information. This better not get out of this room, because, Ems, no one else knows. So if Alex finds out, I'll know it was you, and I'll make sure everyone in town knows how you treat client confidentiality. Are we clear?"

She raises both her hands. "I'm only looking out for you, Chris."

"I appreciate that, but I'll say it again. You're crossing a line. Alexandra is a great girl. You'd find out if you gave her a chance. She's loyal, and hardworking. I want the best for her, and I will *not* sacrifice her well-being for my business."

I gave this some thought recently, did my calculations. If Alexandra dropped out or failed the exam, it would be tight. But I would make it. I'd take struggling financially for a few years if it meant Alexandra would be happier.

And yes, a thousand times yes, if it meant she'd stay here for good. With me.

"I wouldn't want *anyone's* well-being to be sacrificed for *any* business," I say. "Are we good?"

"Of course we're good," Emma says as she wipes the kitchen counter. "Last thing I want is for her to get between us."

I can't hold against Emma that she wants what's best for my business, but this conversation is taking us back to the awkwardness of the evening. Seems to me *she's* trying to get between Alexandra and me. But I can't tell her that.

So I end the conversation by opening the kitchen door and calling Skye again.

Skye reluctantly trails down the stairs, Caroline in tow.

"Mommy, can Skye sleep over tonight? Pretty please?" Caroline asks her, her hands clasped together.

Emma forces a sweet smile. "That's fine with me. Chris? Skye is at home here," she says, laying it on heavy.

I'm so angry at Emma right now, I almost say no out of principle. Not a mature dad reaction, but hey. We all have our limits. But my phone vibrates in my pocket, and I glance at it. Grace is confirming that *us girls* are at The Growler, and yes, Alex is there, too, and they're all having a lot of fun. I didn't ask about Alexandra, but for once, I'm not annoyed by Grace's assumption about what I'm really asking.

I'm rattled by the argument with Emma, even if I'm glad I set her straight. I don't want another argument with my daughter, one I'd have for no reason. And then, there's the fact that if Skye stays here, I could join Alexandra at the Growler. Keep an eye on her.

"Sure, bug, that's fine," I say, feeling like shit. But then, why should I? Skye wants to spend time with her friend, and if that frees me to have that *adult time* Grace keeps telling me about, where's the harm?

I'm rewarded by Skye jumping in my arms, hugging me tightly before rushing upstairs.

There's no reason for me to feel bad. I'm not a bad dad.

When the girls are out of earshot, Emma says sweetly, "Nightcap? I don't want you to leave upset at me."

I'm in a fucking hurry to get out of here now. "I'm not upset at you, Emma. I know you meant well." And that's the truth. "But I should get home. Early start tomorrow." And that's *not* the truth of why I'm leaving.

She sashays toward me, one hand on her hip. "Come on, Chris, you're not gonna stay a bachelor all your life, now, are you?"

I'm embarrassed for her. "Not gonna happen, Ems. We already went over that." I grab my coat from the rack next to the kitchen door. "Thanks for dinner. This was really nice."

"Anytime," she says, her lips drawn in a tight line.

As I reach the door, she pecks my cheek.

Once in the truck, I rub my cheek, suddenly worried about lipstick.

Chapter Thirty-Eight

Alexandra

After Christopher leaves, I stand from the couch. It's still warm, from where he was sitting just now, and his scent lingers.

I can't take it.

He looked *so good* tonight. He was wearing a white shirt, open collar, dress pants, sleek leather belt.

He shaved.

I like him better with a three-day stubble, but that's not the point. He made an effort tonight. He got all dressed up to go to Emma's. Like he was going on a date.

And that frigging hurts.

So I shake the funk, heat up a bowl of soup in the microwave. Then I sit at the cold table in the empty kitchen and eat while I finish memorizing the last chapter of my textbook.

As I'm closing the book, my phone rings. *Sarah*. Yay!

I pick up, shove my earbuds in, clean my bowl and tidy the kitchen while I talk to her.

"Watcha doin'?" Sarah asks.

"Getting ready to go out to the Growler."

"Sounds fun. What are you wearing?"

"Not dressed yet," I say as I get to my room. I strip down to my undies and start curling my hair. "I was thinking jeans, cowboy boots, and my clingy dark green top. What do you think?"

"Sounds sexy. More importantly, what does Chris think?"

My heart sinks. "He's not coming. I'm going with Grace and some other women," I say as I check the back of my hair in the mirror, then move the curler to the front.

"Oh. Girls Night Out? He's on babysitting duty?"

My stomach sinks again. "He's having dinner at someone's. Skye's friend's mom."

"Oh?... Oh." She pauses for a beat, and I can almost hear the wheels turning in her head. "We're cool with that? Did you ever tell me about her?"

"Yeah, Emma. The CPA who makes him homemade yogurt and has her mug and frother and other stuff at his house?"

"Oh." Sarah's silence is telling. "Well, at least it's not her toothbrush."

I take a deep breath. "I guess..." I unplug the curler, plop my hair, and spray it a little. It looks awesome, all curly and stuff. Too bad Christopher won't be there to see it. He usually sees me with my hair pulled back, or worse, in a hair net.

I bet Emma is all dolled up for him.

I dig into my makeup pouch and start on the foundation.

"It looks like I caught you at the right time. Talk to me."

"I know it's not a date, but I'm not stupid. Christopher is maybe the only person who doesn't see how Emma would be a perfect life partner for him. A perfect wife. She's hot, a great mom, a single parent like him, she has a good relationship with her ex, meaning she's levelheaded and has her shit together, emotionally. Something still debatable as far as I'm concerned, if I'm being honest."

"Wow-wow Alex, back up a little. What the hell?"

"She's perfect for him. She runs her own business like a pro. She's a CPA, for crying out loud! She makes her own yogurt."

"So what?"

"So? I don't know anything about taxes, and running a small business, and she does. She does his books, she looks over his contracts, and she brings him fresh eggs from chickens she raises herself. She's like, this perfect small-town wonder-woman."

"And?"

"And I don't even know what hole the egg comes out of!"

"What hole?" Sarah laughs.

"Yeah. The eggs were covered in shit. Do they come from the butthole? Or from the chicken's vagina?"

"Ohmygod, Alex you're too much," she laughs hysterically, then calms down. "And that's important because?"

"It's important because it's a reminder for me why I'm not Christopher's person and cannot be anyone's person."

"Riiiight," she says sarcastically. "Because you don't know if the egg comes from the butthole or not. That's critical to him. Makes perfect sense why you wouldn't be the one for him."

I take a deep breath. Not just because there's no way I can explain this to Sarah, but also because I'm about to apply eye liner, and I need a steady hand.

I do my eyes extra smoky, and for some reason I always have to pull my face down when I do that, so my voice comes out funny when I say, "Point is, we're not a couple. We agreed on that."

"Really. You agreed on that."

"Yeah, really." I don't need her to break down the barriers I put up. She doesn't understand how hard it is for me, to see everything within reach, yet unattainable. I need these mental stops. These reminders that this is temporary. That my real life is something else and that with Christopher, I'm just making it easier while I'm here.

He wouldn't want me for anything more than what we have. Otherwise, why would he go to dinner at Emma's all dressed up like he was? "We said, if I tagged along tonight, we'd look like a couple, so we're not doin' that."

I close the eyeliner thingy, stick it in my pouch, and pull out the mascara.

That I can do with my face straight, for some reason. "I had a good conversation with Barbara," I tell Sarah and update her on our plans for Red Barn Baking. "Even if it's a long shot, I'm excited to be working on making it a better place. Righting some wrongs, you know?"

"I get you, honey, and I'm glad it's working out for you. Just don't give up on yourself, okay?"

"Sarah. This is me not giving up on myself." I think. "It helps me to focus on something where I can really make an impact. Something I have a right to." I apply the last touch of mascara. My makeup is on point, with the focus on my eyes. I'll finish it with a nude lipstick once I'm dressed. I don't want to look like I'm trying to pick someone up.

"You have a right to the happy ever after too, Alex. You're just refusing to see it."

"Not in that way. Not for me," I mumble.

She sighs, exasperated. "Two things. You're wrong about that. And I love you."

"Love you too."

We hang up, and I put on the skinny jeans, cowboy boots, and clingy green top that makes my boobs look awesome without showing too much cleavage. I add gold dangle earrings, an emerald pendant, a stack of rings, and a spritz of perfume, and am ready right when Grace texts me from her car that she's out front.

I look at myself in the mirror.

I look hot.

At least there's that.

"How's the hottest bachelor in Emerald Creek doing?" a girl with long red hair croons my way.

She's a friend of Autumn's, and we bumped into Autumn and Kiara the minute we got to The Growler.

"That would be Chris," Autumn volunteers.

I feel myself blushing. "Um... good. Great, I guess."

"Great?" the red head gushes. "Tell us everything."

I'm pretty sure I'm scarlet by now. Kiara is watching with sadistic fun. Grace comes to my rescue. "Guys, seriously. Leave her alone."

"I want to know if you broke his armor," the girl insists. She's two drinks ahead of us.

What is she even talking about? "Broke what?"

The girl sighs. "He swore off women after Skye's mother—"

"She's not Skye's mother," Grace cuts in.

"Birth mother," Autumn corrects.

Grace shakes her head.

"That's beside the point," the girl says. "What we want to know is, are you breaking him? Autumn says he commissioned a whole bedroom makeover for you. I don't wanna sound crude, but that's kind of... So, did ya? Break him."

Autumn giggles.

Kiara still has her sadistic grin on.

"What?" I'm totally confused.

The girl sighs. "Like I said, he swore off women after... whatever. Bottom line, she ruined him for the rest of us. He needs fixing. Breaking in."

"He's just protecting Skye," Grace cuts in.

The girl ignores Grace. "We were thinking—hoping—that you would break the spell. Make him see that women aren't all bad."

"We?"

"Us girls. We talk. You're perfect for him, by the way—" she says, looking me over from top to bottom.

My heart flutters.

"—because you'll be leaving."

"Oh," I say stupidly.

"No risk of attachment," she explains. "He'll be more inclined to, you know, test the waters again."

I force a chuckle. "Oh. You're funny."

"I'm serious," the red head says.

Kiara hands me my first drink of the evening, an amber liquid on the rocks. "Bambi," she says quietly, "put your big girl pants on. Drink."

The liquid burns my mouth, hits my upset stomach, and gives me an internal pat. My eyes narrow on Kiara. "What's my new best friends' name?" I ask her.

The redhead opens her mouth, but Kiara interrupts her. "Whistle Pig," she tells me, then turns to the girl. "She means the whiskey, honey."

"Come on, guys," Grace says once we all have a drink in hand. "Let's have fun."

As we elbow our way through the dense crowd, I try to shake away the uneasy feeling taking root in my stomach from what the girl said.

It's not too long until a group of guys who know the redhead from her work introduce themselves. I promptly forget their names, but most of them are eye candy, so I mingle in the conversation.

Little things, right?

I realize I miss going out with a man. Tagging along with a group of friends on a Friday night while having someone's arm to latch onto, someone's hand on the small of your back as you enter a crowded space. Someone whose body language tells everyone, *She's mine, and she's the one I'm taking home tonight.* Am I shallow? Maybe. Shallow feels good to me, especially tonight. Shallow keeps me going.

Shallow is where I won't drown.

There's a guy in the group who's making eye contact with me. A lot. He's very tall, taller than Christopher, with ash blond hair, clear blue eyes, and a strong jaw.

He looks like a Viking. And the Viking seems set on me. He remembers my name and leans over to ask me questions like he really cares. After maybe fifteen minutes, I know enough about him.

I do let the Viking slide his hand on the small of my back as he hands me a refill on my drink, though. No harm in that, I think.

Then the girls decide to go play pool, and I move away from him.

He and his friends follow us, and I wish I hadn't accepted his drink. Hadn't let his hand stay on the small of my back like he owned me. A drink doesn't buy you someone.

Men only bring misery.

They also bring massive headaches, I realize as I take my turn at the pool table, and he uses the excuse to wrap his body around me, his hands over mine on the cue. I try to push him back before taking my shot, but only succeed at rubbing myself against his erection.

I elbow him. "Stop it," I say.

Instead, he wraps himself tighter around me.

"I said stop," I repeat, louder.

The energy in the room shifts, and I hear Christopher's voice right behind me. "She said stop."

I freeze, and the Viking digs his fingers in my waist, making me wince.

"Hey, man, get your hands off me. Mind your business," the Viking says, still at my back.

"She *is* my business," Christopher says, making my heart rattle.

The guy releases his grip on me. "You never said you had a boyfriend."

"I—I don't have a—" I begin to protest.

The Viking doesn't have time to process what's going on. Christopher shoves him so powerfully away from me, he crashes against the wall.

Christopher hooks his arm around my waist and flattens it on my belly. "You do now," he grunts. He keeps an eye on the guy picking himself up and moving away from the wall but glances at me. His grip on me releases slightly, giving me the option to uncouple myself from him. There's a question in his eyes, and he's waiting for an answer. I grab his loosening hand and tighten it around me.

In the background, Autumn and the redhead's eyes are glued to us with their mouths hanging, slow smiles building. The redhead gives me a thumbs up and tilts her beer bottle my way, while Autumn mouths, "So hot," and fans herself. I'm not sure where Grace and Kiara are, and I don't have time to find out.

The Viking comes charging at Christopher, who tucks me to the side and dodges him, then grabs my wrist and pulls me out a back door. The door slams behind us, only to reopen a moment later, with the Viking silhouetted against the light and the music spilling into the parking lot.

Christopher pushes me behind him. "Get in the car," he says, and although the guy has his fists balled up, Christopher takes the time to take his key fob out his pocket, unlock the door, and pocket his key as the guy lunges at him. He swerves, and the guy misses, losing his balance and stumbling past Christopher. Christopher grabs the guy's collar and pulls him back toward him, then swiftly head butts him.

One hit. The guy teeters then falls straight back on the asphalt.

Christopher grabs the guy's feet and drags him next to the back door. Sits him against the wall. The guy's head lolls down. Christopher pulls the guy's pants down to his ankles then ties the legs around the guy's neck. Hands on his hips, he tilts his head, seemingly satisfied.

But as he walks back to me, his gaze switches from mild amusement to an intense fire.

I slide into the passenger seat.

Chapter Thirty-Nine

Alexandra

The whole ride back, we don't talk. Almost.

"How was your dinner?" is all I ask.

He clenches his jaw, but that's all I get. Not even a sideward glance, not a single grunt. He called me his girlfriend, and then he dragged me out. Why isn't he talking to me? Is he angry? And for what?

The minute we park, he jumps out of the truck and opens my door before I can unfasten my seatbelt. He makes brief eye contact that zings through my core, then takes my hand and holds it all the way inside the bakery, and up the stairs. Not angry.

Just firm.

Possessive.

Okay, then.

As he drags me past the second floor, he takes his phone out. "Hey," he says. Going by the background noise, he's calling Grace, and they're still at The Growler. "She's home safe… You guys shouldn't hang out there alone." Grace's voice comes through the phone for a few beats, then he says, "She's not my girlfriend. Tell your friends not to spread rumors. I was just getting her out of a situation."

My heart dips at his words, but what was I expecting? And what do I want? *Not to be his girlfriend.*

I should be relieved.

But I'm crushed instead. *Stupid.*

"Close the door," he tells me as we get to my room. He turns a side lamp on. "And take that shit off."

Shit? What shit?

His eyes rake over my body.

Is he seriously calling my clingy green top, my favorite jeans, and my cowboy boots *shit*? I cross my arms, jut one boot-clad leg out to one side, and tilt my opposite hip to the other side. "What's wrong with my outfit? That *shit*'s cute as hell," I tell him with attitude.

He has the nerve—the nerve—to answer, "You didn't wear it with me in mind."

Oh yeah? Um, first, I *was* thinking about him when I was getting ready. And I know that's not what he means but seriously? *Seriously?* I stomp to him. Grab his crisp white shirt and pull him to me. "And did you have *me* in mind when you dressed like Emerald Creek's Most Eligible Bachelor to go to that dinner?"

He flinches. "Then take it off me," he says softly.

My stomach clenches painfully. He doesn't even try to deny it. He dressed for *her*. Jealous rage zings through me. Placing both my hands on him, I rip his shirt open, my nails grazing his chest. Buttons fly around the bedroom. I expect him to protest, but all I see in his eyes is desire.

He shucks his shirt off to the floor while I tug at his belt. Suddenly we're undressing each other hard and furious. I kick my boots off, he pulls my jeans away, and while he grabs a condom, I take off my top and bra.

With his pants mid-thigh, he hoists me onto his hips, pushes us against the wall for purchase, and rips my thin, lacy thong off.

Then he fucks me hard. One thrust and he's inside me. I pull at his hair, bring his head down to my neck, arch my back at his relentless pumping. His fingers dig deep in my ass as he pumps into me. "Babe... Oh fuck... Babe," he says.

He lifts his face to mine, his breath short and hot on my face, and our mouths find each other in a hard kiss, teeth clashing, tongues demanding. He presses his body hard into me and the back of my head hits the wall. I wrap my arms tighter around his neck, fisting his hair. My orgasm is close, my thighs tightening around his hips as I ride him.

"Fuck me harder... harder," I beg. He lifts deeper into me, one hand at my waist, the other under my ass, pistoning me.

"Alexandra, babe. Can't ever get enough of you," he says, and I come at his words, a deep, possessive orgasm where I look him in the eye and still can't get enough of him either.

"I want you to come," I say. "Please." We're both covered in sweat, his hair is matted, and he's carrying all my weight, but still I want him to go the extra mile and fuck me against this wall. All. The. Way.

I want him to lose himself inside me.

He groans, his hips buck, and he grinds in and out of me at a faster rhythm, reawakening my own desire already. Then his cock throbs inside me, he stills, holds me tight against him, and comes on a low growl, his whole body consumed by a shiver, his arms tightening around me. He pumps some more, riding his own, long orgasm. By the time he comes down from it, my limbs are listless.

He steps out of his pants, and I barely have the strength to hold onto him as he carries me to bed, walking over our clothes strewn on the bedroom floor.

He sets us in bed, him partially seated against the headboard, me cradled in his arms, my knees on each side of his torso, the side of my face against his chest. For a while, he just strokes my hair gently, tipping his face to mine when I lift up to look at him, his nose grazing mine, his lips tracing the contour of my mouth, of my earlobe. Then his eyes darken. "I get that you didn't like me going to Emma's. I just wished you'd have told me. Spare me the trouble."

"Trouble? What trouble?" I whisper. "Oh yeah, the Viking?"

He jerks his head up. "The wh—?" Then he drops his head back as understanding hits him. His lips curl up. "Nah, that was actually fun. Hadn't done that in a while."

He sets himself comfortably, adjusting my head on his chest, his hand in my hair. "You hated that, didn't you," he says.

"Um... no. It was hot."

"Me being at her place," he corrects me.

I still, my stomach clenching. Of course I hated him being there. *Playing house*. What does he think?

"It was a friendly visit. There's nothing more to it. The kids were there."

My heart squeezes.

"What?" he asks.

"It's almost worse," I whisper, picturing the perfect family gathered around the table for a nice dinner. The image of domestic bliss.

His arm squeezes around me, like he understands what I'm saying, but I know he can't possibly scrape the surface of my pain right now. So I take a deep breath. The falling apart can wait.

"Hey," he says, in the low tone that makes me melt. "I'm sorry this hurt you. I wish you would've told me, but I should've known. Shoulda read you better."

"It's okay," I whisper.

"No, it's not." He pulls me closer into him, and I move my legs to rearrange myself so I'm straddling him, my knees at his hips, and lower my upper body flat onto his.

I listen to his heartbeat.

One hand comes back to my head. The other one lands on my back, and he strokes me.

God. It feels so, *so* good.

His low voice resonates inside me when he starts talking. "When Skye's mother found out she was pregnant, she didn't tell me right away. I heard it from Kiara. She was planning on giving the baby up for adoption without telling me. She didn't think I'd step up, I guess." He takes a deep breath. "I went to see her—she lived outside Boston. We met at a fast-food restaurant. I asked her how she was feeling, morning sickness and shit like that. The conversation was going well, I thought. Until I told her I'd marry her, take care of her and the kid. She didn't have to worry about anything. I'd sort it out."

He takes a break, and his heartbeat gets louder. Not a good memory.

"She laughed in my face," he continues. "Literally laughed." Another pause. "I didn't think it was funny. At all. But then she stopped and asked me if I was serious. And I said, yeah. She looked at me like I was something the cat dragged in. *Not in a million years,* she said."

God that's awful. I wrap my limbs tighter around him, stroking his shoulder.

"It's okay, beautiful. Long time ago," he says and kisses my hair again. "I didn't really understand where she was, socially. So out of my league, not even funny. I insisted, made a stink, went to see her father. That's when I understood why she couldn't imagine being married to me. She came from serious money. Not just big fat bank accounts. The kind of money that gives you power.

"The guy—her father—was decent. He wasn't going to make his daughter marry me, and I was done with that plan anyway. But he saw my point about wanting the kid, and what difference was it to them anyway? His daughter sure as hell didn't want to keep it. He was a businessman, used to planning for potential trouble. He saw I could be that to them. So he put his lawyers on it, we had court appearances and shit, and a few weeks after Skye was born, her mother was out of our lives for good. Never heard from her again.

"First I thought that was a good thing. Then I saw that maybe it wasn't so great, for Skye. She had no mother, and the other kids around did. So I got her into therapy—that was Grace's idea—and I made sure she had solid female presences around her.

"And that's how Grace takes her to school every morning, and she spends more time at Emma's than I would really care for her to, if I'm being honest. But I think it's good for her to be around a mom, and she asks for it."

I don't interrupt him to say that what *I* believe, is that Skye wants to be around Caroline. But maybe I'm biased. For sure, I'm biased. Emma is stuck up, and Skye is unconventional and fun. Just my two cents here, that I'm keeping to myself.

"So that's why, when Emma insisted on having me for dinner, I couldn't really say no."

"You're a great dad," I say. "Skye's lucky to have you."

He lifts my chin so he can look at me. "I want you to feel lucky to have me too, Alexandra. I never want to hurt you again the way I did tonight."

I shake my head. "It's okay."

"I know I did. I saw it in your eyes when I left. I should have known better. I'm sorry." He lifts his head to capture my mouth in a slow, tender kiss. "What do you want from me, Alexandra?"

I hold his face in my hands, raking through his hair, and my body comes alive atop his. My hips writhe on their own, my middle finds his erection.

What I want from him is too big, too scary for me to even consider.

"Mm?" he insists.

"I want you to want me," I answer against his lips, then dip my tongue into his mouth.

But he flips me on my back, breaking our kiss, and holds my head between his hands. "Fuck, Alexandra, what does this look like to you?" His eyes search mine. "You're the best thing that's happened to me since Skye, beautiful. I don't want to fuck it up." He dives for my neck and inhales me, then kisses me from my neck to my collarbone, then dips to my breasts, bringing me to the edge already. I dig my nails in his shoulders and nip on his earlobes. He hisses my name, grabs a condom, and places himself at my entrance. His locks of dark hair fall around his face, his eyes are the deepest color they've ever been.

"Lemme be clear, Alexandra," he growls. "You're mine, and I'm yours."

His words alone could send me over the edge. As he pushes inside me, I wrap my legs around his waist, pulling him deeper, meeting him thrust for thrust. Our foreheads connect. We smell of fresh sweat and sex, and the only sounds are his grunts, my moans, and my insides sucking his cock in.

We don't last long.

He lets me ride my orgasm first, sucking on my nipple, flicking my clit, and swear to god, it turns into a three-in-one orgasm, three waves one after the other as I come first from his nipple action, then from his expert finger on my clit, and finally, finally, a deep inside orgasm that seizes me head to toe, where I hear myself scream.

Then, only then, he comes, and his powerful body thrusting into mine, falling apart in mine, is the most beautiful thing.

Then he flips on his back, cradles me into him, and strokes my hair until I fall asleep.

I wake up at an ungodly hour when he lifts me off him to get up. I hear his shower.

He spent the whole night with me.

I hop in the shower then follow him to the bakehouse, fix him his coffee, and curl on the couch in the den so I'm closer to him while he practices for the competition.

For the next several weeks, this is how we are. When Skye is home, he tries to crawl back into his own bed. Sometimes he forgets. Or he simply just doesn't want to leave. I'll never know.

Chapter Forty

Christopher

It's Game Night, which means Alexandra is with Grace and the girls, and Skye and me are having an early night at Justin's. Skye plops herself on a bar stool next to me and declares, "I don't like it when Alex-zandra is not with us. And I don't understand why I can't go to Game Night."

"It's for grown-up women."

"Well, that stinks." She punctuates her expletive with a kick on the bar.

I grunt.

I've been doing a lot of grunting lately.

"Daddy."

"Yes, little bug."

"You're doing it again."

"I'm doing what."

"You're being a bear."

"A what?"

"A bear. Grr. Hon. Mph. You're almost a grizzly."

"I'm sorry. Come here."

She slides onto my lap and pulls a deck of cards from the front pocket of her hoodie. She deals five cards on the bar, face up, and gives each of us two, face down.

I guess we're playing Texas Hold Em tonight.

"That legal?" A big voice booms next to us.

"Hey, Declan," I say. Declan Campbell is half of Emerald Creek's police force. "Busted," I whisper-shout to Skye, who giggles and slaps down her cards. "Two pairs! Woo-hoo! Partay!" Then she turns to Declan. "Did you put any bad people in jail today?"

"Matter of fact, yes, I did."

That's interesting. Nothing ever happens in Emerald Creek.

"Are you celebrating?" Skye asks, undeterred by the news.

Declan laughs. "I don't celebrate putting bad people away, no."

"Why not? It's your job. Alek-zandra says we should celebrate every win." She stacks the cards together in her little hands. Maybe she's spending too much time with adults.

"Maybe I will, then. Justin, Diet Coke for me. We're celebrating tonight, it seems."

Justin eyes Skye, holding his tongue for now. "Here you go, Officer. On the house. Thanks for keeping us safe."

Declan shuffles his feet, glancing at me.

Skye slides off the barstool. She knows when adults need to talk. She's a good kid like that. Too good, I sometimes feel. Too perceptive. "Justin, can I take Moose for a walk?"

He hands her the dog's leash. "Stay on The Green," I tell her. "Where I can see you."

"And take poop bags," Justin adds.

"Eww. Okay." Skye stuffs the bags in her coat pocket and heads out. The dog is so tall, he reaches above her midsection.

"I'm wondering who's walking who," Justin says.

"Something on your mind, Declan?" I ask. He never comes into Justin's bar, and he's in uniform. Something's on his mind.

"Old Man Fletcher's not going to be trouble for a while," he says under his breath. "Just thought you should know, seeing how you've been helping Isaac out."

Shit. That can only mean one thing. The person behind bars is Isaac's dad. I'm not surprised. The guy was an asshole. He probably got into it with the wrong person. "How long?"

He takes a long pull on his coke, and says, almost too softly for me to hear, "Depends if the other guy makes it or not."

"Shit," I say under my breath.

"Yup. Thought you'd like a heads up."

That means two things, one good and one bad. The good news is, Isaac's father is no longer an issue as far as using his son as a punching ball. At least for now, and maybe for a very long time. The bad news is, the family lost its primary breadwinner. I'm not sure what his mom does for a living, but I know the dad is—was—a manager at a meatpacking facility, and those jobs pay good money. "Appreciate it," I say.

"No problem," Declan says, and with that, he leaves.

"Tough," Justin says, sliding me a refill. "How old is Isaac?"

"Going on eighteen. He's graduating high school this year."

"He's going to grow up fast."

"Yup. I'm gonna make him an offer."

"How about your other apprentice?"

"What about her."

"Are you making her an offer?"

"She doesn't want to be a baker."

"I wasn't talking about a job offer."

I shoot him an angry glare.

"Told you to stay away from her," he says.

Did not. Told me the exact opposite.

"Should have told you," he says, reading my mind. "But then, I didn't know you were such a pussy."

I don't know what the fuck he's talking about, and I don't care. I take a long draw on the cold IPA.

"I want you to want me."

I *do* want her. Way more than she can imagine. I spend my nights with her, sleeping or making love to her. I spend my days with her, working or just... doing life shit. And yet I can't get enough of her. I want more of her.

But how much does she want me to want her?

And what did she even mean by that? What she said stuck with me, but maybe I'm reading too much into it. She said it after I'd been to dinner at Emma's, and maybe it was just jealousy. It was also right in the middle of fucking awesome make up sex we were having, so maybe that's how she meant it.

"Talk to me, bro."

I huff. Talking is not something Justin and I do.

"C'mon. Spit it out."

"You talk about *your* shit, Tinman?"

"What shit?"

"Right," I say. Been years since Justin's had a girlfriend. Oh, he sees plenty of action, except he goes away for that. Never talks about whatever girl he's had that time. Mentions the pussy, occasionally. "Right," I say again, drawing out the word.

"Come on, I wanna hear it."

"How come you haven't had a girl since high school?"

"I'm talking about you." He wipes the counter, like he's prepping to lay something on it.

"I'm not."

He grunts. "Course not." He grabs a mop and sweeps the entrance to the pub. With the snow almost entirely melted, the ground sloshing and sticking to boots, there are shoe tracks everywhere. It's a full-time job to keep any place clean during mud season.

I follow him, beer in hand, and look at Skye on The Green, talking to Moose. "The baking show is coming up. Couple of months now," I say.

"Yeah?"

"Might need a driver."

He pauses.

"Someone to drive me back." The show lasts three days, and there's little to no sleeping involved.

"Might as well drive you both ways. When is it?"

"Few weeks." I look up the date on my phone as we make our way back to the bar.

"You're a pussy," he repeats after he's entered it into his calendar.

He might as well have punched me with his fists.

I could have punched back.

Maybe I am a pussy. I wasn't always like that. I fought for Skye. God did I fight to have her. And to keep her. She was my flesh and blood. It was instinct.

But I never fought for a woman.

I didn't fight for Skye's birth mother. The minute she turned her back on me, I was done.

Didn't care.

Never missed her.

All I wanted was Skye, and I got her.

But now?

All I want is Alexandra, and I don't know how to fight for her.

"Women want us to fight for them," Justin says. The fucker reads my mind all the goddamn time. "Alex is no different. What's the deal with her, anyway? Looks like she likes it here. Not like that snob," he adds, referring to Skye's mother. "I heard she was looking pretty hot for you the other night when you went all knight in shining armor at The Growler. You bang her after that?"

My jaw clenches and I scowl.

He chuckles. "D'you propose? Did she say no?"

I take my time slugging my beer.

"I don't know, man," he pushes. "Seems to me, you did the manly thing, saved her from the bad guy, got her home, nailed her. At that point she must have been putty in your hands. I'd thought I'd be seeing you two walk in here the next day holding hands and making out in a booth. So. What gives?"

I signal him for a refill on my beer, but instead, he pushes a tall glass of water in front of me. When I don't say anything, he continues, "I heard the most stupid rumor. This one's gonna make you laugh."

I raise my eyebrows.

"Supposedly, you were having dinner at Emma's that night. Doing dishes together, necking in front of the fire with after-dinner drinks. Took her queen-size bed for a trial run. All while the girls were sound asleep upstairs."

My blood boils. The problem with rumors, everyone knows it's gossip. But the truth is, I wasn't paying enough attention to what me having dinner at Emma's would do to Alexandra. Barbara told me, yet I didn't really understand how much Alexandra was closed off about expressing her feelings. Until I had her in my arms that night. Until I saw the devastation on her face, for that one little thing.

I know my apology could never be enough.

"Now were you at The Growler rescuing Alex or were you nailing Emma?" Justin continues, pushing.

"Shut the fuck up," I hiss. Alexandra is so protective of her own self that I ended up hurting her.

He rounds the bar and sits on a stool next to me. "Look, man. I know what went down with Skye's birth mother. I was there."

I raise a hand. He doesn't know the hurt. The humiliation. The loneliness. "Don't." Plus, her and Alexandra? Entirely different.

Different women.

Different stories.

Worlds apart.

No comparison.

He ignores me. "I don't know what went on in your head, back then, and I wasn't there to help you through the shit that went down with Skye." He pauses and strokes his bicep. "But I saw you then. And I see you now. Totally different."

Yup.

"She *gets* you. She's *there* for you. She's *good* for you."

Fuck. *Don't you think I know that?*

"Don't let her go."

I stare at him.

"You're fucking scared, aren't you?" he says.

Scared? "Of what?"

"Of putting yourself out there. Telling her that you need her. That you want her. It's easier to just blame it on her and let her go."

Easier than what? Than being alone, without her, for the rest of my life?

"Look who's talking," I say.

"I'm very happy being single, man. You, clearly, are not."

Chapter Forty-One

Alexandra

We turn the angle of May, and mud season turns into spring: colorful bulbs blooming everywhere, trees still bare, and enough of a chill to sometimes warrant a winter coat.

Spring in New York used to bring me happiness. Here, now, it signals the end of my stay here. Six weeks, give or take, and I'll be gone.

I need my girlfriend from New York.

"Hey, girl, how's it going?" Sarah asks, answering my call. "Are you outside? I hear wind."

"I'm at the river." I stretch my legs out in front of me. I'm plopped on a bench and let the spring sun warm my skin. Skye is riding her bicycle on a small trail up and down the hill, and she waves at me every time she goes up, her tongue sticking out to show me how much effort it is. We're downhill from a white colonial house with broken black shutters. Daffodils spring haphazardly in front of a picket fence that is missing more than a few slats. On her way back up, Skye calls my name at the top of her lungs. I blow her a kiss.

"Are you babysitting?" Nothing escapes Sarah.

I cringe at what she's going to say when I confess, "Just looking after Christopher's daughter. Skye."

"Oh, my. And where is the hot dad?"

I can picture her face, eyebrows lifted, waiting for more.

I hold a sigh. "Playing hockey."

"Oh-kay?"

"*What*."

"How come you're stuck watching the kid while he's doing one of the sexiest things I can think of without showing any skin?"

"Hockey is sexy?"

"Honey. Wake up. Don't tell me you've never seen him play."

Oh, I've been to a couple of games with the girls.

I know exactly what she's talking about.

"For real, why are you looking after his kid when you could be looking at him?"

"She didn't feel like going. It's beautiful out, and she needed the fresh air."

"Oh. Wow. You sound like a mom."

"Oh please." I do feel protective of Skye, though. When she huffed that she didn't want to spend the afternoon inside the arena, I offered to take her bicycling instead. I didn't think twice about it, and I know Christopher was thankful for it.

"Are you guys a real couple, now? I mean, it's been, what, three months?"

Four. "No! Why?"

"'Cause that's what couples do. Look after the kids. Do what's right by them."

"Yeah, well, we're not. We're just having fun." That's become my motto, and it's getting old.

I'm stocking up on memories of sex against the wall of my bathroom, sex on my antique bed, and even sex on the prep tables in the lab.

Memories of his gentle words when we're alone, his hands shaping my body, cupping my face, his lips worshiping mine.

I'm in his constant presence but still starved for him, and it makes our private moments all the more intense. He comes into my bedroom at night, once Skye is sound asleep. I'm often asleep too, but I half wake to his snuggling behind me, warming my back, pulling my waist against him, and before you know it, I'm having a toe-curling—but silent—orgasm, the kind I thought were the stuff girls just made up to brag about but that never really happened in real life.

Some nights, he takes the time to wake me up with a flutter of kisses down my neck and a gentle sucking of my nipples. Other times, he starts by going down on me and licks my folds to oblivion.

I prefer it when he just takes possession of me while I'm still asleep. I wake up to his cock filling me, his whispered curses, the antique headboard knocking against the wall with each of his thrusts. That is the hottest thing to me.

That he wants me that bad.

That he needs me.

"Shut up," Sarah says, when I give her a watered-down but accurate recap of my nights. She's still single, and she won't let me forget that I agreed to give her some sort of sex life by proxy. "There's no way you're not waking up before he's... inside you."

"Try spending twelve hours on your feet, in the heat, six days a week. You'll see."

"How does he do it? He works more than you do."

He's a beast.

"When are you coming up?" I ask to change the subject. It was fun at first, telling Sarah most of what was going on, but as time progresses, I feel more and more protective of my relationship with Christopher.

Even if it's not a *relationship*—relationship.

After what happened at The Growler, the girls were cool, and no gossip transpired—at least as far as we know. We're back to keeping this secret. And I have to reason with myself to not feel a pinch of longing when we're in public—for an arm draped around my shoulder, for a hand trailing down my back or cupping my waist. I miss that. I miss his touch. I miss him claiming me as his.

"Lexie. Are you going to be okay? You know... when you have to leave."

My eyes sting. "Sure! Why wouldn't I?"

She mumbles something that sounds like, "I don't know," and then goes silent.

"When are you coming?" I ask again.

"About that," she says, her voice chirpier. "How about you and I spend a couple of days in Burlington together, before going to Emerald Creek? Would that work? I should get there a week or so before your exam. A girls' getaway."

"That'd be awesome!" Sarah always knows how to lift me up.

"And, after you're done, I'll be backpacking a bit. Care to join, or will you be too busy being important?"

My heart sinks. I already have a slew of emails from Red Barn's lawyers I need to answer, meetings that are being planned by Barbara, situations to address. It's like I can see the clouds gathering. "That'd be great," I say, my voice faltering, "but I don't think I'll be able to."

After we hang up, I wave to Skye that it's time to go. While I wait for her, I snap a few photos of the house. It looks like it's just sitting there, waiting to be discovered by the right family. I notice a For Sale sign and find my caption: *Waiting for a #happyfamily*.

I call Skye again. She's due at Grace's now for some quality time with her aunt, followed by a sleepover, so I offered to drive her. Christopher drove in a friend's car, so I can just use his truck. And, while she's at Grace's tonight, Christopher is taking me out to dinner. I have butterflies in my stomach thinking about it—an actual date. As if I had an actual boyfriend.

Little things, right?

I notice some blue paint in Skye's hair and on her fingers. "Where did you get that paint?" I ask. "At school?"

She rolls her eyes. "Yes," she says. "It's for the Mother's Day gift." She makes as though it's nothing, but my heart falls at the words.

"Oh." I'm caught off guard. "That sucks. I remember those days."

"It's okay," she shrugs.

And she does look okay. She seems unbelievably strong, but I know she must be hiding a lot under the surface.

"Christopher trusts you with his truck?" Grace smiles as she hugs me hello. "I thought he didn't let *anyone* drive it."

"He didn't really have a choice," I answer, plopping Skye's bag at the bottom of the stairs. "Take your stuff upstairs, sweetie," I tell her so she doesn't start leaving a mess in Grace's tidy house.

"I kinda like seeing my cousin having his decisions made for him," she says, picking up her cat. "It's about time."

I have the feeling she's not talking about the truck, so I swerve the conversation elsewhere. "What's going on here?" I ask, pointing at the ingredients laid out on the kitchen counter.

She sets her cat down and washes her hands. "Skye and I are going to make Gram's sandwich bread. Ready, sweetie?" Skye is already rolling her sleeves up.

I'm in awe of this family that can take three or four basic ingredients and make a variety of different foods, each one more delicious than the next. "Who's Gram?" I ask, pulling my phone out to capture Skye's concentrated look as she measures flour.

"Me and Chris's grandmother," Grace answers. "Our mothers' momma. She'd always make that when we were kids. It was a summer staple."

Skye nods. "Back in Maine."

"My mom still makes it." Grace doesn't mention Chris's mom, though.

Things start to fall together. I picture a grandmother lovingly making bread for her family and understand Christopher's passion.

He mentioned a strained relationship with his mother, and I want to know more. For a long time, I nurtured this fantasy of what my life would have been if my mother hadn't died when I was ten. It was always near impossible for me to understand my teenage friends' epic fights with their mothers, and right now, I'm dying to know what an adult could possibly hold against theirs. But with Skye present, I don't ask any questions. And I do realize that Rita was someone's mother—my own mom's mother—so I get that not all mothers are this idealized model I constructed for myself.

"It's great you're doing this," I tell Grace, and I feel my eyes water. I grab my phone and snap more pictures of Grace and Skye baking together, as much to hide my emotion as to capture this beautiful moment.

My own grandmother admittedly built the largest baking empire in the United States, yet she never bothered to teach me anything herself. Here, traditions are passed along from generation to generation.

"Is that how Christopher learned to bake?" I finally ask.

Grace seems to hesitate. "I suppose it inspired him? Or not."

I drop the topic, sensing some underlying family tension that is not my place to dig into.

When they're done with the bread and Skye is in the living room coloring a mandala book, Grace asks, "Wine or tea?"

I hesitate.

"Wine it is." She chuckles. "No need to be reasonable."

"Just a drop, then," I say. Then, lowering my voice, "We're going out tonight."

We clink glasses, and she says, "Look. I get that you guys want to keep it a secret. But I just wanted to say, *thank you*. Christopher has never been happier. It's like his life took on another dimension, and it's all because of you. He's making plans. He's not half as grumpy as he used to be. He's running for New England's Best Baker. He believes in himself, again. He believes in life, again."

I feel myself blushing. "I have nothing to do with the competition—"

"Oh, you have everything to do with it. Believe me. Everyone tried. No one succeeded. But you show up and... ta-da!"

I frown. "But why? I don't get it."

She smiles. "Deep down, Christopher needs to prove himself. He always has. Even though he's an awesome father, successful business owner, pillar of the community, he'll always feel that he's not good enough for the people he loves." She glances at the bread baking in her oven.

My blush deepens. "Christopher doesn't love me," I say. "We're—We're just having fun."

"He may not have told you yet that he loves you, and he may not admit it even to himself, but he does."

Oh, no. No, no, no, no, no. There's no way. It can't be.

My heart beats faster, and I take a longer sip to calm my nerves. "This is not what you think," I say. "I can assure you there's nothing... deep between us."

Except when he falls asleep holding me tight at night.

When he stays entangled with me through the morning.

When he brings me coffee in bed, his eyes boring into me like I'm the most precious being on earth.

It doesn't feel like just sex.

It doesn't feel like sex at all.

"All I can say is, he's never been happier than now," Grace answers. "I hope you two work it out. When you have something so special, so unique... you need to fight for it." Her eyes well up.

"But we don't," I insist, all the while realizing that, if she's right, if there's a remote chance that Christopher has feelings for me, then I'll be breaking his heart. "Like I said, we're just having fun."

"So, tell me this," Grace continues. "Why are you taking care of his daughter like she's yours?"

"Because... I love her. She's— You know how she is." I'm blinking the tears away. "It's got nothing to do with Christopher."

"Honey, when a woman has *just fun* with a man, she doesn't give two cents about the guy's kids. She just wants them out of the way."

I've got nothing to say to that. She could be right. She could be wrong. I never dated a single dad before. Then again, I never wanted a man the way I want Christopher, and I've never felt that Skye was *in the way*.

"When are you supposed to leave?" she asks.

I take a deep, shaky breath. "Mid-June. Right after my exam." I look out the window.

"And why are you crying?" she adds softly as I wipe my cheek.

Because Christopher won't be the only one hurt when I leave. Because I don't know how to fix the mess I created. But I can't say these words. I can't bring myself to think through the depth and consequences of my emotions.

When I leave Grace's home an hour later, Skye hugs and kisses me, leaving a wet trace on my cheek that I actually cherish. The dirt road shortcut from Grace's home is closed during mud season, so I take the long way back. The road takes me by the arena. I check the time on the dashboard clock and slow down, glancing at the long, gray building. People are trickling out. The game is over.

I pull into the parking lot.

Slowly, groups exit, families around their fathers, women clutched to their men, children running around them.

I feel a pang of envy. I try not to project myself, though, because I know how this can be dangerous for me.

And then the thoughts pour out, whether I want them to or not. What would it be like to belong here? If circumstances were such that this could be my life? I could be openly beaming at my sexy boyfriend rolling his muscles, carrying his child in my arms before we all huddled home together in our car. He'd be leaning toward me, feather kiss on my lips, promise of more.

I can't let myself go down this path. This life is not for me, and I can't pretend I'm living it, even on lease.

Or could I? What would it take for me to turn my life on a dime? Could I try and have it all—run Red Barn from here?

As I fish my phone out of my pocket and text Christopher—*Do you need a ride?*—I spot him coming out, his dark curls framing his handsome features, his muscular legs and broad shoulders on full display under his tight T-shirt, a mass of muscles I'm intimately familiar with.

My heart flutters. His charisma is just as strong here as it is in the bakehouse, and even from inside the car where I can't hear a thing, I can tell he's had a good game. The guys surround him, clapping his back. He gives them a small smile back.

What I wouldn't give to have been at the game with him.

To be walking out the arena with him.

He needs a woman on that handsome arm.

As I hit send on my phone, wondering if he'll see the text, I freeze.

Emma snakes herself under his arm, wrapping it possessively over her shoulders, keeping it in place with her hand over his.

Twining their fingers together.

Wrapping her other arm around his waist so she's flush against his hard body.

My heart stutters, then bangs against my ribcage.

I peel off from the parking lot, angry tears blinding me, spurts of mud in my wake.

This is exactly what Rita had drilled into me all those years; You don't let a man into your life. *Men only bring misery.*

My chest hardens at the thought of our date tonight. He apologized for hurting me when he went to dinner with her, and now this?

My phone rings.

And rings.

And rings.

I take deep breaths. The dinging of voice mails and text messages roll in as I take refuge in my room, not knowing where else to go.

Where to hide.

Minutes later, the front door slams, and the whole house shakes as he storms up the stairs.

"Care to tell me what that was about?" he growls as he throws the door open and stands in front of me, muddy shoes, crazy hair, sweaty jersey.

Chapter Forty-Two

Christopher

"What do you want from me?" she says, her eyes brimming with unshed tears.

Fucking Emma. I'm going to kill her. It was all of two seconds. I didn't even know she was there, and then she was snaking her way against me. I pushed her away immediately and grabbed my phone dinging with Alexandra's ringtone.

All of two fucking seconds and she had to see that.

"Why did you take off like that?"

Her mouth gapes. "The nerve," she says and folds her arms against her chest.

"Is this about Emma?"

She huffs, cocks her eyebrow, and shakes her head. "Just—forget it," she says, dropping her arms to her sides. Like this conversation is pointless.

"I'm not gonna forget it. I want you to tell me why you flew out the parking lot, when clearly, you came to pick me up." I know why she did. I want her to own it. Can she do that for me?

Does she care about me enough to fight for us? Call me on my shit? Tell me that what she saw was hurtful? Confusing? Fucking bullshit? That she won't put up with it?

"What am I supposed to do when another woman clings to you? Just ignore it, right?"

"No."

"Then what?"

Claim me. I want you to claim me, Alexandra. I want you to want me the way I want you. I want you to tell me to go fuck myself with my game of hiding around. "Nothing."

She turns her back to me and looks out the window. "I suppose you have new plans for tonight," she drops. She doesn't even want to argue, to call me out for saying one thing and then the opposite.

"No." I take two steps and stop shy of her. The tremble of her body is visible. I place a hand on her shoulder, and she stiffens. "Hey," I say softly. If she'd stayed, she'd have seen me push Emma away. I'd have been with her in seconds. I might even have kissed her in the parking lot. Because—fuck people.

The thing is, I'd make her mine in front of the whole damn town if only she'd give us a chance. If only she'd tell me she's not going back to New York.

But she decided to leave, again. Just like when she saw lipstick on my shirt and went to karaoke, or when I was having dinner at Emma's and she went to The Growler. She might be pissed, but not enough to put up a fight.

She doesn't seem to care enough to do anything about it but run.

"You looked good in my truck," is all I say.

It's getting dark out when I knock on her bedroom door a couple of hours later. I go in before she answers.

Her face is collected, and there's no trace of her previous anger or tears. Is that a mask, or is that how she really feels? Like nothing.

"Oh perfect," she says, turning her back to me, her hands laced at the top where she's fumbling with the clasp of her dress.

Standing behind her, I push her hair aside and kiss her neck, then proceed to hook the clasp of her dress. It's a detail, but it's everything, and it nearly tears me apart before this evening even starts. Me clasping her dress before we go out is a glimpse at what life as a couple looks like.

A life I thought I'd never want.

Until her.

She looked so fucking edible in my truck this afternoon, and even before I stepped out of the arena, I was wishing I'd told her to come pick me up so we could drive home together.

Home.

Together.

I want that so bad.

I want my bedroom to be hers. I want my car to be hers. Fuck, I want my *daughter* to be hers. I want to give her my life.

Because I know how she looks when she's in my arms, I know how she looks when she's with Skye, and that's a thousand times better than when she's on the phone with any person in New York. Hell, even when she hangs up with her friend, Sarah, she has a worry crease that I never see here—not even when she's messing up in the bakehouse.

As I guide her into the restaurant with my hand on the small of her back, I indulge in this fantasy that we've come out as a couple.

Alexandra mellows under my touch, and I wonder if she feels the same.

Can I bring her back to where we were before what happened in the parking lot? Before Emma pulled her stint. We were so good. We were building something. And then her confidence in me fell apart in less than a few seconds.

I need to talk to her. Ask her if she'd consider staying here.

But that's crazy, right? Why would she do that?

Where will she go when she leaves? My mind drifts to the dark side as I mindlessly peruse the menu.

I can't stand the thought of another man with her.

And then my eyes meet hers, and I grind my teeth at the acute awareness that it's way more than that. I can't stand the thought of her away from me. At all.

"Did you make your choice?" the waiter asks, pulling me out of my dark thoughts.

"Alexandra?"

"Oh. Ummm... the fiddleheads. And the perch?"

I close my menu. "I'll have the same." I need to get my head out of my ass and tell her how I feel about her. I brought her to this restaurant because I thought it would show her Vermont also has fine dining. As if pitting Vermont against New York was the way to go. What was I thinking? I'm going about this all wrong. I'm dead on arrival.

"Good evening," the sommelier says.

And here we go deciding on pairings. I'd normally enjoy this, but tonight I'm in no mood. I'm painfully drawn back to a similar scene years ago, when I dressed up nicely and paid for lunch and did everything right, but the woman across the table from me still laughed at me and ultimately looked at me like I was something the cat dragged in when she realized I was serious.

"Skye was making your Gram's sandwich bread recipe with Grace today," Alexandra says. *Shit, I'm not even making small talk with her. I need to pull myself together.*

"Was she, now?"

"I don't think I ever saw those at the bakery."

She's right. I don't sell them. I just don't want to make them.

"You should think about offering those. I mean... once you're done with the baking competition. I know that's pretty taxing, right now. But, starting this summer, you know? Gives you a little time to prepare. I could help you market it in advance, build demand."

Demand for when you're gone?

"From what Grace said, it goes really well with barbecues and for sandwiches?" she continues.

I don't give a shit what I sell or don't sell once you're gone.

"You know what would be great for the summer?" I answer, and she looks at me expectantly. "You."

Her face falls a little. "I—I was thinking of staying a bit longer after the exam, see if I could get some vacation time from Red Barn?"

I huff. Right. Of course. Vacation. *And how about the next fifty years, Alexandra?*

But I can't bring myself to ask her the question. I don't know what she wants, deep down. Is this still about having fun? Or does she want a ring on her finger? Because, if that's what she wants, I'm dragging her to church right this fucking minute.

Hell, if I wasn't close to certain she'd publicly reject me, I'd be on one knee right this minute with a rock the size of Mount Mansfield if that's what it'll take.

"You're freaking me out," she says, her gaze on my hands balled into fists around my cutlery.

Chapter Forty-Three

Alexandra

We get home late at night, and he lets me go first up the stairs. But soon his hand is between my thighs, and I laugh, until my high heels betray me, and I almost fall down on him.

That's when he scoops me in his arms and carries me up the stairs.

When we reach his floor, I glance at his room, then look away.

"I don't want memories of you here. Told you already."

It's bittersweet to hear. I'm not sure what to make of it.

I chase away what Grace told me this afternoon—that Christopher loves me. That can't be true. This is wishful thinking on her part, and I love her for that.

Because, surely, if he did, he'd tell me. He'd want me in his bedroom.

He'd ask me to *move* to Emerald Creek, instead of asking me *to stay for the summer*. I chase the thought away.

I trace the stubble lining his square jaw, grate my nail down his neck, slide it to his shoulder flexing lightly under the weight of my legs, then take a full feel of his biceps.

And sigh.

He chuckles. "Good enough for you?"

"God, Christopher, you have no idea." I wiggle, my panties suddenly itchy.

He sets me on the bed and cups his palm to my middle, and I answer by rocking against him. Wasting no time, he ditches his clothes on the floor and stands in front of me, hunger in his eyes. As I prop myself on my elbows, my eyes naturally fall on his erection, my mouth watering.

"I'm starting a fire," he says. *That fire's been burning for a long time.*

But he means a literal fire, and I get to watch him naked, muscles rolling, as he adds kindle and logs to the hearth while I take my clothes off. Once I'm down to an innocent-looking white demi-cup bra embroidered with blue flowers, matching panties, white garters, and silk stockings, I lie on top of the bed.

"You look like a goddamn bride," he says, smirking.

"I do?" I laugh. "How many brides have you seen without a dress?"

He laughs. "None." Then adds so quietly I can barely hear, "yet." He lies on the bed next to me, slides down to my hip, and nuzzles the garter. "Isn't the groom supposed to grab the garter with his teeth. That true?"

"Maybe? I've heard of that," I say. An uneasy vision worms itself inside me and sits at the bottom of my stomach—Christopher getting married. Christopher with another woman. Someone beautiful, and solid, who aligns with him in so many ways.

Someone like Emma.

"I'd never do that in front of people. Wouldn't want to show my wife's thighs to the whole party. But it *is* fun, hmm?" he says, his teeth gripping the garter, his stubble teasing my inner thighs as he begins to make his way down one leg.

Yeah, Christopher will make a great husband someday.

Just not mine.

And god that hurts.

He gently rolls the stocking and places it and the garter on the side of the bed, then crawls back up for the second garter. My hips rock in need, meeting his fingers.

My mind drifts back to Christopher having a wife, to Skye finally having a mother.

I try to shake the thoughts that are killing my mood.

"You okay?" he says, the second garter now at my ankle.

I hate what's happening to me. That eerie music playing in the back of my head, telling me that the perfect movie I'm in? It's about to take a turn for the worse.

This is not me. I've taught myself to enjoy the little moments of sheer bliss that make life bearable.

And this, right now? This is one of those unforgettable moments that will carry me through all the stuff I don't even know is coming my way.

This is material for memories to make bad days much, much better.

When all this is over and I'm back to a mountain of problems and backstabbers in New York, I'll have this memory of a man so gently unwrapping me. So tenderly kissing me. So passionately making my body come alive under his kisses.

Still, the thought of no longer being here in a few weeks triggers my panic. I can't do soft and gentle in this moment. Soft and gentle is for people who have their lifetimes to explore each other. People who have weddings and garters and weird but fun traditions.

He stands naked and brings the garters and stockings to the chest of drawers. We do have the rest of the night. Which tonight, feels like all the time in the world, and I appreciate that he's not rushing this. That he's savoring every moment of us being together without needing to be somewhere else in a short time, or without risking any interruptions.

This whole night is truly ours.

Yet, my panic takes over, and I get off the bed, flinging myself to him as he makes his way back to me.

"Hey," he says, his lips curling up in the most adorable, surprised smile.

Clasping my hands at his nape, I pull him in front of the crackling fire. "I need you to take me," I murmur as our lips collide.

His brow furrows, and his arms tighten around me. He doesn't need more explanation. He grabs a condom and loses no time rolling it on. Then our mouths mold to one another, and his tongue takes control of my senses.

With one hand cupping my ass, he hoists me onto his hips, then he lowers me slowly to the carpet.

His arm cushions my back from the hard floor, and my body melts into his as he enters me in one powerful move. Not gentle, not slow.

Claiming.

Yes.

How does he know exactly what I need in this moment?

My eyes lock with his, my begging silent. *Fuck me. Fuck the pain out of me.*

And he does.

He fills me. His thrusts pin me hard under him, the veins on his pecs bulge and turn blue, our sweaty foreheads clash as our bodies become one.

Then he dips his head and sucks on my nipple, and my orgasm builds, this time coming from somewhere deep. I moan, a raw, deep sound I don't recognize myself, but I don't come, yet.

Letting go of my breasts, he pins my hands behind my head and sucks my neck.

Our rhythm picks up.

His brow is furrowed and his breathing hard. Low grunts rise from deep in his belly as he plows deeper and stronger inside me.

With each stroke, my lower back scrapes against the carpet. "Fuck me harder," I beg, relishing the burn marks forming on my skin from his rough lovemaking. From the way he wants me. Possesses me. I bring his head to my neck. "Suck me." Then I push his head to my breasts. "Please." I want him anywhere he'll kiss and bite and suck. I need to feel more, to get out of my head.

And Christopher gets it.

He fucks the shadows out of my soul, making me scream and writhe and shake from my orgasm for what seems like long minutes.

"Fuck me," I say again when I come down from it, limbs unresponsive, vision blurred, and he hasn't come yet.

And he does. Oh how he does.

He fucks me so hard that the vein on his forehead is as thick and blue as the ones on his biceps. So hard he throws his head back when he comes with a loud growl, skin slick with fresh sweat glowing in the dancing light of the fire. So hard his eyes roll back, and he nearly crushes me when he drops his body to mine. Oh but I want that crush. The carpet scraping my back. His heartbeat resonating in my whole body. Our skins clinging and slipping. His shaking breath in the crook of my neck.

Later, he carries me to the bed, lays me on the sheet like precious cargo, spoons against me, and pulls the bed covers above our tangled bodies, his hand gently stroking my bare shoulder.

Rain starts pattering against the window, and it's the warmest, softest sound.

The smell of freshly brewed coffee wakes me up. I open my eyes to the sight of Christopher wearing just a pair of low-hanging sweatpants, his naked abs and pecs flexing behind a breakfast tray laden with apple cider muffins, cinnamon buns, orange juice, and coffee.

"Oh, wow," are the first words I can articulate. I stretch my arms above my head and without thinking, I add, "Will you marry me?"

He nearly drops the tray.

Well, that settles it. "Just kidding," I huff.

He smirks and hands me a cup of coffee, then tears apart small pieces of cinnamon bun that he hand-feeds me.

I close my eyes in delight. Not for the food.

For the moment.

I should immortalize this. I reach over for my phone charging on the nightstand and snap a photo of Christopher sitting on the side of my bed handing me a sticky pastry, the breakfast tray between us, my foot resting on his thigh.

In years to come, I want proof that this was not my imagination.

He gives me his crooked smile when I snap the photo.

"Let's get some content for your social media," I say when we're done with breakfast.

"What does that even mean?" he asks, a puzzled look on his face. Then, catching up, he adds, "Don't you have a ton of pictures already?"

"I'd like videos of you. On normal days, I'd be in the way. And I'm supposed to be baking, too."

"Would you like that?"

"I'd love it." I'm beaming.

"Only because you'd love it, then."

Before I can stop myself, I wrap my arms around his neck and plant a kiss on his nose.

He smirks. Something clouds his gaze before he breaks into a wide grin and adds, "Anything for you, pancake."

Once in the bakehouse, he says, "I might as well practice for the competition," and pulls his ingredients out. I set up the ring lights around his workstation then start the video.

I ask him questions, and most of the time he answers, our back-and-forth easy. Sometimes, he's so focused he doesn't answer right away, and I get some great footage. Especially when he looks up at me like he's just discovering me, a huge grin brightening his features. Then, he remembers the question and launches into an explanation with passion, precision, and care.

Four hours later, my stomach rumbles as his confections come out of the oven. "I can't believe you made me work on my day off," he says.

"Right. Like you wouldn't be working if I weren't here."

He grins and kisses me lightly on the lips. "I would be working three times more."

That worries me. "Are you skimping on your preparation because of me?" I can't be the one standing between him and the title.

"You're my good luck charm. I'll be fine."

My heart dips at his admission. The competition means a lot to him—to everyone. And, if he loses, he'll be crushed. I remember Grace's words—Christopher needs to prove himself.

"Even if you don't win, you're the best," I tell him, happy tears rimming my eyes.

"I'll win. When I want something bad enough, I get it."

My heart stutters at his words, and I hide it by scrolling through the videos I took. Surely if he wanted me in his life, he would start by just saying so.

"Show me how this works," he says, motioning to my phone. His woodsy scent warms me when he leans over as I show him. Then, he takes over the phone and practices by filming me.

"You can also do a selfie," I say and adjust the phone's tripod.

"Why would I do that?"

"If you want to talk straight into the camera, like you have an announcement. Or, maybe, down the road, if you want to interact with your customers, you could do a live video."

He grunts. "I don't think so."

"Could come in handy if you're introducing something new. Or a big order just got canceled and you're sitting on inventory. You just hop in and say something like, 'We've got awesome whatever-it-is-you-made, and they won't last long. Come in and get yours!' and then, you just take a bite of whatever you made, or you show it to the camera."

"That's it?"

"Yeah. Just be genuine. You're not trying to impress people with your videos. But before you set out to make a video, you need to know what your goal is. More often than not, you're just trying to get them to come buy your stuff. The thing with live videos is that people get notifications on their screens—so they're sure to see your video. They don't have to look for it."

"You're right. I didn't think about that." He grabs one of the trays he's been baking and starts the live feed. I get behind the camera to check that he's in focus and give him a silent thumbs up.

"Hey, guys, I have a nice surprise for you. I've been baking some sourdough brown bread today." He grabs the bread and rips off a piece of it and shows it to the camera. I see people logging in and reacting already. "I also have some brioche hot dog rolls." Hearts start to trickle up my phone screen. "Since we're closed on Mondays, I'll be dropping them off at Justin's, also known as Lazy's."

I round my eyes at him.

He cocks a questioning eyebrow. "And that's it for today!"

I stop the video and laugh. "Next time, don't give your product away!"

"I thought that was a marketing technique." He grins.

"It can be. When done right. Right now, you're just sending business to Justin."

"I don't mind."

"Of course not, but that's not what you set out to do. Remember to set a goal."

"I'll have to hire you. Because you've just witnessed the extent of my social media and marketing abilities." He draws me against him and closes his arms around me, lifting my chin so my eyes meet his.

"Stay here," he says, and I freeze, senses alert. Why does he want me to stay? To hire me as his social media person? Is that all I am to him? A poor baker, but a good marketer?

"Wh-what?" my voice betrays my hope that he'll say he wants me *for me*, in *his* life.

That everything I shouldn't want, he will give me, without me asking. That *he* wants it.

Only then, maybe, can I take the risk.

His gaze roams my hair, my lips, my face, then settles back on my eyes. "Stay here after your exam. Fuck Red Barn. You don't owe them anything."

It's too early for me to tell him about Red Barn Baking, that I'm about to become the owner of the company. Not until my plan to reform it from the ground up is in motion, and he can accept the secret I kept from him in light of the mission I'm working on.

Nothing is in place yet. I have nothing to show for it. He wouldn't understand.

He takes a shallow breath. He's about to speak, and I stay suspended.

"Bet you'd get a lot of business here," he says, and my stomach drops, disappointment settling in until my toes tingle with the shame of the hopes I held for one weak moment.

I shut my eyes and lay my head against his chest. "I bet I would."

His heart beats fast and hard in his chest, while mine is faltering.

His words haunt me for the next several days.

Maybe he was just being cautious?

Although his words weren't strong enough to win me over, I saw the hurt in his eyes when I wouldn't say yes, and I feel like I'm dying inside.

What's the right thing to do? "Stay" is vague. Does he want me to be his girlfriend? Does he want more? Where will I live? What will we tell Skye? How will I deal with Red Barn Baking?

I call Barbara to help me figure out the last piece.

"Of course you can do whatever you want, but running the company remotely may not be your best option for a smooth transition." She sighs and I hear her shift in her chair. "When they sacked me, there were already factions forming. Pro-Alex and... well, not pro-Alex. The openly pro-Alex got a pink slip, and they're finding other jobs. It'll be tough to rehire them. You'll be left with the other charming group."

Norwood must be leading the anti-Alex group. Whoever else is part of it is anybody's guess. "But they haven't met me yet," I say.

"You might not know them, but they know you. Start building a thick skin, darling."

Great.

Chapter Forty-Four

Alexandra

I'm grateful it's Game Night again. I've been going on and off, and I really need it tonight. There's just too much being thrown at me, right now. I need time off.

I grab a glass of wine and choose to sit next to Laura, Skye's teacher. "Can I ask you a question?" I say once we've exhausted the topics of weather and the play, and we're on our second glass of wine. There's something that's been bugging me, and I didn't know how to bring it up. The wine helps.

"Sure!" Laura smiles, puts her glass down, and clasps her hands, giving me her whole attention.

"This... Mother's Day thing?"

She nods.

"What about kids like Skye, who don't have a mother in their life?" I'm trying to keep this matter-of-fact, but my voice betrays me.

"Mm-hm." Laura nods. "It's—It's tough."

That's it? "What do you do about it?" I frown but try to keep my voice soft. The last thing Skye needs is for me to antagonize her teacher.

"Every child is different, and every situation is different. I discuss it with the guardians or the single parent. Whatever may be the case. We come up with a plan for how to address this for the child."

"Skye seemed—and I know it's not my place—but she seemed... annoyed?"

Laura's gaze leaves mine, as if she's wondering how to answer this. "First off, it is your place to raise a concern if you see one. I'm of the *It takes a village* philosophy, and your bringing this up to me confirms how much you care about her. It's wonderful that she has you in her life. But, to answer your question, and without infringing on the family's privacy... how do I put it? I hope Chris won't hold it against me to share this with you."

She takes a breath, collecting her thoughts. "Although Skye has no legal mother, she knows how babies are made, and that she comes from a woman. And, from what I understand, Chris never encouraged her to hold bad feelings against her. Instead, he made it clear that it was okay for her to honor the person who gave birth to her if she chose to. And, if she'd rather not, she could honor anyone else who had been important to her that year. He made it so it was a celebration of the life she was given. The life she's currently living. Does that make sense?"

Tears line my eyelids. "But—But doesn't she miss her?"

Laura places her hand on top of mine. "You can't miss what you never had, Alex. Like I said, it's different for every child. For every person without a mother. We each have our own story, and we each deal with our losses. Skye doesn't have a loss. She might have questions, and maybe there's latent abandonment issues? But I'd be surprised. She seems very healthy psychologically, as far as I can tell. As far as I know, each year the gift she makes goes to someone close in her life. Chris might have a couple of noodle necklaces, Grace some ceramic vases. I believe her first finger painting is still in Justin's office." She stays silent for a beat, and then, she adds, "How did you deal with your loss?"

My jaw drops. *How does she know?* "Small village," she says, answering my silent question.

"I'm still trying to deal with it," I admit. "Therapy." I roll my eyes then shrug an apology. "It does help, I'm not going to lie. But it's been so long, and the hole is still there. It's... hard. And Mother's Day makes it..."

"I can imagine. But one last thing to keep in mind about Skye. You've become a very important person in her life." Her eyes narrow on me. "You're going to have to figure out a way to stay in her life after you leave."

The rest of the evening goes by in a blur. I'm trapped. What will Skye think of me once she knows I lied to her father, to everyone? How will this impact her as a person? I know what Laura said is true. I have become an important person in Skye's life. I do care about how this will impact her emotionally.

I need to tell Christopher. I need to come clean to everyone. Explain my motivations.

It won't be easy, but I'll explain that I'll be staying here, in Emerald Creek.

It's still me, Alexandra. It was always me, they just didn't know it.

If they loved me then, they'll still love me now, right? I haven't changed. It's what they know of me that has changed. And they won't judge.

They're good people. They'll understand.

I'll tell Christopher.

But I'll wait until after the competition is over, so he can keep his focus. And so the news doesn't come out. He'd hate that. *Contestant Christopher Wright's apprentice is Red Barn Baking heir.*

God he'd hate that.

I have to wait.

CHAPTER FORTY-FIVE

Christopher

Mother's Day always wraps up early at the bakery, and today is no exception. The customers who aren't taking their mothers out swing by early morning, and we sell out before noon. I give Willow the rest of the day off and turn our sign to *Closed*.

I linger in the darkened bakehouse, enjoying the quiet moment. The door to the kitchen is open, the rectangle of light enough to light my steps.

"Daddy would never let me make cake like that. Not a clocking chance," I hear Skye pipe up, and I wonder what the hell she's talking about, so I stop in my tracks and listen.

"And that's why we have Kids' Day," Alexandra answers. "So you can do what you want."

"How was your daddy?" Skye asks out of the blue. Count on her for that.

"I never knew him," Alexandra says after a beat.

"So, you never had one."

"I guess you can say that."

"Daddy says a parent is the person who loves you more than themselves. Like, they could *die* for you." Count on my kid to zero in right where it hurts. After all these years, Alexandra still feels guilty about her mother's passing, and sure enough, she sniffles.

"I suppose that's true," Alexandra whispers, her voice broken.

I hear some shuffling, as if they're hugging. I feel bad for eavesdropping, but this is stronger than me. And I don't want to break their moment.

"Don't cry," Skye whispers back. "I love you. We all love you."

"I love you, too, sweetheart."

"When the red light is off, we can put the cake in the oven," Alexandra says, her voice steadier. "Now, let's measure all this."

Utensils clank, and Skye asks, "Remember a loooong time ago, when I asked you if you were going to marry my daddy?"

My breathing halts as I tense.

Alexandra chuckles. "I do. It was my first night here."

Skye lets out a big sigh. "Well. Now, I wish you could stay and marry my daddy."

"Awww. Honey," Alexandra answers after a beat, and is it my imagination? Her voice sounds a little broken.

I'm shaken, for sure.

"It's okay," Skye continues. "I know you have to go back to New York, and we'll still be friends. But... he'll be sad when you leave. And me too."

There goes my grand plan for protecting Skye from heartbreak.

"Your daddy is strong. And so are you. We'll all be fine," Alexandra says, her voice catching again.

I swipe under my eyes, and Alexandra clears her throat. "Okay, ready?" she says. "Let's make this cake."

I leave the baking house as if I'd heard nothing, and a bundle of new emotions takes over while I'm still dealing with what I just heard.

Skye is wrapped up in a kid-size apron I've never seen, kneeling on a kitchen chair, sleeves rolled up. On the table, there's a bottle of milk, some oil, an egg… and cake mix.

That's right.

Cake mix. In my own home.

And I like it.

I like it because I see the excitement on my daughter's face, and I see Alexandra's smile as Skye reads the instructions out loud from the box, and it just feels right. It feels good. And I want this moment to last forever.

I pull out my phone and snap a photo.

Yeah, I've become that guy.

They both look at me at the same time, and I snap another one.

And, now, a short video as Alexandra shows Skye how to break an egg.

I leave the cake mix out of the frame. Alexandra taught me a thing or two about taking photos. One of them being to leave out anything that could ruin the photo. I'm still partially against cake mixes, so that's not getting in the picture.

The mixer whirs. Using both hands, Skye carefully blends the ingredients while Alexandra holds the bowl.

I approach the table as Skye finishes. "Daddy!" she exclaims. "Want some?"

"Is that any good?" I ask, instantly feeling like a jerk. Sometimes, I can't help myself. I dip my finger in the batter and taste.

Skye claps. "I made it!" she says, as if that should settle the debate. And it does for me.

"Mmmmm. That's why it's so good. Like father, like daughter." Truth be told, the shit isn't as bad as I expected.

Skye raises a scolding eyebrow at me. "Alek-zandra bought aaaall this," she says, her hands gesturing at what's on the table in a swiping motion, "and my new apron! Look! Today is Kids' Day in this family."

"I see that." I smile at Alexandra, my stomach softening as our gazes connect.

"The light is off!" Skye cries.

"How many minutes?" Alexandra asks as she loads the cake in the oven.

Skye reads from the box. "Fifteen minutes or until a knife inser—ted in the center comes out clean."

"Fifteen, it is. Come here and set the timer," she says, then, "Dishes, now," when Skye returns to the table.

"I'll do dishes," I say. "It's Kids' Day. And you've done enough," I say to Alexandra.

"Woo-hoo!" Skye dances around the kitchen.

"Want to bring the cake to Lynn and Craig's tonight?" I ask.

"Yessss!" Skye squeals.

This is what complete feels like. This is the life I want. And I don't want it with just any woman.

I want it with Alexandra.

And I'll have it. No matter what.

I'll have her.

Before we go to the farm, I call my mother, and we switch to a video call. Ryan and Trevor are on either side of her, each with an arm flung across her shoulders, and even Dean, their father, pokes his head in briefly.

The perfect family.

The one I'm not a part of.

"You guys look buff," I tell my half brothers. "Working out?"

"They're getting older," my mother sighs.

Trevor and Ryan have huge grins. "We joined a gym."

I'm reminded of what Alexandra had suggested, that they should work at the bakery during the summers, and the idea is appealing to me more and more.

"I could use some muscle here at the bakery, if you're looking for summer jobs," I say. My mother glances away from the screen—at her husband no doubt.

"Dope!" Ryan says, high-fiving his brother. Both have full-on smiles, and I get that feeling again—we're a band of brothers.

Dean, their father, grumbles something I can't make out. He might be off camera, but he's not letting this conversation take place outside his control. Trevor's eyes cut to the side, and Ryan does a *don't worry about it* eye roll and shoulder shake for my benefit.

As far back as I can remember, Dean has been shoving me to the sidelines of the family, doing everything he could to keep me away from "his sons."

The first time I vividly remember feeling like a second-tier member of the family—the proverbial stepchild—I must have been nine years old. The twins were toddlers. I'd come home from school with a good grade, and my mother was busy getting dinner ready.

Maybe if I got some of her chores out of the way, I thought, she'd have time for a game of cards with me before Dean got home. Like before. When it was just the two of us.

I run the bath and measure the temperature with my elbow, making sure it feels lukewarm. I prepare matching pajamas and clean towels. When the bath is half full, I slowly lower Ryan, who is more outgoing, followed by Trevor, who will do anything his twin does, and I start running the plastic ducks around them. They splash water playfully. I use a washcloth and the baby liquid soap to wash them. Their soft skin and laughs are endearing, and so is the way their big eyes look at me with wonder and happiness.

"Be good boys, or I won't give you your bath anymore," I say as I rinse their baby hair down with the handheld shower, a clean washcloth covering their eyes to prevent the sting from the running water.

I pull the plug from the drain and take Ryan out the tub first. I dry him, put him in his pajamas and set him down. He starts bobbing around, opening the drawers and throwing stuff out. This isn't going to do. The bath is completely empty of water, now, so it's safe for me to dash out of the bathroom and plop him in the playpen without anything happening to Trevor. Ryan is wiggling in my arms, and the playpen is high. My grip on him falters, and he drops onto the plastic surface, wailing more out of frustration than anything else. Echoing him immediately, Trevor shrieks in the bathroom, where I rush back.

I find Dean leaning into the bathtub. "Shannon!" he yells.

I grab Trevor's clean towel and say, "He's just unhappy that Ryan is in the—"

"He could have drowned!" Dean shouts as my mother comes running in.

I feel tears coming up. "But I emptied the—"

"Christopher, what did you do?" my mother asks.

"I was trying to h—"

Dean wags a finger at me. "Stay away from my sons."

I saw it clearly then. My only crime was that I was who I was.

Not his son.

This understanding that I was a second-class person in this household that was no longer a family to me only got deeper from then on.

Ryan and Trevor adored me, but there was this unspoken rule between us that we shouldn't get caught playing together. We broke it, time and time again. When Trevor followed Ryan up a tree, fell and broke his arm, or when Ryan tried a chemical experiment and burned Trevor's eyebrows, Dean and my mother sighed, "Boys will be boys."

But when Trevor got his nose broken playing hockey with me and my friends, no amount of lying on our part could conceal my role in it. He wore his slightly crooked nose like a medal of honor, convinced it gave him the bad boy look that would polish his persona. His father saw things differently, and there were words that were spoken that day that were too hard for me to forgive. I spent the next few months here in Emerald Creek, with my Aunt Shannon and Uncle Dennis. A few months later, I left for a baking apprenticeship in France that lasted two years.

I don't remember whose idea it was that I leave and do something with my hands, but even if it wasn't mine, I was on board with it. I couldn't wait to get out of there and go somewhere I didn't have a past, a history. Somewhere people would welcome me with open arms, even if just to work or learn a trade. I'd made sure of that—that the people I was apprenticing with actually *wanted* me.

I'd been the baggage my mother came with, and I was going to make sure that never happened to me again.

And, later, I made damn sure that never happened to Skye.

In the afternoon, we all meet up at the farm. Lynn, Craig, and the usual suspects are sitting in the sun, sipping wine on the terrace overlooking the apple orchard.

After hugging everyone hello and wishing Lynn a happy Mother's Day, Alexandra takes Skye to the kitchen and reappears on the terrace with the cake displayed on a dish. Skye proudly presents it around, handing half a slice to everyone.

"Today is Kids' Day in..." she starts, beaming, then stops in her tracks. "In our *family*?" She frowns. "Daddy, are we a family?" she shrieks to cover the sound of the multiple conversations going on at once, and manages to make the din die down. "You know, since Alek-zandra and you are not married? But we still love her, and she loves us? And she *lives* with us? Does that mean we are a family?"

It's total silence right now, and amused stares are fixed on me expectantly. I meet Justin's gaze as he takes a long pull on his beer, laughter in his eyes.

I rub my hand on the back of my neck. "Um... no, no, we are not."

Someone boos and stops before I can figure out who it is. Soft laughter ripples through the group, and one of the women says, "Awww. I've never seen Christopher blush."

"Skye, bring me some of that cake," Craig interrupts, breaking the awkwardness.

"Who needs another beer?" Lynn adds, digging into the cooler.

Conversations resume, but I'm in no mood to talk to anyone. I hear Alexandra's laughter cascade, and I put every effort into not looking for her. I just stare into emptiness, mindlessly sipping on my beer.

A hand lands on my shoulder. "Let's go for a walk," Craig says. "I need to check on something."

Grateful for the distraction, I throw my empty bottle in the recycling and follow him down the trail to the orchard.

We walk in silence for a while among the trees in full bloom. Craig stops every so often to examine a flower, flipping it over. He looks up to the sky, seemingly lost in his thoughts for a moment. We reach a small stone lean-to that's used during harvest for workers to take a break. We sit on a bench outside of it, soaking up the dipping sun.

"When I met Lynn," he says after a while, "I knew right away she was the one for me." He rubs his calloused hands together slowly. "It's something you can't explain, but you *know*. You just *know* this is the person for you."

I shift uneasily on my side of the bench.

"Her family wouldn't let me date her," he says before my silence gets awkward. "They told me to my face that I was beneath her. It was hard. You know how it is."

He's referring to Skye's birth mother, and I nod.

"If she hadn't been the one for me, I'd have given up," Craig says. "I'd have walked away. But you don't walk away from your true love." He shifts to the side and looks at me. "You know that. You went through something similar with Skye. You didn't walk away. You fought for her because you already loved your child."

I nod again, not sure where he's going anymore.

"Sometimes, we don't know what the obstacle is, and that makes it harder. Sometimes the obstacle is within," he adds, tapping where his heart is. "It wasn't that hard for us."

"How did you do it? With Lynn."

He chuckles. "I kidnapped her. With her complete consent, I should add. She suggested it."

"You eloped?"

"That's the word. We eloped. Both our families wouldn't talk to us. We worked as farmhands in Upstate New York, got married, and came back only when her parents died in a plane crash, and she inherited this place."

"Wow."

"It was hard on Lynn, you know. Not ever seeing her parents again. Why would a parent do that to their child, I don't know. My parents eventually came around, right after Lynn lost both her parents in the plane crash. Finally saw the light, you could say. I can't imagine doing that to my own flesh and blood."

He picks up a blossom from the ground and turns it in his fingers. "You could say it ran in the family. Her uncle George was disowned by Lynn's grandparents because he got the wrong girl pregnant. Beats me." He takes a deep breath. "He recently reached out to Lynn. Nice fellow. Lives nearby, in the Northeast Kingdom. Apparently, he briefly reconnected with the woman, a few months back. Fifty years later. Lynn's been trying to get him here. We're the only family he has."

His eyes mist. "Imagine that. Lynn recently told me, even though she missed her parents, that she never regretted what she did. That I was worth it." This time, he swipes away a tear. "Even after they both died and it was too late to fix anything, she didn't regret choosing me over them."

I'm a little overwhelmed. I don't know if Craig is trying to tell me something. And, if he is, I'm unclear about what it is.

Reading my mind, he adds, "You're fighting your demons, Christopher, and I'm sure Alex has hers. But, whatever you're up against, know that the fight is worth it in the end. That is, if you think she's the one for you."

When we get to the farmhouse, the group is inside, scattered in different rooms. The women are in the library, making a dent in Craig' spirits while Sophie does tarot cards readings. Some of the guys seem to have gone to the cellar, and Craig joins them. The kids are splayed on the floor of the great room, watching a movie.

I take refuge in the kitchen, wanting to avoid another conversation.

"Hey, kid," Lynn says, affectionately wrapping her arm under mine. "Here. Have some cream pie." I sit down at the kitchen counter, and she slides a generous portion my way.

After two bites, I take a deep breath, and our eyes meet. "Damn," I tell her. "I needed that."

She sits on the stool next to me. "So, tell me," she says, "Why are you two pretending there's nothing between you?"

So much for avoiding another conversation. "It *is* nothing."

"Not to me, you don't. It is *not* nothing. And I'm not asking what it is—yet—I'm asking why you're trying to hide it?" Before I can answer, she adds, "Unsuccessfully."

"We—*I* don't want Skye to get hurt. When Alexandra leaves."

"We're past that point, now, aren't we? Clearly, she knows—"

"She didn't mean it that way."

"Of course not! She's a child. She doesn't need to know what adult love life looks like. But she knows you love each other. Where were you when she all but said it to everyone?"

I rub the sore spot between my eyebrows. "Skye got attached to Alexandra. She's just confused."

"Well, I'd tell you to set things straight for Skye before she gets more confused. But there's more, right? This is not just a fling."

I clench my jaw. "Not for me, it's not," I admit.

"So? You're a fighter. I always saw you fight for what you wanted. What's happening this time?"

"She won't stay. She just. Won't. Stay." I clench my jaw and look at Lynn, then avert my gaze. The tension is too high, and my eyes are uncomfortably wet.

"And why is that?" she whispers, stroking my arm.

"I don't know," I admit. "I've asked her, again and again, but it's always the same nonsense answer about her job."

"Where is her family?" she asks.

"She doesn't have a family. They all passed away."

"Mmm." She looks away for a beat then narrows her eyes on me. "Did you talk specifically to her? About what it would look like for her if she stayed here?"

"She never gives me a chance to get that far. She just shuts down the conversation, saying it's just not possible. Not in the cards for her." I huff. "I should go ask Sophie if that's true."

We stay silent for a beat.

"It seems to me that she needs stability. Whatever is in New York represents stability to her. Here, it's a big unknown. I bet it was hard for her to come, but she did it, knowing she was going back to her environment, no matter what it is. It's something certain. Stable. Where she feels she belongs. What will she do here if she stays after her exam? Is it true what they say?"

"What do they say?"

"That's she's not a good baker. But she's great with her phone and… whatever sort of marketing she does in real life."

I chuckle. "Yeah, it's true." I don't even want to know who says that. Probably the whole town.

"She's going to need more than a few *I love yous* to stay here."

I raise my eyebrow, and she frowns at me.

Her mouth makes a big *O*. "Wait. You never told her *I love you*?"

I groan and dig back into the cream pie.

"Stop hiding, Christopher. You have to say clearly what you want. How is she supposed to know? Talk to her."

Chapter Forty-Six

Christopher

The next few weeks, I mull over what Lynn said. And I know she's right.

As I walk into the den after closing down the bakery, my insides go soft and fuzzy at the sight of Skye cuddled on Alexandra's lap. Instead of occupying the couch, they're huddled together in one of the armchairs, and they look like the poster for happiness. Alexandra lets Skye play with her phone, and she strokes her hair gently, as if she's been doing that forever. I've never been caught in quicksand, but I can bet this is how it feels. Fearing that any move would put me deeper in trouble.

This thing that comes from Alexandra, it's tenderness, and it looks a lot like love to me. And, fuck, it's powerful.

I take it all in.

They both look up at me at the same time, flooring me even more.

Skye flashes a gap-toothed grin at me, and I smile back at the two of them, until Alexandra's soft, piercing gaze is too much for me to handle, and I break it.

As I reach to grab my jar of Maple butter from Skye—I don't know why we still bother putting our name on the lids—Alexandra slides off the armchair and goes into the bakeshop.

"Alek-zandra, what are you doing?" Skye shrieks in my ear, making me jump.

"I have to transcribe some notes from today's work."

"Oooooh, nooooo," Skye said, rolling her eyes.

Alexandra's craftsmanship might be wobbly at best, but her theoretical knowledge is impeccable. And I'm not pushing her to master the practical side of baking, because despite my grandiose speech to her the night of her arrival, I know she'll never be a baker, and that's all right.

In a few days, she'll take her baking exam, administered by a French baker currently working in Montpelier. The way the exam is structured, with a grade close to perfect on theory and a decent grade in practice, she'll pass. That's all we need. Her and me both.

For reasons that don't make fucking sense.

"How about you and I go to Justin's, let Alexandra finish her work, huh?" I say to Skye.

Skye pretends to huff. "I guess," she says.

"What's the matter? You don't want to go to Justin's, now?"

"Only if Alek-zandra comes, too."

"I'll meet you there!" Alexandra says from the bakehouse. "I just need an hour."

We slide into Skye's favorite booth, the one at the front where she has easy access to Moose—who is relegated to the very entrance of the pub—and a prime view of the front door, the kitchen door, and the bar. She likes to wave to people, and she keeps tabs on everyone's comings and goings.

My daughter is turning into the next gen gossip, but somehow, I find that adorable.

"Grilled cheese?" Justin asks her, though there's no reason to. I don't think she's ever had anything else here.

Skye nods with a big smile. "And—"

"And French fries, of course. How about you, man?"

"I'll have a Sip Of Sunshine while I wait for Alexandra. Are you going to join me?"

"Of course."

I look out the window to my bakery, where Alexandra is working.

I wonder what will happen to her if she doesn't pass her exam. Which I don't think there's a chance she doesn't. But still.

Would she lose her job?

Would she still want to go back to New York? She would. There's no way it's only work keeping her there.

I'd have to pay off the grant I received within a year. It would be hard, financially. Still doable. But it's not in my hands anymore.

Skye leans over the table and tugs at my cheeks.

"What are you doing?" I chuckle, pushing her hands gently off my face.

"Smile, Daddy!" She comes over to my side of the booth and tries tickling me.

"Okay, okay." I grin.

She sits back next to me and crosses her arms. "What's the matter with grown-ups?"

"Why?"

"Grown-ups are either sad or worried. Sometimes, angry."

"Who's worried and angry?"

"Miss Hen-der-son was angry this morning with No. Reason. At. All." She pauses to waive to a friend skipping on the sidewalk. "And Alek-zandra was worried."

"Hm. What was Alexandra worried about?"

She shrugs. "Some people in New York."

What else is new. Why won't she let me help her? Why won't she just stay here?

"And you look sad," she adds, poking at my chest and frowning.

"I'm sorry. I'm not sad; I really am not. I am the happiest daddy on earth." I kiss her tenderly, and she snuggles in my embrace. "How could I be sad with you as my daughter? Sometimes, grown-ups are complicated."

I tried to protect Skye by not having a real relationship with Alexandra, but she's getting hurt, anyway. What am I supposed to do?

"Caroline is getting baptized," Skye says out of the blue.

"Is that right?" Did Emma mention something about that? Come to think about it, she might have.

She nods. "She gets to choose her godmother and godfather, because she is old enough."

I don't know much about how these things work, so I settle for a grunt. "That's good. Is she excited?"

Justin comes over with her grilled cheese and fries and two pints of beer. He sits silently across from us.

"If I asked Alek-zandra to be my godmother, would she have to stay here forever?"

Justin cocks an eyebrow, suppressing a smile.

"What do you mean?" I ask, genuinely puzzled as to how my daughter's brain works but still seeing where this is going. Fast.

"Daddy," she huffs. She might as well have said, *Get with the program.* "A godmother replaces your mother in case yours dies. So, if Alek-zandra was my godmother, she'd have to stay here, right?"

Oh. Shit. How am I supposed to answer *that*? There are so many ways her little heart could break again with my answer. "I don't think that's how it works," I say carefully. "Also, being baptized is—I'm pretty sure it's not just about having a godmother and godfather. I think you have to go to mass and stuff. And Sunday school." That's a cop-out, but what else can I say?

Skye's eyes dart outside toward where the church is, at the end of The Green. "Oh," she says quietly. She frowns and tilts her head, then starts picking at her fries.

I might be out of the woods, but my kid is hurting, and I fucking hate that.

"Well, that was interesting," Justin says once Skye finishes her food and goes to pet Moose. "I wonder how long it's going to take that little brain to realize all it'll take to keep Alex in Emerald Creek is for *her father* to take her to church."

"Not all women want a ring on their finger." But the thought of her wearing my ring, using my name, does all sorts of things to me.

"You're not really going to let her go, are you?"

I have nothing to say to that. I look out the window to the trees now full and green. To the window boxes at the bakery. It was Alexandra who arranged them this year, a colorful bunch that match her nature.

"What's holding you back?"

The stab in my chest every time she tells me no. "She can't stay."

"Bullshit. She'll stay if you give her a reason to."

News flash: I'm not a good enough reason to stay here. "I'm not going to take her to church, if that's what you mean."

"Look, man," he says, his voice low so no one can hear us. "I know you swore off women after what... that bitch did to you. But you need to get out of that funk. You need to see what's right in front of you. Don't you see how she's good for you? And for Skye? Since she's been here... you're... you're alive again. And your kid? Are you thinking about your kid?"

"Yeah, I am." I'm angry that he's lecturing me. "That's why we were never supposed to be anything."

"Don't."

"Don't what?"

"Don't pretend that this is nothing."

"It *is* nothing." Despite what I've decided already, it's near impossible for me to talk feelings with Justin.

"I thought you were better than that. If I had a woman like her, if she'd look at me the way she looks at you, hell... I'd never let her go. I'd have proposed already. Hell, I'd probably have a bun in her oven already. Look at her."

Alexandra is stepping out of the bakery, making a beeline for the pub, her short dress flowing around her, showing her toned legs, cinching her waist. My heart stops, and I avert my gaze.

"Don't you talk about her like that."

"What? You said you didn't care about her. You talked trash about her. Now you have a problem?"

"I didn't—"

Anger flares from his eyes. "You said she was nothing to you. *Look at her*, and tell me you won't do what it takes to keep her." He gathers our empty glasses and stands.

Alexandra is steps from the pub's outdoor terrace. She smiles to no one in particular, just happy to be here. Sauntering toward me. She has this aura of happiness, of goodness, that's above and beyond all the sexiness she radiates.

"You don't fucking deserve her, man," he says before making his way back to the bar. Easy for him to say that. He can have anyone he wants.

I ball my fists at him, ready to pounce, the rage I thought I'd tamed years ago suddenly springing back to life inside me.

Alexandra swooshes inside the pub, and Justin grabs her by the waist with his free hand, pulling her against him and giving her a long kiss on the cheek. He whispers something in her ear, and she laughs then makes her way to me, long hair flowing, cheeks rosy, eyes shining for me.

During dinner, I let her do most of the talking. She's excited about her friend, Sarah, coming. Tomorrow, she'll be going to Burlington to meet her, and they'll spend some time there. By the time they get back, I'll be gone for the competition, and that will bring us to when she takes her exam and no longer has any reason to stay here. Even though she said she'd ask for an extension of her stay, it's the end.

Tonight could be our last night together, just the two of us.

I think back to what Craig and Lynn told me when we were there for Mother's Day, and what Justin said, just now.

They're right. It's past time for me to get my head out of my ass and do something.

I'll open up to her. I'll tell her I love her.

She'll say it back.

And, then, we'll figure it out.

Once I know what's so important in New York, I can work out a way for her to stay here. Or lay it to rest—there's always that possibility. But, at least, I'd know.

I'd know what was so much better over there than right here in my arms.

Because god knows, when I make love to her, she's all mine, and there's nowhere else she'd rather be.

That night, I slide into her bedroom like a thief. It's been unusually hot all day, and her window is open, letting some fresh air cool her skin. She's splayed naked on her bed, sheets pushed aside, her hair fanned around her beautiful face.

I cup her cheeks and whisper, "I love you."

I've never said I love you to a woman.

It's fucking scary. Because I really mean it. I love her. And I want to show her my love every day of my life.

Shower her in gifts and kisses.

Take all her scars and all her secrets and make them mine.

Name my bakery after her.

Build a house up in the mountain for us.

Grow a garden for her and Skye.

Have a child with her.

"I love you," I say again, and she stirs. I blow on her skin, from her breastbone to between her legs, and back up. Then I trail my tongue down the same path and stay down at her middle, parting her folds. Her fingers find my head, and I feel her clit swell to life.

I stand to kick my boxer shorts off and meet her hooded gaze. She lowers her eyes to my erection, while her hands trail down between her legs.

I growl and lower myself to her, needing to take her.

Needing to make her mine.

I clasp her wrists and move her hands above her head, then claim her mouth with mine. Her tongue welcomes me, takes me in, while she writhes her soft body against me. Her breasts push up against my chest, and sweat clings our skins together. The musky scent of our bodies fills the air. I move my mouth away from hers to take in her beauty before I lose myself in her. Moonlight gives her skin an eerie glow, as if this were a dream.

In some ways, it is.

"Take me, now. Please," she says.

Her begging almost sends me over the edge, and I do what she says—I take her. She wraps her legs around my hips to pull me closer. "Harder," she asks, her panting telling me she's close already.

"I won't last long if I go harder," I warn her.

"Please," she cries out, and I ram into her, knowing that her asking me to fuck her harder means she's on the verge of orgasm.

And so am I.

As our bodies chase their collapse together, her sucking me in, I want to cry it out loud—*I love you*. Instead, I bury my face in her neck, wrap her hair in my hand, and swallow a sob.

I cannot let go of her.

I cannot lose her.

As soon as she comes undone under me, I let myself go, and we ride our orgasms together, clinging to each other, giving and taking, being one.

After her last tremor subsides, I slide onto the bed and wrap her in my arms. Despite the heat, she takes my favorite after-sex pose, nudged against me, her head on my shoulder, one leg wrapped across my body, her middle against my hip. My arm keeps her tight against me. I wait for her to fall asleep with her mouth open, her tiny snores like purrs lulling me to sleep as well.

But, this time, something feels different. She's sticky.

"Shit!" I push her away from me, like that's going to make any difference. "Fuck, Alexandra, I wasn't wearing a condom. I don't know what I was thinking."

"You weren't thinking." She smiles, her voice raspy. "That's the whole point of l—sex, right?" She pulls me back around her. "I'm on the pill; don't worry."

I'm totally fucking awake and in near panic. I try to sit up, but she won't let me. "Well, we should get tested. Also, you should take a pregnancy test." I run my free hand through my hair. "Just in case."

"Um. Okay, sure." She rubs her eyes and looks at me, squinting. "You need to get tested?" she says, hurt suddenly registering in her eyes. "I guess... I guess we didn't get too much into our histories. I was under the impression... Well, I mean, I shouldn't have assumed... Right... Also, I mean, you don't need to worry too much about me. Should I be worried?" There's a little shock there, a hurt that's not just about the remote risk of an STD. "Like I said, I'm on the pill, if that's what you're worried about."

Her face is falling apart.

I lean over and pull her in my arms. I'm such a jerk. "Come here, beautiful. I'm sorry. This came out all wrong. I just—I just didn't think I'd lose control like that. I'm supposed to always be doing the right thing, and I didn't. But, tonight, seeing you like that, I needed you."

"I needed you too," she murmurs. She relaxes in my arms, and I do too.

"God, you felt so good, Alexandra. I've never had sex without protection, and it was—It was magical."

A playful grin plays on her lips. "Liar."

"It was, I swear! Couldn't you feel the difference?"

"Technically, you must have had unprotected sex at least once in your life... Skye?"

It takes me a moment to understand what she's saying, and when I do, it's a punch in the gut. "One too many drunken parties during a summer with too many parties. I have no memory of that. Might have been a faulty condom, for all I know."

"Well, that's a shame. Or maybe not. I'm your first naked sex partner," she says, cuddling inside my arms.

"You're more than that, beautiful."

She lifts her face to me, and I read hope in her eyes.

I kiss her lips lightly. "So much more," I say against her mouth.

"Christopher," she murmurs against my mouth, her body snuggling tighter against mine.

I pull back from her, hold her chin in my fingers so she's looking at me when I say, "I love you, Alexandra."

Her body jerks and she shuts her eyes briefly. When she reopens them, I read a mix of emotions. Did I come on too strong? Too fast? Too late? But how am I supposed to tell her I love her? What is going through her mind right now? I don't want her to feel pressure. "You don't have to say anything." I dip my head to kiss her again, going for a light kiss, but my heart starts beating like crazy, and I pull her closer to me, kissing the hell out of her, as if it's our last kiss. She kisses me back, wrapping her thighs tighter around me, fisting my hair in her hands, showing me with her body what her mind can't express.

It's not our last kiss.

That answer can tide me over. I pull us gently apart, needing to have some sort of closure over what just happened. Some sort of plan. "We have a lot going on, you and me. You have your exam. I have the competition. We don't need heavy conversations right now." I rub my nose against hers, and a soft smile spreads across her face.

"Just promise me we'll have a talk after all this is over. After your exam, after my competition. But before you go back to New York."

She's full on smiling right now, a fucking sunshine, and she gives me a full body squeeze. "I promise."

Chapter Forty-Seven

Alexandra

"You're glowing," Sarah tells me. "Never seen you in love. It suits you."

We're sitting at an outdoor café in Burlington, sipping white wine to wash down the crêpe we're sharing. She finally managed to take a few days off, and after her visit, she'll be hiking a portion of the Appalachian Trail. I offered to pick her up at the airport, and we decided to spend the night so she could visit the Queen City before her trek.

I smile at her. "I feel... at home in Emerald Creek."

"How about Christopher?"

I take a deep breath and look away. After Christopher told me he loved me, I decided to give myself this day with Sarah to think through it. To make a decision. "I never thought I'd say this, but he's the one for me." Even if I didn't say it back, I love Christopher. I want to make a life with him and with Skye.

I don't know yet how I'll make it work. I don't think details matter when you've met the one.

Sarah's eyes water, and she squeezes my hand. "What's your plan? Work-wise," she asks after a minute passes.

"I'll work from here. Like you said before, I'm not bound to working from New York. There's more to life than work. If I learned anything from this apprenticeship, it's that Rita had it all wrong. Nothing can replace a family. And all men don't bring misery." Tears rim my eyes. "I trust him, Sarah. I love him beyond imagination, but above all, I *trust* him."

"That's all you need, sister." She squeezes my hand, again. "I'm proud of you for going after what you want and need. You deserve it. What did he say?"

"I—I didn't tell him, yet."

Her mouth opens in an *O*, and her eyes go wide.

"I wanted to give myself time to think. And I wanted to have your blessing," I explain.

"Oh girl, you have my blessing. You're—You're like a new woman. A better version of yourself. I'm so happy for you!" She fans herself. "You need to tell him, right now. Did you say his competition starts in a couple of days?"

"Yeah, I'll wait until he gets back to tell him."

"No, you're not. You can't let him hang like that. He needs to know he has your support before he goes."

"I couldn't even say it back," I whisper.

"What?"

"He told me he loves me for the first time last night, and I couldn't bring myself to say it back. I didn't feel a right to, you know? He blindsided me."

"Uh-huh," Sarah says, taking a bite off her skinny pancake. "Didn't see it coming, right?"

Is she being snarky right now? "No, I didn't see it coming. We were just supposed to have a... thing. And okay, I kinda fell for him—"

"Kinda?" Sarah snorts.

"—but why didn't he say anything before?"

"He must have given you some hints."

"Yeah, he'd say things like '*Stay here,*' but not *Move in with me*. Or, '*I could keep you around indefinitely, bet you'd get a lot of business.*' Who says stuff like that?"

"Hm. Wild guess. A guy who's afraid of rejection?"

I take a deep breath. Christopher was rejected by Skye's mother, someone who was going to have his child. And he never felt accepted by his own family.

I should have put my heart on the line sooner for him. "I lied to him, Sarah. What does that say about me? What is he going to think when I tell him?"

Sarah shrugs like this is no big deal. Like my whole life isn't hanging in the balance right now. "If he really loves you, he won't care."

Why didn't I see that earlier? "You're right. God, I've been so selfish. What if I'm not the right person for him? I always—"

She silences me with a finger on my lips. "I don't ever want you to say that again. I've heard you blame yourself too much, and I won't have it anymore. You won't bring anything but happiness to this man. Now, let's get off our tushes and get back to Emerald Creek, pronto."

I should stop texting, because I'm going to end up telling him I'm staying, and that's something I want to say in person. In private. With enough time to process everything. Because I'll also tell him about Red Barn, and that's going to need a conversation.

But I know it will go well. As long as I can explain everything. I know I should have opened up to him earlier about my childhood, but before I knew that our relationship was going to evolve into what it is now, it meant risking whatever we had. And I didn't want that. I wanted to keep the little of him I could have.

He'll understand why I didn't tell him before. And I know he'll accept me for who I am.

No one can be held responsible for who their parents or grandparents are.

* * * * *

It's late afternoon when we get back to Emerald Creek. Sarah takes in the town's charming architecture, the bakery's quaint windows. She takes a deep breath, and her shoulders relax.

"It's so peaceful here," she says. Exactly what I felt when I first got here, almost six months ago.

The door to the bakery opens, and Christopher steps out. Our eyes lock, heat passing between us. It's been only a day, and I've missed him so much. How did I ever think I could live without him?

He hesitates, not knowing how to greet me in public. I want to lunge myself at him and kiss him in front of everyone, but before I can do anything embarrassing, Sarah says, "You must be Christopher," and hugs him, leaving him slightly off-kilter for a beat.

Christopher takes my duffel bag from me to take it upstairs to my room. I feel like I need to stay with Sarah, even if I'm dying to be alone with him and tell him everything. But that will take too long. I need to wait until tonight.

While Christopher is upstairs, I give her a quick tour of the bakery, and we sample maple bacon muffins.

Christopher comes down the stairs, and my insides melt. His gray button-down shirt is tight around his pecs, tucked inside the jeans that hug his hips in a manner that awakens the dirty girl in me.

The things I want to do to him tonight. After we have our talk, and all is good in the world. And before he goes to Boston for the competition.

"Why don't I go with Sarah to check her into the inn," I tell Christopher, "and then, we'll meet up at Lazy's?"

He nods. He looks tired, and I know he's been using my time away to double down on prepping for his competition. If we go to Justin's for dinner, we can cut the evening short.

And be alone earlier.

* * * * *

"You gotta love the creaking staircase," Sarah remarks as we go to her room. "That screams vacation right there. At least for me."

I learn that her room has a breathtaking view of the river and the countryside. Rolling hills, meadows, and pastures for as far as the eye can see. A side window gives a partial view of the village.

I had no idea the inn offered such beautiful views from its rooms. I should reach out to Wendy and Todd, the owners, to offer my help with their marketing.

"Christopher really has you under his skin," Sarah says. "The way he looks at you? Scary hot," she comments while we're freshening up in her bathroom.

"Thanks," I say. "And thanks for not commenting on how hot *he* is." I chuckle.

"I would never."

"Yeah right. Like you never did."

"Because it was never serious for you. This is the real deal, girl. No kidding around for me." She pecks my cheek, and we leave for Lazy's.

The sun starts to dip behind the hill, and the air cools. We walk slowly toward The Green, enjoying the last moments of the day, window shopping on the way. Sarah stops and comments on the displays at the general store.

"I'll take you tomorrow," I say, as I spot Christopher from a distance, crossing The Green.

Emma is coming from the opposite direction, and she waves at him, hurrying her steps. He waits for her on the sidewalk and opens the door for her.

My stomach feels a little queasy, but I chase the feeling.

He's just a good guy, doing the right thing.

Still, I pull on Sarah's sleeve, not liking the vibe I'm getting from Emma in this particular moment. "Let's go," I say.

Chapter Forty-Eight

Christopher

"This really isn't a good time, Emma," I say. I want to spend time with Alexandra, get to know her friend, then take my woman home. She came back to spend time with me before the competition, and yeah, I'm reading a lot into that.

I'm getting hard just thinking about spending the rest of my life with Alexandra.

"I just need a minute, Chris," Emma says.

"You have thirty seconds," I say as I spot Alexandra and her friend down the street. We slide into the first booth. "Spit it."

"I'll make it short," Emma says, pulling out some papers from a file in her briefcase. "Alexandra is Rita Douglas's granddaughter. Heir of Red Barn Baking. Future majority shareholder and commander supreme of said company if she successfully completes her baking apprenticeship at your bakery." She takes a breath. "I thought you should know."

I'm too stunned to respond, so I thumb through the papers she's holding out for me.

Some resolution or other legal shit confirming what Emma just said about the inheritance.

A Profit and Loss Statement, and a Balance Statement, both for Red Barn Baking. Emma wanted to make sure she drove the point home. Can't really blame her for doing her homework. That's her way of looking out for me.

In case I had any questions, the numbers at the bottom of the lines tell the whole story better than any words could have.

I never stood a chance.

The numbers dance in front of my eyes. My stomach clenches. My tongue feels like sandpaper.

Then the bitter taste of bile takes over.

No wonder she thought of me as a little thing to distract herself with while she was here.

I look up, auto-responding to the sound of her voice as she enters Lazy's and introduces Sarah to Justin. Her smile still lights the room, yet slices my heart. I can't believe her duplicity.

Fooled twice by rich women.

Blame's on me.

CHAPTER FORTY-NINE

Alexandra

When we get there, he's sitting at a booth with Emma, and he's looking at papers on the table. He sifts through them. Clenches his jaw. Sets them back on the table.

I'm worried for him. I hesitate for a beat. Is this a private, business moment? Should I wait?

Emma lifts her eyes to me and says something to Christopher. He doesn't look up.

I close the distance between us. Emma is nervously glancing between Christopher and me. Christopher has his eyes set on the papers. He jerks his chin up. Clenches his jaw again.

"Hey, everything okay?" I ask. "D'you need a minute?" I'm standing, Sarah right behind me, and they're both sitting.

Christopher squares his shoulders, and his lips flatten when he says, "Mind explaining this?"

His eyes are steely when he finally lifts them to me.

Emma pushes the papers my way.

I take the papers.

No. Oh no no no no no. No!

They're on Red Barn Baking letterhead. I don't need to read them to know what they are. I drop them on the table.

This is not how it was supposed to happen. I was going to tell Christopher, preface it with some history, and the assurance that I do love him, and that this is just a minor point in my background that I neglected to mention, but that won't make any difference in the grand scheme of things.

Because when two people love each other, they do so without regard to their financial situation or family background. Right?

Meanwhile, Emma catches the papers with a thin smile, stacks them neatly, and puts them back in the file folder with her business logo on it.

The room tilts slightly around me. I want to scream. How dare she take that moment away from me? How dare she get between us?

But I don't let my current anger at Emma take precedence. She's not who's important here.

Christopher will understand. He loves me. He said so just last night. And he knows I love him too. That, too, he said just last night. I understand he's hurt that he didn't hear that from me.

"I can explain, but if you don't want to forgive me for not telling you sooner, I need you to know, I just won't take the exam. I'll forgo everything."

His eyes darken. "Don't," he says.

Emma reaches her hand out and places it on his forearm, as if he needed calming down and she was the only one who could give him that.

My palms are sweaty, my heartbeat out of control. "You think this matters more to me than you? It doesn't. I thought I could have it all. Well, I was wrong. I can't. And I choose you."

"Don't jeopardize yourself, Alexandra. It's useless."

"Useless? I make it right, and you're telling me it's useless?" I can't help the rise in my voice. This is so unfair.

My eyes cut to Emma. "We'll continue this conversation without an audience." Then I turn to Christopher. "I'll be at the bakery."

I get the ugly cry out of the way in my room, cursing Emma but mostly blaming myself.

When I hear the bakehouse door slam, I wash my face quickly and put some moisturizer on my lips. I take a deep breath and look around my room. I'm dreading our talk.

But the make up sex is going to be awesome.

I find him in the bakehouse, leaning against the farthest prep table in the back. I close the door softly behind me, and I lick my lips in search of something to say as I make my way slowly to him, the intensity of his glare like a fist around my heart. "So that's it, huh?" he says, and his eyes say it. He means our relationship is over.

My stomach bottoms and my feet stop functioning. I'm frozen in place, another prep table between us like a wall. "No! What are you talking about?"

His fists clench around the edge of the table he's leaning on. "Can't believe you were going to leave me without even telling me this."

I force my legs to take me to him. To close the gap between us. But I stop midway under the force of his scowl. "I'm not leaving you, Christopher, and *of course* I was going to tell you."

"*Of course?*" he scoffs.

"I—I was waiting until after the competition." He stares me down, and I swallow with difficulty. "I didn't want you to lose your focus."

"How long you been here?" he asks, a mock frown on his face.

Five months and ten days. And each time I thought of telling him, I knew this would happen. I knew he'd feel contempt, and betrayal. "I…"

"You were waiting until the end to tell me what you're going back to, why you can't be with me? A little heads up would've been nice."

Holding onto the edge of the prep table for support, I take tentative steps toward him until I'm close enough to touch him. My breath catches. I need the physical contact. I place my hand on his forearm, but he stiffens under my touch. "I *can* be with you, Christopher. This doesn't change anything between us." Unless I was right, and he doesn't want to have anything to do with the heiress of Red Barn Baking.

But that can't be.

Not him.

"This changes everything, Alexandra."

A thick lump forms in my throat, and tears rim my eyes. Of course it changes everything. It's too much. Too big. *Don't sacrifice your happiness for Red Barn. Don't be your grandmother.* "I told you, I won't take the exam if it means so much to you. Red Barn is nothing to me, and you are my everything."

He hangs his head, chuckling sadly. "Relationships can't be based on lies, Alexandra."

"I didn't really lie to you," I whisper.

His head snaps up. "Don't make it worse."

"Please," I say, squeezing his forearm, but he moves to the side, breaking our touch. The empty table stares at me mockingly. It's where we had our first kiss. Where we got lost in each other. It's where we began. Where he showed me love for the first time.

"You would have hated me," I say, the words barely making it through my tight throat. "That first evening. Remember?" He clenches his jaw but says nothing. His words against Red Barn Baking had been so violent, no way in hell was I going to tell him then who I really was. He couldn't even understand why I would work for them. "I wanted you to *like* me. Since that first day, I would have said anything, done anything for you to like me."

"What about all the time since? Do you really think I would have hated you if you'd told me at some point later?"

I'm so tightly wound my stomach hurts when he looks me in the eye, demanding an answer I don't know I can give him—but I *have* to give him. "I don't know," I whisper.

He exhales, "Really."

My stomach bottoms. "Look where we are, now that you know."

"I wanted *you* to tell *me*. I wanted *you* to trust *me*." He pokes his finger at his chest, his eyes flaring with anger.

I take a shaking breath. "And I wanted you to love me for who I am." The best part of living in Emerald Creek was that no one knew whose granddaughter I was. No one cared. People liked me for who I was. And it was so *liberating*.

"But this is who you are!"

Tears roll down my cheeks, and I don't bother wiping them. "No. No, it's not who I am. I'm not Red Barn Baking. I'm not some rich heiress."

"So why did you take this apprenticeship, then?" he snarls.

I wipe my cheeks with the back of my hand, thinking about his question. Remembering who I was when I arrived in Emerald Creek.

"I was hoping for the love of a dead person. Stupid, I know." He has no idea how Rita's lack of love affected me.

He frowns at me. "I feel like I don't even know you," he says, shaking his head.

The tears start again. "Please, Christopher, don't say that," I beg, knowing what he means by that. How could he love someone he doesn't really know? The more I fell for him, the harder it became to come clean to him about Red Barn. But Red Barn doesn't define me. And as I was falling in love with him, everything tied to my grandmother faded in the background.

"Remember when you told me to focus on the important things when there's too many balls in the air? That's what I did. I focused on *you*. *You* were the most important thing to me. *You* showed me true love. I barely ever thought about Red Barn after the first few weeks here." For months, I'd been happy, truly happy. "I won't take the exam, Christopher. It's that simple. This way, we'll be back to where we were."

"Don't you see?" he shouts. "You didn't trust me! How am I supposed to be with someone who doesn't trust me?"

Oh god. I've been so closed off, so used to protecting myself, I never knew how to trust people. Not even him. My eyes well up again, my bottom lip trembles, and I can't come up with something to say to him that will make him change his mind.

If I couldn't give him my trust, do I even deserve him?

But how am I going to live without him? My heart booms in my chest, then seems to stop. "Please. Don't—Don't do this to us."

"There is no 'us,' Alexandra! I don't know who you are." He runs his hand through his hair. "Hell, I was going to... I was going to tell Skye about us. I was trying to convince you that you'd be happier living here and just being... with me. With us. But all along, I was only a stepladder for you."

I don't have the energy to wipe away my tears. All I can do is shake my head.

"You've blindsided me, Alexandra." He shrugs, regaining his control. "You'll do great. At least Rita taught you deception. That'll come in handy. Nothing I taught you here will help you where you're going."

His words cut deep. "I'm not going anywhere. And you taught me... love, in many different forms."

I wait for him to say something. To acknowledge what I just said. But he doesn't answer, so I say it again, differently. "I love you, Christopher, and you're the most important part of my life," I whisper.

He pushes himself from the table and takes two steps back. "I need to go, and you should too. Get some rest before your exam. Lots riding on it." His sarcasm slits me, even if I deserve it. I've hurt him.

"I love you, Christopher," I repeat, forcing my voice beyond the sobs that threaten. "You'll win the competition. I know it. And I'll be here when you come back."

His jaw clenches. I can see how wounded he is because I kept something from him, and strangely that makes me believe in us even more.

"When you told me you loved me," I continue, "I believed you. And I believe you still do. And the reason I didn't say it back last night—"

He raises his palms toward me. "Stop, Alexandra. Please give me this," he says as he continues backing away from me.

"Okay," I say softly. "But I'll be here when you come back. I won't take the exam. No going back for me."

"Don't," he cuts in. "Don't do that. It won't help. I can't trust someone who didn't trust me." Then he turns around and walks out of the bakehouse into the kitchen, his footsteps receding, until there's nothing but the ticking of the clock.

I wait for him to turn around, change his mind.

I wait in vain.

It could feel like he walked out of my life, but I won't let it be that. I have something worth fighting for, and I will. I'll show him how much I love him.

Still, I don't have the courage to sleep alone tonight, so close to him. So I grab the duffel bag that's still packed in my room and minutes later, I'm in Sarah's room at the inn.

Chapter Fifty

Alexandra

Christopher leaves for Boston the next day without saying goodbye, and I feel suspended.

Surely, this can't be the end.

Surely, he just needs to focus on the competition.

He needs time for himself.

I play back what he said to me.

That I blindsided him.

Didn't trust him.

That relationships can't be based on lies.

What he didn't say, though, is what he thinks about me being Rita Douglas's granddaughter.

Apart from the jab about her teaching me deception.

Does he think less of me because of the family I was born into? Or because of what I hid from him?

Does he actually think less of me?

That thought is unbearable, and I tuck it away.

"Thanks for not saying 'Told you so,'" I tell Sarah the next day. We're sitting in the hotel's small dining room. They serve a breakfast buffet that looks delicious, but I have no appetite.

But since I decided I'm staying here, in Emerald Creek, and I won't be even remotely associated with Red Barn Baking, I whip out my phone and take photos of their homemade granola and muffins, the cute china and silverware, the little bouquets on the round tables. I need to think about my next career.

"Whatcha doin'."

"Warming a cold target," I tell Sarah. I show her the touched-up photos of the inn I've already posted, and those of the breakfast, all with #emeraldcreekvt.

"You're really doing it?"

"Yup."

"M'kay. Maybe still take the exam. Just in case you change your mind down the road? This way, you could still go to the meeting and claim your shares."

"I won't change my mind."

"That sounds a little impulsive to me. I mean, give him a moment to chill out. You two will talk it through after the show. Once he calms down, he'll get over it. And you can still have Red Barn. If you don't take that exam in a couple of days, you're giving it up forever. Think of all the good you could do with that money."

"Okay. I was impulsive. As I can sometimes be. But I *can't* go back on my word. That would be the *worst* thing possible, after *he broke up with me for lying*." I mean, seriously, does she not get it?

"You painted yourself in a corner."

Yes, I did, I get that. "What else was I supposed to do?"

Sarah drops her spoon with a loud clank and throws her hands in the air. "Gee, I dunno! Tell him it was a shit move to start the discussion in front of what's her face? Tell him he needs to cool off before making any decision? Ask him if this is his idea of a couple, breaking things off at the slightest misunderstanding? Tell him you're actually going to need him a shit ton now that you're supposed to run a baking empire and you have no clue what you're doing but he does? And more importantly: Ask him if money is a turn off to him? Ask him if powerful women scare him?"

Her face is red when she finally stops to take a breath.

"Where were you when I needed you?" I ask.

She doesn't answer that non-question.

"You do see my point about the exam, though, don't you? Now that I told him I wouldn't go."

"Yeah, you messed up. If you really want Christopher, I have to say, as much as it pains me, after everything you've been through, if you want to save your relationship, that's probably your last chance."

I'm at peace with giving up Red Barn Baking, if that means I keep Christopher. It might be reckless, and impulsive, but that's who I am.

The competition takes place over three days, and the show is live-streamed. Every home and every business in Emerald Creek is tuned into it. The movie theater suspended its regular projections, showing only the baking competition.

The first day, I take a first-row seat early in the morning next to Grace with Skye nudged between us. The whole bakery team is at the front, and the energy coming from them is electric. They whisper technical comments on which contestant is doing what right. When the camera zooms in on Christopher, you can almost feel the front row holding its breath while the back of the room claps and shouts encouragement.

Someone adds closed captioning after Kiara shouts to the back to *Shut the fuck up*. I silently thank her.

I want to hear his voice, hear his breathing, know how he's doing.

It's a real marathon for the contestants, who only get three to four hours of sleep every night.

At midnight each day, they're given their assignments, and they have the whole day to realize them.

They present to the judges at six.

At five, the streets of Emerald Creek go silent, the shops shut down, and everyone gathers at the theater. Even Sarah, who's decided to stick around for a few days, joins after a day spent hiking the area. The tasting and debating will go on until about ten at night, at which point the judges will announce the winners before handing out the assignments for the next day. Of the ten contestants from the first day, only four will remain for the second.

The third day, it'll be down to two.

To say that I feel guilty for our fight the night before the competition is an understatement. I remember what he told me once, at the very beginning of my apprenticeship—that the dough feels the baker's state of mind and behaves accordingly.

If Christopher doesn't win, it will be my fault. I've inflicted too much hurt upon him by letting him falsely believe I betrayed his trust, and I'm concerned that his head is not in the right place now.

I look for signs that he might be out of sorts, distracted, angry.

I don't see any.

The first day goes well for him, and I sleep better that night. Sure, he looks tense and tired, black circles marking his eyes, but his gestures are assured, and his answers clipped and to the point when the cameras approach him mid-work. He's the Christopher I know in the bakery. And, while no one is surprised, you can sense the relief in the room when the results are in, and Christopher is selected for the second day.

Although a part of me is scared that means he's already moved on from me, I'm relieved for him. He deserves to win, and the world deserves to know what a great baker he is.

Once he wins, people will get to know him better, and hopefully his win will give him a platform to promote his ideas about food, and community, and local production. He has so much to offer the world. So much passion. So much generosity.

I want the world to know him the way I do.

Well, for the most part.

The second day, the four contestants left are up to his level. There's a woman from Boston, another one from Maine, a baker from Burlington, and Christopher. They all have to make the same confections, and there's little left to their creativity. It's all about execution. Creativity will be for the two finalists on the last day.

Today's four contestants are lined up in immaculate and freshly pressed uniforms, their hands behind their backs, their feet slightly apart. Christopher looks more tired than yesterday, understandably, but he's shaved, and his hair looks slightly damp, tamed back. He's fresh out of the shower.

I texted him after our argument, but he never answered. Is he reading his messages when he goes back to his hotel? Is he ignoring me or simply trying to stay focused?

What's important to him now is this competition, and that's how it should be.

The judges start their comments, and my palms become sweaty.

While Christopher's shepherd's pie is clearly the winner, seeing how the judges literally lick their fingers and scoop up the crumbs from their plate, they give the woman from Boston top grade for her rye *miche*, and immediately, the whole room calls the judges partial. My heartbeat picks up.

But her croissants disappoint.

Each dish gets a score, and the tally starts. It's unbearable to watch. At least for me.

Everyone in the front row is displaying some form of stress. Kiara bites her nails. Isaac shakes his leg. Willow pulls hairs from the top of her head.

We're a disaster.

At nine, Skye is fast asleep, and Grace takes her back to her place, where she's been staying since Christopher left for Boston. "I'll watch from home," she says as she slips out during yet another commercial break.

By the end of the evening, it's set: it will be between the baker from Burlington and Christopher. The Burlington guy got a slightly higher score, and the mood is morose as everyone files out of the theater well after ten that night.

There are a couple of cameras on the sidewalk, and a TV van on The Green. Noah, as head of the Chamber of Commerce, is already miked up and defending Christopher and Emerald Creek. A group of people are gathered behind him, and it's a miracle they don't demand on live TV that Christopher get the title already.

I love that about them. That unconditional support and belief in their baker. In their village. The way they stick together.

Kiara catches up with me as I'm leaving. "So, whether Christopher wins or not tomorrow, we want to throw him a party."

"Of course, yeah."

"Can you help? You're good with all the social media and online shit."

Wow, look at that. Kiara is paying me a compliment. I stop in my tracks, and I probably blush. "I'd love to. Who's our target?"

She cocks her head, not understanding my question.

"Who do you want coming to the party?"

She thinks about it. "The party should be just for the townspeople, but if we could broadcast the party and make some noise about us, that'd be great." She glances toward the reporters.

"You want to use the competition and the party as a way to showcase the businesses and the village in general, to attract visitors."

"Exactly."

"Especially if the asshole from Burlington wins the competition. We can still turn that into a win for Emerald Creek, if we play our cards right."

She smiles at my use of profanity. "That's it. I hope we don't lose, though. I don't want to be the one picking up the pieces of Christopher if that happens."

"What do you think his chances are?"

"You heard the theme. It'll be entirely subjective." She shrugs. "It's bullshit."

Tomorrow, it's freestyle. They must create a whole meal celebrating a single bread-based confection and will be judged on their "*creative interpretation of baking tradition.*" Whatever that means.

I don't sleep much that night. I try to send good vibes to Christopher.

I start planning the party, hoping I don't jinx his chances.

The next day, Christopher looks like shit. He's not shaved, his uniform is wrinkled. I'm pretty sure he didn't sleep at all, just went straight from day two to day three without any sort of break. It's seven in the morning when I log into the show from my phone, and my guess is he's been twenty-seven hours without sleep already. And he has about sixteen more hours to go.

This isn't going to end well.

The good news is, the other guy doesn't look any better.

When I get to the theater, the news is that Justin came back from Boston, where he'd driven Christopher, to pick up a list of ingredients Christopher needed for today. Justin and Colton made the rounds of Emerald Creek's producers and drove back down to Boston.

Christopher asked for smoked trout from the Henderson's smokehouse, garlic scapes from Cassandra's plot at the community gardens, cheddar and ice cream from the Kings' Farm, flowers from Miss Angela's patch, and god knows what else.

We're not clear what Christopher is making, and he hasn't given anyone on the show any clue.

I glance at Kiara, and she gives me an *I-have-no-idea* shrug.

Finally, at seven fifty-nine, the countdown starts, and at eight, Christopher and the guy from Burlington pull back from their masterpieces.

Burlington goes first, and he's good.

Like, *really* good.

The stuff he made is impressive, all ornate and beautiful. They're real pieces of art. Carved breads with mini sandwiches nested inside. Soufflés and other elaborate things that look positively delicious.

It'll be tough to beat, but if someone can, it's Christopher.

But after Christopher makes his masterpiece statement—a short presentation explaining his choice—the crowd around me is stunned silent.

And my heart sinks.

We're going to lose.

Chapter Fifty-One

Christopher

Any other time, I would have done something different. But, today, now, this is where my baker's heart is.

The first two days here, I was laser-focused on what was expected from me. I'd shoved all thoughts of Alexandra aside. But, when that bullshit assignment came in last night, I knew there was no point trying to comprehend what the judges wanted.

One word kept coming back to me: pancakes.

I decided to follow my instinct. My heart.

Baking is about community and love. It's about making people feel good and bringing them around a table.

If the judges don't like my interpretation, then so be it.

I'm proud of what I did, and that's all that counts.

Here we go. I look at the judges, one after the other.

"When the people you love are gone, what remains are memories. And one of the best ways to rekindle these memories, is through food. So I made a pancake dinner. You might think pancakes are as American as apple pie, and you'd be right. But they exist, differently, in every culinary tradition. Pancakes are the ultimate soul food, made with simple ingredients, meant to bring a family together around the table, with recipes passed down from generation to generation. And if your recipe consists of a preferred mix, that's fine too. As long as you use real maple syrup." I pause for a beat, again looking at each of the judges. They're wearing their skeptical faces. The hell with them if they don't get me.

"I know that might seem simplistic, but simplicity is what's lacking in our society. And also, at the risk of contradicting myself, pancakes can be quite sophisticated, if that's what you're going for. In any case, whether you want to remain down-to-earth or are going for something more elevated, pancakes will always call to our sensory memories, those created early on in our childhood. For me, they will always be associated with love. And for the viewers out there, here's the takeaway: If you want to tell people you love them, make them pancakes."

Justin pushes himself from the reception desk and marches toward us, hauling his carry-on. "Let's get the fuck out of this fucking place," he barks.

Okay.

"'Bout time," Colton mumbles as we follow him to the parking lot.

We throw our bags in the truck bed, Colton flicks the truck doors open, and Justin folds himself in the back seat.

"Good call," Colton says under his breath as he takes the driver's seat.

After the show ended last night, we wanted to get back home, but couldn't find Justin. There'd been a power outage, and word was that he might be stuck in an elevator, but he didn't pick up his phone, and, anyway, power was eventually restored and still no sign of Justin. Colton and I crashed in a double, and in the morning, a very pissed off Justin showed up with no explanation, said he had business to tend to, and started a half-hour long argument with the front desk, the gist of which we had no clue and gave no fucks.

We just wanted to get home, and he was being a diva.

Colton finally breaks the silence. "That was brilliant, man, what you did. I didn't know you could make so many dishes with pancakes."

"Thanks," I answer simply. I blew the judges' minds with my sourdough pancake batter base, interpreted both sweet and savory to form the basis of a whole meal. Blinis and smoked Vermont trout with a side of whipped cream and freshly picked garlic scapes, cheddar soufflé pancakes, chocolate silver dollar size pancakes with a side of ginger ice cream, and the proposal pancake—a hibiscus pancake topped with pansies holding an engagement ring.

"If anybody would know that, it'd be you. Proud o'ya."

I tilt my chin toward Justin. "What happened to him?"

"Hell if I know."

After a while driving in silence, Colton says, "So, Alex, huh."

Last thing I want to talk about.

"I had someone that sweet look at me the way she looks at you, I wouldn't let her go that easy. Wouldn't matter she didn't fully disclose her circumstances."

"Yeah?" I don't want to argue with Colton.

He shrugs. "Not telling you what to do. Not in your shoes. Just saying, that's what I'd do."

I keep staring out the window. My cousin usually doesn't speak much.

"She and Grace're tight. See her at Ma's sometimes."

Right. He's been around Alexandra more than I thought. He understands.

He's not done with his pep talk. "You got a shit start in life, man. You deserve a woman like her."

I chuckle. "Thanks, man, but she got better things to do than be stuck with me."

He glances my way. "Stuck? A'right, man. Whatever." He flicks the radio on to a country music station. After an hour I switch to rock, and that's the extent of our disagreement.

And then we get to Emerald Creek.

The town is decorated to the nines, with balloons and twinkling lights and my name plastered on all the windows.

It's embarrassing.

Embarrassing and great.

"Alex organized the celebration party for you. Tonight by the river," Colton says.

I shuffle my feet. "How do you know Alexandra did this?"

He shrugs. "Kiara. You look like shit, dude," he says as I step out the car. "Get some sleep."

The bakery's been closed for a few days, and it's quiet inside the house. The exhaustion of the past few days catches up with me, and I haul my ass up to my bedroom.

I glance at the door to the hidden staircase, shove my feelings down where they can't bother me, and get some sleep.

I wake up with a throbbing headache, take a long shower, a couple of aspirins, then drag myself to the river, guided by the sounds of the band.

This should be one of the best days of my life so far, yet I feel like shit. There's nothing worth celebrating for me. I already know I'm the best baker in New England.

Cocky? So what.

But I'm doing this for Emerald Creek. This community always came through for me. The least I can do is give them this. I plaster a smile on my face and walk toward the sound of music drifting up from the riverbanks.

I navigate through the swarms of people who slap me on the shoulder, hug me, or take selfies with me. The band interrupts their gig for a second to announce my arrival and to remind people to use the bakery's hashtag when posting photos of the event on their social media.

Is Alexandra still here? That's something she would do. Uneasiness settles in my stomach. I don't think I can bear to see her.

"There he is!" My mother's voice startles me from my thoughts.

I narrow my eyes at the sight of the family assembled in a circle. I hug Mom first, then my half brothers, Ryan and Trevor. They're as tall as me now, and what I saw of them in the videos is confirmed. They're filling in. I feel out their muscles teasingly, and they reward me with huge grins.

Finally, I shake hands with my stepfather, Dean, who's standing awkwardly to the side. "I suppose congratulations are in order," he drops, a smirk on his face. He's bouncing from one foot to the other, like a kid who's been chastised. My mother must have lectured him on the way here. At least he's making an effort.

"Thanks, yeah. And thanks for coming."

"Oh—We had to come to pick up Skye, anyway. Your mother doesn't like to drive long distances. Figured we'd kill two birds with one stone."

Mom interrupts him before he puts his foot deeper in his mouth. "We thought it'd be a nice opportunity for the whole family to celebrate together. Dean, let's go find Shannon and Dennis and let the boys catch up."

"Dude, you rock," Ryan says when they're out of earshot.

"Yeah." Trevor chuckles. "Look at this crowd, all for you." His eyes glimmer with genuine pride and joy, and they both laugh and look admiringly at me.

Fuck, I've missed these little buggers.

The video calls we try to have each week now, mainly for Skye's benefit, are no replacement for the real, physical presence. "You guys have anything lined up for the summer? I could use some help in the bakery."

"Ohmygod that's a great idea!" Grace exclaims. I turn around and see her and Alexandra swinging Skye between them. They crept up on me, and now I'm caught in Alexandra's gaze boring through my core, and I want to be anywhere but here.

I focus on Skye running to me and dousing me in kisses. "I love you, Daddy. Now, Caroline can't say you're not the best baker in the whole wide world."

I hug her tight and close my eyes. "You already knew that."

Grace is greeting her cousins and saying, "If you guys are in, I'll talk to your mom and dad about working here."

Skye pinches my cheeks and pulls them apart. "Yes," she says. "Now smile."

I try to smile as I set her down. Alexandra is standing back, looking like she wants to leave, but Skye starts pulling on her yellow summer dress, introducing her to her uncles.

The dress shows her shoulders, hugs her breasts, and stops right above her knees. All I can think about is how soft her skin is.

How sweet she tastes.

How deeply moving her kisses are.

And how I'll never have her again.

The twins' eyes light up at the sight of her, and Ryan pulls her into a hug that lasts several unnecessary beats. Little shithead.

"Alexandra is—*was*—our apprentice," I say. "She's leaving the day after tomorrow."

Chapter Fifty-Two

Alexandra

A bottle of wine and a whole box of tissues into the night, Sarah asks again, "You're really doing that?"

"Yes," I sniffle. "Red Barn is already a half-lost battle anyway, and it's not one I feel like fighting anymore. Not without him to support me. I—I didn't—couldn't find the words to explain myself to him. I need to *show* him."

"No bad ass girl boss in your future?"

"This is my only way to show him I love him. I'm a bad ass girl boss with her priorities right."

"M'kay."

"There's so much more to life than running a multi-million company that does no good at all. Look at Rita. I don't want her life. No thank you."

As if on cue, my phone rings.

Barbara.

"Hello," I croak.

"Calling to wish you good luck, my love. We have champagne on ice here. Are you driving back right after the exam? There's no rush. You should stay and spend some time with your celebrity lover. Maybe we'll come up and celebrate with you. Jerry! You down for a trip to Emerald Creek? Why haven't I thought about this earlier? We can all drive back down together like the big happy family we are, right on time for the general meeting. It's not for another two weeks."

"Barb. I'm not going."

"Pardon? What did you say? I'm getting hard of hearing."

Is she joking, or is she really getting hard of hearing? She's pushing seventy. "I'm not going to take the exam."

"What is that? I'm not following."

"I'm giving up on Red Barn. I can't do it. Won't do it."

"And why is that? We have it all figured out. Jerry has been pumping me up to be your mighty right hand. Like with Rita, but better."

I take a deep breath, and the words spill out, as well as the tears. I tell her how I was exposed, and how that affected my relationship with Christopher. "Red Barn has caused me so much pain, Barb. So much. I can't take it anymore. In a way, I'm relieved the choice is made for me. I feel like I have a real direction, now."

"Well, that's quite the grand gesture," Barbara says. It's followed by silence, not even the sound of her drawing on a joint and exhaling. "You might regret that, you know. It's a lot to give up on."

"I know. I understand that. And when I was thinking about it, when I was gearing up to come clean to Christopher, I thought the upside would be that I would receive his guidance, you know? We'd be a team. He would have been the perfect person to help me. Guide me." Tears well up again. "Everything is ruined now. He won't even listen to me. I can't get through to him. He's convinced I lied, and that's all he sees. It's my fault though, and I have to fix this. And I'm sorry, Barbara, he is more important than Red Barn to me. I love him. He's who I want in my future."

"Of course, honey. Of course. And you've tried everything?"

"The only thing left is for me to renounce Red Barn by not taking the exam. That's all I have left. Red Barn was never going to be my long-term future anyway."

She grunts her assent. "That makes perfect sense, in a way."

That sounds like an easy win. "How so?"

"Rita thought Red Barn was the solution to her personal problems, when it was really its source. She wanted to impose that on you, and for some time you followed. But then circumstances forced you to see the light. You're choosing love. That's powerful. I'm proud of you." There's the sound of voices muffled by her hand on her phone, then she says, "Jerry can't wait to meet you. We'll see you soon." And she hangs up.

I look at my darkened phone screen.

"Well, that went well," Sarah says.

I'm about to dissect what Barbara said when I'm interrupted by a knock on our door. We exchange a look, and Sarah gets up and cracks the door open.

"You again? You have some nerve." Sarah is trying to keep her voice low, but the tremor in it is telling.

"Please, I really need to talk to Alex."

The voice grates like nails on a chalkboard. Didn't she torture me enough already? I hide my head under the pillow. If Emma's here to examine the physical effects of her manipulation, I won't give her that satisfaction.

"How did you know where to find her?" Sarah asks. "Just leave her alone already. You got what you wanted."

"It's not what I wanted," Emma answers. "I was just looking out for Chris."

The welcome sound of a door shutting in her face is immediately followed by a rapping on the door again.

I muffle a scream. The woman has no shame.

"There's something she needs to know," Emma insists. "Please."

Sarah lets out an exasperated sigh. "I'll meet you downstairs," she says, locking the door. She pulls her jeans and a sweatshirt above her short and tank-top pajamas. "Bitch isn't coming in here. I'll make sure she leaves and doesn't bother you anymore," she says to me.

I wait until the door shuts behind her to pull myself together. I stand, go to the bathroom, do my business, and splash water on my face.

I'm normally not a sobber, so the red blotches on my face are a surprise. I really don't care right now.

I brush my hair and tie it in a ponytail, then apply some moisturizer.

Feeling halfway human, I plop on the bed, waiting for Sarah to return.

Then I decide I might as well put my jammies on, but the room phone rings.

And rings.

I look at it. I guess it's for me?

"Hey, boo," Sarah's voice comes out gloomy. "You're gonna wanna come downstairs."

"Really?"

"Yeah. Really," she whispers.

Shit.

I go downstairs.

There's a small sitting room off the lobby with four blue wingback chairs and a coffee table. Sarah and Emma are sitting on opposite sides.

I glance at Emma, who's studying her cuticles, and sit next to Sarah. She's holding a document. I'm not fond of those right now.

What now?

Sarah takes a deep breath. "You know how you were going to prove your undying love to Christopher by giving up on Red Barn? Not going to the exam?"

"That's what I'm doing." I nod. However hurt I am right now, that's the only thing I can do to prove my love for him.

"We have a problem," Sarah says. She turns to Emma. "Go ahead."

Emma looks up and takes a deep breath. Her chin pointing to the papers Sarah is holding, she says, "If you don't go to the exam, or if you fail, Chris loses his grant. And if he loses his grant, he's at risk of losing the bakery."

"What the hell are you talking about?" I take the papers from Sarah and start reading.

Emma's eyes are ruthlessly narrowed on me, as if I'm the accused in a particular brutal murder and she's the prosecutor. "Chris got a grant from the Red Barn Foundation, several years ago. That grant stated as a condition that he may be asked to take in an apprentice on short notice. If he did get that request, he had to accept the apprentice *and* the apprentice needed to be successful. No dropping out, no failing the exam, or else the grant is due back, in full." She looks at me, a harsh expression in her eyes.

I skim the grant, confirming everything Emma is saying. Confirming that I'm that apprentice. I remember her words from the first time I saw her doing books at the bakery.

Sarah clears her throat. "The grant is massive, Boo. It covered everything. Building, equipment, start-up costs. It's how he was able to start a bakery in a remote place like here. Why didn't he tell you?"

My heart is beating so hard in my chest I can't breathe. What I'm reading confirms this as well.

"He didn't want to put pressure on me," I whisper.

I turn to Emma, and my anger flares. "Why didn't you tell me?"

She pretends not to understand. As if her telling me now is enough.

"At Lazy's, the day before the competition," I say. "When you told Christopher I was to inherit from Rita Douglas. I said I wouldn't take the exam, if it meant so much to him. I told him I didn't care about Red Barn enough to lose him over it, and I could prove it by not going to the exam. And when I said that, you put your paw on him, as if to calm him down. You could have said something to me. You should have told me then, what this meant for Christopher."

"It wasn't my place."

Air wooshes out my lungs. The nerve!

"Why didn't Chris say anything?" Sarah interjects before I have time to ream into Emma.

"Christopher would never force anyone to do something for his benefit," I say. And that's why he never told me, during my whole apprenticeship. It would have been a lot of pressure on me. On anyone in my position.

Emma turns to Sarah, ignoring me. "Chris is proud. Too proud to ask anyone for help. That's the only reason he hasn't told Alexandra. That's why I came tonight."

"You're so full of shit," I spit. "You waited until I was so deep into promising him I'd do it to show him my love. You could have intervened at any time. You could have come during the competition."

"I can't disclose client information like that. Surely, even you can understand that." Her disdain is palpable.

"So why the fuck are you here now?" I say between gritted teeth.

She widens her eyes. "I thought you'd understand why."

"Oh, I understand, Emma. Because you can make it look like I changed my mind. Like I lied to him again, led him on. Like I don't care about him."

"You couldn't stand seeing them happy together, could you?" Sarah snarls at Emma. "If you hadn't interfered, hadn't told Chris about Alex's grandmother, none of this would have happened. They would be happy right now. He'd know the truth, would have heard it from Alex, and he would have supported her taking the exam. But you couldn't stomach it."

Blood swooshes in my ears.

"I was only looking out for him," Emma answers, her chin trembling. "You can't tell him I told you."

"Honey," I say, standing up and dropping the grant papers on the coffee table. "We, contrary to you, are not in the business of ruining people's lives. But he'll find out eventually. This is a small town. There are no secrets. But you are already know that, right?"

I lean toward her. "One last thing. No matter what you do, you'll never love him the way I do. And he knows that."

I only get a few hours of agitated sleep. I'm high-strung when I get to the big hotel where the baking testing takes place the next day.

I take deep breaths and calm down.

I need to pass. No choice.

I concentrate. Think one last time about my purpose. And understand Christopher's focus, on screen: this needs to get done.

I try to channel his strength.

My assignments are easier than I anticipated, and I don't encounter any problems. I'm asked to do brioches, croissants, a baguette, and a specialty bread.

I take a moment to plan on paper the order in which I'll prepare each bread, so I'm done in the allotted time, demonstrating my organizational skills in the bakeshop. I also write down the proportions from memory, so I don't mess up at the last minute. No more overflowing dough for me.

I finish with fifteen minutes left for the cleanup. It might be the last time I ever do anything related to baking, so I tackle it like a personal cleanse. A clean slate before I begin a new chapter in my life.

"You have been taught well," the examiner tells me. He speaks with a French accent. "Who iz your master?" he asks, looking down his list.

Master?

"Ah yes," he says. "Monsieur Wright."

He harumphs. Cocks an eyebrow. Jots down his notes. "He will receive your results by electronic mail," he says, straightening, then walking away, hands behind his back.

"Did I pass?" I ask, forcing him to turn around.

"Mais oui, bien sûr," he shrugs with a frown.

Torn, I deflate. Then I remember why I did this.

It doesn't make me feel better.

Chapter Fifty-Three

Alexandra

Two weeks later

*

The last biting sun rays duck behind the mountain. "One more hour," Sarah says, "and that should do it."

Now that it's cooling down, I feel like I could go on for hours. I don't feel my legs anymore, and the blisters on my feet are healing.

When Sarah picked me up from the exam, I asked her if I could join her on her backpacking trip. I needed to get away. And I needed a buffer between my time in Emerald Creek and my move back to New York. Between my scorching love story with Christopher and the next slice of my life, at Red Barn Baking.

Something to ease the pain. To make the transition less brutal.

While I was in Montpelier taking the exam, Sarah grabbed all my stuff from my room, dumped it in Grace's garage, even my phone—especially my phone—except whatever gear I needed for backpacking. She arranged for everything to be picked up and shipped to New York. She told Grace I'd come back soon to say a proper goodbye, once the dust settled.

I also wanted Skye to know I hadn't abandoned her. That I would still be in her life, even if I knew that was probably not going to happen long term. But I can see myself coming back to Emerald Creek for a visit, staying at Grace's, and seeing Skye there.

For the first two days of the hike, when I wasn't breaking down sobbing against a tree, I'd focus on the searing pain of the blisters on my feet to get out of my head.

"Breathe into it," Sarah, who believes yoga cures everything, kept saying. I could have killed her. Until, one day, I tried it. And maybe it was the dehydration—water is freaking heavy to carry on a trail—but it worked. Breathing into your pain makes it go away. "It's because you're telling your body it's all right, so it stops acting up and sending you pain signals."

"So, I'm tricking my body."

"You gotta do what you gotta do to make the pain go away."

And that's been the theme of this trip. I've been trying to work through my pain without ruining Sarah's hiking trip. Which means, she's done most of the talking.

"It's okay to cry, you know," she says that evening, while we're both on our backs, staring at the stars. We're at a camping ground along the Appalachian Trail, and surprisingly, there's only one other couple, on the opposite end. "You're allowed to grieve, no matter what I think of him." Sarah thinks that Christopher feels differently about me because of who my grandmother is. She's totally missing the point. He feels differently about me because I lied to him, effectively rejecting him by not being open about who I was and why I really was here. That rejection revived some old wounds. I should have known better than to do that to him.

"What about tricking my pain?"

"That's for your body, boo. Your emotional pain? You need to acknowledge it. Express it. Meaning, push it out of you."

I groan. "Hanging up your therapist plate anytime soon?"

She chuckles. "Come on, tell me one good thing and three bad things about him."

"What's that? A campfire game?"

"Ha ha. I'm listening. Start with the good thing. Only one."

"He's the ultimate caretaker," I whisper. The memory of his hands holding my hair back when I was puking after I got drunk at Justin's sticks in my head. We hadn't even kissed yet, and he'd picked me up, carried me in the glacial night, held me over the porcelain bowl, tucked me in bed, left water and aspirin and the best coffee ever on my nightstand.

"M'kay. Three bad things now."

I sigh. There isn't one bad thing about him.

"Boo. I'm waiting. Nobody's perfect. He's only human. Show me his ugly side. Come on."

"He's a stickler for rules. Baking rules." Although I'd messed up more than once in the kitchen, the ultimate disaster I created when I confused yeast and flour was probably the worst. He'd been upset and broody, but he hadn't let anyone other than him take care of me. He'd applied ointment on my elbow, ensured nothing was broken, and took me off baking duty.

"Rules, barf," Sarah says. "Now I really don't like him. Okay, second bad thing about him."

After a beat, I answer, "He can't shoot a video to save his life." He was so cute that morning in the bakehouse, when I showed him how to do a selfie to sell product. He ended up telling people to go grab his stuff for free at Justin's. Later, he got into it on his own, but his shoots were always off focus, tilted, and jumpy. It was so amateurish it was actually good, in an avant-garde kind of way.

"Whaaat? You can't be with a guy who doesn't understand how to make a decent video. Come on, Alex, I'm disappointed in you. What were you thinking?" She's playing with me, and she knows I know it, but it's good to be talking about Christopher with my best friend without it being dramatic.

It's gotta be a stage of grief.

"Alright, last one, and it better be good."

Good? *He* was good in so many ways. I wrack my brain to come up with something bad about Christopher.

Images of him flow to me in response. Gently blow-drying my hair. Giving me advice when I was overwhelmed. Patiently teaching me his craft. Admiring my photography. Bragging about my social media skills.

I let out a heartbroken sigh.

"He let you go, Alex," Sarah says. "That's a fucking bad thing in my book. His loss, but I'll never forgive him for the pain you're going through. There. We got three. Time to move on."

I take a deep breath. "I'll be okay, boo. I come from a strong line of women." The truth is, I see where Rita was coming from. I don't need a man for my life to be complete. "It's going to be good to focus on Red Barn Baking."

"Work will help you get through this," Sarah says, surprising me. "But don't you let it become the end goal."

I take my best friend's hand and squeeze it tight.

Chapter Fifty-Four

Christopher

It's Justin's community dinner at Lazy's tonight, so I haul my ass out there. Sophie posted on Echoes that I'd be dragged there by force if I didn't show, and I know she means it.

Since Alexandra left, I'm a mess. I can't even bring myself to reopen the bakery. My staff is on paid leave, courtesy of too much financial security that I honestly hate right now. Just as much as I hate myself.

Skye is still in Maine with Mom, but not for much longer. I need to pull myself together before she's back. So I shower, shave, find some clean clothes, and cross The Green.

When I walk in, Colton is giving Justin a hard time for his attitude. "You been in a shit mood since we came back from Boston. I thought you always got some when you're out of town."

Kiara slides onto the stool next to Colton. "What's up with that, by the way? What's wrong with the women around here?"

"I don't shit where I eat," Justin snaps.

"Lovely," Haley says. "Mom and Dad would be proud of you," she adds sarcastically. "Good thing they're late."

"As usual," Justin growls.

Fuck. He's in as bad a mood as I am. "What's up, man?" It's time I get my head out of my ass and actually give a damn about my friends' problems. "You worried what's gonna happen next door?" The owner of the fine dining restaurant adjacent to Lazy's had a heart attack. There was no love lost between the two, but their businesses are linked somehow, and the guy's passing is going to shake things up for Justin. I'm not sure how, but I bet that's what eating at him. Word has it he had an epic argument with their new manager.

He wipes the squeaky clean counter, says nothing.

"Come on, man. What's up? Colton's right—"

"Just drop it. Nothing's up. You been moping around for weeks now, your business is still closed, but when you finally get out of your cave, you think you can give me lessons or somethin'?" His anger is palpable, hitting me in the stomach. Fuck.

"Hey, cousin," Grace says, wrapping her arms around my middle and squeezing me. "You okay?" she whispers.

I shut my eyes and hug her back. "I don't know," I admit. I've been trying to reach out to Alexandra, but I still haven't heard back from her.

"She'll be back," Cassandra says. I open my eyes and see a group of women assembled around me. I let go of Grace and shuffle my feet.

"She just needs time," Wendy says.

"Space," Kiara adds.

"Just keep trying," Autumn says.

Emma huffs. "Seriously, you guys aren't helping him. You need to leave it be, Chris. Honestly, I could never understand what the hype about her was anyway. You'll see diff—"

"Do yourself a favor, Emma, don't trash talk Alex," Grace says. A couple of the women look embarrassed.

Emma quiets and shrugs like it's no big deal.

"Alex is the kindest, most generous person I know. What's wrong with you?" Autumn says, and Emma blushes, catching onto the vibe coming from the women.

I know Emma is only looking out for me, offering me a clumsy way to cope. She means well, but she clearly doesn't know where this barrage is coming from. "Told you you should have tried to get to know her better, Ems," I tell her. "Your loss."

"Oh, Emma was close to Alexandra. Weren't you, honey?" Wendy says.

Emma turns a deep shade of red. "No, not really. Not at all." She looks a little panicked.

"Welllll," Wendy draws out. "I wouldn't say that." She glances at me, then her eyes narrow back on Emma. "Or else why would you pay her a long visit in the middle of the night after Christopher broke things off? You told me you came to offer support. That's what friends do."

Emma offered support to Alexandra after I broke things off? What is Wendy talking about?

"Dee Dee!" Kiara interjects. "What the hell? Everybody knows Emma couldn't stand Bambi."

Wendy turns to Kiara. "Remember the night of the party for Christopher?"

"What about it?" I ask.

"Alex came to stay with her friend at the hotel."

I close my fists, remembering what a selfish asshole I'd been. I've been going over that night a million times. I can live with myself for being angry at her after I heard from Emma that she was inheriting

Red Barn. It was impulsive of me, but I'm not perfect, and I had my reasons.

But I can't live with myself after I had a few days to calm down, after I won the competition, after Alexandra threw me a party and was still waiting for me, sweet and forgiving and fucking way more than I ever deserve. I'll never forgive myself for pushing her away. There was no reason other than my stubbornness. I hurt her, I lost her, and even if by some miracle I win her back, I'll never forgive myself for that.

Honest to god, I don't give a shit what family she's from, how much or how little money she has. I love her, the core of who she is, and I let my past, my demons, fuck with me and get the better of me. I let my fear of being hurt again jeopardize my future. Alexandra was not like that. I should have known better.

"Anywho," Wendy is saying, "Emma came to the inn late at night, rang the doorbell seeing as it was past midnight. Remember?" she says, turning to Emma. "You said you *absolutely* had to talk to Alexandra. I remember telling Todd after letting you in, and I slipped back in bed, *'Well, that's what friends do. They show up when the going gets rough.'*"

Emma's face goes from deep red to ashen, and blood coils in my veins. Did she really do that? "What the fuck did you tell her?" I groan, knowing the answer.

She bites her lip and says nothing.

"I told you!" I boom. Grace's hand on my arm reminds me we're in a public space, and I bring my voice down. "I told you you had no right to share that information with her. I told you what would happen if you did."

"Chris. I was looking out for you," Emma says, then straightens her shoulders. "End of the day, I was looking out for her as well, seeing as—"

"Don't you dare," I hiss. "Don't you dare say you were looking out for her."

Cassandra protectively wraps an arm around Emma, who's shaking now.

"I should drive you out of business, like I said I would," I continue.

"Now, now. No one is driving anyone out of business," Cassandra says. "Come on, sweetheart, let's talk about all this somewhere else," she says, thankfully walking Emma out of my sight.

Wendy narrows her eyes on Emma as she walks away, then turns to me. "I'm sorry I didn't say anything earlier. Might have saved you and Alexandra a lot of trouble."

I run a hand through my hair. "Don't be sorry. Bottom line, it's all my fault. I should have known." I should have known Alexandra would have been true to her word. I can't believe I was angry and bitter when I received her results via email. Selfish bastard. She did it for me. She sacrificed herself so Skye and I would have financial security. Why did I not see earlier that Emma played her dirty card?

I blamed Alexandra for not trusting me with her secret, and meanwhile I couldn't even trust her love.

How do I fix this?

My phone buzzes in my pocket. Stupidly hoping it's Alexandra, I look at the screen.

It's not her. *Of course it's not. I still have her phone.*

But it's Barbara, and she's been leaving me messages to call her back.

Maybe it's time I do just that. Maybe she can help me.

I leave Lazy's to take her call.

Chapter Fifty-Five

Alexandra

The next day, we say goodbye to the Appalachian Trail in Bear Mountain, New York. We check ourselves into an inn that offers hearty dinner options. It's a little on the pricey side, but after more than two weeks on the trail, we need the indulgence. We'll spend the night, then make our way back into the city by bus tomorrow morning. Then onto the subway to haul ourselves all the way back to Brooklyn.

After dinner, I plop on the bed while Sarah is in the shower. Such luxury. When it's my turn to clean up, I take extra time shaving, wash my hair three times, and finish their outrageously good-smelling conditioner. I loved my time away from civilization, but I'm ready to go back, now. And even if I have a pinch of apprehension at the idea of running Red Barn Baking, I'm looking forward to having so many things on my plate there's nothing—no one—else I can think about.

The next morning, I dig out a summer dress and sandals Sarah somehow threw in the backpack. I give the dress a quick iron and slip it on, relishing feeling feminine again. I've lost weight over the last couple of weeks, and my legs and tummy are toned from the hiking, but my breasts still fill the low-cut dress in a sexy way. I tie my hair in a French braid and finish my look with a clean cotton hat and sunglasses.

As we check out, the front desk clerk narrows her eyes on us. "What's wrong with her?" Sarah whispers as we leave.

I shrug.

The bus stop is a short walk away, and we're early for the ride to New York City. There's a diner nearby with outdoor seating and a sign that says Ice Cream All Day.

"That qualifies as breakfast, right?" Sarah asks.

"It's dairy," I confirm.

We sit under an umbrella, bask in the sun, and relish the cool taste of ice cream cones on our tongues.

Once I'm done eating the last crunchy part of the cone, I pull my hat down and close my eyes behind my sunglasses, enjoying the quiet. From here, we'll hear the bus pull up. Sarah goes to the bathroom, and for a moment, it feels like it's only me out here.

"Holy effing shit," Sarah whisper-screams as she comes back.

I open one eye at her. She's holding a bag of candy and a gossip magazine. The kind with paparazzi photos of celebrity close-ups.

I close my eyes, again. It can't be the candy, so I wonder what the Kardashians might have done again to rile Sarah up.

"'Sup?" I mumble, wanting to know what the rest of the world has been up to while we totally checked out.

"Hello?" she says.

I open my eyes, again. She shoves the magazine in my face, so close I have to push it away to actually look at it.

When I do, I'm staring at myself.

There's a full front-page photograph of me with the words, *Where is she?*

I sit up and gasp. "What the actual f—?"

The diesel engine of the bus rumbles as it comes to a stop. There's no time to figure this out now. I roll the magazine up, with my photo on the inside, tuck my hat lower over my sunglasses, and tiptoe behind Sarah as if that will make me less visible.

Sarah leads us to the very back of the bus. It's empty now, but it'll fill up as we make our way into the city.

I take the window seat, where no one can see me. Pull the magazine out and start reading the text on the cover. 'New England's best baker loses his one true love, and now, he won't bake.'

And, then, below, a subtitle: 'Help us find her.'

Sarah starts laughing uncontrollably. She's on her phone, earbuds on. "Oh my god, Lexie, this is priceless."

"What? What's so funny? It's not funny!" I hiss as she hands me one of her earbuds.

We huddle over Sarah's phone, watching a news segment from last week.

"The country is on a frantic search for Alexandra Pierce, Christopher Wright's former apprentice and now lover. Alexandra disappeared abruptly two weeks ago, and Wright is desperate to find her. Police refuse to list her as a missing person, as there have been sightings of her on the Appalachian Trail."

The segment cuts to *Officer Declan Campbell*. "People are entitled to their privacy," Declan says. "We have reports that she is alive and well, and just... doing her thing."

"And what would that be?"

"I'm not at liberty to disclose."

"Why not?"

"It's a matter of protecting her privacy."

"So... you can't tell us anything?"

"I'm afraid not."

"Anything you'd like to say to Alexandra?"

He nods. "If you're watching, please come back. We miss you, and don't take this the wrong way, but we miss our fresh bread too."

The camera pans out and focuses on the bakery, then zooms in on the sign hanging at the front door. *Closed until further notice.*

The screen switches to the anchor. "News outlets got wind of Christopher Wright's plight when the recent winner of the popular TV show, New England's Best Baker, started posting videos addressed to Alexandra on his bakery's social media feeds."

"Dammit," I growl, digging deeper in my seat.

Sarah's thumbs fly over her phone's screen as she opens the bakery's social media. There are a number of notifications of the bakery having been live in the past couple of weeks. All the videos are posted.

Sarah scrolls to the oldest. "Let's do this in order," she says, plunging her hand in the bag of candy.

I almost snap at her that this is not some prime-time show. This is my life we're talking about. But I bite my tongue. She's been putting up with me for over two weeks. Her plan was not to be my emotional crutch.

She wanted some quiet connection with nature before she goes back to her crazy New York life, and instead, she had to put up with my sobbing for a few days, then my brooding. We never really talked about her, and I realize I've been a shitty friend. She's been here for me the whole time, and I don't know how I would have gotten through this without her.

Except judging by my heartbeat, I don't think I'm actually *through* anything yet. I have a physical need to see Christopher on the screen. To hear his voice.

And to hear what he has to say.

In the first video, the camera pans haphazardly, like someone hit the Start Live Video button and then decided to set the phone somewhere. Finally, the image settles on the inside of the bakehouse. The room is slanted, and I figure the phone must be slightly crooked in the tripod.

I'd told Sarah to leave the tripod, the ring light, and the lens Christopher gave me on my bed. It does something funny in my stomach when I understand he's using the tripod. The first time I showed him how to make a live video was in the bakehouse, pretty much right where he is now.

A chair comes into focus.

The chair where I was sitting when Christopher organized a blind tasting—and ended up tasting me.

Sweet bitterness grips me at the memory. But, before I can dwell on that feeling, Christopher comes into the frame and sits on the chair. He's off center, and slanted like the rest of the room, and the light isn't good. But all that matters to me are the dark circles beneath his eyes and his disheveled hair.

"Alexandra," he says. He's looking straight into the camera, and he's a little stiff. "You left your phone at Grace's, and I don't know how to get in touch with you. I thought maybe I could do a video like you showed me, and you'd see this somehow." He shuts his eyes for a beat and takes a deep breath. When he reopens his eyes, he's looking at his hands, and his voice is a little muffled. "I don't know where to find you. I need to talk to you." He looks into the camera then down at his hands, again. "Shit." He stands, kicking the chair away. His footsteps sound while he's off frame, then the video ends. I look at the date. It was the day after I left Emerald Creek.

Sarah clicks on the next video. It's dated from the next day.

He's sitting in the same chair, and the room is still crooked, but he used the ring light, and he seems to have tamed his hair somewhat. "I need you, Alexandra. I need *us* again. I never should have reacted the way I did. I'm sorry. I'm sorry for hurting you."

He stands, the pattern of his plaid shirt blurry, then the frame moves until his face fills the whole screen. "I was stupid to be upset at you for what you didn't tell me... Fuck, I hate this video thing. Can you please make it so we can have a private conversation?" The image swerves, showing the ceiling. It looks like he's back on the chair now, as if he's waiting for an answer. "All right," he says, and the video stops.

The next video is several days later, and this time, he's in the kitchen, and he's holding the phone in his hand. "I don't know if you don't want to talk or if you're not getting these messages. I know you left your phone here, but I can't imagine you're not online from another device. So maybe I did something wrong in the settings. I hope that's what it is, because fuck it, I miss you. I miss you so much. I want you here. I never should have pushed you away."

He scrunches his face and gets closer. "What the hell," he says. "Who the fuck are these people," he mumbles. "Why are you writing messages if you're not Alexandra." His face appears distorted, and something—probably his finger—obscures part of the screen for a bit. "Why did I push her away? I was an idiot... What the fuck are these people writing? Get the fuck out of my video! How do I stop this? Don't you guys have a life? Yeah, I do have a life, and I'm trying to fix it, you moron."

The screen shifts, and there's background noise, then Justin's voice comes across, echoing in the background. Then it's Christopher again, the image swerving so much it makes me seasick. "I'm not on the phone. I'm sending fucking video messages to Alexandra, and all I get are a bunch of losers giving me dating advice."

He squares the phone and frames it on his face, again. "Send her flowers," he mumbles, clearly reading the messages floating on his screen. "I DON'T KNOW WHERE SHE IS! She checked out. Left her phone and just vanished... I don't know how she's going to see the videos! On her computer. Or on her friend's phone. Her name? Sarah... No, I don't know Sarah's last name." The video shifts off screen, his voice muffles. "I'm banking on a bunch of losers to help me find Alexandra, that's what I'm doing." He must be talking to Justin.

"What losers?" Justin's voice comes through clearer, now.

"Those people on the video."

"You mean the die-hard followers of your social media accounts that get instant notifications when you go live?"

"What do you mean?" Christopher is so clearly confused my heart pinches for him.

"The people messaging you while you're live are people who love your bakery. And morons like me, who follow you because they're your close friends."

"Shit," Christopher says. He focuses back on the video, and Justin's head appears behind him, grinning. "Sorry, guys," Christopher says, running his free hand through his hair. "I... I have no idea what I'm doing."

"Clearly," Justin says. "Someone says 'clearly' in the chat." Christopher clenches his jaw, then Justin adds, "I'm Justin."

"Nobody cares who you are," Christopher grunts.

"T-tt-tt," Justin says. "Someone's asking who the cutie is."

The video stops.

Sarah giggles then stops herself. "Are you okay?" she says as she gives me a side hug. "Do you want to just jump to the last video?"

I don't know if I'm okay. My legs are antsy, and my stomach is tied in knots. "Just keep going," I tell her.

The next video is several days later. Christopher's stubble has grown. He's in the dark, holding the phone in his hand, and as it moves around, I recognize the contours of the armchair in his bedroom.

"Alexandra. I know I should have told you how I felt earlier. I'm not good at talking, and that's something I need to work on. Also, I don't like being in the spotlight, but here I am. So, I guess that's a start. I hate that I have to say this in public, but I don't have a choice. If only I knew where to find you, I'd speak to you in person. I just want to hold you and never let you go, and I shouldn't have said I didn't want you here. The truth is, I *did* want you here. I've wanted you right fucking here since the moment you walked in."

I know that, by *here*, he means in his bedroom, except he's not saying it because this is a public video. He knows that I'd understand. And, somehow, the fact that we're sharing this little bit of inside knowledge makes me feel closer to him.

"You kept saying you were going to leave. What was I supposed to do? I needed to protect myself, Alexandra. I might be a grump, but I've discovered something since you came into my life."

He pauses.

"I'm breakable."

And his voice actually breaks a little. "And I didn't know that. I wasn't breakable when I left my family at the age of fifteen. I wasn't breakable when I built my business from the ground up. I wasn't even breakable when I fought for Skye. With Skye, the kind of love I had for her before she was even born is the kind that made me a thousand times stronger than I really am. But the love I have for you, Alexandra, is the kind that breaks me. I knew it all along, and I tried to fight it, and here I am. Shattered into pieces."

Tears are streaming down my cheeks, and Sarah nudges herself against me. Christopher stops talking for a moment, and the image moves away from him. It's blurry until it adjusts on his bed. He slowly moves it to the nightstand, where a picture of me and Skye replaces the old picture of Skye as a toddler. I recognize the selfie we took in the kitchen, the one I'd emailed to Christopher so Skye could keep it. The image pans to the other nightstand, where my phone is charging. My heart skips a beat.

He has my phone?

Next, he directs the camera toward the closets. The doors are open, and my clothes are hanging there. He must have picked up my suitcases from Grace's and unpacked my stuff.

In his bedroom.

He says nothing. This is for me only. He doesn't want other people to know. Only I can understand. "If this isn't what you want," he whispers, "I'll bring it all back. I just... I just wanted to feel you around me."

My heart explodes.

I shut down Sarah's phone, ignoring her protests that there are more videos. For now, I need a moment. I'll get back to the videos when my heartbeat is close to normal.

I take a long gulp from my water bottle and stare outside the window to the landscape blurred by my tears. I try to tame the emotions that come rushing, if only because I'm sitting in a bus that gets more crowded every stop we make. But I can't ignore that he loves me the way I love him, and that we both want the same thing. I might be strong enough to be without Christopher, but I know I still want him and won't feel whole without him.

"Are you okay" Sarah asks, leaning her head on my shoulder.

"I'm good," I say, faking a brave smile.

The next video, Christopher is at Justin's, sitting at the bar, his face filling the whole frame. "Before I get started today, I just want to post an update that I haven't heard anything from Alexandra. So, as far as I know, she probably hasn't seen my videos. Or, if she has, she doesn't want to have anything to do with me. Anyway, here we are." He looks around and then back at the camera.

"I've been getting a lot of questions about why she left me. What happened between us. I'm not sure where to start. It's kind of this gradual accumulation, and then this small thing that sent everything overboard."

He narrows his eyes again, reading the comments. "*Say it as it is.*"

He takes a shaky breath. "What happened is, I pushed her away. And so, she left. Simple as that."

His gaze leaves the frame. "I made her pay for other people's mistakes. I have this tender spot, you see, and without knowing it, she struck me right there. And it was more than I could take, at the time." His eyes are misty, and he squeezes his eyelids tight. "It was nothing she did."

He focuses on the bottom of the screen, again. "*Lots of fish*—Are you crazy? Have you been listening to anything I said here? Alexandra is the one for me. Fuck this."

The video stops.

The last time the bakery was live is three days ago. The image opens on the ceiling of Justin's pub, then swerves to a pint of beer.

Christopher clears his throat, and Justin's voice comes through. "Dude, stop the videos already. That's not what your social media is for."

"The fuck do you know about my social media?" The image swerves all over the pub again. "Alexandra said that before I start any campaign, I need to set goals. Well, my goal is to get Alexandra back. There. Ya happy, now?"

"You had too much to drink, buddy."

"That I have. That I have. But I still know what I want. I want my Alexandra back."

"You should get back to work. Bake us some bread."

"Not until I find Alexandra."

"Will you get back to work when you find her?"

"That I will."

"Even if she doesn't want to be with you?"

The image is fixed, now, showing us the pub's ceiling again. "She'll be with me."

There's shuffling noise in the background. The image swerves around again and then becomes dark. "Come on," Justin says, "let me help you."

Sarah's phone rings, interrupting the video. It's a New York number that looks familiar. Sarah picks up, and Barbara's anguished voice fills our earbuds. "Sarah, are you with Lexie?"

Sarah hands me the other earbud. "Hey, Barb, it's me. I'm with Sarah. We're on our way to the city."

"Thank god you're back! What were you thinking, disappearing like that for almost three weeks?"

"What are you talking about? We've been gone two weeks, tops. Meeting is—when is the meeting again? June 30?"

"Exactly. Tonight. At five." *Toni—?* What's today?

Shit. Shitshitshitshitshit.

I check the time on Sarah's phone. That's in three hours.

"Where are you right now?" Barbara asks.

I look out the window. "We're... crossing the Hudson."

"To Grand Central?"

"Yes." We were going to take the subway to Brooklyn from there, but looks like we might need a change of plans. If the meeting is tonight. Which it always was. I just lost track of time. I guess the Appalachian Trail has a way of making you lose track of time.

"Okay. I'll send a car for you at the station," Barbara says. "You need to go to Red Barn Baking directly."

"Okay."

"Okay? You sure?"

"Yeah. I mean, I don't have a choice, right. The rest of my life starts today. Might as well get on with it."

"Do you need me to bring you some clothes?"

I look down at my bare legs, my sandals, my dress. At least I shaved. I washed, conditioned, and braided my hair. I'm not wearing any makeup, but I have a nice tan. I shrug. "Sure, why not. Maybe some eyeliner and mascara, too. If you can. More importantly, can you give me an update on the law firm you found?"

"They'll be meeting with you first thing tomorrow morning. That's all I could do. I don't have a timeline or pricing yet for everything you want to do."

"Great. No problem. How about the consultant?"

There's a silence on the line. "That was tougher to figure out, but I think you'll love who I found."

"Wanna tell me about them?"

Her voice is a little distant, as if she's talking away from the phone. "I don't have time right now, sweetie. I still have a lot of paperwork to prepare for the meeting, and Robert isn't exactly helping. But don't worry, everything will be all set. See you later!" The line goes silent. Barbara signed off. She's busy.

The phone reverts to Christopher's video.

There's two minutes left on it, but it's all background noise of walking and going up stairs. Some grunting. Christopher's navy-blue comforter.

Then it goes dark, and there are no more videos.

"Do you want to call him?" Sarah asks.

Yes, yes I do want to call him. I want to hijack the bus and tell the driver to take me straight back to Emerald Creek. I want to be in his arms, his mouth claiming mine. I want to revert time.

But I'm a strong woman. I'm expected at Red Barn Baking in a couple of hours. Barbara is working hard for me. And a lot of people's lives are going to be better thanks to me. So I'm going to focus on this, for now.

"No, I'm not going to call him."

Chapter Fifty-Six

Alexandra

The company car drops me off at Red Barn Baking and smoothly pulls off the curb to drive Sarah straight to our Brooklyn apartment. The perk of owning the company, like Sarah said.

My best friend is way more excited than I am by this whole turn of events in my life.

The offices at Red Barn Baking are just as sterile as I remember them. No smell, controlled temperature, hushed sounds of computer clicks and voices behind doors.

I go straight to Barbara's office, only to find it occupied by a new face.

Right.

Barbara was let go.

For now.

But I know she's here, because she said so herself.

I make for the conference room two doors down—because where else would the meeting take place—and am greeted by familiar faces.

On the longer side of the table, facing the windows, the same man and woman from the law firm who handled Rita's will. They're wearing light-colored suits this time around. It's summer. Neat piles of documents in front of them like six months ago, except thicker, with colored little stickers poking out for signatures. The man is nervously flicking his pen. The woman shoots glances at me, like I'm about to do something as outrageous as take a pee break in the middle of a meeting again.

Barbara is sitting across from them, with equally neat files in front of her. The top one is labeled RBB 2.0.

Nice.

She winks at me. I smile back. We'll hug later. No point rubbing anything in.

The spot at one end of the table—under the poster of a red barn in a picturesque Vermont landscape complete with hot baker in plaid flannel shirt holding a big, wholesome bread that is definitely not on the menu of any Red Barn Bakery anywhere in the country—is occupied by Robert's usual accessories: A fat, black fountain pen with a stylized snowflake on the cap—I've been told it's expensive; A notebook in leather binding; A bottle of Perrier, and a crystal glass with our logo etched on it.

The logo is killer.

We're totally keeping the logo.

Everything else is up for discussion.

Except maybe the poster. My eyes keep returning to the baker in the painting. Something about the way his hair falls over his left eye. Something about his shy grin.

I take my seat at the opposite end of the table.

My eyes fall back on Barbara. "We're missing a few people," I tell her.

Robert strolls in, checks his watch, loudly pulls out his chair and slumps into it. Avoids making eye contact with me.

"I thought we could bring them in for the second part of the meeting," Barbara says, glancing at Robert, then at the lawyers.

"Right." We didn't have time to iron out all the details, so glances and insinuations will have to do. Not having my phone isn't helping the strategizing of all this. "Let's get this over and done with," I tell the lawyers.

"Before we go any further," Robert interrupts me. "I'd like to present that the board's offer still holds."

He's kidding, right?

I glance at the lawyers, and they look near panicked. This was not planned. At least there's that. I'm not the only one thinking he's lost it.

"It looks like Mr. Norwood is confused as to the purpose of this meeting," I say. That sounded in control, right? I don't want to be bitchy, but enough already.

The woman clears her throat and jumps in. "We're here to formally confirm the transfer of shares of the late Ms. Douglas, representing the controlling majority of Red Barn Baking." She looks at no one, only focusing on the paperwork the man next to her hands her, one document at a time. She does all sorts of lawyerly things to them, stamping, signing, all the while explaining what she's doing and what each document represents. A recap of the conditions in the will. A formal acknowledgment of my successful completion of the apprenticeship. More stuff about the exam. A formal transfer of shares. A thorough scrutiny of all the above.

As she completes each pile, the man brings them to me to sign.

Robert is getting very pale.

We're almost there.

"There, all done," the woman says, visibly relieved. "Would you like to continue without us?" she asks.

They were not only Rita's lawyers, they're also Red Barn Baking counsels, so having them around for the next part might prove useful. I'm about to fire Robert. "Why don't you stay."

I've never fired anyone in my life. It's the fucking scariest thing. I have to fire a guy who's had so much power over me, and who used to scare me, you'd think I'd take some level of sadistic pleasure in it? I don't.

He looks at me. Stands from his chair, grabs his expensive shit, and says, "If you think I'm gonna be working for you, think again. Consider this my resignation. You got witnesses, save us some paperwork. Good luck running this fucking place."

And just like that, he's gone.

Well, that was easy.

Must be beginner's luck. In the moments that follow, the room fills with the top people in the Finance, Marketing, Product, and Assets departments. The heads of departments take seats. Their seconds stand behind them.

I don't like that one bit.

"Greetings, everyone," I say. "Thanks for being here. First things first, let's make this a little more workable." I grab the edge of the table. "Everyone standing, go grab a chair. Everyone sitting, please stand and help me move this mammoth out of the way."

There's a bit of hesitation, and then one by one everyone starts moving. After much pushing and shoving, we have the conference table nudged sideways, against the far wall, right below the projection screen. Within ten minutes, a group of people with sleeves rolled up are talking to each other, pushing, pulling, then sitting in chairs arranged in a large circle where everyone fits.

"That wasn't working," I say once the voices quiet down. I take a seat within the circle, my back to the door. At any time now, the consultants will get here, and I want to be able to greet them personally. "With everyone's help, we turned a stifling room into a convivial gathering. This is what I want to do with Red Barn Baking."

I go on to explain the broad lines of my vision, and as I'm doing so, Barbara leans into my ear, and says, "The consultant just arrived in the building." I nod and continue rolling out my plan. There's an absolutely mouthwatering smell invading the room, and for a beat, I wonder if I'm manifesting the smell of bread as I'm talking about the soul-deep connections we make around bread.

"I'm counting on each one of you to give your honest opinion of the feasibility of all this, but I do need you to be fully on board if you're going to stay with RBB. There will be no hard feelings if you decide this is not for you, and you'd rather pursue your career somewhere else." I pause for effect. "That being said, I'm told our consultant is in the building, and—oh my god." There're baskets of bread being handed around, making their way to the table in the back, which is quickly set up like a buffet. People are standing up, attracted to the smell. "Whoever dreamed this up, you have a promotion already," I say giggling.

Then I turn around to greet the consultant and my giggle dies in my throat while my knees buckle and the room spins.

Christopher is leaning against the door jamb, holding a dark suit jacket over his shoulder. "I like your vision, Ms. Pierce," he says in a low, rumbling voice. "I'd be honored to help you bring it to life, if you'll allow me to help."

I steady myself on the back of a chair while our eyes lock.

He came. He came here.

All the way here.

To help me.

His gaze all but eats me up, top to bottom and back up again. His eyes are circled with fatigue, and he's lost weight. But his gaze is full of love, so intense I can feel it. He came for so much more than to help with Red Barn.

Our eyes are locked for what seems like an eternity, saying all that we cannot yet tell each other. Sorrow. Love. Forgiveness. I'm so overwhelmed by the force of it, that I shut my eyes momentarily. When I look up again, Christopher is walking past me, into the room, and as he does so, his fingers lightly touch mine, the burn radiating to my core.

Turning around to face the room, I open and close my mouth twice, without any effect.

Barbara jumps in, closes the door behind Christopher, and introduces him as the consultant for Red Barn's Makeover—as we are now calling it—and also as the baker who made all the breads and confections everyone's started sampling.

I plop back in my seat. People follow suit, and I let Christopher take over the meeting. He wraps his jacket on the back of a chair, then chooses to stand in the middle of the circle. The sleeves of his crisp white shirt are rolled up to his elbows, and his aviator sunglasses hang from the top button of his shirt, reflecting the light.

The moment he starts talking, he owns the room.

No one seems to notice my reaction to his presence. People are too busy staring at him, drinking in his words. Everyone is mesmerized by his charisma, his passion, his ideas. He makes this conference room look small.

I should probably be interjecting, commenting, proposing, but my mind is racing in all sorts of directions. *Did I read him right? Is he really here because of me?*

His voice rumbles softly across the room. He's standing in the middle of the circle, slowly walking around.

My heartbeat is so loud the people sitting next to me must hear it.

"... being in tune with the communities that each bakery serves," he's saying. "Let's be mindful of established traditions while adjusting to newcomers."

Or is he here only because Barbara begged him to? She would be one to guilt-trip him.

For all his groveling over video, part of it might have been out of guilt and worry and part of it due to alcohol.

Until we've talked this through, I don't know what the future holds for us.

I can't know how he really feels about me.

If he wants anything other than a consulting gig.

He's turned one-eighty now, and I lift my eyes to him.

His gaze rakes over me. I uncross and recross my bare legs.

I need to keep it together.

Maybe he's just here as a consultant. He did call me Ms. Pierce, after all.

God, I can't wait for his presentation to be over.

"Happy Fourth of July! Enjoy the long weekend if I don't see you tomorrow," I tell everyone as they file out of the room with wide smiles. "We have a long road ahead, but we have a solid road map."

I have a good feeling about Red Barn Baking now.

But as Barbara exits the room and closes the door behind me, leaving me alone with Christopher, I don't know where to even begin the conversation with *him*.

It's so strange, seeing him right here. You'd think he would seem out of place, but he doesn't. Not at all.

He props himself against the table in the back, his gaze hungrily devouring me.

I take a tentative step toward him, then another, through the maze of chairs strewn across the room.

He doesn't say anything, so I stop.

He extends his hand and pushes himself from the table.

In an instant, my hand reaches his, our fingers twine, and we both freeze.

"Is it true what you said, on the videos?"

He pulls me closer to him. "You saw them?" he asks, his voice betraying his surprise, his lips curling up.

"This morning, on my way here," I explain. I can barely find my voice, I want him to hold me so bad. "Is it true, what you said?"

"Said what?"

"That you wanted me back."

He pushes a stray hair behind my ear. His hand warms my neck, and goosebumps trail down my body. His gaze caresses me softly, until his eyes darken. "I never let you go, beautiful."

My heart thumps, my legs weaken, and I lean into his touch.

His other hand softly cups my hip and trails around my waist, pulling me closer to him. "I was stupidly angry. Dealing with my own shit. Never should have let it get in the way of this," he says, his head dipping.

Our lips clash and our mouths meld to each other, our tongues reclaiming their familiar territory without missing a beat. There's no hesitation, no question.

We belong together.

Within seconds, I'm coiled around him, one leg wrapped against his hip, his hands kneading my ass, my hands fisting his hair.

A knock on the door startles him, and I feel him pull away. I pull him deeper into me.

I own this freaking place. There's got to be some perks, right?

"I like the new leadership style," Barbara says behind me.

We keep kissing.

"Whenever you're ready, the new lawyers are here. Last item on the agenda before the weekend."

She closes the door softly, and we continue our makeout session.

"I like your leadership style too, Pierce," Christopher says as we come up for air.

"Yeah?" I brush his nose with mine, nibble on his lower lip, and say against his mouth, "I apprenticed with this awesome baker. Got it from him."

Chapter Fifty-Seven

Christopher

There are so many cars in the driveway at the farm, I park the truck on the grass. Skye hops out on her own and runs around the back of the white house to join the pack of kids running around.

I quickly round the front of the truck to get to Alexandra's door.

It's a perfect day. The air is brimming with Summer fun—the smell of Justin's smoker, the laughter of children, the chirping of crickets, the sun up high in the bright blue sky.

And my girl.

Alexandra slides down into my arms, and I keep her there, nudged between the open door and the seat of the truck, soft and pliable against me, exactly how I want her, exactly where she belongs. Her body hums under my hands, and I can't help but run my fingers under her flowing dress, against her soft thighs, up to the thin strap of fabric she wears as an excuse for panties.

I growl in her neck, and she half giggles, half sighs in response. I fist her hair, pulling her head back so I get her lips right where I want them.

"Christopher," she says.

"*What.*"

"You're messing me up."

I claim her mouth, and her willing tongue says a different story. Messing her up is what she wants.

"Sure hope so," I groan when I come up for air.

She exhales softly, her puffy lips and lidded eyes telling me she feels exactly the way I do.

"I can't wait till tonight," I say, stepping back and watching her smooth her dress and comb her hair with her fingers.

"Mhmm," she purrs in response.

This is going to be a long day, but god am I going to enjoy it.

Skye is more than on board with Alexandra being my girlfriend, and with that out of the way, I know I'm not going to keep my hands off her today. I'll have her right by my side, on my lap, or under my arm. I'll have her every which way that shows she's mine.

No more pretending we're nothing to each other.

No more guys taking advantage and flirting with her.

I hand her the basket of buns I baked for the patties and hotdogs, and pull out the assortment of pies I made early this morning.

Alexandra freezes. "Why is *she* here?" she asks, her chin jutting toward Emma, who's in the backyard.

I shrug. "Everybody's here. She's the CPA for King's Farm. It's Sunday. I guess she had nowhere else to go."

Alexandra's lips are a thin line, her brow is creased. I hate that I'm partially responsible for that. As much as I've joked I like the look on her when she's jealous, I know the hurt and insecurity is real for her.

And I know how to fix it.

"Come here," I say as Emma turns around and fixes her gaze on us.

Pushing the pies back inside the truck, I grab Alexandra by the waist and pull her to me with one arm. My other hand cups her nape and angles her just right. Dipping my mouth to hers, I nibble at her entrance. "Babe. It's only you. It's only ever been you. Kay? Now show her how you kiss your man."

Her cheeks flush, and her eyes light up. God, she's so fucking beautiful. She's shy and hesitant but I will have none of it. She's mine, and I'll make sure she feels it. I fuck her mouth with my tongue, dipping her head back, my hand gliding from her waist down for a nice ass grab. She responds with the sexiest whimper, her body molding against mine, her tongue getting in the game. With her free hand, she grabs my hair and pulls it, all the while pushing my mouth harder against hers.

Yes.

That's what I'm talking about.

Mine.

When we nudge apart, she gives me a small sigh. She stands taller. Her eyes are bright. Her confidence is back.

That was easy.

Emma is nowhere to be seen. I straighten Alexandra's hair and dress, turn her around and give her a slap on the butt. "Let's go," I say, grabbing the pies, and pulling Alexandra back into the curve of my free arm as we make our way to the farmhouse.

After we say hello to Lynn and Craig, we drop the breads and pies on the kitchen counter laden with a bunch of other foods.

I point to two large, brown, open boxes lined with checkered wax paper. "Where'd that come from?"

"Fresh whoopie pies made this morning by Kiara."

I growl. "Babe, you gotta taste that." I tear a piece of the sandwich cookie and finger feed her, grabbing her against me.

Justin is fixing drinks and winks at us. "Sex on the beach for you guys?" It's good to see him so happy about us. It warms my heart. Although, it's a little over the top for him, but I'll take it.

Alexandra gives him a dreamy smile. I take a bite and have to admit, Kiara is onto something with those. Never tasted anything like it.

Then Alexandra wraps her mouth around my fingers, licking the filling off, and my mind drifts in a totally opposite direction.

"Jesus, get a room," Justin growls. "This is a PG gathering." His gaze drifts to a pretty brunette I've never seen before. And what's that about?

"Such a prude," Alexandra teases him. "The kids are outside," she adds before drifting away from me to stand on the wraparound porch. The truth is, we're not demonstrative around Skye. We don't want to make her uncomfortable. It's sort of an unspoken agreement we have. But when she's not immediately around us?

Forget it.

I grab us two Switchbacks and join her, my arm gliding loosely around her waist. From here, we have a breathtaking view of the King property, all rolling pastures and meadows lined by wooded areas in the background. Beyond the hill is a pond you can't see from here, and creeks, and more farmland, and hundreds of acres more just waiting to be put to better use.

The King children are in their twenties and early thirties. Justin found his calling at the pub, and there's no saying what Ethan, the eldest, will do with his life when, or if, he leaves the military. But the three youngest, Haley, Hunter, and Logan, are involved in expanding the farm business.

Their perfect family life used to be bittersweet to me. I loved it for them, but I felt like I'd never get to experience it for myself, even if they did everything they could to make me feel part of their family.

But now, with Alexandra by my side, I feel differently. We're building something together too. We'll work on making Red Barn Baking a model in the baking world, a business built to do good on the local scale. And we'll be a family soon.

Justin crosses the porch to tend to his smoker down on the lawn, next to where Craig is firing up the barbecue. Kiara and some kids are preparing s'mores, and Colton is hauling logs next to the pit for tonight's bonfire. Everyone here has their place, and so do I.

Having Alexandra in my life makes me whole. I don't feel like a misfit anymore.

Justin walks back to us. "Meat is about ready, and Dad is going to start grilling. Wanna bring the buns down to the picnic table?"

"Sure." I turn to Alexandra, but her attention is elsewhere—on a couple inside the large family room.

She frowns. "What's Barbara doing here?"

When we left New York a couple of days ago, Barbara didn't mention coming up to Emerald Creek. All she told *me* was, *'You break her heart again, you'll answer to me.'*

"Is that... Jerry?" Alexandra adds on an exhale, her face suddenly pale, her cheeks blotchy.

"Who's the woman with Uncle George?" Justin asks as Alexandra walks away from me to greet Barbara.

Is this family ever done with secrets? I close the distance keeping me from Alexandra.

Something is up, and I'm not letting my girl deal with this on her own. I tuck Alexandra right back where she belongs, under my arm, and I like how she fits perfectly there. How she relaxes into me. How she clearly belongs there.

Whatever shit is going on between Barbara, Uncle George, and Alexandra, I won't let it affect her. We are our own little unit. No one gets to pop our bubble of happiness.

Chapter Fifty-Eight

Alexandra

Barbara and the older gentleman are sitting at the bay window overlooking the pastures, but you can tell from their expression that they're not seeing them. They're deep in thought. Barbara pats the man's arm, and he wipes away a tear. I heard Justin say it was Uncle George, and that's a relief.

I'm not prepared to meet my mom's father yet.

Barbara stands and tilts her head, then takes tentative steps toward me, her arms outstretched. "Honey." She's not her usual self. Something's wrong, and she doesn't know how to tell me.

A rush of emotions surface. The memory of sensing your life is about to tilt on its axis, and there's nothing you can do about it.

Christopher's arm wraps around my shoulders, and the tension eases away. Nothing can affect me when he's with me. Feeling his physical presence, knowing he would sense my need for support, is all the strength I need.

"What—what are you doing here? Is there a problem at Red Barn already?" I glance at Uncle George, waiting for Barbara to introduce us formally.

I've heard about him. He's Lynn's uncle and was estranged from the family a long time ago. They recently reconnected.

"Uncle George," Justin confirms, hugging the older man.

"Honey—" Barbara starts.

"Get us a couple stiff drinks, Justin, please," Uncle George interrupts her kindly, "and let's sit down, shall we?"

He has a soft voice, a gentle demeanor. I can see why the King family brought him into their fold so easily. No matter what happened in the past, he must be a good person to have around.

Moments later, we're seated around the round table that fits in the bow window, and Justin has us fixed up with amber liquid in rocks glasses. All our eyes are fixed on his Uncle George, but he twitches this way and that.

"Come on, Uncle George, bottoms up," Justin says. I jerk my head at him. Ironically enough for a bar owner, Justin is usually the last person to encourage any drinking. His eyes are fixed on George.

George, who needs liquid courage to say something. Something that involves us, since we're seated together.

What is Barbara up to? Should I be worried?

"What's going on?" Christopher groans under his breath to Justin. I'm nudged against him, that's how I hear.

"No fucking idea," Justin mutters back.

"Oh for Chrissakes!" Barbara says. She downs her bourbon and slams the empty glass down. "Uncle George is Jerry. Your grandfather," she says to me. "There."

My jaw slackens. Christopher's arm tightens around my shoulders as he pushes the glass of bourbon my way.

George clears his throat. "Thank you for the nudge, Barbara." His voice is still soft, a contrast to Barbara's nervous outburst.

Her statement wasn't exactly full of tact, definitely not a nudge, but at least it's out.

George lifts his clear blue eyes to me, and quickly they mist over. "I am your mother's father." With a trembling hand, he pulls out a worn leather wallet from his back pocket, shifts through the compartments, and produces a plastic sleeve protecting the photo of a baby.

"Rita sent me this. And then, nothing." His voice breaks, and Barbara reaches out to pat his forearm.

I turn the photo in my fingers. It's a baby. It could be any baby. I know it's my mother, but strangely, I don't feel like this is my drama to contend with. It's his, and I can help him get through this.

I hand him the photo back.

"She passed," he says it as a statement of fact. A regret. Barbara twitches in her chair.

"A long time ago," I say. I feel his guilt, his regrets, and they're weighing him down. Where's the fun man I heard in the background of phone conversations with Barbara?

Christopher's hand traces soothing circles on my back. "You don't have to do this now," he says for my benefit, but loud enough that everyone can hear.

This, his support, his understanding, is all I need in life. Nothing can affect me with him in my life. "It's fine," I tell him.

I have everything I want and need.

A man who understands me. Friends. A real family, one forged in love.

George should have the same. And Barbara.

"We can't fix the past, but we can design our future." I raise my glass toward Jerry slash Uncle George slash Not Ready To Call Him Grandpa Yet.

"Holy fucking shit, Bambi! That was profound." Kiara plops onto an empty seat and takes my glass from me. "Why the gloomy faces?" she asks, suddenly tuning into the atmosphere around the table. "You guys should try my whoopie pies!"

Justin jumps in. "Uncle George here, turns out to be Alex's grandfather."

"That's cool," Kiara says, unfazed. "So you guys are cousins. Nice. Now can we all put some smiles on our faces and have some fun like the big happy family we are?"

And just like that, the evening lightens up.

Chapter Fifty-Nine

Alexandra

Three months later

"Pancakes! Ready to go?" Christopher pulls my back to his front and kisses my nape. Shivers of pleasure roll through me, and I drop my head against his strong shoulder. I'd rather stay at home this afternoon. Be lazy. Sneak in a quickie while Skye has a playdate.

But it's a beautiful fall day, and Christopher is excited to show me all that Vermont has to offer during this glorious season. We've been on hayrides and gone apple picking, taken bike tours and had cider tastings. Today, he wants to go for a picnic.

He seems so excited about it, I don't find it in me to protest. To use my morning sickness and afternoon slumps for an excuse. He'd get worried over nothing.

"Ready," I breathe into his kiss.

He palms my breast and groans. "Ah fuck. That's the best."

I blush under his compliment and writhe under his hand. Christopher already has a child, but he's never been with a pregnant woman. My pregnancy is not only a total surprise, it's also a first for both of us. I revel in those little wins. Those first times I can give him.

It means the world to me, that I'm giving him something new. Something no one ever has.

Christopher is taking his role very seriously—no surprise there. He's over-the-top protective and oversees everything I'm eating like I'm some athlete on a mission to win the Olympics. He raided the bookshop of every book available on pregnancy. He talked with the apothecary about supplements.

I'm hard at work on the nursery. My nesting instinct is already kicking in, and with Autumn's help, I'm already turning one of the empty rooms down the hall from a bedroom into a nursery.

Yup, my social media business is doing so well I can afford a decorator! Sure, she's cheap, and I pay her in kind only with my marketing skills. But still—it's a nice feeling.

As for Red Barn Baking, the process of changing the business model is moving along, but it's slow. I've appointed a new CEO to drive the effort. I have weekly online meetings to follow her progress, and Christopher consults on the new stores opening, but we've decided our life is here in Emerald Creek.

I slide a plaid flannel shirt over my long-sleeve T-shirt and step into my hiking boots. Skye has a matching pair, and she grabs my hand after tying hers. Christopher carries our picnic bag and swings his arm over my shoulders.

We head out of town through the covered bridge, toward the hills covered in flamboyant trees. Reds, yellows, and oranges are ablaze, standing even brighter against the evergreens and the lush pastures.

Skye kicks her feet in the piles of crunchy leaves. Christopher is unusually silent, his hand twirling in my hair.

We hang a left midway up the hill and end up on a dirt road covered in a canopy of maples, oaks, and birch trees. Through the foliage, the sun shines, flecks of gold on our feet. Between the branches, we see the village down below, bordered by the river, the lake in the background.

It's glorious.

And when the church bell chimes, perfection.

We continue quietly up the hill, the trail taking us deeper into the woods, the village lost behind us, until we reach a clearing at the top. The view is even more breathtaking, hill after hill rolling into the horizon, green and blue and seemingly endless. Peaceful. Majestic in its simplicity.

My eyes water at the view. "It's beautiful up here."

Skye points to a meadow below us. "Daddy, can we picnic down here?"

"Pick a spot," Christopher says, leaning over to kiss me while Skye runs downhill.

I could have walked a bit more—it really is a gorgeous day for a walk in the woods—but I'm not going to complain about this beautiful view. And maybe if we get home sooner, then we can... be *playful* sooner?

I'm so horny since becoming pregnant.

Skye plops on a flat grassy area and taps the space next to her for me to join her.

Christopher sits on my other side and uncorks three sparkling apple ciders. We clink our bottles and stay silent, the view enough for us. After we finish our sandwiches, I let myself fall flat on my back.

"Beautiful, scoot over." Christopher slides a stadium blanket under me.

So protective.

Pregnancy makes me horny. It also makes me sleepy. Soon I'm dozing off, and I feel the blanket being pulled atop me. I'm vaguely aware of some rustling and whispering, and then Skye says, "Daddy, can we have dessert now?"

"Sure. Babe?"

I wave my hand, eyes still closed. "I'm good, thanks."

Christopher clears his throat. "Skye made these galettes herself."

I pop up. "You what? That's awesome! I'm so impressed." I take the galette Christopher hands me. "It—my god! It looks perfect."

She nods. "Daddy helped me."

That's so cool.

We start eating in silence. I'm really not hungry, but I don't want to hurt Skye's feelings. It's not a hardship to eat the flaky pastry, I must admit. It's perfectly done. I recognize Christopher's masterful handiwork, but I love that he is now involving Skye in his passion.

"Oopsie. I got a fortune message!" Skye says, looking at me with excitement.

"Did you?" Christopher asks, a glimmer in his eye. He looks at my pie and I swear I see him blush slightly. "How about you?"

"Do I have one?"

"You better," he groans.

I've only taken one bite off my pie, so I tear it in half until I find a piece of paper. It's rolled on itself so that the writing is on the inside. I unroll it carefully, the almond filling slightly sticking to my fingers.

It's upside down, so I turn it around, but already I recognize Christopher's handwriting.

"Will..."

Oh.

My.

God.
Will.
You.
Marry.
Me.

Dropping the pie on the stadium blanket, I launch myself at Christopher, nearly toppling him over. He wraps his strong arms tightly around my waist, and I straddle him.

He leans his forehead against mine. "Alexandra, you brought me back to life. You showed me the meaning of happiness. You made us a family. Will you do me the honor of being my wife?"

"Oh my god yes. Yes! A thousand times yes!"

He grabs my ass with his hands and moves me closer to him. "Close your eyes," he says to Skye, and she giggles while he kisses me tenderly.

"Can I read my fortune cookie now?" Skye asks.

"Sure, little bug."

"Alez-zandra," she says, and I turn to her. I glance at the paper and recognize her handwriting, not Christopher's. "I don't want a stepmother." She pauses, and my heart sinks. Her eyes lock with mine, and by the glint in her eye, I know something is up.

I just don't anticipate the bomb she drops on me.

"So will you please a-dopt me? I want you to be my real mother."

My jaw falls open. I figured Christopher might propose eventually, but I never thought Skye would point blank ask me to become her mother.

"Pretty please?" she adds.

I'm so overwhelmed with emotion.

Responsibility.

Honor.

Before I tear up, I pull her into our embrace. "Oh my god I'm going to be a mom! You guys," I sob.

Skye's puzzled gaze goes between her father, me, and my belly.

"But you *chose* me," I blabber. It's too much for me to explain, so I just shut up.

Skye ties her little hands around my neck and sighs. "I just wanted to be your first baby. Also, your name is too hard to say."

We stay in a group hug a moment, Christopher rocking us gently.

"Daddy," Skye's voice comes out muffled from where her face is buried in between us. "You forgot something."

"Just taking my time, little bug. Enjoying the moment." His chin strokes the top of my head. Both their heartbeats resonate through my chest, and I don't want this moment to end either.

Skye lifts her head. "But it's *part* of the moment."

"That's right." He takes my left hand and slides a simple diamond ring on it, his eyes on mine. "There," he says, his voice thick with emotion, his eyes shining. Then he dips his head to kiss his daughter's hair. "Thank you, little bug. Couldn't get it right without you."

Then Skye wiggles her way out, and she starts packing our picnic while I pull my head back just enough to find Christopher's mouth again.

"I love you so much," I say when we pull apart.

When our house comes into view, Skye runs ahead of us. "She said yes!" she yells at the top of her lungs.

A whole group of people pour out of the bakery, clapping and cheering. Grace, Kiara, Willow, Autumn, Cassandra, Sophie, Willow, Haley, Lynn, and Craig, and so many others. The whole team from the General Store. Wendy and Todd from the inn and their children.

Justin and his wife.

Christopher seems unfazed.

I look between them and him and start laughing. "Oh my god Christopher! Did you do this?"

He doesn't answer, just lifts me effortlessly, gives me a chaste kiss, sets me on the ground, then wraps his arm tightly around me as we join the group.

We get there just in time to hear Skye say, "She's ho-normal. But she'll be okay."

I giggle into Christopher's shoulder at her words. I love this kid so much, I can't wait to call her my own.

Wait.

Justin is *married*??

How did that happen?

It's all in The Promise Of You. Continue reading for a sneak peek, or scan the QR code for the whole book!

Didn't get enough of Alexandra and Christopher? As a thank you for signing up to Bella's newsletter, download a bonus scene on www.bellarivers.com/bonus-scene-nlyg or scan this QR code:

The Promise Of You

SNEAK PREVIEW (CHAPTER ONE)

Chloe

Breathe in, breathe out.

I got this.

I clench and unclench my hand around my leather backpack-slash-laptop bag, and glance at my reflection in the mirrored walls of the office building. Nothing weird like greasy paper stuck to my four-inch heels or a pigeon dropping on my elegantly understated pantsuit.

I got this.

I deserve it.

I check my phone screen. Thirty minutes early.

My meditation app interrupts its ocean sounds to announce *Fiona wants to connect via video. Answer?* I've been dodging Mom's calls this morning because I don't need another one of her lectures on how I should live my life.

But my sister rarely calls, and when she does, it always brings a smile to my face. And it's always on video. A lightness spreads through me as I accept the call and her feisty face fills my screen.

"Hey. Did Mom call you?" she asks point blank.

My chest tightens. "Why?"

"Uncle Kevin died."

I blow air as dull sadness over my uncle's passing replaces the tension I always feel where Mom is concerned. "Oh no." Images of my uncle's big belly trembling with his hearty laughter blur my vision. "How's she doing?"

"Not great. You know how she gets."

Yeah, I can just picture it. Mom sobbing, Dad mumbling, *'Another asshole gone.'*

Another lovely day in the Sullivan household.

"Funeral is next week. Think you can make it?"

"I'll make it." Uncle Kevin was a nice guy, and even if I haven't seen him or my aunt Dawn—or my cousins, for that matter—in what must be now over ten years, they hold a special place in my heart. And not only because summer vacations at their home in Vermont is one of my favorite childhood memories.

They were good people.

"How about you? Can you make it, or will you be touring?" I ask her.

"Nah, couple concerts got canceled." Her eyes shift to the side. "I'll try and make it."

"What's the holdup?" I ask.

"They're kinda behind on payments, and last-minute flights from Europe at this time of year are going to be through the roof. But it's Uncle Kevin. I'll make it work."

"D'you need money?"

"Nah, I said I'll make it work."

"I'll send you money."

"I don't want charity, Clo. It's annoying enough."

"Charity? Who's talking about charity? Consider it a loan. You can repay it by playing at my wedding."

"You have that kind of money sitting around?" She grins. "Damn, sis. I wish I had my shit together the way you do."

"Um, hello? *You* are a rock star. I mean, how many people can actually say that?"

"I'm not a rock star. Just a rock musician. I think a lot of people call themselves that, these days."

"You write your own music, do your own thing."

"And am currently starving doing so."

I lower my voice and glance nervously around me. "Well, I'm up for a promotion," I whisper into the phone. A much-deserved, well-paid promotion that will be handed to me in exactly... twenty-two minutes. "I'm feeling generous. That okay?"

Through the video I can see her blushing. "Did you mention a wedding earlier? Did I miss something? Did he propose?"

I was wondering what took her so long. "Um... no. But I think this *promotion*"—I lower my voice again—"is going to speed things along." I step away from the building's entrance and cross the street for more privacy.

Fiona narrows her eyebrows. "That's whacked, Clo. Although I will say, when a man marries a woman for her money, that could mean progress for the rest of us? Maybe?"

I chuckle, seeing where she's coming from. "To be honest, Tucker and me, we're going through a rough patch." I sigh. "Basically, he's saying I'm not spending enough time at home. I work too many weekends and evenings."

She tilts her head. "And this promotion is going to help how?"

"It's a move to a cushier department. More pay, less stress, less hours."

"Really." Doubt seeps from her tone.

It does sound counterintuitive, but there it is. It's a bigger job, one where I would have a large team working for me. After the initial few weeks or months settling in, I'll have more free time. I think.

"What's this job about?"

"It's..." I hesitate on how to best describe it to her in few words. Tucker hasn't asked me about it, and it's the first time I've had to explain it to a lay person. "It's financial analysis on the feasibility of opening new breweries." My new team will do the grunt work that requires travelling, as well as weekend and evening calls and meetings. If I play this right, I'll be able to wind down, put my mark on this department, and fix things with Tucker, all while having a job I think I'll love. A job that will feel more like I'm running my own thing. "Trust me, Fi, I got this."

"I trust you. You're a kick-ass boss woman, even if Tucker doesn't appreciate it."

Not this again. "Fi..."

"You know how I feel about him."

"I do." Fiona has made that clear. She's not a fan of my boyfriend. Moving on.

"And you wanting to marry him gives me anxiety, and the fact that Mom and Dad would be beyond themselves happy is further proof that something's seriously whacked when it comes to him."

I roll my eyes. "I gotta go, Fi. Wish me luck," I say and touch the four-leafed clover at my neck.

"Good luck in the elevator." She chuckles. "Here's to hoping it doesn't break down on you."

"Not funny," I answer, forcing a smile, my stomach clenching. I'm extremely uncomfortable in small, enclosed spaces, and my worst fear is to be stuck in an elevator. Not that it's ever happened to me, but Fiona teases me about that every chance she gets.

"Proud of ya, putting yourself through that shit twice a day for a career," she says before shutting down the connection.

Make that six times a day, what with lunch break or outside appointments, and the ride up and down to the apartment.

I quickly access my banking app to send her money for a flight, put my phone on silent, cross the street, and enter the building feeling awesome about myself.

Thirty minutes later

Assholes.

I can't believe they're doing this to me. The voice sounds tinny, remote. *"New management is shifting our focus, Chloe. The whole department is let go. It's not just you. God, if it were me, we'd keep you."*

Crap. Crapcrapcrapcrapcrap.

"An uber competent, ambitious person like you won't have trouble finding a much better job elsewhere. Your severance package will give you all the time you need..."

I struggle to keep my composure. I remind them my plan could make the company millions in profit over the first three years.

These ignorant assholes don't seem to care.

I bite the inside of my cheeks until I taste blood.

I take no time packing all my stuff in the brand-new moving boxes provided by HR. They also thought of the packing tape. With a whole department let go the same day, they had to prepare. Make it as clean and quick as possible.

I take the emergency staircase down, avoiding the clusters of dejected colleagues all carrying the standard-issue box, lined up at the elevators. All cramming an already suffocating small space.

My fern is heavy. That bugger needs a lot of water. Which means, it's not only heavy, it's humid, and the humidity is seeping through the box. Add to that the fact that HR didn't extend the courtesy to provide bubble wrap, which means my photo frames clink against each other. I set my box on the sidewalk and schedule a car from my phone. I'm not carrying that stuff on the subway.

My next job, I'm not getting too comfortable until I'm the boss and no one can fire me. My next job, I don't want to deal with small spaces.

I haul myself and my belongings into the car; three and half years' worth of work and all I walk out with is this one little box.

On the upside, Tucker should be happy. I'm going to be home the next few days or weeks until I find the right job, not only for me, but for the two of us. I want our relationship to work, I really do, and I know I'm to blame for the dry spell we're in.

I lean over and ask the driver to swing by the mall and confirm that he'll wait outside, meter running.

The upside of being home is, I won't be so tired in the evenings. I wouldn't mind picking up the bedroom action where we left it off a few months ago. I mean, it's not like I'm fending him off. He's not showing any interest either. But with one of us to focus on that, we should be good.

So I charge through the mall and pick up a few necessities at Victoria's Secret. And on the way out, I stop at Whole Foods and grab fresh lobster, onions, and cream. I already have everything else I need to make Tucker's favorite dish. That and a bottle of Chardonnay and

I'm ready to go home. I'm not going to let a setback at work take over my whole life. It's midday. I have literally hours to prep a romantic dinner and an even more romantic evening.

Chloe Sullivan does not give up. She always gets what she wants.

Operation get-this-show-back-on-the-road has begun.

Fifteen minutes later

I press the elevator button with my elbow, balancing my box from work, the pink bag from Victoria's Secret jammed inside it, groceries precariously plopped on top, my backpack with my laptop, and the bottle of wine acting as a counterweight to all the shit I'm carrying in my arms.

The doors slowly open, then close on me. *Breathe in, breathe out.* Another elbow press on the panel, the elevator hiccups up, and I clench my jaw.

But I've hit rock bottom already this morning. I'm not getting stuck in the elevator now. The Law of Averages says so.

I get to my floor, no problem. See?

Steadying my box on my hip, I unlock our front door and enter the apartment backward, pushing the door open with my backpack, then letting it shut softly. I close my eyes.

I can do this. Being let go is not the end of the world.

For most people, Chloe, but for you? Pretty much is.

I turn the little voice off.

Reality is beginning to catch up with me, and I need to get a grip.

Eyes still closed, I focus on my breathing. On the smells.

There's a weird smell.

Something sweet. Flowery.

I open my eyes.

What.

The.

Fudge.

I kick my shoes off and set my stuff on the kitchen counter. I resist the urge to call Tucker to bitch about him lending our apartment as a fuckpad to his loser brother.

Whatever.

There's a bra on the back of the couch, a blouse on the floor, jeans on the coffee table, and the trail of shoes and underwear continues down the hallway.

To

our

Bedroom.

G-ross.

And really—*the nerve!*

I stomp down the carpeted hallway, dark except for a ray of light seeping from our half-open bedroom door. Not enough for me to see inside the room.

Plenty enough to hear.

The woman has her full volume on.

Come. On.

This is like a porno soundtrack, without the lounge music.

No music? The guy is lacking in the atmosphere department. I'll have to tell Tucker that. We'll have a good laugh.

Meanwhile, this is my place, and I need them out of here.

I'll clear my throat, knock on the door, push it open, say a few words, then retreat to the kitchen so they can leave decently—I hope. It'll be awkward but what the heck. Not *my* problem.

I'll have to wash the sheets. *That's* really annoying.

I'm getting pissed at Tucker now.

The woman picks up her moaning, and the guy grunts.

He grunts just like Tucker. Brothers, I guess.

God! I so do not want to be here right now. I train my eyes to the floor as I prepare to push the door wide open, not wanting to see anything. Still wanting to get them out of here right. Now.

But then the woman moans, "Oh, Tux... my god... Tux!"

My hand pushes the door, my eyes fly up to the bed, and the thump of my heartbeat covers the rest of their sex noises as I struggle to just stand there. To not collapse, or scream, under the humiliation.

The anger.

The shame.

I expect them to jump and grab the sheets to cover themselves and say something absurd like "It's not what you think," but they're so deep in it. And I'm so totally in the dark of the hallway, I go unnoticed.

I've lost all sense of touch, as if my skin were building a shield around me. There's a voice-over in my head making commentaries, helping me process what I'm seeing.

Tucker has his face snug between her legs. She's undulating under his mouth. They still have no clue they have an audience. At some point he lifts his face and says, "On your knees," and they end up both facing the oversized mirror on the side of the bed. I have a prime view of his narrow ass ramming into hers. Her face looks vaguely familiar, but she has one of those pretty blonde faces. Could be anyone.

Is she faking? He's not that *good.*

When I'm close to throwing up, I go back into the kitchen on wobbly knees, shove my box with my fern in the pantry, the pink lingerie bag and the brown grocery bag in the trash, and quietly leave the apartment, taking the emergency staircase down to the street, blood swooshing through my ears, my mouth dry, my eyes wet.

I walk the streets for hours, trying to quiet my heart. Trying to shut down the thoughts in my head. When did I start meaning so little to him that he could do... *that*? Why am I feeling dirty and ashamed? Like I did something wrong. Something to deserve that. God! This has to stop.

And why did I leave the apartment instead of yelling at them? I wish I'd had the guts to throw them both out. I don't like confrontation, and I always thought that made me a better person. Until now. My fingernails dig into the palms of my hands, forming pitiful little fists.

Eventually I end up at a coffee shop and wait until it's my usual time to come home. I don't have the energy for a fight. I'm too defeated.

We never have sex like that. He says he doesn't like going down, that it's gross. But he sure didn't mind going down on another woman. In our bedroom.

I guess I'm the problem.

And then there's the matter of losing my job.

My throat tight, I swallow my shame.

Eventually the sun dips over the buildings, and I walk into the apartment. Tucker is at his usual station on the couch, watching a game on TV, fully dressed, no trace of any woman. Not even a faint smell.

He looks so *normal*. Does this happen often? Like, regularly?

I sit on the armrest of the couch. His gaze cuts to me. "Hey," he greets me and looks back to the game.

I wipe my hands on my thighs. "Hey... So. I was here earlier," I say, struggling to keep my voice from trembling.

His face whitens. "*Why* were you here?"

I fight to control the quiver in my voice. "I *live* here." Again, I can't believe his nerve. Really? *Why* was I here? I stand from the armrest. "You have thirty minutes to pack your shit."

"Come on, Chloe. It's not what you think."

I knew it! I knew he'd use that stupid phrase.

"Tux? She calls you Tux. You need more details?"

He stays silent but still doesn't budge from the couch.

"Thirty minutes, Tucker. Get the hell out of here."

He doesn't bother looking at me. "It's my place, Chloe."

"What?"

"Lease is in my name."

A-hole. Crapcrapcrap. "I'll take it over," I say with way more confidence than I feel. Sure, I already pay two thirds of the rent because Tucker makes way less than I do. But paying the extra third will be a stretch, and then there's the matter of losing my job.

"No you're not. Like I said, it's my place. You can't find it in your heart to be cool about what happened, feel free to go."

"Cool about—" Is he effing nuts? I don't want to argue about the blonde in our bed. I can't believe he'd even—actually, yes, I can believe it. But I'm not leaning into the argument going that way, because I know what lies there: my responsibility. "You can't afford the place," I say instead. "Don't be a dick."

He stands and towers over me. "Gave you your chance, Chloe. You just burned it. Now *I'm* breaking up with you, and *you* got thirty minutes to get the hell outta *my* space." He plops back on the couch and adds, "Sick of your shit."

Sick of *my* shit?

What shit are we even talking about? Me working too much?

This argument hasn't even started yet, and I can see how useless it would be. There's nothing to discuss.

I cross my arms. "I'm going to need to rent a U-Haul. And I'll need time to pack. And it's already night."

He disappears into the bedroom and comes back with a duffel bag. "Move out by tomorrow night," he says before slamming the door on his way out.

My eyes well up. Three years together, the last six months not so great, but *this*? I never saw this coming. What did I miss? How can he just write me off like that? My vision blurs as I think back to the blonde. And here I was thinking he'd be proposing soon. What an *idiot*! I don't know if I'm more hurt or ashamed.

I shake myself out of my pity party and call my mom. I misjudged the situation, me, Tucker. Clearly, I missed so many things. I need to focus back on my family. Starting with Mom, who's just lost her brother.

She's shaken, and I hardly recognize her voice as she tries to quell her sobs. "I wish I'd seen him more often," she manages to say.

"They lived far away. Don't beat yourself up."

"Not that far. Anyway," she continues, forcing fake strength into her voice. "The funeral is next week. Do you think you can make it? Maybe Tucker too?" She likes Tucker, and so does Dad. He's everything they want in a son-in-law. Good family. Successful, even if he makes less than I do. It's only a matter of time for him to be fast-tracked by his father into a brilliant career.

Shame washes through me when I tell her what happened—the PG-13 version.

"Oh, honey." Is that disappointment in her tone? It can't be. She's probably sad for me or upset. "Boys will be boys. And men have needs. Are you sure he was getting what he needed at home?"

My toes curl. No, he clearly wasn't getting what he needed, or wanted. But is it entirely my fault? Really? And can't my own mother stand by my side, even if I'm to blame for Tucker straying?

Also—cheating? Is that something she would let Dad get away with?

And in our bed? Not that that matters.

God, I don't even know what to say to her.

My voice is unsteady when I ask her, "Um... do you know what day Uncle Kevin's funeral will be?" That's a safer conversation than discussing if my dreams of a blissful marriage were shattered by my callous boyfriend or by me being too self-centered.

"Next Monday. Daddy and I will be staying at the lake house. It's only an hour away from Kevin's. Why don't you go there right away, get yourself centered. Maybe see if Tucker will come to his senses and join you there. It's very romantic. I always loved it."

I didn't know Mom loved the house on Lake Champlain. It must be the recent loss of her brother that's making her sentimental. Dad and she bought the house fairly recently, and I'm not attached to it. But it'll be a perfect place to lick my wounds while I look for another job and another apartment. "Thanks, Mom." And no, I won't be asking Tucker to join me and reconsider.

"I'll text you the door code."

"Thanks."

"And talk to Tucker, honey."

"Bye, Mom."

Breathe in, breathe out.

I go to the bedroom and pack my clothes in suitcases. Then I make a mental inventory of all the things that are mine here, the things that made this apartment feel like a home—at least to me. I don't want to leave anything behind.

At least not objects.

My disillusionment can stay behind. Because really, what does it say about me that I just didn't see it coming? Didn't suspect anything was off? Dry spells happen, don't they? It shouldn't be anything else than just that—a spell.

The next day, after a few short hours of restless sleep on the couch, I buy packing supplies and rent a U-Haul, thankful my secondhand Honda Civic came with a hitch.

I'm on autopilot while I sort through three years of a life in common. The Moroccan carpet is definitely mine. The coffee table, too, and I'm not leaving it here, even if it's a nightmare to carry down the steps alone.

While I pack the rest, I try to shut down Mom's voice in my head. Try to ignore her questioning, but still it pops in my thoughts. What did I do wrong? Was working long hours to make a good living a wrong thing to do? Is being ambitious and driven wrong? Was it wrong to want it all? The career, the husband, and happiness to top it off?

It looks like it was. Because it's all gone now. Even our friends, I realize, are really all his.

Guess what, Chloe? It's time to let that go.

Driving out of the city, my nerves are raw. But it's only because of the trailer behind my car. Because thinking about Tucker as I glance in my rearview mirror before changing lanes, a sense of relief washes over me. It's over.

And what does that say about me?

On my way to the lake house, I stop by Aunt Dawn's. Her pain is fresh and raw, her house is full, and I feel awkward for only a minute. I haven't seen my aunt and uncle and my cousins since I was a teenager, and I feel guilty that these are the circumstances that bring me back to them. I used to spend time here a lot during the holidays and summer vacations. Somewhere during my teenage years, that stopped, and I'm not sure why.

I stay only long enough to hug them all, drink some apple cider, and be on my way. Aunt Dawn and my cousins Brendan, Daphne, and Phoebe are under the shock of their sudden loss. But their welcome is genuine, and I leave their home feeling their pain but also feeling the warmth of reconnecting with family.

I've missed that.

Then I'm alone at the lake house. I spend my days applying to jobs in a desperate, frantic, and therefore random manner. I spend my evenings drinking too much wine, alone.

I know, I know.

But this is temporary.

Mom and Dad and Fiona eventually get here, and the loneliness is replaced by some massive family tension.

"Did you talk to Tucker?" Mom asks for the umpteenth time as she's preparing a dip platter.

I throw my head in my hands and scratch my scalp. "What are you doing, honey?" Mom asks softly, seeing that I'm about to lose it but not seeing that it's over her reaction and not Tucker's effed-up behavior.

"Gonna catch up with Fi," I say, then go down the wooded path where Fiona disappeared.

I find her throwing stones in the lake. "Hey."

"Uncle Kevin is still dead. Shoulda stayed home, woulda saved you a load, woulda saved my nerves." She throws another pebble, watching it ricochet.

She's had the usual lecture about her looks—piercings, tattoos, and colored streaks in her hair. Nothing out of the ordinary, especially in her world. Why can't they see that? "Maybe there's a song in there," I say to try and lift her spirits.

A bitter chuckle escapes her lips. "Yeah, maybe." She turns to face me. "I'm too old for that shit, Clo. I don't think I'll ever bother coming back."

My heart constricts at her words, but I understand her, I really do. Still, I try. "They mean well."

"Mom and Dad treat you like shit, and you, of all people, should see that."

"They treat you just the same."

She turns her back to the lake to look at me. "Right, and I don't put up with it."

Right. "I just don't want the confrontation."

She closes the space between us to hug me tight. "I'm sorry that asshole hurt you. But I'm not sorry you broke up. Please tell me you're not getting back with him."

"Of course not," I reply without hesitation.

She settles her face in my neck. "Good," she mumbles on a last squeeze before letting me go and throwing stones in the water again. "How about the job hunt?"

"What about it?"

She shrugs. "How's it going?"

"Um... I been thinking."

She turns to face me, pebble in hand. Tilts her head and reads my mind. "Fuck no."

"I'm tired of working for strangers. I want to work for myself, and at this stage in my life, working for Dad is the closest I can get to that."

Fiona rolls her eyes dramatically. "UGH," she yells, her bark echoing on the hills. "*You* are your own woman. *You* don't need anyone. *You* are the kick ass person who inspires me daily."

She's right. No offense, but I am all that. So why do I hope against reason that working for my father is a good idea? "He's our dad. You don't get to choose your family."

"You won't change him, Chloe. And maybe he *will* show you more love and appreciation if you work for him. I really hope he does. But I'm not holding my breath. And, Chloe? I love you. I really do. I'm proud and fucking happy you're my sister. But my family? My family is my band. I hope you find that someday."

Something breaks inside me at her words. We exchange a long glance, defiance, and anger, and in the end love, so much love. When our eyes water, Fi turns back to throwing stones in the lake, while I go back up to the house.

"Rhonda is retiring at the end of the month," is my father's answer to my carefully worded opening about me having an interest in joining his firm.

"Rhonda is your receptionist," I answer stupidly.

"Start at the bottom, show your worth."

I take a deep breath. "I have an MBA, Dad. Maybe I can start at the bottom in an actual department? Or as Luther's assistant?" Luther is the CFO. Being his assistant would at least put me in the mix of things, get me acquainted with the business. I mean, surely Dad is thinking about a succession plan or just retirement down the road? I know there's time. I'm in no way thinking I should push him out the door. But look at Uncle Kevin. He died suddenly, and now they're scrambling to figure out who's going to run the restaurant in Emerald Creek.

Just that should give Dad pause.

"Darling, you don't know your place. If I hired you for one of them top jobs, guys would talk. Nobody cares about your fancy em-bee-ey. And, I'll have you know, a receptionist *is* important."

My toes curl in my shoes, and I can almost feel the hair raise on the back of my neck. There's no point arguing. Just like I did with Tucker, I shove the feelings away, and put a thick lid on them.

"I'm not sure that's right for me, Dad."

"Didn't think so, honey."

"What's with the U-Haul?" my cousin Brendan asks. Uncle Kevin has been laid to rest. Aunt Dawn and Mom face their grief together, both heavily medicated and slightly inebriated, which is not the best combination but the one that works right now. Brendan and I are sitting on the steps that lead to the wraparound porch of his parents' house. The reception is coming to an end, but despite the reason I'm here, I find peace. I don't want to go just yet.

Fi and I drove here in my car so we'd have some alone time before she flies back out, and so we don't have to spend another hour or so in a confined space with our parents. And yeah, I'm not dealing with unhooking and re-hooking the small trailer, so it's here with me.

"Broke up with my boyfriend."

"So you U-Haul your shit everywhere? That's kinda dramatic," Brendan says sweetly. He's always been nice in a quiet, mountain-man kind of way.

I count on my fingers. "I lost my apartment. I lost my job. I don't know where I'm going to end up. And I didn't have time to plan, what with Uncle Kevin passing."

"His timing was shit, I'll give you that," he manages to joke.

I place my hand on his forearm. "I'm really sorry about him, Brendan. I mean it. I'm sorry I didn't keep in touch more, but you guys mean a lot to me. If there's anything I can do, you know, just... I'm here." That's the kind of stupid thing I'm prone to say at a funeral. What the hell can I do now? "I can stay a few days and check in on Aunt Dawn while I'm at the lake house, you know. In case you need to go back to your cows or..." What does Brendan do again? Some real Vermonty stuff.

"Sheep," he volunteers with a smirk.

"Right. Sheep."

We fall silent for a while in the gentle glow of twilight.

"Actually, there might be something you could help with while you're here."

"Yeah? Great!"

"I don't know anything about restaurants," I say. After everyone left and Fiona got a ride to the airport, Brendan and I moved to the study, a dark paneled room with a legit desk, shelves with trophies, deep leather armchairs. Aunt Dawn is there, too, and Brendan's younger sisters Daphne and Phoebe. They see this as a business meeting.

"But you're a businesswoman, sweetheart," Aunt Dawn says. "A restaurant is just a business like any other. It's actually much simpler. Just a few employees. One location. Preparing dinner. How complicated can it get? I mean, you've managed whole departments. And your recent bump in the road is not on you."

She knows all this about me, and I haven't even stayed in touch? The warmth of her love spreads through me like sunshine. She continues her plea, but she's already won me over. How could I let her down? She needs someone to run the restaurant while they put it on the market. It needs to stay open for them to get the best price out of it. They believe that considering how well the restaurant is doing, it shouldn't take more than a few months to sell. I'll be paid a fair salary. And it'll add hands-on experience that would factor favorably on my resume. "There's a chef, right? No cooking involved on my end?"

She cackles. "Your uncle Kevin couldn't cook to save his life, bless his heart." The meds are definitely at work in the relaxed way she's dealing with all this, but she still has her wits about her. "It's just a numbers game, honey. I'm sure you'd have a lot of fun doing it while you get back on your feet."

I sometimes watch reruns of *Restaurant Disasters*. It doesn't look remotely fun. But I get what she's saying. And from what I know, the restaurant my uncle owned is a small, fine dining place with a stellar reputation. Not the stuff that draws audiences on TV.

I'll just be tucked away in the office, making sure bills are paid and remittances are posted.

"The restaurant lease comes with the cutest cottage, so you won't have to worry about finding a place to stay. It's adorable, and your uncle Kevin barely used it. It's all yours!"

I glance at Brendan, and see him nod, visibly relaxed.

"When do you want me to start?"

Read Chloe and Justin's story in The Promise Of You!

Acknowledgements

When I started my writing journey, I was always in awe of authors' acknowledgement sections in their published works. Where did they even meet so many people? How did they manage to get so much help? Surely this would not be my fate, I thought. I knew close to no one in the writing world. I was going to have to do this alone.

But when you set out to do something with the kind of grit that writing a book requires, the universe has a way of putting the right people on your path. Things happen. And as in any heroine's journey, alliances form—or, it seems, there cannot be a journey.

First and foremost on this journey came my Redbirds tribe: Teresa Beeman, Ariana Clark, Diana Divine, Michele Ingrid, and Kenna Rey. We met over three years ago during a writing boot camp led by Alessandra Torre, and are still meeting weekly. This book wouldn't be here without their weekly cheer, our constructive discussions, and the friendships of fellow aspiring writers (some of them now published) who understand each other's struggles and insecurities.

On the way I also met Sarah Barbour, Gia Stevens, Abigail Sharpe, Lisa Stapleton, and Sarah Hawthorne. I've loved every one of our late-night plotting sessions over zoom, as you West Coast dwellers were bright out of work and I was ready to call it a night.

The indie community at large is also incredibly supportive, and I wouldn't be in the position I'm in without groups such as Melanie Harlow's Author Facebook group, the 20 Books to 50 k Facebook group, and especially the Author Conference talks every morning on Club House (even though as I write this, I realize this may not be where the meetings are held in the very near future). I've spent countless mornings listening to your conversations and taking notes while working my other job. Your generosity in sharing your knowledge is truly inspiring.

This list would not be complete without the incredible number of book reviewers who took a chance on a new author, read this book, and shared it with the world. From the bottom of my heart, thank you.

Last but not least, this book would not be what it is without the stellar feedback and guidance of my truly amazing editor, Angela James. Thank you so much for giving in to my request to leave the niceties at the door and give me the naked truth of where this book was succeeding and where it was going to fail without prompt remedy. If I didn't reel from the metaphor, I'd say Angela is the midwife to my books.

About the author

Bella Rivers writes steamy small town romances with a guaranteed happily ever after, and themes of found family and forgiveness. Expect hot scenes, fierce love, and strong language!

A hopeless romantic, Bella is living her own second chance romance in the rolling hills of Vermont. When she's not telling the stories of the characters populating her dreams, you can find her baking, hiking, skiing, or just hanging around her small town to soak in the happiness.

Her newsletter is where Bella shares progress on her writing as well as sneak peeks into upcoming books, the occasional recipe from her characters, and books from other writers she thinks her readers might like. You can also find her and interact with her on social media. To subscribe, browse her books, follow along on social, or get in touch, visit www.bellarivers.com

Made in the USA
Monee, IL
04 August 2025

22597668R00312